Keep up to ... **,**
and specials from J. R. Rada by joining his mail list at https://bit.ly/3CILHI6. When you sign-up, you'll get *Polderbeest* as a FREE gift.

Other books by J. R. Rada

Finishing the Charge (Gettysburg Tall Tales & Short Stories)
Kachina
Kuskurza (e-book)
The Man Who Killed Edgar Allan Poe
Polderbeest (e-book)
Welcome to Peaceful Journey

BEAST

THE COMPLETE SERIES

by
J. R. Rada

AIM
PUBLISHING

BEAST: THE COMPLETE SERIES

Published by AIM Publishing, a division of AIM Publishing Group.
Gettysburg, Pennsylvania.

Printed in the United States of America.

ISBN: 978-1-7352890-4-5

Beast: The Complete Series was originally published in e-book format as:

- *Beast: The Past Present*
- *Beast: The Hunt Begins*
- *Beast: Man or Beast*
- *Beast: Sins of the Father*
- *Beast: Freedom's Sacrifice*

PUBLISHING

CHAPTER 1

JULY 3, 1993

Robert Armentrout kept looking back over his shoulder as he hiked the C&O Canal Towpath. Out of the corners of his eyes, he saw dark figures moving behind him on the trail, but each time he turned to look directly, he and his wife were always the only living things in sight.

In front of him, Diane hummed a country song as she walked with her bouncing stride. He would much rather watch his wife's shapely legs and butt move, but the shadow figures kept distracting him. He thought it might be another hiker, but when Robert turned... nothing.

He sighed and told himself he needed to rest, and if possible, sleep. It was getting dark, and it would be hard to see the dirt trail soon. They had walked their twenty-five mile goal for the day, and Richard wanted to make camp for the night. Better yet, he would have preferred to find a place to stay in Fleetwood, but they had passed through there an hour ago and hadn't seen another town since.

If they waited too much longer, they would be making camp in the dark, which was never fun.

He and Diane had been on the trail for six days now. She wanted to reach the end in Cumberland tomorrow night. Robert thought that would be nice, but he doubted it would be the case.

The C&O Canal Towpath was 184.5 miles long running from Georgetown, near Washington D.C., to Cumberland, Maryland. The Armentrouts had started in Georgetown and covered 153 miles so far. That meant they would be hiking at least another eleven hours before they finished the trail. They had been averaging about eight hours a day. The math was betraying them.

Robert enjoyed taking his time on hikes. He enjoyed stopping to photograph the sites. He had even taken a swim in the Potomac River two days ago. For him, hikes were all about the journey. Diane just wanted to get from point A to point B as soon as she could. For her, it was a race.

"What's that song you've been humming since we left Fleetwood?" Robert asked.

"It's called 'Romeo.' It was playing on the radio in the store," Diane answered and immediately started humming again.

"Singing about me again, are you?" Robert teased.

"Don't you wish," Diane said in tune with the music.

Robert wiped the sweat from his forehead with his handkerchief. He still hadn't become animal enough to use the back of his arm. Give him to the end of the week.

"I thought you didn't like country music," he said as he stuffed the white handkerchief into his front pocket.

"I like this song."

Near another of the dozens of abandoned locks along the long ditch that was once a major commerce route, the towpath turned west abruptly. They starting hiking away from the Potomac River, which they had been paralleling until now.

Robert looked back over his shoulder toward the river and thought he saw something dart upward into the trees. He stared for a little while longer but didn't see any movement.

"Look at that," Diane cooed. "Isn't it gorgeous?"

The sun was getting low on the horizon, and it was right over the towpath, so that it looked like they were walking right into the sun.

Robert held his hand over his eyes to act as a visor as he looked into the setting sun, but when he caught a whiff of his underarm odor, he lowered his arm. So much for his deodorant's long-lasting protection.

He sat down on the ground and leaned back against a tree. If it wouldn't have hurt his pride to say so, he would have announced he was too old for this sort of vacation. Next year, he wanted to take a Mediterranean cruise and sit around while people waited on him.

Fat chance of that happening with Miss Fitness helping plan their trips.

"Did we buy any milk in Fleetwood?" He had a craving for a nice cold glass of skim milk right now.

"You bought a pint and drank it. Anything more wouldn't have kept," Diane said.

She turned to take a quick picture of him as he leaned against the tree. He flipped her the bird just as she took the shot.

"That ought to make a lovely picture for the photo album," Diane said sarcastically.

"I want an eight by ten for the living room." His wife turned back to taking shots of the scenery and he flipped her the bird. "And I know that milk wouldn't keep, but I want my cow juice," he said as he struggled to his feet, which was nearly impossible with a fifty-pound pack on his back. "Do you suppose there's a 7-Eleven at the top of the hill?"

"You're lucky there was a store in Fleetwood. This is an isolated stretch of the towpath." Diane started hiking again. She waved for her husband to catch up. "C'mon, I want to get another mile before we settle down for tonight."

Robert groaned.

"We should have stayed in Fleetwood. We're not that far from it, and the cashier at the grocery store said there was a bed-and-breakfast just outside of town," Robert said, hoping he might persuade to turn back. Sleeping on the hard ground was messing up his back as much as carrying the pack.

"We're not hiking to stay in a hotel," Diane said.

"No, we're hiking to give ourselves coronaries. What beautiful words! Bed and breakfast," Robert shouted dramatically.

"Stop complaining, you wimp," Diane teased.

Robert reached forward and yanked on Diane's blond ponytail. She yelled and almost fell backwards.

"You wouldn't want to stay in town, anyway. Look at the friend you made while you were there, that guy who kept calling you Mueller," Diane told her husband.

"You can have him. I'll take the cute redhead in the grocery store," Robert taunted.

"She's too young for you, Hon. Forget the hike. She would give you a coronary. Besides, the big guy is your friend, not mine. You told him so. You shouldn't have agreed with him."

"It got him to leave us alone, didn't it?"

When they had walked out of the grocery store in Fleetwood with the supplies they had bought, a man had walked up to them. He had the flat-appearing features of someone with Down's syndrome. He was also at least 100 pounds heavier than Robert, with arms as large as Robert's head.

"Are you Mueller?" the man had asked.

"Afraid not," Robert had said as he dipped his plastic spoon into his chocolate ice cream.

He and Diane had started walking toward an access trail behind the country store. The huge man had continued following them.

"Are you Mueller?" he asked again.

"No. My name's Robert Armentrout."

Robert felt a little nervous then. The big man was agitated Robert kept telling him "no," and that was the last thing Robert wanted a man the size of a gorilla to be.

"Are you Mueller?" the man asked once again.

Feeling angry as well as scared, Robert stopped walking and turned to face the man.

"Yes, I'm Mueller. What's your name? What do you want?" Robert snapped.

The man's face had gone white, and he had turned and run off so fast his arms had almost dragged the ground. It must have been Robert's own anger that scared the man off; he almost felt sorry for losing his temper. The man had meant no harm, but he had certainly been a pest.

Diane pointed some interesting landmark out to Robert. He could have cared less what it was. He just wanted to lie down and sleep.

"Uh-huh. Gorgeous," he muttered.

He saw the shadow figure out of the corner of his eye again. He turned quickly and wished he hadn't. Thick hands closed around his neck, and he felt himself lifted off the ground.

He tried to scream, but he couldn't get air into his lungs, let alone make a sound. He saw the side of the tree rushing toward his face. He closed his eyes so he wouldn't have to see the moment of contact. It was bad enough he would have to feel it.

Diane heard an odd sound, like a melon breaking open. She stopped walking to see if the sound repeated.

"Did you hear that noise, Hon?" she asked her husband.

Robert didn't answer. Was he listening for it to be repeated, too? "Robert, did you..." She turned and saw an empty trail where her husband should be. "Robert?"

She retraced her steps on the trail, hoping to see him sitting on the trail, having tripped or something just as stupid. But if that had happened, why hadn't he yelled out for her to stop?

"Robert! Where are you?"

No one answered her call.

"I don't like this, Robert. If this is your way of getting back at me for not wanting to stay in that..."

Something rustled the branches over her head and then was still. She looked up, trying to see if she anything, but the canopy was too thick and it was getting dark.

Something splattered on her cheek and she jumped back.

"Oh, crap..." she muttered, which was exactly what she thought it was. A squirrel or a bird had rustled the branches and then crapped on her face. She wiped away the mess on her face. It didn't smell bad. It smelled faintly of ... she couldn't place the smell, but it wasn't crap.

She took her flashlight from her belt and shined it on her fingers.

They were red with blood. The meaning of the sight took a moment to register. "Robert!" she screamed as she started running.

She had only gone a few feet when she heard a crash in the trees above her head. The body fell to the ground with a heavy thump, bouncing slightly against the hard-packed trail. It was Robert, but his head had been smashed nearly flat and his face looked like it had been dragged across a cheese grater. It was shredded and bloody. His nose and one of his eyes were missing.

Diane screamed again and ran in the opposite direction. She could hear something breathing hard off to her right. It sounded like some panting animal keeping pace with her. But animals would run from her. Whatever was in the forest had probably killed Robert.

She slipped out of her pack so she could run faster. It dropped behind her, and she felt a surge of speed.

She and Robert had crossed a paved road only about a half mile or so back. If she could get back to the road, she would be safe. There would be cars there, and she could stop one and get a ride into town.

The thing pacing her now sounded like it was running in the trees above her. She tried to run faster. There was a crash and breaking of branches, and the thing was running on her right again.

Diane thought she saw a headlight of a passing car break the darkness of the forest. She screamed again, but it wasn't loud. She needed her breath to keep her running. She was almost safe. She just needed to reach the road.

The large hands grabbed her on either side of her head. She screamed and was running in the air as the unseen thing lifted her off the ground.

"Mueller's friend, you bad, too." The voice was very throaty, and she thought she recognized it, but she didn't have any time to place the voice.

The hands squeezed inward, and Diane joined her husband.

CHAPTER 2

JULY 6, 1993

Daniel Levitt had been taught from childhood that Nazis were nothing but vermin to be hunted and killed. They had no feelings. They were inhuman. Then he saw one commit suicide.

The crowd at the Baltimore Zoo stood shoulder to shoulder along the railing so they could peer down into the pit where the two grizzly bears lived. Most of the people watching the bears were children whose faces barely rose above the three-foot cement rampart. One bear walked back and forth in front of a cage that was disguised with plaster boulders so that it looked like a cave. The second bear climbed onto a rock at the edge of the moat that surrounded the fake cave. He reared up on his hind legs, and the children watching from the railing yelled with delight.

Daniel glanced away from the massive bears to fan himself. The day was hot and humid, and he was not the only person among the crowd he saw trying to stay cool. He stepped back into the shade of a large tree and watched the old man standing to his far right. This was who he was here to see. Not the bears.

Because Daniel was average height and weight, he blended in easily with the crowd and did not stand out. To further conceal his features, he had pulled a black-and-orange Baltimore Orioles cap snugly over his brown hair so that his brown eyes were in shadow.

The old man laughed with his grandson as the two bears wrestled with each other until they rolled into the water-filled moat. Laying his arm across his grandson's shoulders, the old man hugged him.

It was only a small act of love. Not unusual to see such things in the zoo. Lovers walking hand in hand. A toddler riding on his father's shoulders. A little girl kissing her mother. All those things were seen and dismissed as commonplace, but this act of a grandfather hugging his grandson caused a twinge in Daniel's chest. It wasn't supposed to happen this way.

Where was the hate he was supposed to feel? Why did he only feel guilty?

The foreign feeling might have surprised him if it had indeed been foreign. It wasn't. He had come to expect the feeling lately. In fact, he had even given it a name. He called it his conscience, and it had been a long time since he had heard from it.

Until three days ago, the old man had only been a file to him.

Case number GH17543. The old man, whom Daniel watched hug his grandson, had been born Gregor Heinsdorf in Dusseldorf, Germany, on August 16, 1913. By all accounts, he had been a pleasant child, much like his grandson would be. Then he had grown up and joined Hitler's SS. As a prison guard at the Maidanek Concentration Camp in Central Poland, he had brutally beaten and killed the Jews interred there. Some reports from survivors, and there were few, said he had taken an odd delight in his job. He whistled Handel's Messiah as he whipped starving Jews tied to a post.

Now Gregor Heinsdorf called himself Greg Heinz. He was a grandfather and retired Baltimore City policeman, and Daniel was watching him display an emotion the Maidanek prisoners had never seen from him. Had not only Heinsdorf's name changed but also his personality as well?

Of course, Adam would say, "A leopard can't change its spots. It may lose its teeth, but if you turn your back on it, it will rip you to shreds."

Daniel glanced back at the bear. He didn't want to stare too intensely at the old Nazi. One bear slid into the moat to cool itself off. The bear's 400-plus pounds hit the water with a loud splash, and the grizzly disappeared underneath the surface to reappear a moment later floating on his back. The bear was lucky. It might be imprisoned, but it was fed a scientifically prepared diet of perhaps not the most-delicious food in the world, but it kept the grizzly healthy. He was given plenty of room to play and kept clean. Funny how an animal could be treated better than a human.

How many people had died in Maidanek Concentration Camp? About half a million was the best guess. No one would ever know the truth. At the time, no one had really cared to keep count. Daniel's people had died because they hadn't been given the same conditions as this bear.

He stared at Heinsdorf from the corner of his eye.

Are you remembering Maidanek, old man? Daniel thought. *Is this what the Jews were to you? Nothing more than animals to be watched?*

He looked away occasionally in case Heinsdorf sensed he was being watched. To have avoided detection for so long, the old Nazi must have developed some sort of sixth sense or third eye to keep himself hidden away from investigators.

Gregor Heinsdorf was eighty years old, according to his birth certificate. Yet, he looked twenty years younger, and he acted thirty years younger. Daniel had watched him walk through most of the Baltimore Zoo without tiring. He had even kept pace with his grandson, who rushed from animal to animal with a ten-year-old's energy. Heinsdorf and his grandson turned away from the bear pit and headed up the hill toward the monkey house. Following behind at a safe distance, Daniel kept Heinsdorf in sight while allowing other people to walk in between them. He wasn't too worried about the old man running away. Heinsdorf might be youthful, but he was not young. Still, he didn't want Heinsdorf to know he was being followed. At least not until the Nazi hunter could figure out what he would do now that he had verified the old Nazi guard's identity.

Adam Goldstein, the man who had sent Daniel to Baltimore after Heinsdorf, would have exposed Heinsdorf in public. Even if Adam could have caught the old Nazi alone in a dark alley and killed him with no one being the wiser, Adam still would have gone to the media with his evidence. Public humiliation was part of the way Daniel's employer extracted his revenge on the Nazis. The Nazis had committed their crimes against the Jews in the secrecy of the concentration camps, and Adam delighted in taking that shield of secrecy away, exposing Nazis for what they were.

Daniel wasn't so sure that was the way to work, or at least not *his* way to work. He had exposed Nazis in public and private, and of the two, he preferred his role remain a secret. When he revealed a Nazi to the public, he revealed himself as well. People saw him as a bounty hunter... a grudge holder... a persecuted Jew taking his frustration out on the world. And it didn't help that the remaining Nazis were old men. They had grandchildren, like Gregor did, and they reminded people of their own grandfathers. Arresting a person like that in public didn't humiliate him, it humiliated the one making the accusation. People saw Daniel as a bully picking on old men when he exposed eighty-year-old men as war criminals.

Daniel stood in front of the African gorilla's cage, alternating his gaze between the huge, black beast and Heinsdorf, three windows away from him. Heinsdorf's grandson, Jeffrey Heinz, raised his hand to tap on the glass of one of the chimpanzee cages. Gregor put his hand on the young boy's arm and pointed to the "Do not tap on the glass" sign. Jeffrey lowered his arm, and Gregor ruffled his grandson's hair.

Obey the rules. Just follow orders. That was the excuse most of the Nazis had used at the end of the war. They had just been following orders from their superiors. They weren't responsible for what they did. Gregor still seemed to follow orders, and he was teaching his grandson to do the same thing. Only this time, it looked like Jeffrey would turn out to be a law-abiding citizen, not a sadistic killer.

Jeffrey led his grandfather by the hand out of the monkey house toward the children's zoo. Daniel gave the gorilla one final glance. It didn't notice his departure. It was too intent on picking something from between the toes of its leathery, hand-like foot. Daniel hurried on, glad to get out of the musty, animal-smelling exhibit and into the fresh air.

It had taken him six months to find Heinsdorf, and now that he had, he wasn't sure what to do about it. He had come across Heinsdorf's name when he and Adam were studying some of the old records the U.S. War Crimes Commission had amassed at the end of World War II. In exchange for his freedom, a documents forger named Vincenzo Thomaselli had provided the commission a list of names of the Nazis for whom he had created false papers. U.S. Army investigators had later discounted Thomaselli's testimony as lies. The investigators claimed Thomaselli was trying to buy his freedom and would have said anything to avoid prison. However, Daniel had noted in his research that many of the people listed as Thomaselli's clients had been provided with false documents that had allowed them to escape Germany.

Daniel had created a list of the people Thomaselli mentioned who had not been captured, and that was his first contact with the name Gregor Heinsdorf. With further research, he found that Heinsdorf had been an executioner at the Maidanek Concentration Camp. Multiple witnesses testified they had seen him torture inmates to death and whistle while he did it.

Now, Daniel was watching this same man walk through the aviary in the children's zoo with a ten-year-old boy. Was this man Gregor Heinsdorf or Greg Heinz? Was there even a difference? Daniel wasn't so sure anymore.

Feeling conspicuous among the parents and children as he walked from area to area, Daniel tried to stay as far away from the pair as he could. He had no children tagging along with him as he walked through the people-sized beaver's dam, groundhog tunnel, squirrel's tree, and bat cave. These large dioramas allowed children to have fun while learning something about the animal habitats. The sliding board that led from the top of the squirrel's tree to the bottom served only to make him feel even more foolish. Unlike Heinsdorf, who rode the slide with his grandson, Daniel opted for the stairs.

He thought Heinsdorf might have recognized him at the beaver's dam.

Most of the dioramas had an entrance on one end of the display and the exit on the other to keep a steady flow of traffic moving through. The beaver dam was different. Daneil hadn't realized that and had followed the Heinzs into the re-created dam. Daniel walked in a single-file line that went beneath the beaver pond. The portion of the tunnel that went underwater was made of clear Plexiglas so that the kids could see the beavers swimming above them in the pond. The tunnel then dead-ended with a series of fish tanks showing salamanders, turtles, minnows, and frogs. The air was damp and cool. Daniel was enjoying the respite from the heat when he realized the single-file line reversed direction at the fish tanks and retraced their steps back to the original entrance. Before he could back himself out, he came face-to-face with Heinsdorf coming out of the dam as he walked through the clear Plexiglas tunnel. Daniel quickly looked away, but then he realized Heinsdorf didn't know what he looked like or that he was even following him. After all, who would expect to be on someone's "Most Wanted" list after nearly half a century? So Daniel turned back and tried to act nonchalant.

At the end of the children's zoo, a snack bar and a picnic area invited weary parents to rest and spend money. Ignoring the sugary smell of cotton candy, Daniel stepped up to the young cashier and ordered a Diet Coke and a soft pretzel with mustard while he continued to watch Heinsdorf. As he waited for the attendant to spread the mustard on his pretzel, Daniel saw Heinsdorf come out of the barn, which was part of the petting zoo and the final exhibit in the children's zoo.

When Heinsdorf walked toward the snack bar, Daniel suddenly lost his appetite. His first impulse was to run and hide, but then he reminded himself that Heinsdorf did not know him. This man had not even known Daniel's father, who had been confined in Auschwitz, so there was no chance of even noticing a family resemblance.

The old man walked up behind Daniel in line. Daniel stiffened, but he tried hard not to turn around. He passed the cashier a five-dollar bill and waited for his change.

"Why are you following me?" Heinsdorf asked in a casual voice.

Daniel choked on the piece of pretzel in his mouth. How had Heinsdorf recognized him? Daniel took a deep breath and turned slowly to face the old Nazi.

"Were you speaking you me, sir?" Daniel said, pretending ignorance.

The old man stared at him. His face reminded Daniel of Jackie

Gleason's. It had the same bulldog-with-a-mustache look and the same ever-present frown.

"Yes. I may be old, but I'm not blind, young man. I saw you enter the zoo only a few people behind my grandson and me, and I've seen you everywhere my grandson and I have gone today." Almost fifty years of life in Baltimore had replaced his German accent with a Baltimorean one. Like the hug, it was another incongruity Daniel found hard to reconcile.

Daniel tried to smile, but he could tell it looked forced. It felt forced. "I do not know what you are trying to infer. I am sure many people have followed the same attractions both you and I seem to have followed. I cannot say that I remember seeing you throughout the zoo, though." Of course, most people in the Baltimore Zoo wouldn't have an accent that was a melting pot of half a dozen different lands.

Daniel took his change and started to move away with his drink and pretzel.

"That may be," the old man said, following him, "but how many single adults without children walk through the children's zoo?" Daniel stopped walking. He knew he had been conspicuous inside the children's zoo without a child, but he hadn't realized just how conspicuous. "Tell me the truth. I'm an old man. I don't have the time to wade through a lie. And you better not be a supremacist looking for an idol. I busted punks like you when I was a cop, and I can still hold my own if I have to."

Daniel looked over his shoulder at Heinsdorf. "That will not be necessary."

He walked over to a bench which faced the petting zoo, and sat down. Why couldn't Heinsdorf leave him alone? Why did he have to force the issue now? And here, of all places?

"Do I know you?" Heinsdorf said as he sat down beside Daniel. He stared intensely into Daniel's face. "No. No, I don't. I would remember you. I'm very good with faces. I learned to be walking a beat for over thirty years."

Daniel shook his head. "My name is Daniel Levitt."

Daniel watched the old man's face for a reaction, but he saw none.

"You're the man who caught Albert Gossamer?" Heinsdorf said.

"Yes."

So the old man kept himself up to date on which Nazis had finally run out of places to run. Albert Gossamer had been the last Nazi Daniel had publicly exposed in 1989. It hadn't been a pleasant situation for either

Gossamer or Daniel. A few people had even jeered Daniel as he led away the old man.

"Then you are also the man who killed Rolf Mentzer?" Heinsdorf asked.

Daniel shook his head. "No, that was another man, my employer."

Heinsdorf frowned and rubbed his eyes. "I knew you would come after me someday. Not you personally, but your kind. I thought you looked too young to be a Nazi hunter. So you are part of a second generation of vigilantes, eh?"

Daniel's back stiffened so that he looked like he was sitting at attention. "I am not a vigilante. I am a detective, here to verify your identity and have you arrested for crimes you committed against the Jewish people during World War II," Daniel said with too much defensiveness in his voice.

Heinsdorf leaned closer to Daniel and poked him in the shoulder. "You are a killer seeking revenge. Nothing more. Look at me, I will never live to see a trial. I'm an old man. And even if I did, it would be a kangaroo court. There would be no justice for me. Both you and I know I'm telling the truth."

Daniel shrugged and tried to remain undisturbed. "That is not for me to say. I am only the hunter, not the judge and jury. I will say this, though. No matter how slim a chance you have in court, it is more than you gave the Jews at Maidanek. Maybe your executioner will whistle Handel's Messiah for you as they hang you."

Daniel was trying to work up his anger against the man with little success.

"How much of a chance did you give Aria Mueller?" Heinsdorf asked Daniel.

Daniel looked away quickly so the old man wouldn't see the pain in Daniel's face at the mention of the woman who haunted his dreams.

Heinsdorf sighed. "So you will take me now, I suppose? You will arrest me in public to humiliate me and then drag me off to the nearest police station like some common hood."

"I had not planned on having you arrested here, but you have forced me to choose that way by approaching me."

Heinsdorf shook his finger in Daniel's face. "How could I ignore the obvious? You were sloppy. I've lived most of my life looking over my shoulder. I can recognize a tail when I see one. You didn't act like a Nazi hunter. You acted like a man who wanted to be seen." Heinsdorf paused.

"If you arrest me now, you'll create not only a second generation of vigilantes, but a second generation of victims, too. Did you realize that?"

"What are you talking about?"

Heinsdorf nodded toward the barn. Jeffrey had walked out and was staring at them. He looked so small standing alone in the crowd with only a G.I. Joe T-shirt and blue jeans on.

"My grandson is a fine boy. He doesn't know what I once was, nor do his parents. He will grow up to be a fine man. I've tried to teach him right from wrong. He is just now reaching the age where he can understand the war. I do not want him to glorify Hitler because his grandfather was a Nazi. I also believe Hitler was a mad man." Daniel started to say something, but Heinsdorf held up his hand. "Please, let me finish. It's true I believed in him at one time in my youth. Many of us were carried away by his words, but with age and distance, I have come to see him as history sees him. My point is, if you arrest me here, my grandson will hate you. You, of all people, should know how the seed of hate grows and consumes a person. Someone had to plant the seed in you. You must only be about thirty. You weren't even alive during the war."

Heinsdorf was right. Daniel was only thirty-five, and he knew what hatred could do to a man. He had seen hatred for Nazis consume his father, making him a bitter, vindictive man. Daniel would not allow it to happen to him if he could help it. The problem was, he wasn't sure that he had a choice.

"I do not hate. I seek justice," Daniel said.

"Is it justice when no one cares anymore? Most would say justice has been done. Others would say living with the ghosts of the past and looking over my shoulder all my life is justice. Obviously, you don't." Daniel did not confirm or deny the statement. "Let me ask you this: Who will care if I am caught? Do the families of those I killed know that I'm the one who killed their relatives? With so many pressing problems in the world today, what is one old Nazi?" His eyes narrow quickly as he met Daniel's stare, then widened in expectation.

Daniel had never spoken with a Nazi like this before. His job had been to expose them and bring them to the authorities. But this! This was different. He wasn't sure how he should handle this conversation. Heinsdorf didn't even sound German any longer.

"What would you have me do? I cannot turn my back on those you have killed," Daniel said.

The old man pursed his lips and raised his eyebrows. "No, I suppose you can't, but I do not want to taint my grandson with our evil. And don't fool yourself, the evil you accuse me of is an evil we both share. Only I have forsaken it, and you have embraced it. You, and others like you, keep it alive. You don't allow it a chance to die as it should have all those years ago."

Daniel reached into his pocket for a pair of handcuffs. He would keep Heinsdorf from running until he could find a policeman.

Reaching for Heinsdorf, he said, "I have heard enough."

Heinsdorf grabbed his arm. "Not here. I'm begging you, and I've never begged for anything. Give me a day to satisfy your needs of justice on my own."

"Why?"

Heinsdorf pointed to his grandson. "If I can, I will satisfy you and not implicate my family. The evil must end."

"What do you want to do?" Daniel asked.

Heinsdorf shrugged. "I don't know yet, but I will do something if I must. Follow me if you want, but don't interfere for a day." Daniel realized he must have looked skeptical because Heinsdorf added, "You've waited this long, what's one more day?"

Daniel sighed. Then he slowly nodded. He held up his index finger.

"One day."

CHAPTER 3

JULY 6, 1993

Kendall's Country Store was nearly deserted on Monday mornings. That was the reason Eva Lachman shopped for her groceries at that time. In the afternoons, especially on Friday, people crowded Kendall's six aisles, hurrying to finish their weekly chore. But on Monday mornings, fewer eyes looked at her and fewer minds wondered why Eva bought what she did. Both cashiers would be sweating from working so quickly, trying to check everyone out as quickly as possible. However, this Monday morning, the store was so empty it made even Eva uneasy.

She straightened her cart and pushed it into the narrow aisle between the checkout counter and the candy stand. The college-age cashier put down the accounting textbook she was reading and smiled at the old woman.

"Good morning, Tina," Eva said to the young girl.

"Good morning, Miss Lachman. Looks like you're my first customer today," Tina Rourke replied as she scanned the bar code on a gallon of whole milk and multiplied it by six.

Eva liked Tina. The girl reminded her of how a young person should look. Happy, innocent, and untroubled by life. This was not how Eva had looked at Tina's age. What might Eva's life have been like today if she had looked like Tina fifty years ago and not like a Jew? What would her life have been like if she had been able to play as children are supposed to play? What would it have been like if she could have met and married the man of her dreams? She would never know, would she? The Nazis had made sure of that.

Eva returned Tina's smile. No use dwelling on the things she couldn't change.

"Looks like I'm your *only* customer this morning," Eva said. As far as she could tell, only three people, including herself were in the small grocery store; and she was the only customer. Even the butcher's counter wasn't open yet. Kendall's might be the only grocery store on the eastern end of Allegany County, but there was a reason for that. There just weren't that many people in this area of Maryland.

Tina nodded. Her red curls bounced around her head like small springs. "A lot of people stocked up for the holiday weekend last weekend. Business probably won't start to pick up again until tomorrow."

Eva remembered Sunday had been Independence Day. Sunday night, the noise from the fireworks display the volunteer fire department had put on in Hargan's Field had frightened Jacob at first. He had cowered in the hall closet, thinking the farm was being bombed. Once he realized the noise accompanied the colorful fireworks, he had gone into the backyard with Esau and watched the sky as the rockets exploded and flowered with bright red, blue, yellow, green, and white petals.

"I guess you'll be able to get your studying done then," Eva commented as he tapped the hard cover of the textbook.

Tina manually punched in the price of a box of herbal tea the scanner didn't recognize. "I just hope I don't fall asleep studying this stuff. Accounting is boring. I'll be glad when this class is over. The finals for the first summer term are coming up next week and accounting will be a monster."

The word jolted Eva, and she stared at Tina to see if the young girl meant the comment as an intentional jibe. Tina seemed unperturbed, and Eva passed the comment off as a coincidence.

She touched Tina's hand lightly as if brushing something away and said, "You'll do fine."

Tina nodded as she punched the price of a multi-pack of razors into the cash register. "I hope so. I don't want to be a cashier all my life." She packed the groceries that she had pushed to the back end of the checkout counter.

Eva reached across the counter to get a *TV Guide* and noticed the cover stories on the tabloids. The newspapers sat in racks below *TV Guide* with bright, full-color pictures and large headlines. One proclaimed Hitler was still alive and well in Germany. To support the claim, the blurry picture on the cover supposedly showed Adolf Hitler. The thought of Hitler still being alive sent a chill through Eva's body.

Although she knew she was the only customer in the store, Eva looked guiltily from side to side, making sure no one was watching her. No one was behind her in line, and Tina was concentrating on bagging the groceries. Eva hesitated a moment, then grabbed the tabloid and dropped it onto the moving conveyor belt, quickly covering it with two loaves of rye bread so that only a small corner of the photo of Hitler showed. Even if the article had only a grain of truth among all the lies, she needed to find the grain. If Hitler still lived, she wanted to know.

When Eva finished emptying the contents of the cart onto the conveyor belt, she asked, "Is the rest of my order out back?"

Tina nodded. "A bushel each of peaches, bananas, apples, pears, and plums." Tina counted off each item on her fingers. "I'll add them onto the end of your total. You know, I still don't understand how you and Jacob can eat so much fruit."

Eva tried to keep the worry out of her voice as she said, "I think Jacob could be a fruit vegetarian. He positively loves any type of fruit and eats them day and night," Eva told her. "Besides, all those carbohydrates give me energy and keep me healthy. Not to mention that the fiber keeps me regular. And you know how important that is for someone my age."

Tina smiled at her.

Eva glanced out the large plate-glass window at the front of the store. Bob Halethorpe walked out of F & G Hardware carrying a brown bag and crossed the street. She watched him walk to the corner and cross Hanover Road. A BMW stopped for the light at the corner of Main and Hanover partially obscuring her view of the hardware store. She could see the passenger in the car or at least the back of his head.

A stranger, she thought, *but he won't stay here long, not with* a *car like that.*

Fleetwood was too small a town for most people, and Eva liked it that way. But, a man with the money to afford a BMW would not. He would be at home in the city with all its pressures and prying eyes.

The passenger in the car turned his head to look to the right and Eva saw his profile. Her breath caught, and she clenched her eyes shut.

Memories rushed forward with the slight nudge and took control. She was no longer in the country store, but lying on her back on a metal table.

A red light shined in her face casting a red glow over everything in the room. A green, sticky liquid that smelled like vomit covered her body. The red light made her eyes water, but she refused to look away. She didn't want to see what was off to the side of the room. Maybe it wouldn't notice her. Maybe it would let her be this time. She didn't want it to happen again. Although she could feel the cold from the metal table against her back, she was too frightened to shiver. Over the scent of the foul-smelling liquid, she smelled a musky odor that almost overpowered the smell of the liquid. It made her dizzy and unable to keep wits about her, but she knew this was not a dream. It had never been a dream. It was a nightmare.

Fear caused her mouth to go dry. She licked her lips with her tongue, which felt thick and rough. She wanted to moisten her mouth just enough so that she could beg the doctor not to let it happen.

The thing off to her right growled, low and guttural.

She twisted her head to the left, away from the sound. A soft hand patted her cheek. The touch was meant to be comforting, but it might just as well have been a choke hold around her neck. She shuddered.

"Darwin is harmless, Eva. He would never hurt you. He loves you," the doctor said in German.

Eva looked up. In the colored light, the doctor's white clothes looked red as if he were covered with blood. Dr. Mueller wasn't looking at her but across the table, probably at Darwin. Eva was staring now at the same profile in the BMW.

"Miss Lachman?" an unfamiliar voice said.

The voice startled Eva, and she unwittingly turned her head in Darwin's direction.

Who could it be? There hadn't been a woman in the room with her and Dr. Mueller. Not even a nurse. Mueller couldn't risk anyone learning of this experiment. Darwin was not in his cage. There wasn't even a cage off to her right. Instead, a woman only a few years older than Eva, who was in her teens, stood in front of her. The woman had curly, red hair.

She couldn't be German. Not with that hair, Eva thought.

The details around the woman changed. The red walls of the laboratory faded into shelves filled with boxes of cereal, jars of peanut butter, and cans of vegetables. Finally, Eva recognized Tina Rourke.

"Are you all right, Miss Lachman? You looked awfully pale suddenly," Tina asked her.

Eva tried to smile, but her lower lip quivered thwarting the attempt.

Instead of denying how she felt, Eva said, "I do feel a little under the weather, I guess." She wanted to run out of the store, but she took a deep breath and forced herself not to panic.

She opened her purse and pulled out seven twenty-dollar bills. Her hand shook as she passed them over to Tina. The cashier eyed her curiously. Tina opened her mouth to say something but closed it without uttering a word. Eva glanced nervously over her shoulder out the window. The BMW was gone and with it, Dr. Mueller. *If* it had been Dr. Mueller. Of all the places in the world for him to come, what would bring him to Fleetwood? She had come here specifically because she doubted he ever would. What would bring him into her life again after all these years? And if he had come, would she really recognize him after all this time? The answer to that question was easy. Even as aged as he was, Eva could not forget Dr. Mueller's dimpled chin, sloping forehead, and straight nose. His blond hair had turned white, but that was to be expected. If she had been closer to the man in the BMW, she was sure she would have seen his blue eyes. They were part of the perfect Aryan's features, weren't they? And hadn't Mueller been the perfect Aryan?

She had seen his profile, but had she seen him? Again, she asked herself: Why would he come to Fleetwood?

Jacob and Esau. She jumped as if she had been struck. The change Tina had just placed in Eva's hand spilled over the conveyor belt. Eva looked at the change on the checkout counter, then at Tina. Eva's self-control faded, and she started crying.

"I'm sorry," Tina apologized. "I'm just being a klutz today." Eva knew the girl was lying. Eva had dropped the money, not Tina.

Tina quickly gathered up Eva's change and put it in the old woman's hand. Then she gently closed Eva's hand over the change. Eva blindly dropped the money into her purse.

"Are you feeling ill, Miss Lachman? I can call Jacob to come and get you," Tina offered.

Jacob. Esau.

Dr. Mueller wanted her sons.

Eva shook her head. "No. I'm fine. Jacob's home doing chores. I can drive myself home," she blurted.

Tina nodded but still looked concerned about Eva. Eva tried to smile again. This time she must have been at least halfway successful because Tina smiled back.

Eva pushed the cart filled with her bagged groceries through the automatic doors and stopped it outside. She looked up Main Street in the direction the BMW had driven. It wasn't parked along the road. She had hoped she could get another look at the man just to be sure. Had Mueller come to take her sons away from her?

She shivered from a sudden chill and took a step back from the road as if she thought Mueller might be watching her from a hiding place further up the road.

She hadn't seen Mueller she told herself. Seeing the story about Hitler in the tabloid had scared her. It had started her imagination up. That was all. The man in the BMW was just a stranger riding through town. He was probably five miles outside of Fleetwood already. Just passing through on his way back to the city.

Jacob and Esau were home. They had to be home. Esau couldn't leave the farm, and Jacob would never leave without permission. And, both boys knew better than to let anyone onto the property. They were safe at the farm. No one, especially Mueller, could get her sons there.

Eva took another step backwards and felt something press against her back. She jumped forward and spun around. Behind her stood a large Coke machine. She had backed into the corner. Sighing, she collapsed against the red machine, scolding herself for her foolishness. After the way she had acted in Kendall's, Tina probably thought she was a senile, old woman.

Was she senile? She had imagined seeing Mueller once before, but that had been in the late 1940s. Never since then.

Until now.

What if he had come back? Would he recognize her? What would he do to Jacob? What would he do to Esau? Eva started crying again.

CHAPTER 4

JULY 6, 1993

Daniel watched Heinsdorf walk through the crowd of zoo visitors, leaving him sitting in confusion on the bench. He rubbed his cheek wondering if he could feel his marks of shame that a mirror would show.

The old man stopped in front of his grandson and held out his hand.

The boy glanced over at Daniel, then he took his grandfather's hand. Jeffrey said something to his grandfather, and Heinsdorf shook his head. The boy laughed, and the two of them started walking toward the exit from the children's zoo.

Had Daniel made a devil's bargain with Heinsdorf? He would know within a day. What would Adam say if he knew about this?

Daniel stood up and started walking after Heinsdorf and his grandson. The boy was about the same age Daniel had been when he had beaten up a young boy in Israel simply because the boy's name had sounded German to him. He remembered the blind fury he had felt pounding at the boy's face with his fists until a passing adult had pulled him off the battered boy. The boy's family had complained to Daniel's father, but Ira Levitt had simply told the family they should change their name to something less offensive to a Jew's ear. That was the evil seed Heinsdorf had referred to. Even then, it had infected Daniel and turned him into a creature of hatred. And instead of weeding it out, Daniel's father had nurtured the seed in his son. The memory brought an unpleasant realization Daniel hoped Jeffrey Heinz would not have to realize someday.

His mission from Adam had been to confirm whether Greg Heinz was Gregor Heinsdorf and if so, to expose him, so the Israeli government would ask the United States to revoke Heinsdorf's citizenship and extradite him to Israel.

Daniel had completed the first half of his mission. Heinz was indeed Heinsdorf. The man had admitted it. So why wasn't Daniel calling Adam right now to tell him to have a press conference? Why weren't the Baltimore Police leading away one of their own in handcuffs? Daniel wished he knew why.

Adam would probably say he was getting soft. Adam would show him the pictures of the Jews being liberated from the concentration camps after the war. They looked like skeletons with skins. Many of them were so weak they couldn't walk or even stand up on their own. Still, those were just photos. They were someone else's memories. Not Daniel's. He had no memories of the war. He hadn't even been born until more than ten years after it had ended. All he knew, he had learned through the understandably biased Jewish eye, in particular that of his father, an Auschwitz survivor.

Daniel almost laughed. He thought he was such a worldly person. He had traveled over most of the world, hadn't he? But in all his growing and learning, he had missed one basic truth most children learn before they are a dozen years old. Sometimes adults lie to children. Santa Claus, the Tooth Fairy, all Germans are Nazis. Sometimes the lies helped the children deal with life; and sometimes they helped the adults deal with life.

An itch under his eye reminded him of what would happen if he exposed a repentant man... another mark of shame.

Heinsdorf's grandson protested for a few moments as they walked through the main gate and out of the zoo into the parking lot.

"Sorry to have spoiled your day, Jeffrey, but right now your grandfather has other things on his mind than seeing the elephants in the African habitat," Daniel muttered to himself. And the truth was, he did feel sorry. A boy should be able to enjoy his boyhood and not have to face what Jeffrey Heinz would learn in a day.

Heinsdorf helped his grandson into the car, what looked like a police-surplus Cavalier. As the old man straightened up, he glanced across the roof of the car and saw Daniel standing by his car. When Heinsdorf climbed behind the wheel of his car, Daniel did the same and followed them out onto Druid Park Drive. He might be stupid to have made the deal he did with Heinsdorf, but he wasn't a complete idiot as to let the man drive off without following him.

Heinsdorf drove his grandson back to the townhouse that Jeffrey's parents owned in Owings Mills. Heinsdorf's son had followed his father's example and taken a job concerned with law, but not as a police officer. David Heinz was a lawyer with Taylor, Brasturn, and Pullman in the city. From everything Daniel could find about David, the lawyer was an honest Democrat with no Nazi sympathies or connections.

To Heinsdorf's credit, he made a point of staying in Daniel's view. He stood on the porch in the front of the townhouse declining his daughter-in-law's invitation to come inside. When David came out, the three of them stood on the small front porch talking. Daniel couldn't hear what they were saying, but he guessed Heinsdorf was probably saying his goodbyes. Whatever the old man was planning on doing wouldn't involve or implicate them. But Heinsdorf was a family man, and he would try to ease the pain his absence would cause his family. Heinsdorf hugged his son and kissed his daughter-in-law goodbye. Then he ruffled Jeffrey's hair and turned back toward the car.

David and Helen Heinz watched their father climb into his car. Daniel could tell by their confused and worried expressions they thought something was wrong with him, but they couldn't guess at what it was. Who would suspect a retired Baltimore City cop of being an ex-Nazi? Heinsdorf smiled cheerfully and waved to them as he drove off.

Daniel waited a moment and followed Heinsdorf. He wished he knew what the old Nazi was planning on doing. He had agreed to give the old man a day to put his affairs in order and distance his family, but from what he knew about the man, he had very few affairs to put in order. Greg Heinz was a retired police officer who lived in a row home in Baltimore and kept his money in a federally insured bank. Other than the time spent with his family, Heinsdorf lived alone. No poker games left unplayed with his old buddies. No girlfriends having to finish life without a mate. No senior centers with one more empty chair where he spent his afternoons. His entire life was his family, and Daniel had just watched him give that up.

After following Heinsdorf for fifteen minutes on the Baltimore Beltway, the old man pulled into St. Mark's Church in Catonsville. It was a small stone church with beautiful stained-glass windows, which would now cost so much that they could not be replaced if they were ever broken. He thought the old man might go into the chapel and ask a priest for forgiveness for his past sins. He was prepared to follow Heinsdorf into the chapel, but the old man walked around the side of the building instead. Quickly changing direction, Daniel found himself in a graveyard behind the church. It was a small graveyard with probably no more than a hundred old markers in it.

Daniel stood at the corner of the church and rubbed his cheek as he watched the old man. Heinsdorf knelt on one knee in front of a grave. The man Daniel watched pray in the cemetery was a completely different man than the one who had kept up with a ten-year-old boy in the Baltimore Zoo. Greg Heinz had been an energetic old man with a broad smile. Gregor Heinsdorf was a stooped old man with pale skin.

Curious, Daniel approached the man quietly from behind. When he got close enough, he could read the name on the grave marker: Julia Heinz. Beloved wife of Greg. Loving mother of David. From the dates on the marker, she had died two years ago. Daniel wondered if she had ever known the truth about her husband.

"Please, allow me these few moments with my wife," Heinsdorf said without turning around.

Without replying, Daniel walked back to the corner of the chapel and waited. Heinsdorf's shoulders shook as he cried. Feeling like a voyeur, Daniel turned away. After a few minutes, Heinsdorf walked back past him on his way to his car.

He stopped, looked at Daniel, and said, "Thank you."

From the church, Heinsdorf drove downtown. Although it was Saturday, traffic in the city was still heavy, but it was moving faster than it did on weekdays. If he hadn't known better, Daniel would have thought Heinsdorf was trying to lose him in the crowd. However, the old man did not make any quick turns or speed up unexpectedly. He seemed to drive with no destination in mind. Daniel was sure he had passed the intersection of Mount Royal Avenue and Charles Street at least three times.

After half an hour of aimless driving, Heinsdorf parked his car on Charles Street a few blocks below Mount Royal Avenue. He climbed out of his car and stood beside it. Daniel drove past him and found another parking space a half block beyond Heinsdorf's. After Daniel had parked, he climbed out of his car so that he could watch the old man and follow him on foot, if necessary.

Heinsdorf was still waiting next to his car watching the traffic rush past him even though he had several opportunities to cross the road.

As Daniel approached him, Heinsdorf looked over at him. He raised his hand and gave Daniel a short wave. Then he dashed into the middle of the street.

Daniel hesitated for a moment, but when he realized what was happening, he yelled, "Heinsdorf, stop!"

Daniel wasn't sure whether Heinsdorf stopped because Daniel yelled or because it was part of his plan to keep his family free from having their lives torn apart when he was deported. Whatever the reason, the old man stopped and stood in the middle of the Charles Street.

Behind him, a horn blared and tires squealed. The driver of an eighteen wheeler bearing down on the old man tried desperately to stop. He spun his steering wheel hard to the left, but he was too close. Daniel was also too close. He could see the panic and fear in the truck driver's face as the man realized he would hit the old man. Heinsdorf's face showed no such fear. He just closed his eyes and waited. He looked almost... peaceful. Daniel couldn't understand it. The man was content to die.

Daniel turned away just before the truck hit Heinsdorf, but he couldn't turn away from the sickening thud of the impact. A woman on the sidewalk screamed. Daniel hesitatingly turned back. He had to see. He had to be sure. Heinsdorf was lying in the road twenty feet closer to him than when he had been standing. His body was twisted at an unnatural angle. Though Heinsdorf's back was toward Daniel, his head was staring over his left shoulder so that Daniel could see his face. What was left of it. One side of Heinsdorf's head was a mass of blood as if the old man had slid along the road on his face after the truck hit him. The thought made Daniel's stomach queasy. What was worse, Heinsdorf seemed to stare at him. It was an accusing stare. One that said, "Are you happy now? Is this how you wanted to see me?"

But it wasn't how Daniel wanted to see him. Before a judge and in jail—yes. A bloody mass of flesh lying dead on the road—no.

Daniel turned away from the corpse and shuffled back to his car.

Behind him, he could hear the truck driver protesting his innocence. In the distance, he heard an ambulance's siren blaring. He climbed in his car, took a deep breath, and drove away.

CHAPTER 5

JULY 6, 1993

With a loud grunt, Brad Kendall heaved the last bushel of fruit into the bed of Eva's pickup truck. He set the bushel of peaches on the tail gate, caught his breath, and pushed the bushel towards the other four bushels of fruit near the front of the truck bed. Finished, he stepped back and wiped his hands against each other. Eva stood next to the truck door, tapping her foot against the pavement. She looked up anxiously any time a car passed the parking lot along Hanover Street.

Brad Kendall was a small, wiry man, not much larger than Eva. He was not the Kendall who owned Kendall's Country Store, but the only son of the man who did. On a normal day, Eva might have teased Brad about his thin build, but not today. Today, she just wanted to get home.

She had to make sure the boys were all right. If she had seen Mueller, they were all in danger.

Brad closed the tailgate and sighed. Sweat from his exertions soaked the back of his white shirt.

"All loaded, Miss Lachman," Brad said as he wiped his forehead with the back of his arm.

Eva nodded curtly and climbed into the cab. She started the truck and raced the engine. Brad shrugged and walked back inside his father's grocery store through the rear door.

Eva ground the gears as she pulled out of the parking lot onto Hanover Road. The engine grated, and the truck hesitated until she got it completely in gear. She would have corrected Jacob for such a foolish mistake. Now, with fear rising in her throat she only hoped Jacob would be around to make such a foolish mistake again.

On Hanover Road, she pushed the truck up to eighty miles per hour.

The old truck shook and complained about the high speed, but it went faster. She ignored the pot holes in the road and simply drove through them and held onto the steering wheel when she was bounced into the air. Her seatbelt kept her head from hitting the roof. Some of the fruit flew out of the baskets and onto the road when she bounced through the pot holes, but she didn't even notice them. Even if she had, she wouldn't have stopped or slowed down. What would having fresh fruit matter if she didn't have her sons to eat it? She didn't care if Chief Montgomery saw her speeding or not. She just knew she had to get home and make sure her sons were safe.

"Please let them be home," she muttered to herself.

Mueller had already taken her parents from her. She couldn't let him take her sons, too.

The Lachman farm covered 102 acres of Allegany County. Eva had bought it with money from the trust her parents had set up for her and from the settlement after the war on the properties the Nazis had stolen from her family. In 1965, when she bought the farm, Allegany County was called country. Now Interstate 68 made it easy for people to travel to the area from Cumberland and Hagerstown. Too easy, if you asked Eva.

The Lachman farm was a farm in name only. No harvest came from it. Its border was bounded with a ten-foot-high, chain-link fence topped with barbed wire. Everyone in Fleetwood knew about it. They called the farm, "The Prison," and chalked it up to Eva's eccentricities just as they did her enormous weekly fruit purchases. No one cared what she did as long as she continued spending her money in town. However, if the townspeople could have seen the second fence that ran around the farmhouse, they would have considered Eva truly crazy. This fence was also ten-feet tall and topped with barbed wire. It circled the small three-acre area around the house. Access onto the farm and into the house was through two remote-controlled gates that spanned the driveway.

Eva didn't even slow the truck down as she approached the outer fence. She just started pushing the button on the dash to open the first gate and kept pushing it until she got within range for the small remote control to work. The gate slowly rolled open, and she barely missed crashing into it as she sped through the opening and down the long driveway.

Once through the gap, she punched the button once more, and the gate reversed its direction as it closed. If Mueller hadn't come already, she didn't want to give him the opportunity to walk right onto her property. She had the fences built to keep people like Mueller out more so than to keep Esau on the farm. She pushed a second button, and the interior gate opened. A third button on the driver's-side visor raised the garage door.

She stomped her foot on the brake pedal as the truck entered the garage. The truck slid forward as the wheels locked. The frozen wheels squealed against the concrete. She braced herself against the seat and pressed on the pedal even harder, but it was already to the floor. Blue smoke spewed from the squealing tires. The truck slowed rapidly, skidding past the usual stopping point toward the garage's far wall.

She closed her eyes expecting the truck to go through the wall and into the backyard. Instead, it halted with a strong jerk as if to remind her how close to an accident she had come. She opened her eyes and saw the truck had stopped about two inches from the wall. She slammed the gear shift into neutral and turned the engine off.

Jumping out of the truck's cab, Eva rushed for the door that led into the kitchen. She fumbled with her keys for a moment until she found the right one. The foul-smelling smoke from burned tires made her eyes water so that it was hard to tell one key from another. She was yelling before she even opened the door.

"Jacob! Esau! Boys! Where are you!"

She ran through the kitchen almost falling against the wooden table.

Jacob would be in the living room, watching cartoons.

He wasn't. The living room was empty, but the television was turned on. Some talk show host was talking to a group of female bodybuilders who had once been men. It looked like Jacob had stepped away to go to the kitchen, but he hadn't come back. He certainly didn't watch mindless talk shows. Where was he now?

"Jacob! Answer me! This is not-hide and seek!" she screamed.

No one answered her. Suddenly, all she could think of was the last time she had seen her sons. Jacob had been watching cartoons on the television and Esau had been playing his newest game on his computer. She shouldn't have left them alone this morning. But she couldn't very well take Esau into town, could she? Instead of leaving them, she should have stayed home. The groceries could have waited. Of course, she hadn't known she would see Mueller in town.

She ran to the back door and looked out on the yard. Sometimes Esau couldn't hear her if he was outside at the far end of the yard. Maybe both of them were outside. She whimpered when she saw the back yard was as empty as the living room.

She was too late. Mueller had captured her sons.

CHAPTER 6

JULY 6, 1993

With a hard gulp, Daniel swallowed the last mouthful of Jim Beam.

The liquor burned his throat, but he was too drunk to care. What's a little burn compared to murdering a man?

He tossed the empty bottle into the waste can next to the desk. The glass rattled dully against the plastic basket as it tipped over. The bottle rolled out onto the floor of the hotel room toward Daniel as if it were calling him to pick it up.

He tried to stand up from his chair. It wasn't the easiest thing in the world to do, but after three attempts, he stayed upright. He staggered across the room to the bathroom. His stomach made him feel like he was standing on the deck of a boat being tossed about in a storm. That's what he got for drinking on an empty stomach.

He was tired, but he didn't want to sleep. He was terrified of what he might dream. As he passed the mirror over the bureau, he turned away so he wouldn't have to look at himself. He didn't want to see the scars each case left, his marks of shame.

What he wanted to do was splash some cold water on his face, but the bathroom was so far away. Why hadn't he gotten a smaller room? *Because there were no smaller rooms*, he reminded himself through his stupor. One size fits all. Taking a step past the bed, his feet and knees betrayed him and he fell back against the twin bed.

He had started drinking at six o'clock, just after he saw the news clip on the local news about Greg Heinz's suicide. The newscaster hadn't called it a suicide, though. He called it a tragic accident. An old man who couldn't move quickly enough struck down by the speeding traffic. Heinsdorf's plan had worked. He had kept his past from his family and paid for any crime he might ever have done.

Daniel thought such courageous actions ought to be toasted by the only person who knew the truth. So Daniel had toasted Greg Heinz with one shot of whiskey after another.

He raised his head and saw the telephone sitting on the nightstand.

Adam would expect his call about now. He would be waiting by the phone in his office above a small diner in Israel; waiting for his various operatives to call in with their progress reports.

What if Michael didn't call in? The idea appealed not only to his drunken side, but his sober side as well. What if he simply changed his name and wandered off to find himself a new life like Gregor Heinsdorf had done nearly fifty years ago? But look what had happened to Heinsdorf. He remembered the dead man's vacant stare and his bloodied face as he lay in a heap on Charles Street. Daniel's stomach tightened and for a short time. He thought he might vomit.

Daniel could never hide from Adam, nor would he try. The man would locate him if for no other reason than to make sure the Nazis hadn't killed one of his operatives.

Adam Goldstein was the founder of the Committee for the Prosecution of War Criminals. He was the chairman of the committee, and the war criminals he was concerned with were old Nazis. At sixty-seven, Adam was aging himself, but his hatred for the Nazis and their ideals was still as new as it had been when he had been sent to Dachau in 1943. His family of ten had gotten on the crowded cattle cars in Stupsk. Only nine had gotten off at Dachau. Of the nine, only four were actually selected as slave laborers, and of the four, only Adam walked out of the camp when it was liberated in 1945.

From that time on, Adam Goldstein had been an angry young man, but his anger had no direction. He found a focus for his energies when he saw the outcome of the Nuremburg trials. From his new home in France, he invested the money his father had left behind in banks in London, and he began collecting information from the European Jews in Jerusalem about their war-time experiences. This was the meager beginning of the Committee for the Prosecution of War Criminals. With Adam's guidance, it had grown from a committee of one to two dozen committed men. Since 1949, the Committee had been responsible for the exposure and imprisonment or execution of fifty-three Nazis.

Of that number, Daniel was now responsible for six exposures making him one of the most-effective committee members. Adam had recruited him in 1978 when the committee chairman discovered Adam's father had survived Auschwitz. The experience had left Ira Levitt unable to walk, but his son was healthy and ripe for recruitment. At that time, Daniel's hatred for anything German had blazed. But with time and experience, the fire was now only a few, hot coals, which he often tried to extinguish with alcohol. It was hard to maintain a flaming anger at an unseen entity, and it was nearly impossible to want to seek vengeance on old men and women.

That was all it was. Pure vengeance. Once the prosecution of the Nazis had served a purpose. It reminded the people of the atrocities committed by the Nazis in the name of Nazi idealism. It had been Jewish justice but not anymore. The prosecutions had succeeded and history had recorded for eternity the barbarity and menace of the Nazis. This is the same history that would be taught to the children through their history books. They could see the survivors of concentration camps looking like skeletons wrapped in tissue paper. They could see the ovens covered with bone ash. They could see atrocities being committed in propaganda photos. They could see pictures of young Nazis and believe these men were monsters.

Who would believe someone's grandfather was a monster? This sort of persecution of Nazis was becoming counter-effective for the committee and other Nazi-hunting organizations. For every Nazi tried, ten people thought the Jews were seeking vengeance, and perhaps ten more thought the Nazis had been right.

Daniel picked up the phone and contacted the overseas operator.

Through slurred words, he told her the number he wanted to reach and waited while she connected it. It took two minutes, but finally a throaty voice answered the call on the first ring.

"Hello."

The voice of God speaking. Ira Levitt's god and now his son's. Daniel said nothing. He just waited.

"Hello?" the voice said again.

"My subject is deceased," Daniel said, trying to gather enough strength to sound coherent. He tried to distance himself from the anguish was telling him to feel, but he was unsuccessful.

"Daniel, is that you?"

Daniel heard Adam rustling papers or maybe it was static over the line. Either way, he waited for it to end.

"Yes. It is me."

"What is this talk about Heinsdorf being dead? You didn't shoot him, did you? I can't protect you over there. America is not Africa."

Daniel winced at the off-hand reference to what he considered his greatest sin from which there would be no redemption.

"Heinz killed himself today." He deliberately used the name Heinz.

That was who had died on Charles Street. Greg Heinz, not Gregor

Heinsdorf. Heinsdorf had died many years ago.

Daniel saw the bloodied face and heard the soft body thump against the hard truck. He wished he had another bottle of Jim Beam, but he doubted even that would be enough.

"Why would he kill himself?" Adam asked.

"He knew I knew who he had been. He discovered I was following him and asked me for a day to prepare his family for what would follow." Daniel hesitated. "And I gave it to him."

"You what! That was a foolish thing to do, Daniel. You should have gone right to the police."

"He did not want to involve his family. They were not part of what he did," Daniel said in his own defense. "He had enough honor at least not to involve innocents." If only Ira Levitt had had as much honor.

Daniel raised himself off the bed and propped a pillow under his head.
"But he could have gotten away," Adam said.

"He did not."

There was a long silence on the line, and Daniel wondered what his employer was doing.

Finally, Adam said, "Fine. I'll close his case file then. Are you still in Baltimore?"

"Yes, but I will be leaving tomorrow. I would rather not stay here." Daniel rolled onto his back and held his arm across his eyes.

"You don't have to. I have another assignment for you."

Daniel felt hot even though he knew the room was cool. He wiped his damp forehead on the white bed sheet.

"I do not want another assignment right now. I want to come home. I need to rest. It is too soon to send me out again," Daniel pleaded.

"You'll want this one. It's not often you get a second chance at the man who killed your brother and sisters, not to mention who destroyed your father's legs."

Daniel rolled onto his stomach. "You know where Mueller is." Daniel's comment was not a question so much as it was an exclamation of surprise. Karl Mueller had killed Daniel's four brothers and sisters and his father's first wife while they were confined to Auschwitz, and his experiments had left Ira Levitt's legs like twisted twigs unable to move or support the weight of his body.

"Yes. He's in a town called Fleetwood."

"I have never heard of it."

"It's in Western Maryland."

"Maryland? Your reports said he was in South America."

"He was until a week ago. He and his son flew into National Airport then. I'm still trying to trace their passports. Anyway, they rented a car for two days until they purchased a new BMW in Wheaton. We need confirmation of our information and someone to lead the police to them. I want it to be you, Daniel. It's fate. God has brought him to you this time. This time you won't fail. I can feel it."

Mueller. Dr. Mueller. Mueller the Mauler.

In 1981, Daniel had tracked Mueller down to his home in South Africa. He had prepared to arrest the man, but a leak in the local police department had tipped off Mueller that he was being hunted. Daniel had arrived in time to see Mueller and his family racing to catch a flight out of the country. In a brief exchange of gunfire between Mueller and Daniel, Mueller and his son had gotten away, but Daniel accidentally killed Aria, Mueller's wife.

Aria Mueller became another innocent victim of World War II over thirty-five years after the war had ended. Daniel hadn't meant to kill the woman. He hadn't even been aiming for her. He had shot at Mueller, but the bullet had ricocheted off the plane's bulkhead above Mueller's head and struck Aria in the heart.

"Daniel, will you take this assignment?" Adam asked from across an ocean.

On his bed, Daniel cried silently. "Yes," he told Adam.

Was the only way out of the cycle to die? That was Heinsdorf's answer. Would it be Daniel's too?

CHAPTER 7

JULY 6, 1993

The coming of night brought no relief for Eva. Neither Jacob nor Esau had come home, and her mind only allowed her to imagine the worst. They must be dead. Her sons had never been without her for so long, and she couldn't protect them where they were now. Esau had never even been off the farm before, and she allowed Jacob to make only brief trips into town. He liked to walk the two miles into town when she allowed him.

But now Mueller had her sons and he would surely kill them.

Her body shook slightly as she began crying. For most of her life she had protected Jacob and Esau; not only from the Nazis but from those who would lock them up and study them or kill them simply because they were different. For years, she had sacrificed a normal life only to fail them in the end; to fail them because she had become too complacent with her life. Her old age had weakened her enough that she had been careless. Esau had no experience dealing with people face to face and Jacob did poorly at it. Despite their size and strength, they would be no match for Dr. Mueller.

She collapsed onto the couch in the living room and buried her face in the throw pillows. She pounded silently on the cushions with her fists. Why did he have to come back? A few more years and she would have died in peace. Hadn't she gone through enough already? Hadn't he taken enough from her already? Did he have to take her sons, too?

If only her father was still alive. She could trust Papa. He would tell her what to do. But Mueller had taken his guidance away from her forever. She sobbed even louder. They had all been nothing more than vermin to the Nazis. Her entire family... her people... had been vermin, laboratory mice, and firewood.

A hot salty smell assaulted her nose, and she pressed her face deeper into the throw pillows. She knew her imagination was creating the scent from her memory, but she didn't deny the smell of hundreds of unwashed Jews crammed together on a cattle car. It had been real once, just as the Jews had been alive once. They had been pressed against each other for hours. It had caused the temperature in the boxcar to rise. People were sweating and there was no way to clean themselves. They were lucky if they could even raise their arm to wipe the sweat from their brow. The Jews had to perform their bodily functions in their clothes, and that only added to the smell within the confined space. Those people at the sides of the car were lucky. At least they had fresh air to breathe. Eva had not been one of the lucky ones. The crowd kept her stuck near the center of the boxcar between her parents.

Her feet ached. She wished she could sit, but there was no room.

She wished she were back in her house lying on her comfortable bed. Did they even have a house any longer?

The Nazis had come to Eva's home the night before or the night before that one. She wasn't sure which. However, she was sure of their rifles and pistols. The brown-suited men had arrested her father, her mother, and herself as enemies of the Fatherland. The Nazis had herded them into the boxcar as if they were nothing more than cattle. The Nazis didn't even give them seats to sit on. They could pack more Jews into the rail car if there were no seats taking up the space. No longer did the Nazis even pretend that the Jews they arrested were only being relocated to work for the good of the Fatherland. They were being led away to die, and they knew it.

Many others shared the boxcar with Eva and her family, so many that all they could do was stand even if there had been seats to sit on.

Everyone was forced to stand crammed against each other. Elbows poking in stomachs. Short people not being able to see over the shoulder of the person next to them; not that they could have seen anything, only more misery. Sometimes, a person's nose would touch another person's nose as they stood face to face, and they maintained this position for days. Eva was pressed between her parents so tightly that when she had fallen asleep (or had she passed out?) she remained standing.

She raised her head off her father's chest looking into his weary face. The darkness in the rail car only accentuated the deepening lines in his face. His eyes were closed, and she wondered if he was awake.

Even as she wondered, her father opened his eyes. "Ah, Eva, you are awake? Did you have a good nap?"

"I suppose, Papa."

He stroked the back of her head with his right hand. His left hand was pinned at his side by the crowd.

"Good, good," he whispered.

"Will we be wherever they are taking us soon?"

Her father's stroking paused for the briefest moment, then continued smoothly.

"We will get there when we get there. We are in God's hands now. He will either deliver us, or we will soon join him."

Eva laid her head on her father's chest again. She could hear the steady beat of his heart. She heard it above the sound of the train rolling over the tracks and even above the people moaning from the pain caused by standing on their feet for two days.

The train slowed suddenly throwing her back against her mother.

Her mother grunted in pain.

"I'm sorry, Mama."

Ruth Lachman leaned her head against her daughter's because she could not raise either of her hands.

"It's all right, Eva. It was not your fault," Eva's mother assured her.

Eva looked to the side of the car. Bright light showed through the slats of the car. It was too intense to be the twilight of another day. Perhaps it was a town, but she couldn't tell where she was.

She heard a high-pitched squeal of the wheels against the iron tracks as the train slowed to a stop. Everyone looked toward the side of the car; toward the door. She heard a shout, then the sound of the boxcar door on the adjoining car opening. The boxcar expelled its passengers with a rush of air like a collective sigh. Then their door was unlocked. It slid open, and she saw more Nazis. Always the Nazis.

The people with her spilled onto the platform eager to breathe fresh, cool air and sit down or move freely. Many of the Jews collapsed on the floor of the boxcar once their surrounding support of other people moved onto the platform because their legs were too numb to move. Even on the platform, the Jews were confined, just not as tightly. Nazis lined the edges of the platform keeping the Jews within their circle. The only place where the Jews could get off the platform was at a ramp at one corner. The people formed a single line and slowly hobble off the platform.

At the bottom of the ramp was another Nazi. He had blond hair and blue eyes–the perfect Nazi ideal. Tapping his foot impatiently on the ground, he looked bored with his job. He either pointed the people coming down the ramp to a truck convoy or toward a waiting area beside the platform.

Behind the Nazi, in the distance, she saw the wire fence that marked the boundary of the concentration camp. Beyond the fence, she saw a wooden building and towering, brick smokestacks spewing out black smoke into the light of early dawn. The sign on the station read "Auschwitz." Eva shuddered. She had heard the rumors of what went on here. Her parents had talked about it during the night when they thought she was asleep. Their talk was of torture and death, things that had given her nightmares. Her parents had wanted to run across the border, but they decided that would only draw attention to themselves. So they had stayed and remained as inconspicuous as they could. In the end, they had not even dared to venture out of the house. Their ruse had not lasted for long.

Would this be the end of her now? To die in the ovens of Auschwitz? Eva was only thirteen. She had never kissed a boy yet. She had never traveled outside of Germany to Paris, London, New York, and Cairo. She was just a child. Children weren't supposed to die!

Eva stood with her parents near the middle of the stumbling pack of Jews making their way down the ramp. She hoped the Nazis would point her toward the trucks. She wanted to sit down. Just for a little while at least. She was tired of standing. She was going to die anyway, wasn't she? The least they could do was to allow her last few minutes to be free of pain.

As she came down the ramp, the young Nazi making the selections smiled at her. Although he was quite handsome outside, she knew he was ugly inside, and she did not smile back. The Nazi pointed her toward the waiting area beside the ramp. She limped to the side and waited for her parents to join her.

When they came down the ramp a short distance behind her, the Nazi at the bottom pointed them both toward the trucks. She started toward them, but another Nazi pushed her back in the waiting area. She fell against the man behind her, and then both she and the man fell to the ground. The nearby soldiers laughed at them as they struggled to untangle themselves and stand.

"They're my parents. I want to stay with them," Eva said to the soldier who had pushed her.

"Stay with your group," the man barked.

"But they're my parents," she pleaded.

She stood up and tried to run past the guard to her parents.

"I said stay with your group!" The soldier grabbed her by the arm and shoved her back toward the waiting area again.

"Papa, help!" Eva called.

Nearly to the trucks, Aaron Lachman heard her scream. He stopped walking and turned to look for her. When he saw her back by the platform, he started toward his daughter, but another soldier making sure everyone got on the trucks stopped him. Aaron tried to push by the man, but the soldier jammed his rifle butt in her father's stomach. Eva's father doubled over and fell to his knees. Her mother dropped to his side and hugged him.

He looked up and called to Eva, "Wait for me at the gate! I'll meet you at the gate!"

She nodded she understood. The soldier pulled at her again. She turned and walked toward the waiting area. Looking back over her shoulder, she saw her mother helping her father to her feet. He was still holding his stomach, but at least he didn't look hurt too badly. His face looked very pale, though, as if he might be sick.

"I'll wait for you, Papa," she whispered to herself.

When she had been freed, she had waited, too. She had stood for a full day in the freezing cold waiting for her father to join her by the gates. The trees she had hidden among had done little to keep her warm. Her clothes had been rags and every time the wind blew, a chill had rushed up her back. By then, the twins had been born. Jacob had cried continually unless she rocked him, and Esau had kept trying to crawl away. But she had waited because she had known her father would come. He had said he would, and he had never lied to her.

But he never came. She had looked at the large smokestacks over the incinerators inside Auschwitz and realized that was where her father had gone, and he would not be coming back. He could not keep his promise to her this time.

Mueller had sent her parents to the gas chamber. Now he had taken her sons as well.

CHAPTER 8

JULY 7, 1993

Despite what the sign he had passed only moments ago said, Daniel found it hard to call Fleetwood, Maryland, a town. But the small green-and-white sign said Fleetwood was home to 1,925 people. Now that Daniel was in the heart of the town and he could see how large it was, he doubted it.

The business district was an eight-square-block area flowing from the intersection of Hanover Road and Main Street. He knew it was the business district because the intersection had the town's only traffic light.

Daniel passed through the light and turned into the Sunoco station for gas and information, if any was to be found. Fleetwood appeared to be the type of town Mueller would hide in. Isolated and unknown. Except, why would he come to America to hide? The only worse place he could have hidden would have been Israel. Now wouldn't that have been a sight? Karl Mueller the Israeli.

Daniel stopped his ten-year-old Corolla next to the self-serve pump and climbed out of the car.

As he filled his tank, he looked over the town. His first impression had been right. Even when you slowed down, Fleetwood still wasn't much to see. Besides the gas station, a grocery store, a hardware store, and an antique shop sat on the other three corners of the intersection. On Hanover Road, he could see a dry cleaner, a diner, a veterinarian hospital, another antique shop, a beauty salon, a video store, and a feed store. On Main Street, a bank, a post office, a shoe store, a doctor's office, a Dollar General, a clothes store, the sheriff's office, and a barber shop filled the block. Beyond the business area, he could see three steeples marking the locations of churches. This was the vision of America he thought could be found only in old movies.

The gas station attendant walked out of the office to watch Daniel finish topping off his tank. He wore dirty, gray coveralls, which had a name tag sewn to the chest that read, "Bill."

Daniel put the nozzle back in the slot on the side of the pump. Bill wiped his greasy hands on his coveralls. The coveralls were already so dirty Daniel wasn't sure whether wiping his hands put more grease on the coveralls or Bill's hands.

"That'll be ten bucks," Bill said as if Daniel couldn't read the pump's display.

Daniel took a ten-dollar bill from his wallet. "This seems to be a quiet town," he said as he passed the money to the attendant.

"Yup."

Bill shoved the bill into his pocket.

"Is there a hotel in town? I do not see any signs for one," Daniel asked.

Bill stared at him. Daniel assumed it was because of his accent. His voice didn't have the twangy accent of Western Maryland. Because of the different languages he knew, Daniel had learned to speak with more precision than the natives of the country used themselves.

Bill shook his head. "The closest thing we got is the Maryland House. It's a bed-and-breakfast place. If you ask me, it's nothing more than an old boarding house, but calling it a bed-and-breakfast inn lets old Charlie Hardesty charge that much more to folks who want to stay. And lots of those politicians from Washington like to come out here for a quiet weekend. They stay there. Of course, they're using my tax money to stay there when they could just as well have stayed at a Motel 6. Hancock has some hotels. It's about twenty miles to the east of here."

"I suppose the Maryland House should do for me," Daniel said.

When he saw Bill's friendliness retreat 'a bit, he added, "My boss is paying for it, and I guess he would only want the best for me."

Bill laughed, and the friendliness returned. "How do I get there?" Daniel asked.

Bill pointed over Daniel's shoulder. "It's down Hanover Road about two miles. There's a sign on the right and long driveway that will lead you to the house. Can't miss it."

"Thanks," Daniel said. "I appreciate the information. I guess you get asked questions a lot. You are probably the first person to see all the strangers who come into town."

The man shrugged. "Only if they're low on gas. Otherwise, they could buzz right on through and I'd never see them, just their cars. Those politician's cars, though, are all fuel hogs. Not a one comes into town that doesn't stop and see me."

"I assume you know most of the people who live here pretty well?" Daniel continued.

"Yup," Bill agreed.

Daniel straightened up. "Have you had two men visiting in town lately? One man would be in his eighties and the other man would be about your age. Their last names are Mueller."

The mechanic frowned and his forehead wrinkled as he eyed Daniel suspiciously. Daniel stared back unwaveringly.

A tall, muscular man rose from his chair in front of the office and lumbered over to Daniel and Bill. He had a thick sandwich in one hand and a half-gallon carton of milk in the other. He stood about six-feet tall and probably weighed 250 pounds. Because he had a heavy brow ridge, Daniel thought the man looked like he might have Down's syndrome.

"Who are you looking for, Mister?" the man asked. His voice was deep and had an unnatural ring to it, though Daniel wasn't sure why he thought that.

"Jacob, hush up. Go sit back down and eat your breakfast. I'll call your ma in a minute," Bill said to Jacob. From his adult-talking-to-a-child tone of voice, Daniel decided Jacob probably was mentally challenged.

Turning back to Daniel, Bill said, "He's not playing with a full deck if you know what I mean. He was sitting in front of my door this morning complaining that he was hungry. I used to give him a free candy bar now and then because I felt sorry for him, you know? So I guess he thought I would treat him to a breakfast if he asked. Of course, the way that man eats would bankrupt me. I don't see how his ma can afford it."

Daniel glanced at Jacob. "It looks like you gave him food to eat."

Bill smiled sheepishly. "Yeah. I guess I'm an old softy. I don't have no kids of my own, and Jacob ain't nothing but a big kid, so we get along. As soon as he's done, I've got to go call his ma to come and get him. She's an eccentric thing. I can see why Jacob turned out the way he did. Take care, Mister."

Bill turned away and started walking back to his service bay, then he stopped and turned back to Daniel.

"Why do you want to know about these two men? You don't look like a cop, and you sure don't sound like one," he asked.

"I am not," Daniel replied.

"Then why should I tell you anything? Loose lips can cost this town money. Those Washington-types spend a lot of money in town, but they don't always come out here with their wives, if you know what I mean. And like I said, their cars like the way I treat them." Daniel nodded. "If I was to say I knew where these two men were, and I'm not saying I know, mind you. But if I was, you might cart them off to the town jail. That means you'd be taking money out of this town, including the money that would be spent here."

Daniel pulled a fifty-dollar bill out of his wallet and held it up in front of Bill's face. The man stared at the money. Money spoke every language fluently.

"Maybe I can put my own money into this town or at least parts of it," Daniel said.

Bill reached for the money, but Daniel pulled it away.

Looking frustrated, Bill said, "No. I don't know nobody named Mueller. I don't think there's anyone in town by that name. Anyways, at least not one that's stopped by here." Jacob started to say something, but Bill silenced him with a harsh look. "Do I get the money, anyway?"

"On one condition."

"What?"

"I will be staying in town for a little while. I will probably visit here occasionally and ask you the same question. I will give you fifty dollars to keep watch, and if your answer ever changes, I will give you another fifty dollars when you tell me where the Muellers are staying."

"Did those men do something wrong? Is that why you're looking for them?" Bill asked.

"To find that out, you would have to give me a hundred dollars," Daniel said.

"But you only gave me fifty."

"My information is worth more than yours." Daniel handed the fifty-dollar bill to the mechanic. Bill said nothing. Daniel turned and walked to his car. Jacob followed him.

"Mister, I've seen a man named Mueller," Jacob said.

Daniel paused and looked at the retarded man. Did he really know something or was he just talking?

"Jacob, don't bother the man." Bill turned to Daniel. "He's harmless, but he's slow." Bill twirled his finger around his temple.

"Where do you know him from?" Daniel asked Jacob.

Jacob hesitated. "I've seen him down by the river sometimes." He paused and looked around. "I take walks down there sometimes when my Mama lets me come to town. She lets me go alone as long as I'm back before night," he added after a moment.

Daniel rubbed his face. He had been driving over two hours to get here. All he wanted to do now was rest, but if this man knew where Mueller was, Daniel might be able to end his business now. Of course, he hadn't been able to end it in twelve years. What made him think he could end it now?

Because Karl Mueller had made a mistake that was why! He had come to America with its strong Jewish population. America with its computerized technology to make the hunt that much easier.

Why had he come to America? That was the question that begged to be answered. However, Daniel could live without the answer if he could only see Mueller dead. Ira Levitt's justice would be satisfied, and Daniel could get on with his life. It was too late to try to become a doctor again, but maybe he could be a nurse.

"How do you know the person you saw was Mueller?" Daniel asked. Jacob frowned. "Because I heard one man call the other man Dr. Mueller."

Doctor? Daniel was suddenly attentive to Jacob's story. He had mentioned nothing about Karl Mueller being a doctor. Maybe Jacob had seen him.

Jacob was still staring at Daniel waiting for a response. "How do I get to where you saw him?" Daniel asked.

"It's down by the river. You'll have to park your car by the bridge and walk through the woods. I can show you the way. I know all the trails through there."

Daniel opened the door to his car. "Okay. Let's go."

Chapter 9

JULY 7, 1993

When Esau Lachman opened his eyes in the morning, the first thing he saw was the sky shining through the branches of a cluster of maple trees. The leaves were bright green, mostly; some were turning brown as they withered in the July heat. Beyond the leaves was the sky; light blue with an occasional patch of white of a passing cloud. The leaves seemed to break the sunlight up into individual rays. The sight confused Esau for a moment until he remembered where he was.

He was free!

He stretched out his long body to its full length, then folded his arms behind his head to watch the morning sky. The clouds slid lazily by, and he watched their progress through a small opening in the canopy of leaves as they passed overhead. He tried to associate the shapes with something real as he often did when he watched the clouds from the farm. One was a loaf of bread. Another was the pickup truck. A third looked like a rabbit.

He took a deep breath. His broad chest swelled even larger. The air smelled sweeter. Yes, sweeter. It wasn't tainted by stagnation like the air around the farm.

He chuckled, and the forest went silent. The birds chirped a quick warning and then shut up. Animals moving in the woods froze until they could identify the sound as a friend or enemy.

Esau sat up in the leaf-and-branch bed he had made the night before. He brushed the leaves from himself. Wrapping his arms around his knees, he rocked back and forth, humming to himself. After a minute of doing this, he let himself roll backwards into a rear somersault. He stood up and stretched his arms as far over his head as he could.

He wondered what his mother was doing and thinking right now. She worried about him. His mother worried a lot. He hated that she would fret over him, but this was more important.

He felt young, although he was almost fifty years old. This was the way he should feel all the time. Freedom made him feel young. He wondered if he would still feel that way when he returned home because he knew he would eventually return. He loved his mother too much to stay away from her and torment her by his absence. Would the memory of his time spent free burn forever in his memory keeping him young or would it gradually fade? If it faded, he might leave again for another trip like this one.

Esau wondered what Jacob had thought when he found him missing yesterday morning. Whenever their mother left them alone, Jacob thought of it as his job to babysit Esau. Jacob was probably too stupid to realize how his brother had escaped. Esau considered himself stupid for not thinking of it before. The chain-link fence surrounding the house and yard had been built to human specifications, not to his. It had been simple to pull apart the wire bands that held the fence to the posts and then pull the fence up so he could duck under it. That way the fence wasn't destroyed. And since it wasn't obvious how he had left, he might be able to use the same way again. So simple and yet, it had taken him twenty years to realize it. Maybe Jacob wasn't the only stupid one in the family.

Esau jumped up and grabbed the thick maple branch above his head. Lifting his feet, he let the branch take his weight. It sagged under his 350 pounds, but it did not break. He swung his legs up over the branch and let his body follow until finally he was sitting on top of the branch. With his legs dangling playfully in the air. He laughed again. A hush fell over the woods, but he didn't care. He meant the animals no harm, and they would learn that soon enough just as the forest animals around the farm had learned. In a way, he was one of them.

His stomach rumbled. Esau rubbed it to quiet it down. He should have brought himself some food for his trip. He had been so excited at the discovery of an escape route from the farm that he had left without planning what he would do while he was free. Next time he would bring a lunch.

If there was a next time.

He jumped down from the branch. With plenty of farms nearby, he should be able to find enough food and vegetables in the fields to fill even his stomach. And if he was careful, no one would see him. That was the important thing. He could crawl in low under the height of the plants, take what he wanted, and be gone just as quickly. If someone saw him, the same thing would happen that had happened in Poland so long ago.

He was older now, and more cautious. He wouldn't make the same mistake again.

The river was closer than the fields. He was thirsty, too. First, he would drink, then he would worry about finding food.

Perhaps he would go home tonight. His mother would punish him but it would be worth it. Every man and beast should know freedom at least once, even if it lasted only two days. His two days had been the only two days of his life that he had control of since the day of freedom he had known when he was ten. When Esau went home, he would always know he had chosen to go home and not been forced to do it like before.

It was good to have this time to live and to think. Especially to think.

That was what had caused him to want to leave in the first place. He had finally realized that the reason his mother kept him hidden was not because she was afraid someone would hurt him. She was afraid that someone would learn the secret she tried so desperately to hide. And that secret was him.

CHAPTER 10

JULY 7, 1993

By the time dawn came, Eva had cried herself to sleep, finally giving in to exhaustion and falling asleep at two in the morning. It was a tenuous sleep, though, filled with dreams of what Mueller might do to her sons. Dreams of torture. Visions of killings. She could see her sons crying out for her in her dreams but she could do nothing to help them. They were at Dr. Mueller's mercy, or lack of it, now.

She slept until the sun rose high enough to shine directly through her window. Because she had been too upset to remember to pull the shade last night, the sunlight shone directly on her face. Eva rolled away from the bright light pulling her blanket over her head. She sobbed gently to herself beneath her covers. She was alone. Mueller had taken her family from her again.

After a few minutes, she stopped and listened. It was too quiet in the house. No voices arguing or laughing in other rooms of the house. No feeling the heavy footsteps that sometimes shook the floor of the old farmhouse. Downstairs, the television was silent, showing neither Esau's horror movies nor Jacob's cartoons. Nothing at all because Mueller had her sons.

She clasped her hands together in front of her as she prayed. "Blessed God, I know Jacob and Esau aren't normal in the eyes of the world, but they're my sons. I love them. They're the only things that came out of that time that don't scare me. Mueller's the real monster, not them. Please keep them safe from that monster. They are innocent. Please don't take them from me." It sounded more like she was begging than praying, but if it would bring her sons back to her, then she would beg. Whatever it took, she would do it without question.

Right now she didn't know what to do. God was the only one she could talk to about her sons. He was the only one who understood what she was going through. Didn't the Christians say God had sacrificed his own son for the sins of the world? Yes, God knew her pain. And if anyone could somehow return Jacob and Esau to her, it would be God. She had to trust in him, at least until she knew what she could do, if anything.

She climbed out of her bed and walked to the walnut bureau to brush the tangles out of her long, white hair. Tucked in the lower corner of the mirror frame was an old picture. It showed Jacob and Esau when they were only five. The old woman they had been staying with in Poland had taken the photograph with her new camera. At first, Eva had been frightened the wrong people might see the photo. She'd had nightmares then, too, about Dr. Mueller finding her and the twins and taking them back to Auschwitz to finish the experiments on them.

Then she had looked at the photograph and had seen her twins forever saved on film. At five, Jacob and Esau had already been as different as night and day, at least in personalities. It wasn't until puberty that Esau started having problems with too much body hair. When Jacob reached puberty, his protruding mouth, nose, and brow actually seemed to shrink, or it may have been that the rest of his body suddenly grew. At five, they both looked more like little boys. Oh, their skins were dark and there was the beginning of a brow ridge. They even had body hair at that young age, but despite that, despite everything, they were her little boys.

She held the photograph clutched to her chest. Now the photograph was all she had left to remind her of her sons. This thought brought on another fit of crying.

If only she could have remembered to get the license plate number of the BMW. She had panicked at seeing Mueller again, and he had driven off to take Jacob and Esau right from their own home. How stupid of her! She deserved whatever Mueller might do to her as payment for her foolishness and laxness. She should have been more careful about leaving the twins at home alone. She should have been more careful about covering her tracks when she moved to America. It was her fault that Mueller had found them, but it was Jacob and Esau who were having to pay the price of her carelessness.

She could report Jacob missing to Chief Montgomery. He might find something out about Mueller. He'd have to find it out on his own, though. She wouldn't be able to tell the sheriff that she thought an eighty-eight-year-old Nazi had kidnapped her sons. He would never believe that. And she couldn't tell him about Esau. No one even knew Esau was alive. The town knew about Jacob, but if she said both her sons had been kidnapped, people would ask questions she wouldn't want to answer. Esau's identity was the one thing she hadn't been careless about for all the good it had done. Mueller had found Esau and would make sure he really was dead.

She sat down on her bed and wondered if Jacob and Esau were still alive trapped in a cage somewhere watching Dr. Mueller prepare his experiments. Or were their bodies already buried in some unmarked ditch or burned to ash in some incinerator? Would she be able to sense it if they were dead? She had heard mothers could sometimes feel such things. If it were true (and she prayed it was), then the twins were still alive. She had felt nothing to lead her to believe otherwise.

Eva knew she had to help her sons, but she wasn't sure where to start. With the sheriff? Or should she search on her own? Maybe she should wait for Mueller to contact her? She swore to herself she would find her sons. If they were alive, she would find them and bring them home. If Mueller had hurt them...

She sat up straight and slammed her hand on the headboard.

No, she wouldn't let him hurt them. Somehow, she would find him and she would stop him before he killed her sons.

CHAPTER 11

JULY 7, 1993

Daniel pulled his car off Hanover Road onto the packed-dirt shoulder near the bridge. The car shimmied a bit on the rough road, but he kept it under control and parked in the shade of the oak trees so that the interior of his car wouldn't heat up under the morning sun.

"Karl Mueller lives in the forest?" Daniel said skeptically when he turned off the engine.

Jacob seemed to think about his answer and then he said, "No, only animals live in the forest. The doctor has a house. You know that. You are trying to fool me."

Jacob looked angry at the thought that Daniel tried to fool him. His eyes narrowed and his brow furrowed as he stared at Daniel. It gave Jacob an almost ape-like appearance. It was not pleasant to receive such a look. Daniel wondered if Bill the mechanic hadn't been mistaken when he said Jacob was harmless.

Daniel shook his head to assure Jacob he wasn't trying to fool him.

Maybe Jacob knew where Mueller was, but Daniel wasn't so sure the large man could collect his thoughts enough to lead Daniel to the Nazi.

Daniel wanted to end this hunt quickly. If he could capture Mueller, he would have an excuse to leave the committee. He would have accomplished what he set out to accomplish when he joined the committee. His father, not to mention the others Mueller had killed or maimed, would be avenged. Daniel could then retire without arousing suspicion or questions and live his life as he wanted to live it, not as his job dictated.

Jacob got out of the car and stalked into the forest taking large, loping steps. It surprised Daniel how fast and quietly the man moved. It was almost as if Jacob were an animal himself. One moment, Jacob was sitting in the Corolla, and the next, he had disappeared into the thick green of the forest. Daniel walked to the edge of the trees and saw Jacob following a well-worn trail further down the gently sloping hill. Daniel jogged quickly down the hill to catch up with Jacob.

"Why did you come here?" Jacob asked when Daniel finally fell into step alongside him.

"I told you. I am looking for Dr. Mueller," Daniel said slightly out of breath from his jog. He needed to exercise more, but it seemed he was stuck in a library or traveling in a car most of the time. Visiting a local gym was hard for him when he was tailing a suspected Nazi for eighteen hours a day.

Daniel wiped the sweat from his forehead. He wished he had driven on to find the Maryland House and collapsed in a bed instead of following a mentally challenged man through the forest. No telling where they would wind up. If Jacob got them lost, they might take hours to find their way back to the road.

But he knew Mueller was a doctor, Daniel reminded himself.

"Why do you want to find him?" Jacob looked straight ahead as he spoke as if he were looking for something.

"That is my business," Daniel answered.

Suddenly, Jacob spun around like an overweight ballerina. His open hand slapped Daniel on the shoulder flinging him five feet into the air. Even if Daniel hadn't had a hangover from his previous night's excess, he still couldn't have avoided Jacob's hand. But his headache was certainly a factor in his inability to defend himself.

Daniel landed hard on his shoulder. He was too stunned to feel any pain at the moment. As he staggered to his feet, Jacob rushed at him. Daniel could feel the ground shaking beneath his feet. He froze for a moment until he realized what was happening.

Daniel tried to sidestep Jacob's charge, but he was too slow. A thick-skinned hand grabbed him by the back of the neck and jerked him into the air as if he only weighed only a few pounds. Jacob spun Daniel around and switched his grip to the front of Daniel's throat. Jacob's large hand nearly encircled Daniel's neck.

Now Daniel could see Jacob's face more clearly than he had before.

In his anger, Jacob looked more animal than human. His hair was black and coarse and came down far on his forehead ending where his brow jutted out. He was dark-skinned. Not tanned, but not black either. His eyes were narrow slits in the shadow of a slightly too-heavy brow. His nose rested nearly flat against his face. His nostrils flared with each breath.

"You know Dr. Mueller!" Jacob yelled. "Where is he?"

Daniel was sure he was going to die. He had come so close to being free of all the madness only to have fate snatch him away before he could enjoy it. Not that he didn't think he deserved to die. After all the misery he had caused to others, he probably deserved to die. He had taken away Aria Mueller's life and driven Greg Heinz to take his own. Why shouldn't he suffer and die as they had?

"I do not know," Daniel said in a hoarse whisper because it was all he could manage. "You said you knew where he was."

"You're a Nazi. Nazis are bad. Dr. Mueller is bad!"

Jacob shook Daniel by the neck, and the Nazi hunter almost passed out from lack of air. Stars exploded in his vision. He would be unconscious in moments and that would leave him at Jacob's mercy, if the big man had any mercy.

Daniel kicked up between Jacob's legs sinking the toe of his boat shoe into Jacob's crotch. Even though the shoe was soft-toed, Jacob howled in pain and let go of him. The massive man grabbed his crotch with both hands and rolled back and forth on the ground. Rubbing his throat, Daniel scrambled away trying to find the path he had hiked down, but the fall had disoriented him. He was no longer sure which way he had come into the forest.

Jacob stood up and growled louder. Daniel looked over his shoulder and saw Jacob slowly approaching him like a beast of prey cornering its quarry. Daneil had no doubts from Jacob's expression that the huge man wanted to kill him.

From somewhere nearby, Daniel heard another loud growl. For a moment, he wondered if Jacob had a partner, but this growl was definitely from an animal. When Jacob stopped advancing, Daniel knew his attacker was just as surprised as he to hear the sound. Jacob spun around in a circle, scanning the trees. Daniel thought about trying to run to the car, but he didn't want to draw any attention to himself. At least not until he thought he had a better chance of getting away from Jacob.

Jacob hissed at the forest. He took a deep breath and pounded on his chest. He looked like an ape trying to protect his territory.

Daniel heard a rustle of movement off to one side. It moved closer, then up into the trees, but Daniel saw nothing. Suddenly, there was a loud crack of wood snapping and a small tree crashed down. Jacob jumped to the side, and the tree hit the ground where he had been standing.

Jacob screamed again and beat his chest. However, he did not seem as confident now as he had been. Without a glance back at Daniel, he ran off deeper into the forest.

Daniel sighed and collapsed onto the ground. He lay there for a half an hour allowing the fogginess to clear from his head. His throat was sore and would probably be bruised tomorrow. His back hurt from the fall and he didn't really want to walk, but he knew he had to. Jacob might change his mind and come back for him.

Why had Jacob's attitude changed so suddenly? He'd acted like a simpleton at the gas station, but in an instant, he had changed into a murderous animal in the forest. Jacob would have killed him, too, if that other animal hadn't drawn him away.

And what had that animal been? It had moved quickly and could stay hidden. It also had to be very strong to knock down a tree. What kind of animal could do that? A bear? Maybe, but he doubted bears could move that quickly. Besides, a bear wouldn't have tried to scare Jacob off by knocking a tree down. It would have approached Jacob and challenged him. Whatever the beast was, it was certainly not something he wanted to meet out here in the forest. He had already had his share of doing battle.

Daniel leaned against a tree so that he could stand and staggered toward the path that lead to his car. Jacob had run off in another direction deeper into the forest so he didn't think he had to worry about the retarded man waiting to attack him on the path. Even so, he looked over his shoulder every few seconds. He could see or hear nothing, but he still felt like something was watching him. He quickened his pace.

He rubbed his throat where Jacob had choked him. The tightness in the skin told him it was swelling. He told himself that both Jacob and the unknown beast were gone. He didn't convince himself.

At the edge of the woods, Daniel stepped behind a wide-trunk oak and studied his car across the road. Had Jacob circled around him in the forest and returned here ahead of him? Was Jacob quietly waiting for him to walk to his car so he could attack again?

Some Nazi hunter he was. He had allowed Jacob to lead him into a trap and nearly choke the life out of him.

Had Daniel locked the doors when he had gotten out of the car? Yes, he remembered locking his door when he climbed out. What about Jacob's door? He hadn't checked the passenger-side door. The crazy man might have left it unlocked. If Jacob had come back to the car, he could have climbed inside and taken Daniel's pistol from under the dash. He shivered until he remembered Jacob hadn't even seen the pistol and Daniel hadn't mentioned it to him.

He didn't think much about his 9-mm Beretta nowadays. In fact, he made a conscious effort not to think about it. That pistol had only brought death, but not the proper death. He wished he would never have to touch it again. Yet, he had kept it with him even after he had killed Aria Mueller.

Daniel recognized the weapon's defensive value, especially in his line of work. Just the threat of pointing it in someone's face had saved his life more than once without resulting in another death. Having a pistol didn't necessarily mean someone had to die. Not if he was careful. He wished he had had enough sense to carry it with him into the forest, though.

He should have known better than to walk into such an isolated place with a stranger and no protection, but Jacob had seemed harmless at the time. Even the mechanic in town had said he wasn't dangerous, just mentally challenged. Now he wanted that pistol. He knew he would feel safe... at least safer, with it in his hand. Jacob might be strong, but a bullet was stronger and faster. The only problem was would he be able to pull the trigger and kill Jacob if that was what it came to? Could he bear to have another Aria Mueller on his conscience? He doubted it. He already had too many ghosts to deal with.

Daniel waited five minutes... ten minutes... fifteen minutes and still nothing stirred around the car. No tell-tale knee or elbow poked briefly into his line of sight of the car. He didn't see a mysterious pair of feet moving underneath the car. All was still. All was quiet.

Approaching the car from the driver's side, Daniel duck-walked toward the car. Since the driver's side was further away from the forest, he thought that Jacob, if he was in the car, might not expect him to approach from that side. He also hoped the driver's side door was still locked. The locked door would delay the crazy man's attack long enough so that he could run across the street and into the forest again.

He crept around the front of the car trying not to slip on the gravel and dirt on the shoulder of the road. A loose pebble might alert Jacob that he was approaching. Turning quietly, he moved along the driver's side fender. Finally, he was next to the door.

Lightly resting his ear against the door, he listened. He could hear nothing from inside the car. He took a deep breath and stood up. The inside of the car was empty. With a sigh, he rested his forehead against the side of the Corolla. His hand shook as he took his car keys from his pockets. The keys jangled annoyingly against each other and against the side of his car. He tried to insert the key in the lock, but he missed the keyhole three times.

Finally managing to open the door, Daniel jumped into the driver's seat and shut and locked the door. He made sure that the passenger door was locked. It wasn't. He pushed the button down. Only then, did he feel safe. He had a shield between himself and Jacob, and, more importantly, between himself and that thing in the forest. Daniel wasn't sure which one presented the most danger to him.

He had never truly faced his own death before today, he realized. In all his searching and stalking of other humans, he had always been the confident hunter and his prey had always been weaker, or at least less prepared than he. The challenge had been in the hunt, not survival. But today had been different. Today he had been careless, and Jacob had turned the tables on him in an instant. He had become the prey and Jacob the hunter, and without a doubt, he knew the crazy man would have, and could have, killed him if that tree-climbing beast hadn't interfered. Daniel reached under the dash of his car and pulled out his pistol. A magnet glued to the underside of the dash held the hidden holster for the pistol. He held the 9-mm pistol in his hand gently, but it comforted him as if it somehow made him invulnerable.

He had to go back into the forest. He didn't like being attacked by a crazy man, and he wanted to make that known to Jacob. He was also curious about what could have scared Jacob away. It had to be large, but Maryland woodlands weren't known for large animals that could climb trees. Had it been another person? It would explain why Jacob had become so easily scared. He had thought there might be a witness to his crime, but somehow that answer didn't seem right, either. Jacob had been terrified and angry at the same time. But could a man have knocked over a tree?

Besides, Daniel had heard the beast growl, low and rumbling like approaching thunder. It had definitely been an animal sound. No human would have made a sound like that.

Daniel opened the door and stepped out of the car. He shut it quietly behind him so as not to alert anyone. He told himself he was being foolish. What did it matter what had been in the forest? It had scared Jacob away, and that was enough, but was it enough? Had the other person been a partner of Jacob's who aborted the mission at the last minute? Or had it been as it sounded, a beast?

The clearing was empty and silent as he had expected it to be. He really didn't expect for Jacob to come back after him, at least not here. Daniel stood in the center of the clearing and looked at the thick growth of trees and brush around him. Amazingly, an open spot in the thick, green canopy let the sunlight shine through.

He turned around in a small circle trying to orient himself to where he had first heard the growling sounds coming from the trees. They had come from behind the brush almost opposite of where the trail led into the clearing. He held the pistol out in front of him as if he expected the beast to be behind the brush watching him still. If something came out of the forest for him, whether it was Jacob or the beast, he would be ready for it.

The brush around the path was thick, and he didn't see how he could go through it. At least not easily. He wasn't sure he was curious enough to crawl through the thorny brush to satisfy himself. He followed the path along the brush line until he found an opening; then he passed onto the opposite side and moved back the way he had come. Much of the ground behind the brush line was clear of debris except for a few fallen branches. The exposed earth was soft underfoot. He stopped where he judged the beast's noises to have come from and looked down.

Footprints in the ground, a half of dozen of them, marked the beast's path across the ground as it moved from one tree to the next. Bare feet were clearly outlined in the soft earth. They looked large enough to be a size fifteen or sixteen. Daniel put his own foot beside the print and it was dwarfed in comparison. He wondered if this was how people felt when they found a footprint of Bigfoot. The foot had five toes and resembled a human foot except that instead of being lined up with the other four toes, the big toe stuck off from the side of the foot and looked as if it might be turned on its side. All the toes were longer than most human toes, and the foot was wider.

Daniel was struck by the image of the gorilla he had seen in the monkey house at the Baltimore Zoo playing with its toes. But the gorilla's foot had resembled a large hand. This print was large, but it was definitely a foot. It was wider than a normal foot but shaped more like a hand, but a deeper impression at the back of the print definitely marked where the heel was. The side toe wasn't opposable like the gorilla's. Just off to the side like a malformed toe.

What kind of creature made this type of footprint? Certainly none that Daniel had ever seen or heard of.

Then the second, more disturbing, question occurred to him. Why was that kind of creature in a forest in Maryland?

CHAPTER 12

JULY 7, 1993

The yard behind the brick ranch house was large and well-kept. Joseph Speer looked out of the large rear window, appreciating the landscaping in the back yard. It was obvious the owners took good care of their property. Large oak trees filled the yard and offered cool shade in the hot July sun. A split-rail fence ran around the edge of the property. The grass was a rich shade of green and neatly trimmed so that it resembled a golfing fairway.

His mother would have loved this house if she had been alive to see it. Would he ever own such a house, and would he ever have a wife and children to share it with?

He shook his head and tried to keep from crying. Who was he kidding? He would never lead a normal life. This piece of Americana would never be his life, at least not until his life was his own, and he could make his own decisions. Only then would he have a chance to live the life he wanted to live. He might even find Regina again and bring her back here. She would love this place just as he did. He chuckled at that bit of foolishness. Regina would surely be married with children by now. Still, he couldn't help but imagine her standing beneath one of the massive oaks, looking out over the field of green. He saw her wearing a white summer dress. Her dark hair was tied behind her head in a ponytail. She was walking barefoot through the grass, holding her sandals in her hand.

The owner of the house and Joseph's father conversed a few feet behind Joseph. It was small talk about how friendly Fleetwood was and how the townspeople would make the Speers feel like a member of a close-knit family. Joseph almost laughed when he heard the woman say that. What would she say if she knew she was talking to the dreaded Dr. Karl Mueller–"Mueller the Mauler," as the Jew writers for the newspapers liked to call him? Would this killer of Jews be welcome in Fleetwood then?

Joseph still wasn't sure why his father had insisted they come to America. Things had been peaceful in Brazil. No one suspected them, and people had begun to forget about the war. The Nazi hunters had all but vanished. Then three months ago his father had received a letter from the

United States, and now suddenly they were here.

Joseph blinked and his vision of Regina vanished from the yard. He sighed and turned from the window. His father sat on a blue-pastel sofa staring at the owner, who was a slightly overweight woman in her mid-thirties. Her arms moved rapidly in exaggerated motions as she talked. Albert Speer–that was his father's name now–was an old man with folds of loose skin hanging from his chin and a thin layer of white hair covering his head. He sat next to the woman, slowly nodding his head. Joseph asked himself once again if this man could have killed the thousands of people he was said to have killed.

Perhaps. Then again, it could be another Jewish lie, probably spread by the Nazi hunter who killed his mother. That was more likely. The Jews accused the Nazis of wanting every Jew dead, but they were just as bad. His mother hadn't been a Nazi, only married to one. That hadn't mattered to them. They had killed her anyway. Her life had been worth more than the lives of ten... of a hundred... of a thousand Jews.

Albert Speer coughed hard, and Joseph hurried to his father's side.

His father's cough was worse than it had been last month. Joseph didn't need to be a doctor to know that. The cough was deeper and more filled with phlegm. If Joseph could recognize the difference in the cough in that short a time, he knew his father was sick. Albert coughed into a handkerchief, and Joseph glimpsed a puddle of dark-green phlegm before his father stuffed the handkerchief in his pocket. The stubborn old man wouldn't go to see a doctor. It was true that doctors made the worst patients. As far back as Joseph could remember, he couldn't recall his father ever going to the doctor, no matter how sick he had gotten. Perhaps his father was afraid that as a patient, the doctors would treat him the same as Mueller the Mauler had treated the Jewish prisoners.

Albert regained his breath and patted his son on the thigh. Then he looked at the owner and smiled at her. Her hands had stopped moving, and she now sat on the far end of the couch. Her expression made Joseph think she was worried more about having an old man die in her house than if his father was all right.

"Forgive me," Albert said, "I am getting over a case of bronchitis I had last month." It was a lie, but a sharp glance from Albert told Joseph not to contradict him.

The woman smiled, but her eyes still looked worried. "I'm glad you're feeling better." She let the comment hang in the air, waiting for Albert to agree. When he didn't, she turned her attention to Joseph. "I was just telling your father what an ideal home this would be for the both of you, Mr. Speer. It's far enough away from D.C. and Baltimore not to be affected by their fast pace of life, but close enough, so that you could get to either city within two or three hours," the owner said, giving the house one last pitch.

She had already spent an hour showing them the house, but as soon as Karl had seen the large basement, Joseph knew he would rent the place. A large area that couldn't be seen easily was just the place Karl needed to set up his laboratory. Not that he had any human patients to carry out his experiments on nowadays. However, he was still very interested in the fields of genetics and biotechnology.

Joseph nodded in agreement with the woman's comment. "Would you and your husband be interested in selling rather than simply renting this house out?" he asked. Not that he believed his father would let him purchase the house, even if it was for sale. He just wanted to entertain the dream, if only for a little while longer.

Karl's grip tightened on Joseph's thigh. "No, Joseph, we only need to rent for a few months. No more."

"But..." Joseph began to say, then he saw the look in his father's blue eyes harden. This was a look that sharpened into a point, and it was aimed at Joseph. *Yes*, thought Joseph, *this man could have killed 6,000 Jews.*

Joseph looked at the owner and said, "If we were to give you a check for the first- and last-month's rent and the security deposit now, could we move in immediately?"

The owner frowned momentarily at the loss of a sale, but quickly regained her smile. "We'd still have to sign the lease, of course, but we can do that tomorrow after you and your father have had a chance to rest up," the woman said.

Joseph pulled a checkbook from his pocket and wrote out a check. He glanced at the amount left in the account. It was more than enough to live off if he ever got a chance to live. He ripped the check from the book and passed it over to the property owner. She took the check, glanced at the amount, and smiled. Joseph wondered how much she was overcharging them for the house.

"I'm sure you'll be happy living here, and if you decide you want to buy this house, just let me know. I'm sure we can negotiate a great deal for you on this place."

The woman held out her card, but Joseph ignored it. Why should he take it? There would be no future sale. All his future held for him was a return to Brazil in a few months. How could he return to living in a small bungalow on the outskirts of Rio de Janeiro when he had seen this?

Karl reached out and took the card from the woman's hand. He took her hand in his and kissed the back of it. "Thank you. We will call you if we change our minds."

She seemed satisfied with the promise and turned to leave. Joseph showed her to the door and locked it behind her.

When he returned to the living room, Karl said, "She suspects."

"She suspects nothing, Father. Her mind was filled with the thoughts of the money she will earn from renting this house to us," Joseph told him.

Karl shook his head quickly. "She suspects," he repeated.

Joseph shrugged and walked back to the rear window. He hoped he would see Regina again, but all he saw were the trees and the rolling hills. It was enough. He could be happy in this home if his father didn't spoil it. For a few months at least, he would know what it was like to live and not simply exist. Perhaps he could endure Rio de Janeiro with the memory of America in his mind. Their return was inevitable, of course. Eventually, someone would realize who Albert Speer really was.

"You still haven't told me why we had to leave Brazil. If you want to remain hidden from the Nazi hunters, you don't come to a small town in America. They extradited a Detroit auto worker on trial a few years ago. They have no mercy here. The Jews are too powerful. You should go to a large city where you would be just another face. If you are caught here, they will extradite you. Don't you understand that?"

With an effort, Albert stood up and walked to his son. "I don't want to remain hidden for now, or at least, it is not my main reason for coming here to this town."

"Then why are we here risking our freedom?"

"There is something here I must do before I am unable to do it," Karl said in almost a whisper.

Joseph hated it when his father was cryptic. His father had been that way all of Joseph's life. The entire truth had to be coaxed from him one sentence at a time. Sometimes he felt like a dentist having to perform one painful extraction after another. He had been twelve when he had finally learned who his father really was, and even then, it took another year until he had learned the full story of Karl Mueller.

"And that something you need to do is here? In this little town? What could you possibly need to do here that you are willing to risk exposure to accomplish?" Joseph asked.

"Before you were born, I did many things in the thrall of Hitler for which I am not proud. Many of those things are forgotten now. Many of the people I did them to are dead, but one thing remains that I must resolve before I die. Because I stepped over the boundaries of nature, I must set things right once again."

Joseph shook his head. Pulling more teeth. More cryptic speeches.

What other secrets was his father still hiding? "I don't understand. You're talking vague nonsense."

Karl shrugged and shuffled back toward the couch. For a moment, he looked just like Joseph had earlier when he had shrugged and walked toward the window. "Perhaps, but if you knew the entire truth, you would be in as much danger as I am. If those who still want to see me tried for my research during World War II felt they could learn the truth from you, they would stop at nothing to learn it. Not even your death." The old man paused, and Joseph wondered if his father was remembering Joseph's mother. They certainly hadn't stopped Karl Mueller by killing Aria Mueller. "We should wait another hour until darkness has come to bring in the equipment."

Karl shook his head. "No, it's boxed up. No one can tell what it is." Karl laid his hand on his son's arm. "Joseph, I am the old man. If anyone should be impatient, I should. You know as well as I do I am dying." He glanced out the window. "How far are we from the farm?"

"No more than four and a half miles." He pointed out the window. "The farm looks more like a prison camp, if you ask me. It has a tall, chain-link fence topped with barbed wire running all around it. By road, we are ten miles away. What is at this farm?"

"I can't say yet." Karl rubbed his chin. "I have to make contact first."

"Contact? What are you talking about?" Give the tooth another yank.

"There is someone I must talk to before I can act. I must ask her forgiveness for what I have done, and what I will do. She will probably not understand it, but I must tell her for myself. I will do it tomorrow," Karl told Joseph.

"Do what?" Joseph grabbed his father by the shoulders and spun him around. "What are you planning to do? Does one of the death camp survivors live in this town? You can't go around asking each one of them for their forgiveness." Karl pushed his son's hands away from his shoulders. "I don't intend to, only this one."

"Why? Why's this one so special?"

"Because she is."

"Why won't you tell me the whole truth?" Joseph jumped to his feet.

"You never have! I'm at as much risk as you. The Jews don't care whether they kill you or me. The dead son of a Nazi will make them almost as happy as the dead Nazi himself. Look what they did to Mother." Joseph leaned close to his father's face. "You may be ready to die, but I'm not. Don't take me with you into your grave. What have you gotten me into?"

Karl frowned. "What I do is for your protection."

"No, it's not. What you do is for your protection. You are afraid if I knew the truth I would leave you."

Karl reached out with more speed than Joseph would have given him credit for and grabbed his son's forearm. "Would you?" he asked, trying to keep his voice calm.

Joseph hesitated. "No," he admitted. "You are my father. I swore to Mother when she died I would care for you and watch out for you, but how can I watch out when I don't know what you have led us into? I don't want to spend time in an Israeli prison watching you die."

Karl touched his son's face lightly with his fingertips. "I would tell you so much if I was not so afraid. Your mother did not know at first, but when she did, she almost left me. It would have been better if she had, but in the end, she stayed because she realized the person she had heard stories about and the person she had married were not the same."

"If you trusted her, why don't you trust me? I'm your own flesh and blood."

Karl nodded his agreement. "I know. And the time will come when I will tell you all there is to tell, but that time has not come yet. Perhaps after this is over." The old man nodded. "Yes, after this is over. That will be the best time to talk. Until then, trust me, Joseph."

Joseph closed his eyes and sighed. "I do, Father."

He turned and walked back to the window. He looked out over the back yard, then closed his eyes.

Where are you, Regina? Where are you, Mother? You both belong here. This place will never be a home without you.

He leaned his forehead against the window and cried. He would never be free from this life.

CHAPTER 13

JULY 7, 1993

When Melissa Partridge relieved Tina Rourke from working the cash register at two in the afternoon, Tina was finishing her review of a chapter on promotion for her marketing class at Allegany Community College. She had a lot of time to study during the morning since the amount of traffic in Kendall's Country Store had been unusually light. Brad Kendall probably would have been better off not opening the store until ten o'clock instead of eight. The two extra hours would give them more time to stock the shelves, especially now since they still looked empty from the holiday weekend rush that had emptied them.

"He's making up next week's schedule," Melissa warned Tina as she moved out from behind the register.

Quickly scanning the store, Tina thought there were still fewer people than usual in the store. She dropped her text into her bookbag, swung it over her shoulder, and carried the canvas bag into the office with her cash drawer.

Brad Kendall was sitting at one of the two desks in the office, putting together the work schedule for the next week. Brad liked to think he ran Kendall's Country Store, though it would have surprised his father to hear it. Earl Kendall made sure the managers in his stores ran a tight ship, but Brad let things slide. When Brad was in charge, shelves could be found empty during peak times and cashiers could study during lulls in business. Not that Tina minded, but eventually Earl Kendall would realize his Fleetwood Store could do much better. Then he'd either replace Brad or ride him hard. Either way, things would swing 180 degrees from the direction they were going now. Tina hoped it was after she graduated.

Brad was a frail-looking man. His arms were thinner than Tina's. Of course Tina worked out regularly, but her arms weren't that big. In the summer when he tanned, Tina thought he looked like the mascot for Mister Salty pretzels, the pretzel-stick man. Even his hair, a pale blond, looked as if it might snap if someone tugged on it. Tina considered Brad to have an almost complete lack of appeal, but Brad thought of himself as a stud. He never seemed to be without a date on Friday nights, and Tina had even seen him with some girls more than once. Something about the man must have appealed to certain women. Maybe they liked to date a man who they knew wouldn't make a pass at them, or if Brad did make a pass, they could easily handle him.

Whatever his appeal to women was, it eluded Tina. She liked exactly the opposite type of guys. Big, hulking men tended to catch her eye. Not fat men, either. They had to be in shape like bodybuilders. She liked the way their abs rippled and their shoulders jutted out from their necks. Not that she liked dumb jocks. Far from it. A Herculean body was just the most-obvious aspect about the men she went for. Her boyfriends also had a certain gentleness about them she suspected they had developed from realizing how much they could hurt someone if they pushed too hard. Whatever the reason, it was that contrast of personality and body that drove Tina wild. Unfortunately, Tina was not the only woman who appreciated those qualities in a man, and quite a few of her boyfriends also responded to the lures of other women besides her.

Tina sat down and started counting out the money, checks, and coupons in her cash drawer. She tallied up the numbers and wrote the figures down on a piece of scrap paper.

"Tina," Brad said from the next desk.

Tina held up her hand to tell Brad to wait until she finished double checking her figures. Her second count matched the first. It usually did, but she always liked to make sure. Brad might not care much, but Earl certainly would. When she finished, she looked up to see Brad leaning over her shoulder trying to look down her blouse. Tina brought her arm up to scratch her nose and nonchalantly cut off Brad's view.

Brad backed off a step and said, "I'm making up the schedule for next week. I can give you Saturday night off if you'd like to go down to Hagerstown to Bantam's Roost with me."

This wasn't the first time Brad had asked her out. It almost had become a game between the two of them. How many times could Brad ask her out before he came up with a date she couldn't refuse? And how many ways could Tina say "no" without hurting her boss's feelings?

Even if she had considered Brad attractive, she wouldn't have gone out with him. A high-school friend of Tina's, Cheryl Latham, had not only warned Tina of the dangers of dating the boss, but she had demonstrated it. Cheryl was working as a secretary for an accounting firm in Cumberland when she started dating one of the partners. Only when she became pregnant with her boss's child did she find out he was married and had two kids. Cheryl had the child, lost her job, and now lived in a small apartment on Cumberland's south side.

"I don't think I'll be able to Brad. I've got my summer-semester finals coming up and I need to study," she told Brad.

It wasn't a lie. She was struggling to maintain her "A" in accounting.

Tina had a 3.9 GPA at Allegany Community College, up from the "B" she had gotten her first semester when she still enjoyed partying more than following her dream of getting out of Western Maryland.

"I can arrange the schedule so you are off for both Friday and Saturday. That way you can study one night and go out with me the other night," Brad suggested with a wry smile.

Tina sighed. Why couldn't the men she liked be this persistent in trying to date her? Instead, they made and broke dates casually with her. Brad continued to pester her at work, and an obscene phone caller bothered her at home. Did she attract only oddballs? She could handle Brad easily enough, though he was like a persistent itch that she needed to scratch continually, but the obscene caller was beginning to rattle her. She had changed her phone number and somehow he had found it out and continued calling her. Last night, she had blown a whistle in his ear when he called. She wondered if she could blow a whistle and get rid of Brad.

"Brad, do you remember Doc Winings?" Tina asked.

Brad nodded. "What's he got to do with you being able to go out with me?"

"Well, Louise Belcher used to be his nurse. She was a gorgeous woman. One of those women with the perfect Playboy-type body. Then one day people started noticing her body wasn't so bunnyish anymore. It was bulgyish. Louise was pregnant, but she wouldn't name the father. Small towns being what they are, rumors started that Doc Winings was the father. People started deciding they wanted to go elsewhere for their healthcare, and Doc Winings' practice disappeared. No one would have even taken their cats to him to get hairballs removed. When Louise went into labor, she decided to name the father. It turns out he was a state senator down in Hagerstown. She didn't want to ruin his reputation, but she destroyed Doc Winings without even trying."

Brad's eyes looked a little glazed over. He shook his head and asked, "Who told you that?"

"Kay over at the diner. She knows just about everything that goes on in town."

"Well, what's that got to do with me and you?" Brad asked.

"Brad, you know I've got a reputation for being a little wild. If I were to date you and something like that happened to me, what would people think? I could ruin your reputation, Brad."

Brad thought about what she had said. After a moment, his face turned red. "You can't fool me, Tina. You think you're too good for me. I've seen you around campus with those big jocks!"

Tina chose her next words carefully. She had to if she wanted to keep her job. "Brad, we're friends and that's all. I've never said or done anything to make you think otherwise. If you don't want to be my friend, that's your choice."

Brad seemed about to say something, but stormed out of the office, slamming the door behind him. Tina picked up her bookbag and left a moment later. She wondered if she would have a job to come back to tomorrow. If Brad fired her, she could start yelling sexual harassment. The threat of a lawsuit would calm him down quickly enough. However, she would prefer not to. She liked to handle things on her own and didn't need Uncle Sam sticking his nose in her personal affairs.

As she walked toward the front door, she stopped by the magazine rack and grabbed the latest issue of *Muscle and Fitness*. She flipped through it and glanced at the pictures. She carried the magazine up to the register where Melissa was sitting.

"Looks like he finally learned the meaning of the word, 'no,'" Melissa commented.

Tina smiled. "It took him a while. The problem is, I don't think I'll have any weekends off for a long time."

Melissa glanced at the cover of the magazine as she rang up the price. A bodybuilder and a fashion model were on the cover with their hands around each other's waists.

"She doesn't look much like she lifts weights," Melissa said.

"She probably doesn't. She's just a pretty model to get the men to buy the magazine," Tina told her as she handed Melissa a five-dollar bill.

"Do you like these guys?"

"I think they're pretty sexy."

Melissa shook her head and handed Tina her change. "Too much muscle for me."

Tina had to bite her tongue to keep from laughing. Who was Melissa to judge what too much muscle was? The forty-five-year-old woman had to weigh close to 200 pounds. She barely fit behind the cash register, and she probably had forty percent or more body fat. Not to mention a cholesterol count of 250.

Tina stuffed the magazine in her bookbag and walked outside. Because the store was air conditioned and she had started work when it was still cool outside, she wasn't prepared for the heat. Tina started sweating almost immediately. The temperature was over ninety degrees outside with high humidity. Her clothes would be soaked with sweat by the time she walked home. Just another typical Maryland summer day.

The only other way back to the small house she rented was through the forest behind the store. The forest surrounded the C&O Canal, which ran along the north side of the Potomac River. If she followed the trail, it would take longer for her to get home, but she would be in the shade most of the way there. She could get off the trail at the Hanover Road bridge and walk the rest of the distance to Tyler Road, where her house was.

The choice wasn't hard to make.

She walked to rear of the store where the parking lot was. She tried to avoid the bubbling patches of tar because tar was almost impossible to get off her shoes. The trail ended just behind where Brad had the dumpster. Walking around the dumpster, she found the trail and started down it.

The trail was well-worn and at least fifteen degrees cooler than it would have been walking on the road. Not too many people used the trails much, except for kids who wanted to make out in private. Most people preferred following the road, even if they walked. To get from the center of town to the Hanover Road bridge was a quarter mile shorter walking the road. Tina liked the trail, though, as long as the sun was out. Otherwise, following the trail was nearly impossible, especially at night, unless she had a flashlight.

She took the lower loop of the trail which would make her walk even longer. But the lower loop ran closest to the creek. She couldn't see the river yet, but she could hear it tumbling over the rocks as it headed west.

She stopped walking when she reached the river bank. About a half a mile up river she could see a group of kids swimming. Jumping off the bridge, one boy cannonballed into the water. He disappeared in a large splash and reappeared a few seconds later, laughing loudly. They were too far away for Tina to understand clearly what they were saying. She could see they were having fun, and that was the important thing. She wondered why they never came further down river. The water was just as deep here and there were plenty of good diving rocks and sturdy trees for a rope swing.

Tina sat on the river bank and dangled her feet in the water as she looked through her magazine again. The water felt icy compared to the warm air, but she didn't mind. She put the magazine off to the side and lay on her back with her feet still dangling in the water.

She watched the kids up river splash for a few minutes. They were probably pleasantly cool, even in the heat. Tina stood up. She would not lie in the shade in sweat when there was a cool creek right at her feet.

She looked around. No one was nearby. Few people used the trail. She unbuttoned her blouse and tossed it on the ground. The rest of her clothes quickly followed.

She dove into the water. The coldness of it startled her and when she surfaced, she gasped. Rolling onto her back, she floated down river a short distance. The sun warmed her breasts, stomach, and face.

Tina wondered what Hank Ellison, her date tonight, would think if he could see her now. She hoped Hank enjoyed looking at her with her clothes on. She knew she certainly enjoyed looking at him. When he had asked her out last weekend, she had been excited, but she had stayed calm so she wouldn't appear too anxious.

She rolled over on her stomach and started swimming back up stream. Enough enjoyment for now. She had to study for her finals before Hank came to pick her up tonight.

Tina came out of the water and wrung out her red hair. She put her bra and blouse back on. When she reached down for her panties, they weren't there. She looked under her bookbag, but they weren't there either.

At first she thought an animal might have carried them off, but the panties had been under her skirt. If an animal was going to take something, it would have taken what was on top, not what was buried under something else.

She looked around self-consciously. She didn't see anyone, but someone must have been watching her. Had her whistle driven her obscene phone caller to become a voyeur? She hoped not.

All the same, she wanted to be away from here. She wanted to be up river with other people and away from whoever had been watching her.

CHAPTER 14

JULY 7, 1993

When the phone hanging on the wall next to the kitchen doorway rang, Eva Lachman looked at it as if it was a person speaking a foreign language she couldn't understand. It rang again, and she continued staring at it trying to understand the odd language.

Was it Dr. Mueller was calling to taunt her? Calling to tell her he had ended what he had started in 1944? Her sons were dead. Eva held her hands against her ears trying to block out the annoying sound. Jacob and Esau couldn't be dead. Not after all she had done to keep them alive. They couldn't be dead. It wasn't fair.

She ran from the kitchen up the stairs to her bedroom, but she could still hear the phone. An extension on the nightstand in her bedroom rang twice more, then stopped. By the time the ringing ended, she was squatting in the tub in the upstairs bathroom. She cried and allowed herself to slide into the dry tub on her back.

Where was Jacob? Where was Esau?

The phone rang again and Eva screamed. She kicked her feet against the sides of the tub and screamed as loud as she could. If she was loud enough, she might drown out the sound of the ringing telephone.

Would that change anything? She had tried to run away from the phone before, but it had only rung again. Why was Mueller taunting her? He should be dead by now.

She stopped screaming and kicking. What if it was Jacob or Esau calling for help? How could she know? If it was Mueller, she didn't want to talk to him, but if it was one of her sons, she had to talk to them. She had to warn them about Mueller and tell them to get home quickly so that she could protect them.

Eva clenched her brown eyes shut and shook her head in indecision. She made her choice and jumped from the bathtub and ran to the phone in her bedroom.

Snatching the receiver off the hook, she held it to her ear and said anxiously, "Hello?"

"Miss Lachman, this is Brad Kendall." It wasn't her sons, but at least it wasn't Mueller either. Why was Brad Kendall calling her?

As if he heard her thoughts, Brad said, "I'm calling because I need to know if you want your regular fruit order next week. If you do, I need a deposit from you. You forgot to leave one with Tina this morning."

He sounded angry. Was he mad at her simply because she forgot to leave her money for next week's fruit order? Eva nodded and waved her hand in the air. Then she remembered she was talking on the phone.

"Yes, please fill my normal order. I'll get you the deposit by Thursday afternoon," Eva told him a bit too abruptly.

"That would be fine."

She thought Brad would say goodbye and hang up. Instead, she heard silence on the line.

"Anything else?" she asked.

"Well... um, are you all right? You weren't acting like yourself this morning and you sound a little tense now."

Eva shook her head. No one must know. No one. She took a deep breath and tried to collect her thoughts before she spoke.

"I'm fine, Brad. I just had a terrible migraine headache this morning that was bothering me, but I took some aspirin when I got home. I feel just fine now," Eva lied.

Brad hesitated. "Okay, then. I'll look for you to stop by Thursday afternoon."

"Goodbye, Brad, and thank you for reminding me."

"No problem, Miss Lachman. You're one of my best customers." Eva hung up and wondered if she would ever need the large order of fruit she had just ordered. Without her sons, she would have no need for the massive amount of food. It was for them. Just as everything she did was for them.

What would she do now that they were gone?

She walked to her bed and threw back the blanket and sheets.

Shoving her arm in between the box spring and the feather mattress, Eva felt cold metal. Grabbing the grip, she pulled the old gun out and held it up to the window. It was a .45 automatic. An American soldier had given it to her when she had thought she had seen Mueller in 1950. She hadn't had to use it then because she never saw Mueller again. However, she had put the gun under her bed just in case. Just knowing the pistol was near at hand acted like a sedative that helped her sleep at nights. She had nearly forgotten about it until now.

Eva dropped the clip into her hand and saw that the pistol was still loaded. Good. She shoved the clip back into the grip. She was surprised she still remembered how to work the pistol. Her fear at the time must have ingrained the soldier's instructions in her memory.

She walked back down the stairs to the living room. She absorbed the silence and walked to the corner near the fireplace. Sitting down in the rocking chair, she laid the pistol in her lap and started rocking back and forth.

Mueller would come for her now. She was the only one left. He would come for her, but she would be ready for him.

Karl Mueller replaced the phone in the cradle. The number he had tried to call was busy. Joseph walked into the kitchen and stared at his father standing next to the phone.

"You're crazy. Do you know that?" Joseph said. "When that woman figures out who you are, she'll have every Nazi hunter in the world after you. Probably even the Mossad. If you're so eager to die, put a gun to your head. It would be much quicker."

Karl frowned at his son's disrespect, but Joseph ignored him. He reached into the refrigerator and pulled out a can of Coke. Pulling back the tab, he chugged half of the cola quickly.

"She will tell no one I am here," Karl said quietly.

Joseph arched his eyebrows. "Oh, really. Show me a Jew who's not afraid of the Nazis, and I'll show you a traitor."

"This woman is afraid of something more than one old Nazi."

"What would scare her more than seeing the man who put her through hell about fifty years ago?"

Karl shook his head. He would not talk about it. He stood on his shaky legs and turned to walk out of the kitchen. "You would not understand," he said.

"You would not understand. You're too young to know," Joseph mimicked his father's voice. He followed his father into the dining room and then the living room. "Let me tell you something, *Father.* I'm forty-two-years old. That's about ten years older than you were when you got yourself in all this mess. I'm not a baby anymore. I never had a childhood. You took that from me. So what you have here is an adult who doesn't like being led around like he was only ten years old."

Karl sat down on his sofa. He turned on the television with the remote control. He quickly changed the channel from the John Wayne war movie to a rerun of *Happy Days*. Karl did not want to be reminded of his past with images of American soldiers killing hundreds of Germans. These were the same men Karl had once tried to save, but his efforts had put him in the mess he was in now. He switched the channel again. Someone was interviewing women who had given their babies up for adoption and were now trying to find them.

"I am not keeping you with me," Karl said. "The doors are not locked. No fences surround the property. You are free to go." He was only bluffing, but he could show no weakness in front of his son. Couldn't Joseph understand Karl was doing this as much for his son as for himself? With this task complete, he would be free to die, and Joseph would be free to live whatever life he wanted to live.

Instead, Joseph stood in front of Karl with his hands on his hips staring at his father. Joseph's body shook, and Karl was sure that his son wanted to fly into a rage.

"Stay or go. I don't care which, but if you stay, remember who the father is and who the son is," Karl added.

Joseph pressed his lips into a thin, tight line and sat down in the chair. Karl had known he would. This argument had not been their first and it would undoubtedly not be their last, especially if Joseph ever learned what Karl intended to do while he was in Fleetwood. Joseph could never understand the necessity of this trip.

"I hate you," Joseph whispered.

Karl waved his hand in the air. "You hate too much. You hate me. You hate the Jews. You hate the Nazis. Is there anyone you love?"

"I *loved* Mother."

Karl's eyes fell to the floor and Joseph smiled. He stood up and walked out the front door leaving his father sitting alone in the house.

When Karl heard the door close, he looked up. Alone in the room, he walked to the kitchen window, which looked out over Deer Run Road. Joseph backed the BMW out of the driveway and drove down the road toward town. He wondered what sort of places his son visited during these times he needed to be alone. Even in Brazil and Africa, Joseph had left for hours at a time to be by himself. He had never learned where he went, and Joseph always shrugged and refused to answer him when Karl asked directly. Karl was not the only one who could be cryptic. Perhaps, Aria had known. If she had, she also had not told her husband.

He turned away from the window and started for his bedroom. The coughing fit hit him fast. Usually, he could feel it welling up in his chest, but this time it was at his throat before he realized it. He grabbed at the edge of the sink and leaned over it. He spit up part of his soul, dark-green phlegm mixed with blood. It terrified him to see his own blood in the sink, but he had expected it. He had expected it for years. Karl turned on the water and washed the disgusting sight down the drain. He did not want Joseph to see it, at least not yet. He didn't want Joseph to know his father was nearly dead.

He started again for the bedroom, but his legs shook and he wondered if he could make it. Sitting down at the kitchen table, he looked down the hallway where the door to his bedroom stood open. It was no more than thirty feet away, and yet, he couldn't walk the distance.

His strength was fading faster than he had expected. Karl might have to rely on Joseph more than he wanted to complete his mission. He hoped it would not come to that because he doubted Joseph would help him. He thought that unlike himself, Joseph had grown up with a sense of morality. Obviously, Aria had instilled it in him because he did not share his son's idea of morality. He could push his son only so far, and Joseph was at his limit now. There was no telling what he might do if Karl pushed him over the edge.

He crossed his arms on the table, leaned his head down, and cried. It was not right. He wanted to set things right. He was willing to do it. Perhaps in the end, he had finally found his own sense of morality. He certainly knew now what was right and what was wrong and what he needed to do to make sure that right triumphed.

You waited too long.

No. He told himself. It had taken him years of searching to find Eva.

He had not been lax in his task, only unsuccessful.

He laughed at himself. *You could have found her years ago if you had truly wanted to. You were afraid* of *her. You still are. You are afraid to admit your mistake to her. You are afraid to humble yourself* to *her. You are afraid to die.*

Karl was not afraid to die. He was dying now, and he was not afraid.

He only wanted to complete his mission.

If you hadn't been afraid to die, you wouldn't be in this unpleasant situation. But you were and you still are. You were afraid to die in the war so *you created something you wanted to die in your place. You were afraid to die after the war because you thought you could still avoid facing your sins. Now it is unavoidable, and you are still afraid to die. You just want to make sure you don't die alone.*

He sobbed hard at this thought. It was not the truth, he knew, but it was close enough to the truth to scare him. Yet, afraid or not, he must continue until he found redemption.

He raised his head toward the ceiling. "Lord, preserve me until I have killed the spawn of my ignorance. Then you may take me in whatever way you want, but allow me to complete what I have begun."

His legs stopped shaking, and he took it as a sign that he would complete his mission. He stood up and shuffled toward his bedroom. He didn't stray far from the wall in case his legs failed him again. However, he made it to his room without falling.

The room was furnished when they had rented the house. It was the most extravagant room Karl had ever seen in over a decade. Though it would not impress anyone used to the wealth of America, for someone who had lived in a three-room bungalow in Brazil, it was opulence at its grandest. His poster bed was queen size and sat below a pair of canyon-landscape photos. A walk-in closet was to the left of the bed, and it embarrassed Karl that he did not have garments enough to fill it. A private bath opened in the wall to the right, a desk stood beneath the window on the left wall, and a low bureau with a mirror over it stood opposite the bed.

He had hung a sheet over the mirror because he did not want to have to look at himself in his fallen state. He had once been so handsome. His skin smooth. His blue eyes bright and attentive. His blond hair vibrant, not brittle as it was now. He had once looked as Joseph did now, except that his son had softer features like those of his mother.

But what had he seen when he looked in the mirror when the owner had given him a tour of the house? He had walked by the mirror and seen an old man staring back at him. An old man with wrinkled, loose skin hanging under his chin and thin, white hair. Only the eyes were the same. They burned with the intensity of a man on a mission just as they had when he was younger. He was so shocked by the person in the mirror that he had staggered back and sat down on the bed. How long had it been since he had seen himself in a mirror? One had been on the plane that had taken him and Joseph from Africa to Brazil. But that had been in 1976. He had been only middle-aged then. Now he was an old man.

With great effort, he stooped down beside his old cedar chest at the foot of the bed. He opened the large chest and reached down beneath the blankets and comforters until he felt the squared edges of the cold steel. He pulled the gray-metal box from the bottom of the chest, closed the chest, and set the box on top of it. Fumbling with the small set of keys in his pocket, he eventually found the key he wanted and unlocked the box. Beneath the personal pictures inside the box were a dozen notebooks. He pulled the one off the top and opened it up.

The first thing he saw was a black-and-white photograph of who he had been. The handsome Karl Mueller. He was not the fiend the Jews called "Mueller the Mauler." At least he hadn't been when the photo had been taken. He turned the page and more photos slid out. He saw himself posing in front of the University of Berlin science building in a lab coat. Another photo showed him in a school picture taken when he was nine.

He stopped for a moment and sighed over his wedding shot. Aria had been so beautiful. Her brown eyes were soft and always gentle, even during their worst times. Her light brown hair, which usually hung to her waist, was tied in looping braids behind her head. He could almost see the redness of her lips, although the photo was black and white. She had been loyal to the end. How he missed her. Without her, he couldn't bridge the gap between himself and Joseph. Aria had been the bridge and the peacemaker. He turned the page again and saw his degree in science. It was a fragile, yellowed piece of sheepskin, but it was the cause of his problems. No. He shook his head, not the cause, only the verification of a foolish man's pride. Karl Mueller had been the scientist who thought he alone could save the Aryan nation from destruction.

What an idealist! What a fool!

He remembered the day he had enlisted in the SS two years before the war. He did it not because he had political ambitions, but because he wanted to aid the Fatherland in purging itself of the ineffective Weimar government. Once the war began, he had been among the SS divisions sent to replace the decimated troops as they fell at Rostov in the Soviet Union. As he and his troop jumped off the train eager to be in battle, they had watched a much larger troop of dead bodies take their place on the train.

He and the rest of the Nazis had found out that the Russians were not the Poles. As warriors, the Russians were admirable; as enemies, they were devastating. They intended to fight the invasion of their homeland.

Snipers picked off individuals whose heads rose too far above cover. Tanks became firebombs as artillery targeted them. Frontal attacks by the SS ran into protected defenses and walls of bullets. It was in one of these attacks that Lieutenant Mueller fell.

The field hospital had been inferior, and he had been lucky they hadn't amputated his leg. The doctors did what they could, though, and passed him on. He had spent six weeks recuperating in the hospital behind the front lines. He had been able to get out of bed after two weeks, but he had still been too weak to return to the front lines as a soldier. So he had used his limited medical training to help the overworked doctors. He had seen the beautiful Aryan soldiers cut into pieces. Arms missing. Eyes missing. Blue eyes blank with incomprehension. Blond-haired men dying. It was too much for him to endure. The future of the Fatherland existed in the hearts and minds of these young men, and they were dying. Dying under the bullets from the inferior, vicious Russians.

There had to be a way to reconquer Germany's territory without losing its future. The Reich had to survive to bring humankind into its next evolutionary step. Hitler could create the Aryan nation, superior above all others, the leaders of the world.

One day while lying in his bed, he realized the answer. The next week he requested a transfer to Auschwitz to act as the camp doctor. However, he had a different agenda than tending to the Jews. While Hitler wanted to create the perfect soldier, Dr. Mueller wanted to create an expendable soldier, and he found his answers in Auschwitz.

CHAPTER 15

JULY 7, 1993

Joseph Speer had driven away from the house not knowing where he was going; not caring where he was going. All he knew was he had to get away. He couldn't stay in that house any longer at least not with his father there. Such a shame, too. The house had held such potential when he had first seen it. He had dreamed of turning it into a home, of making it the place he ran to when he needed to think.

But his father had changed all that as he always did.

Just another of Joseph's foolish dreams. He would never have a home. Just as he would never have a wife. Just as he would never have children to carry on his father's destructive blood line. Joseph had given his life to his father, only to realize his father had wasted it.

He turned the BMW onto the south side of Main Street and headed north into Fleetwood. He looked at the beautiful trees covering both sides of the road, but they now seemed to loom over him. Watching him, someone was always looking for him. At a break in the tree line, he could look out over the valley and see for miles, but all he thought of was how he could kill himself by running the car off the road and over the side of the mountain into the valley below.

It would be one way of escaping his father, but he could never do it.

He had bound himself to the old man before he knew what such a promise would entail. Still, it had been a promise Joseph had made to his mother and he would never break it.

When he was fifteen years old, he had finally found out the entire truth about his father. Not that his father had volunteered the information, but Joseph had put together the scraps that he had been told by his father and mother; he had listened to his parents' conversations when they thought he was asleep, and he had done some research on his own. Realizing the truth about his father had terrified him. The newspapers and books on World War II said Karl Mueller had tortured and killed hundreds of Jews in medical experiments as a camp doctor at Auschwitz. He had disappeared at the end of the war, but even then he had left a trail of dead bodies, people who had tried to hinder his escape, until he had crossed over the German border and vanished from his hunters.

Could such blood run in his veins? That was what terrified him now. That at some future date he would act as monstrously as his father had and kill hordes of defenseless people. He was a peace-loving man, as his mother had been peace loving. He did not want to be a killer or even the son of a killer.

After learning the truth about his father, Joseph had decided then to run away. He would be a free man to form his own future. He would go to Egypt where no one would know him. Perhaps from there he would sail to Italy, maybe Portugal. After all, there was no reason *he* should stay in Africa. The Nazi hunters sought Karl Mueller, not Joseph Mueller.

So he had packed his few things: two changes of clothes, a Bible, a comb, and a machete. He should have left Kenya without so much as a goodbye to anyone. If he had, perhaps he might be happy today. Joseph would certainly be free from his promise to his mother. He hadn't left, though. He had waited until his father left to visit someone in Moyale, the city they lived near, and then Joseph had gone to his mother to say goodbye.

She had cried in his lap when he told her. He had stroked her hair and felt like such a terrible son for wanting to leave her. He had his father's blood in him after all. He had pleaded with his mother to stop crying. He offered to take her with him, but instead, she had begged him to stay. Before he knew it, he had promised he would stay with his father and try to protect the man from himself when all Joseph wanted was to be free of the man.

He had kept that promise for thirty years now, but every day his urge to be away from the man grew stronger. One day he would leave his father. Of that he was sure. But it would not be today or even tomorrow. The future. Always the future.

It only made him hate his father more.

He parked the car along Main Street in front of the Farmers and Merchants Bank. He took his wallet out to see how much money he had. Twelve dollars. Before he put his wallet back in his pocket, he looked at the worn photograph of his mother he carried in his wallet.

Such a beautiful woman. Long, light brown hair that she liked to wear braided and wound on top of her head to keep it off her neck. Lively brown eyes that the black-and-white photograph could not capture, but that he knew were there just the same. A warm, loving smile. He felt his heart breaking again to know he would never feel her embrace again.

Then he felt his heart turn to steel. After all she had done to hold the family together, to make sure her husband was not left alone, Karl had left her alone when she needed him most.

Karl Mueller had left his wife to die at the feet of that heartless Nazi hunter, Levitt. And why? Because Karl Mueller wouldn't allow himself to be captured by a Jew, even if it would have saved his wife's life. At the moment he had seen his mother collapse with a bullet in her chest, his bond to his father had cracked like an eggshell, but his hatred of Jews had flared until it overwhelmed his hatred for his father. Hatred consumed him. Realizing this, Joseph he believed his father's blood would always taint his life.

Anguished, he thought if the Jews wanted to wreak their revenge on the Nazis, fine. But leave the innocents alone. Just because the Nazis had condemned themselves to Hell by slaughtering innocents, should the Jews repeat the stupidity? What had his mother done to bring harm to a Jew? Nothing, but a Jew had ended her life.

He slid the wallet into his rear pocket and climbed out of the car. He fed the parking meter a quarter and started walking down the street. He had no specific purpose for being here. It was just some place to be away from his father for a few hours. Let the old man wonder if his son would come back. Of course, he would. They both knew it, but let there always remain the doubt. At least Joseph had an illusion of independence.

He had such places wherever he lived. Hideaways that weren't poisoned by his father's presence. The hills above Moyale and the alleyway bars of Sao Paulo in Brazil had been such places. Now he would find a hideaway in Fleetwood.

He passed the shoe store and the grocery store without even slowing. Crossing Hanover Road at the light, he turned right and walked east for no particular reason. Midway down the street, the diner caught his attention. It reminded him of the bars of Brazil, but this was not a dangerous place where a man might lose his life. This was a bright establishment with normal people sitting in it. It was a place where he could lose himself in American customs and retreat to his private thoughts until he had gathered the strength to return to his father.

He pushed open the door to Kay's Kitchen and scanned the room.

Only half a dozen people were here at this time of day and one of them was paying his bill as he prepared to leave. Joseph paused in the doorway deciding where he wanted to sit. As he waited, the man at the cash register turned away and bumped into Joseph before he could stop himself.

"Excuse me," the dark-haired man said.

Joseph thought he detected an accent other than American in the man's voice, but there were so many American accents. How could he be sure?

For a moment, his eyes met the stranger's brown eyes. Joseph knew this man. He was sure of it, but how could that be? He didn't know anyone in America. The stranger lowered his eyes and stepped around Joseph to go out of the diner. He turned and watched the man go, half tempted to rush after him and ask him his name.

"Can I help you?"

Turning back, he saw a middle-aged woman staring at him from behind the cash register. He smiled and nodded.

"I'd like to see a menu please."

This place felt right to him. It was right. He had found his hideaway from his father.

He didn't notice Daniel Levitt, full from his dinner at Kay's, climb into his Corolla and drive back to Maryland House.

CHAPTER 16

JULY 7, 1993

The orange tabby meowed loudly at the side door. Then it reared up on its hind legs and stuck its claws into the screen that kept it from getting into the house. From inside the small house, Tina put her marketing textbook aside and hurried to the door.

"Pandy, shut up. Do you want the neighbors to throw us out?" she cooed to the cat.

She slid open the screen door and the large, orange cat waltzed into the living room. The cat glanced up at her and then strolled into the kitchen expecting to be fed. Sliding the screen shut, Tina shook her head.

"Not even a hello?" Tina asked.

She originally named Pandy Pandora. However, when Tina had taken the cat to the veterinarian to have her fixed, the vet had told Tina that her female cat was a male. So as not to cause her new cat any undo embarrassment among the other felines, Tina immediately changed his name to Pandemonium. That way, she could still call the cat Pandy for short, and it seemed an appropriate name. Sometimes the cat would rampage through the house chasing after a fly. Other times Pandy would leap onto her textbooks while she was studying.

She followed the cat into the kitchen. He was standing next to his empty food dish staring up at her with an impatient look on his face. As soon as Tina entered the kitchen, Pandy began walking in and out between her legs. She reached down and stroked his back.

"What a kiss up. You know I'll feed you."

She took his box of Meow Mix from the cabinet under the sink and shook a handful of morsels into his bowl. Pandy immediately forgot about Tina and set himself to eating.

Tina shrugged and went back into the living room. Even her cat was rejecting her. So far, it had not been a good day. First, Brad had tried to ask her out again. Then, someone had stolen her panties at the creek. When she got home, there was a message on her answering machine from Hank Ellison breaking their date for tonight. And now, even her cat was turning his back on her.

Maybe she should have gone out with Brad.

Tina shuddered. She really must be desperate if she was considering that. Brad was okay as a boss but only as long as he wasn't near her. She had caught him too many times leering at her. Once he had asked her to climb a ladder to stack some extra boxes on the top shelf in the storeroom. She had thought nothing of it at first and had climbed the ladder. Brad handed her the boxes, and she stacked them on the top shelves. Then she noticed what Brad did when she turned away to stack a box. She turned back quickly to tell him about some out-of-date stock she had noticed and saw Brad looking up her skirt! Tina had worked at Kendall's Country Store for almost a year now, and she was sure that for every time she caught Brad being crude, there was probably a time or two that she didn't notice him.

Tina turned her attention back to her text and Maslow's Hierarchy of Needs. She was sure this would be a question on her test tomorrow. She wanted to ace that test and keep her GPA at 3.9 or better.

Just as she got comfortable again on the couch, the tape player clicked off. She sighed and walked across the living room to the cassette player and put in a new tape.

Tina barely managed to read a page in the textbook before the telephone rang. She glanced at the wall clock mounted over the television. It was eleven o'clock. Who would be calling her now?

Her obscene called? No, it wouldn't be him. Not so soon after the last time and not after getting a whistle blasted in the ear.

But most of the town would be asleep by now. She should be asleep by now. In fact she would have been if it wasn't for her test tomorrow.

The phone rang again and Tina answered it rather than let it ring. It was against her nature to let it ring when she could pick it up. Someone must want to talk to her really badly if they were calling this late. It might be an emergency or maybe her mother calling from Fort Ashby to tell Tina her Granddad Douglas had died. If she let it ring, she would wonder who had called her for the rest of the night and wouldn't be able to study.

But what if it was him?

What if it wasn't? It was too soon for him to call.

Tina picked up the phone just as it trilled again. "Hello."

Nobody answered, but the line was open so there must be someone on the other end.

"Hello, is anybody there?"

"I want you," came a whisper on the other end.

At first she thought it was a connection, then she realized the person was only whispering. It was him!

"You need to speak louder, I have a tape playing," Tina said as she looked around for her whistle. Some people just had to learn the hard way. Maybe another blast from her whistle would deafen him.

"You need a man who can make you feel like a woman, one who can make you scream with passion once you spread your legs for him."

Tina shook her head. "Listen you, I..."

The caller cut her off. "Do you know what I would do if I were with you right now? I'd snap all the buttons off your blouse."

Tina unconsciously grabbed at the front of her blouse to hold it together as if just by speaking the caller could rip open her blouse.

Where was her whistle? It must be in the bedroom. That was where she had been when he called last night.

"Then I'd run my tongue allover your body."

The skin on Tina's stomach tingled. She wished she had the whistle so she could let loose with a shrill whistle that would be heard all over town. No one in Fleetwood ever complained about obscene phone callers, though.

What should she do? Would the whistle even discourage him? It hadn't last night. In fact he had even called back sooner. She had to discourage him so that he would never call back.

"... then I would flip your skirt up over your head and pull your panties off with my teeth..." the obscene caller was saying.

The voice sounded vaguely familiar, but since he was whispering, it was hard to tell whether or not she was imagining the familiarity.

"... I'd make you whine, babe. I'd make you whine and beg me for more. You'd forget your uppity attitude real fast..."

Tina closed her eyes and tried to concentrate on the man's voice, but she just kept hearing the filth he was saying. The more she focused, the more her mind imagined his hands on her, his tongue on her, and his body in hers. She shivered. She couldn't keep listening to this filth. It wasn't doing her any good. He was probably just taking her silence as encouragement.

Maybe she could give him some of his filth back.

"You know," she broke in on what the man was saying, "You probably couldn't even get it up if you saw a woman."

The obscene caller stopped. "What?"

"And even if you could get it up, I still probably couldn't see it."

Tina laughed. She could hear the caller sputtering on the other end of the line trying to come up with something to say. Before he could, Tina said, "Well, it's been, uh, interesting talking with you, Little Dick."

And she hung up.

CHAPTER 17

JULY 7, 1993

Eva Lachman tried to sleep, but she couldn't relax enough to sleep no matter how hard she tried. Her boys were out there somewhere. Dr. Mueller could be torturing them right now. Or they might be running for their lives, trying to get back to her. Were they dead or alive? She didn't know which, but she knew she wouldn't be able to rest until she did know.

She lay on her bed staring up at the ceiling, cotton sheet pulled up to her neck and the old pistol resting comfortably on her chest beneath her hands. The pistol was only a small comfort, though. She was protected, but Jacob and Esau were in danger.

Where were they? What would she do if Mueller had already killed them? She had to assume they might be dead even though every time the thought crossed her mind, her chest tightened. Both of them had been missing now slightly longer than a day. She had heard nothing from either of them. They certainly would have called her if they could have.

She started crying, and sometime after midnight she finally fell asleep to dreams that hadn't troubled her in over thirty years. Dreams that Dr. Mueller's reappearance had caused to become reality again.

The prisoner nurse knocked on the metal door to the lab. She had once been an attractive Jewish woman, but now her dark hair was stringy and her elegant clothes were replaced with a loose, gray tunic and ill-fitting shoes that caused her to shuffle when she walked to keep the shoes from falling off her feet.

"Come in," said a voice inside the lab.

The prisoner nurse pushed open the heavy door so that Eva could see inside.

Dr. Mueller stood alone inside the room. He mixed the contents of the two test tubes in a small jar. Pouring the two clear liquids together, they formed a cloudy liquid similar in appearance to skim milk. The scent was overpowering, worse than even spoiled milk. Eva could smell it from the doorway. The mixture smelled like sweat mixed with coal, but it was not intended to please a human's nose as she would soon discover. Dr.

Mueller swirled the jar gently in circles for a minute until the liquid cleared once again. That done, he picked up the atomizer from the research bench and twisted it onto the top of the jar.

"I've brought Eva Lachman, Dr. Mueller," the nurse announced.

She shuffled through the doorway leading sixteen-year-old Eva by the arm. Eva was even more-poorly dressed than the nurse. The young girl did not look up as she entered the room. Her head hung forward as she stared at the floor. Karl Mueller could only see the stubble of brown hair on her shaved head.

Please don't let this happen to me again, God, Eva thought to herself. *Let me die first before it touches me, before it violates me again. If you have any mercy, you'll strike me dead now.*

Mueller nodded to the nurse. Her name was Anne. Eva did not know her last name, but she did not need to know or want to know. Anne was enough. Anne was a traitor.

"Thank you, nurse," the doctor said curtly. "You can go now."

A moment of panic flashed across the nurse's face. She looked from Eva to the doctor. As Dr. Mueller stared at her, she parted her lips and ran her tongue around them. Eva saw the action and wondered how the nurse could hate her people so much that she could love or at least act like she loved a Nazi. Not only was she a whore, but she was a traitorous whore.

"I will need to see you later," Dr. Mueller said to the woman.

Smiling, the nurse turned and left. Mueller turned his attention to Eva, and she shivered under his stare. The doctor had attempted this procedure twice already without success. At least she didn't think it had been successful, otherwise, why would he need to do it a third time? The last time, three months ago, the experiment had broken her hip. Even that sharp, aching pain of a broken bone had not hurt nearly as much as the humiliation of knowing what was happening to her, and Mueller would make her endure the pain and humiliation for a third time. He did not care about her feelings. The only reason he waited three months for her hip to heal was because the straps that held her still through the experiment would not have been as effective if she had worn a cast.

Before these experiments, Eva couldn't imagine anything more painful than Nazis whipping her back so many times it was red with blood. She couldn't imagine anything more humiliating than stripping nude so that a Nazi soldier could body search her, probing and prodding with sadistic glee. But she discovered something was far worse than both these things. Dr. Mueller had found it and did not hesitate to use it.

Eva stared at her feet not wanting to make eye contact with the doctor. Her body was still thin from poor nutrition, even though she ate better than most other prisoners. Dr. Mueller had tried to improve her health since his initial examinations not out of kindness but out of necessity. She had to endure near-daily injections of various concoctions. She didn't know what they were. Most were clear fluids, but many were green. A few were even blue and red. One had been bright pink. Eva endured the shots, although some made her nauseous and dizzy. She ate not to make Dr. Mueller happy, but because she wanted to live. People around her died every day for lack of food. Who was she to turn away food when it was offered to her? Not eating would not stop the experiments. Eva wanted to live, even if it meant helping the doctor. Was that why the nurse gave her body to the doctor? Some of the other women could see that Eva ate better than they did, and they had started rumors she was like the nurse, giving her body willingly in exchange for food.

How could they know how close to the truth they were?

Yes, she gave her body, but not willingly and certainly not to Dr. Mueller. She could never tell the women the truth, though. No one must know, except her father. He would help her. He loved her.

"How long has it been since the beginning of your last menstruation, Eva?" Dr. Mueller asked.

She trembled, but said nothing.

"How long has it been since the beginning of your last menstruation, Eva?" he said again more sternly.

She looked up and stared at him. Her brown eyes were slightly cloudy, an effect of the tranquilizer the nurse had given her earlier. However, she could still remember the two failed experiments enough to fear a third.

"Two weeks," she answered, her words slurring slightly.

Dr. Mueller nodded. "Good. You are ready then. Follow me."

He picked up the small jar filled with the foul-smelling liquid he had mixed and walked to the locked door that led into his private research laboratory. This was where Dr. Mueller conducted the experiments that only he and his subjects knew about. And many times his subjects never left the room. If they died, he incinerated their bodies in a single oven that was attached to the laboratory. Mueller unlocked the door and let Eva walk through first. He followed her inside and locked the door behind him.

Would she leave this time?

She certainly hoped not. Not if it meant she would have to endure a fourth experiment.

Eva stood by the examination table that she was all too familiar with.

She turned, so she did not have to look at the cage where Darwin, the gorilla, stood watching. Darwin was a 500-pound African gorilla. Mueller had intercepted him on his way to the Berlin Zoo or so he had told her.

"Disrobe," Mueller ordered.

She pulled the baggy, gray dress over her head and dropped it onto the floor. She was wearing no undergarments beneath.

Mueller flipped his hand up motioning for her to climb up on the steel table. Eva barely flinched when she lay against the cold table. The sedatives were slowing her reactions. She laid her feet in the stirrups and Mueller fastened the buckles across her calves and thighs so that she could not move her legs. Next, he tied her arms to the head of the table and fastened a final strap across her stomach to immobilize her completely.

Using the atomizer, Mueller sprayed Eva's body with the sticky fluid, concentrating most of it around her groin. The smell was worse than the latrines around the camp.

Eva cried, but Mueller ignored her. "I want my Papa," she whimpered.

Mueller continued to spray her body until the bottle was empty. To her left, Eva could hear Darwin rattling the bars of his cage as the first scent of the mixture reached him.

"I want my Papa," she said again.

"Cry all you want. Your father will not come. He is ash in a rubbish heap. But you... You are participating in a grand experiment. With your help, good German boys will not have to die fighting in wars."

Papa dead? Mueller was lying. Her father had said he would meet her at the gate when they were free, and her father would never lie.

Darwin growled and rattled the bars of his cage again. He was excited now. More excited than he had been the first time. The spray must be triggering the correct responses from him. Mueller would not have to prod and encourage the beast this time. He would take Eva on his own. Eva was not sure whether she was relieved or even more frightened. Relieved that it might mean the end of the experiments, but more frightened that this might be the most brutal of all the experiments.

Mueller walked over to the cage where Darwin paced back and forth.

"Can you do it this time, Darwin?" he asked. "Will you take evolution to its next step?"

The gorilla stopped pacing and rose up on his legs to touch the top of the cage. He puffed his chest out and pounded on it with his fists.

Mueller smiled and nodded. He took the key from his pocket and unlocked the door to the cage. Then he quickly scurried over to a corner of the lab and waited. The large ape seemed to sense he was no longer a prisoner. He pushed the iron door with one hand, and it swung open easily.

Sniffing the air again, Darwin then stood up looked at Mueller. The gorilla pounded on his chest. He bellowed a loud roar. Eva clenched her eyes shut. She wondered if the soundproofing in the walls was thick enough to muffle the roar or if people just ignored what was going on in the lab. Wouldn't anyone help her? No. What would it matter? Just another Jew. So many of them died each day, the scream of one more would mean nothing especially to the guards. Eva didn't need to die, she realized. She was already dead, sentenced to Hell.

Darwin rushed toward the examination table on both his hands and feet. He stood up next to Eva and puffed out his chest. Eva whimpered and turned her head away. She could feel his hot breath on her bare neck. Darwin stared at her and then put his nose on her stomach and sniffed. Eva tried to pull away. She sucked her stomach in as far as she could, but Darwin leaned further forward. He stood upright again and cocked his head to the side as if he was trying to decide whether Eva was human or a female gorilla in heat.

Making his decision, Darwin moved to the foot of the table between Eva's legs. Eva saw Mueller check the time and scribble his notes into his log while she screamed.

CHAPTER 18

JULY 7, 1993

Karl Mueller rolled over on his bed. The mattress immediately remolded itself to his body. It was too soft. He wasn't used to such luxury. The mattress molded around him like Aria's body once had, and his pillow made his head feel like it was on a cushion of air. This was a far cry from the hammock he had slept in for almost fifteen years.

Thanks to central air conditioning, the temperature in the bedroom was cool and comfortable with no humidity, unheard of in his bungalow in Sao Paulo. This was too much opulence for him. He was undeserving of such a place to live.

In Sao Paulo, he could have lived in a home like this. He certainly had enough money to live in even a better home than this one. It had been his choice not to indulge himself. Poverty had been part of his penance for his many sins. Why should a man who had let his wife die in his place live in a state of grandeur? Why should a man who had broken the laws of nature live a life of ease?

He felt the tears form in the corners of his eyes. In the darkness of the room, he let them flow freely. No one could see him cry; no one could hear his sobs. He should be living in a tent somewhere suffering in the high heat and humidity. This was not the home for him. For Aria, perhaps, but not him.

He sighed and wiped his eyes on his sleeve.

Aria deserved so much more than he had given her. His wife had given him unconditional love, loyalty, understanding, mercy, and a son. He had returned to her fear and death.

Joseph complained to him when he wouldn't see a doctor. A doctor could help you live, Joseph complained. Did Joseph think his father a fool? Karl avoided doctors not because he thought he could cure himself, but because he wanted to die. He wanted to die suffering. He would have to repent of much if he were ever to return to his wife.

Gravel crunched under wheels as Karl listened to a car pulling into the driveway. The headlights flashed briefly across his window casting oddly shaped shadows on the opposite wall. Though he knew it was only

Joseph returning from wherever he had found to run off to, Karl checked just to be sure. He had not lived to be eighty-eight by being careless.

He parted the curtains just enough so he could see outside. Joseph climbed slowly out of the car and stretched. He glanced at his watch, then at his father's window. Karl pulled back deeper into the shadows. Shutting the door, Joseph leaned against the side of the BMW. He pulled a cigarette from his pocket, lit it, and slumped back.

Karl climbed back into his bed and waited to hear his son come into the house through the kitchen door.

Not only had Karl failed Aria, but he had failed Joseph as well. His own flesh hated him, but could he expect anything else from his son? Karl hated himself. Living on the run was not the life to raise a child in, but Joseph had been forced to endure it much the same as Aria had. Living without a mother and without affection from your father was no way for a boy to live, and for that, Joseph would never forgive his father. And Karl didn't blame him. He preferred it that way.

Karl heard a key rattle in the kitchen door and the clank of the dead bolt disengaging. The door opened, closed, and then he heard Joseph's footsteps across the floor of the kitchen.

The cough came without warning. Karl's throat trembled and spewed out green phlegm onto the blanket. Burying his face in his pillow, he hoped Joseph hadn't heard. He didn't want pity. Let Joseph hate him. That was the way it should be, but his illness brought out Aria's qualities in Joseph as he tried to care for his father, no matter how badly Karl treated him.

Once the coughing stopped, Karl listened. He did not hear Joseph approaching. He must not have heard.

Karl closed his eyes. Why had Joseph even stayed with him? He had done nearly everything he could to drive the boy away and yet still he stayed. The poverty, the lack of affection, the arguments. Anyone else would have left. He had hoped his son would. Joseph would be better off without his father. Why didn't he leave?

Maybe the Lord was showing mercy on him. Perhaps the fact that Joseph was still with him was proof that the Lord approved of his mission.

Maybe his son still loved him.

Karl looked at the blanket soaked with his sickness. He pulled it off the bed and tossed it away from him onto the floor. He didn't need it, anyway. What he needed was mercy and forgiveness.

CHAPTER 19

JULY 7, 1993

Jacob Lachman sat at the river's edge with his arms wrapped around his knees, rocking back and forth. It helped calm him when he was worried. Thinking clearly was too hard for him if he couldn't concentrate, and concentrating was so hard to do, anyway. Too many things went on around him that diverted his attention.

He wasn't dumb. Jacob knew his mother and brother thought so, but they were wrong. Esau had even called him retarded once. Jacob had tried to look up the word in his dictionary, but he wasn't sure how to spell it. So he had asked Mama.

"Where did you hear that word, Jacob?" Mama had asked. She smiled when she asked, but Jacob could sense her tension. Her entire body was stiff. She didn't like the word.

"Esau called me it. He said, 'You're too retarded to be human, Jacob, and too stupid to know it.'"

Mama had frowned. Retarded must be one of the bad words.

"I wouldn't have said it, Mama, but Esau said it first, and I wanted to know what it meant. But I couldn't look it up in the dictionary. It has too many letters," Jacob said, quickly putting the blame on his brother.

Esau was a bad boy, anyway. Why else wasn't he allowed to go into town? His mother allowed Jacob because Jacob was a good boy. Jacob was only bad sometimes like the time he ate Esau's pet rabbit. Mama had punished him then, and he couldn't go into Fleetwood or watch cartoons for an entire week. But Mama never allowed Esau to go into town. He must be a very bad boy.

Now that Jacob thought about it, he never had learned what retarded meant. It was a bad word, and he never said it. But what did it mean?

A raccoon quietly approached the river's bank alongside the huge man. Jacob stopped rocking and growled at the raccoon. The throaty, rumbling sound froze the raccoon in place, poised on the bank as if had been stuffed and mounted. It stared up at Jacob, deciding whether or not it should bolt. Jacob didn't give it a chance to decide. His hand shot out quickly and snatched the raccoon up by the neck. The raccoon growled in defense, but Jacob cut off the sound as he clenched his fist. He felt the small animal's throat collapse and the faint snap of bone as the raccoon's neck broke. He brought the dead creature up to his nose, sniffed it, and flung it into the river.

He heard a splash and then silence. He could barely see the ripples the carcass caused in the darkness, but he didn't care. Jacob wrapped his arms around his knees and continued rocking, continued thinking.

Dr. Mueller's friend had gotten away from him. Esau had helped him. Why? Esau hated Mueller as much as Jacob did. That was one of the few things he had in common with his brother. So why had Esau helped Mueller's friend?

Jacob knew the answer, of course, because he was smart. Esau had helped because Esau was a bad boy. But was he bad enough to help someone he said he hated? That would take more thinking.

Jacob would have killed Mueller's friend if he had had the chance.

He would have snapped the man's neck like the raccoon's and left him as food for the animals in the forest. Not that any of them would have wanted to eat the dirty body.

He clenched and unclenched his fists. Killing Mueller's friend would have felt good. Killing the raccoon had felt good, and Mueller's friend was much bigger than the raccoon. Killing the man would have been much more fun, and Jacob's mother would have been proud of him for killing Dr. Mueller's friend.

But Esau had helped the man. Esau was bad. He was evil. First, he had run away from the house to play when he knew Mama never let him leave the fenced-in yard. Then he had helped Mueller's friend get away from Jacob. Finally, he had caused Jacob to be bad because Jacob had to leave the house without telling his mother he was going to try to find his brother.

Esau was bad. Esau would have to be punished. That would be fun to watch.

Jacob liked to see his mother punish Esau, but this time his mother wasn't around. It was up to Jacob to punish his brother. He would give his brother the punishment he had wanted to give Mueller's friend. That would be even more fun than watching his mother punish Esau. Jacob would put his brother's neck between his hands and squeeze as hard as he could. His brother would scream and yell, but Jacob was stronger and he would squeeze until his fingers touched each other on the back of Esau's thick neck.

Jacob smiled and rocked back and forth furiously. So furiously in fact that when he rocked back his head would touch the ground, and when he rocked forward, he was standing on his feet even though he was in a squatting position. In his mind, Jacob saw his brother's eyes bulging, saw his brother's nose flaring trying to draw in air, heard Esau's last, desperate hisses as his throat closed off under the pressure from Jacob's grip. It was a good punishment. Good punishment for a bad boy.

This amused Jacob, and he rolled onto his back and giggled. Suddenly he stopped giggling and lay still. He had heard something. He was sure of it.

Had Esau come back to scare him again? Jacob clenched and unclenched his fists. If Esau was in the woods, Jacob would show him who the good brother was.

Come and take your punishment, Esau.

Jacob stood up quietly and waited to hear another sound. It came a few moments later.

"Come on, Shannon. You're just being paranoid. No one's out here, especially not your father. We told him we went to the movies remember?"

It was a male's voice, but not Esau's. This voice belonged to someone younger than his brother.

Jacob moved slowly toward the voice. It wasn't far away. The boy was probably on the trail or not far from it.

"I'm not being foolish. I told you I heard someone laughing." This time it was a girl's voice that spoke.

"Well then, I know it wasn't your father." The male voice laughed loudly, but the female voice didn't.

Jacob moved closer to the voices. He was large, but he could move as quietly as any animal. The boy and the girl were on the other side of the trail across from him. Maybe only a hundred yards away. They must have heard him laughing, but they weren't sure.

Had Esau sent these two to find him? What if they were helping Esau because Esau was afraid to take his punishment from Jacob? That would be very foolish of him. These two young people would not be much more trouble to kill than the raccoon had been.

Jacob stared through the trees and bushes. He caught a flash of pale skin on the other side of the trail and then it was gone. He saw white material for a moment and then it too was gone. A girl stepped onto the trail.

She was young; no more the eighteen. She was wearing blue jeans and buttoning a red shirt. She was pretty like some of the models in the magazines Jacob ordered. The pretty girl looked up and down the trail as if she was expecting to see someone.

Was she looking for him? Esau must have sent them. Otherwise, why would they be out here in the middle of the night? Why would the girl be looking around if she wasn't looking for Jacob? Good girls and boys stayed at home unless they went somewhere with their mothers.

The boy stepped out onto the trail. He wasn't wearing a shirt. He was skinny and did not have the muscles Jacob had. Of course, no one except Esau had the muscles Jacob had. The boy slid his arms around the girl's waist and nuzzled her neck.

The girl pushed his face away. "Billy, I think we should go back. I don't like it out here. I feel like someone's watching us."

"Just Mother Nature. C'mon, Shannon. Nothing's gonna hurt us out here. It's not the wilderness, you know."

The boy ran his hands over the girl's chest and she moaned. It was a strange way to be looking for him, Jacob thought, but at least their attention was diverted from their job.

Jacob jumped out onto the trail growling. Both Billy's and Shannon's eyes went wide as they saw Jacob. Shannon tried to run into the woods, but Billy held her in front of him. Instead, she started screaming. Jacob slapped with his large hand her to shut her up. He did not want her screams to bring Esau to help her. Shannon's head snapped to the side, and she slumped forward in Billy's arms. He let her go, and she fell to the ground.

Billy turned to run, but Jacob jumped over the girl and grabbed him by the shoulders. He took Billy's head in one hand and smashed it up against the trunk of a tree growing beside the path. The boy's scream ended sharply as his head hit the tree. Jacob slammed the boy's head against the tree again and again until he heard the satisfying sound of bone breaking. Then Jacob knew he was finished. Good punishment for a bad boy. Maybe Jacob would do the same thing to Esau.

Jacob let the boy fall limply to the ground then he turned his attention back to the girl. She was trying to stand, but she was still groggy from Jacob's smack and moved unsteadily. She looked over her shoulder and saw Jacob stomping toward her and whimpered.

"Where is he?" Jacob said. "He's hiding from me."

Jacob would use this girl to find his brother. Then Jacob would punish Esau the way he had the boy.

The girl whimpered loudly. She held one hand over her chest and continued to back away from him. Jacob stepped on her foot so she could go any further.

"Where is he!" he shouted.

Shannon stopped crying as her eyes glazed over. It was the same look Jacob had seen in the eyes of Esau's pet rabbit right before Jacob had killed it. At first, the rabbit had shivered and tried to get away. Then it had stopped struggling and sat still until Jacob killed it. The girl was like the rabbit. She was ready to die.

Jacob reached down and put a hand on either side of the girl's head and lifted her off the ground so not even her feet touched. She must be in pain Jacob realized, but she didn't even yelp. He pulled her face close to his so that he could look into her eyes. There was nothing in there. Her eyes looked dead even if her body wasn't.

"Where is he?" Jacob asked once more, anyway.

When she didn't answer, he squeezed his hands together.

CHAPTER 20

JULY 8, 1993

Esau Lachman's dark-brown eyes flared open. Even in the almost utter darkness, his eyes did not dilate. They were small pricks of black in a sea of mahogany brown. His mouth opened in a silent scream, and Esau grabbed his head with both his hands using them like a net to shield his head from something unseen. The imagined pain was so great he could even feel it in himself. His heart raced and his breaths came nearly as fast as the thump, thump, thump of his heart. He touched his head lightly feeling around the sides of the crown. He had to be sure no bones in his skull were broken or more misshapen than usual. He had to be sure it was all truly just a dream. No, not a dream, a nightmare.

He thought he could even smell blood and gore although none was on him.

Esau rolled out from under the hollowed-out area of the riverbank where he was sleeping. It was a place where the river had worn away the bank giving him a roof over his head as he slept. He was not the first animal to use the place as shelter. Further back in the hollow, he had found a muskrat's lair, but they had come to an agreement earlier that neither would bother the other.

Such was Esau's way with animals.

The creek was only a few feet in front of him. He stepped into the water and allowed its cold bite to clear his head. Bending over, he splashed his face. As he brought his hands up to his face, he saw his hands were shaking. Realizing he was not only shaking, but sweating as well, he moved deeper into the water up to his waist.

He was more relaxed now. The phantom pain was gone. Honeysuckle and moss replaced the odd smells. His breathing and heart rate were all normal.

It was all because of the dream.

No, it hadn't been a dream. Dreams had a distinct quality to them.

They were visual and auditory, but this had just been sensations. An evil sensation. And yet familiar. He had felt something like it before but he couldn't remember the circumstances.

Then he had felt the second sensation. This one was not familiar, and it was one of great pain. His head throbbed at the memory of the pain. He had felt it contract smaller and smaller as if being squeezed out of shape. Then just when he thought his skull would burst from the pressure being created, he woke up.

So if it had not been a dream, what was it?

The first feeling had been like a whisper in his head, and it was a voice he understood. Esau closed his eyes and tried to recall the first feeling. He was afraid to feel the second again. It had been too painful. A wild fear seized him that his head would actually burst if he tried to remember it.

The first sensation, while it had been hostile, had been familiar. He thought he might be able to recognize it if he concentrated. To remember this feeling and try to understand it was safer.

Esau put his hands over his ears to help drown out the extraneous sound from the river and the forest. He hoped it would help him concentrate better on the feeling, on the voice. He tried to recall the sensation he had heard in his head.

Eeeeeeesssss. Daaaaaaaahhhhhhh.

He clenched his eyes shut, trying to filter out the interference. All interference. If only he was deaf, he would understand.

Eeeeeeeesssssaaaa. Daaaaaiiiihhhh.

He could almost understand the voice. It was deep and throaty, but familiar. He should know whose voice it was. He felt he knew the voice. He just couldn't put a name with the face.

Esau. Die.

The voice was Jacob's. His brother was coming after him.

CHAPTER 21

JULY 8, 1993

Karl woke in the morning with the sunrise. His room was still dark because the curtains were drawn, but he knew it was morning because he could see the morning light peeking around the edges. He rose and shuffled into the master bathroom. Blinking as he turned on the lights, he stood in front of the sink.

He took a bottle from the medicine cabinet and shook out two pain killers. They were codeine-based and highly addictive, but he would probably be dead before the addiction took hold. South American doctors were not as conscientious about what they prescribed as American doctors. Joseph didn't know about the pills. If he did, he would have taken them away to keep Karl from becoming addicted. What mattered was that the pills worked and allowed him to continue his work. He swallowed the pills quickly and washed them down with a mouthful of water.

Staying close to the wall in case he fell, he walked down the hallway toward the living room. As he passed by Joseph's room, he noticed the bedroom door was open. He could see his son sleeping peacefully under the sheets. Funny how Joseph looked like a ten-year-old boy when he slept. The tension that seemed to be ever present in his face faded when he slept. Karl stood in the doorway and stared at his son.

This was the sort of life Joseph deserved; it was the type of life he wanted to live. Never having to worry when he saw the police coming in his direction. Being able to live in relative comfort with indoor plumbing and air conditioning. Having a mother to cook breakfast for him in the morning.

Many people might consider that lifestyle boring because it was so common, but that was just the reason why Joseph would want it. It wasn't common to him. It was unknown and mysterious in its own way.

Maybe when everything was done here, things could change. Maybe then they could remain in America in another small town. He knew he only had a few more months to live, so it didn't matter if staying in America would draw the Nazi hunters to them. He'd have to take precautions until he died, but after that Joseph would be free to live.

Karl turned and went into the kitchen. The more he thought about the idea of remaining in America, the more he liked it. When the twins were dead, it would cleanse his sins. The balance of nature would be straight once again, and he could die in peace. Perhaps then he wouldn't have to sacrifice worldly things as part of his penance. During his last few months, he and Joseph could enjoy themselves. Maybe Joseph would even learn to love him again. Maybe Joseph would even miss him when he died.

He could start changing things today. The first move would have to be his. He had to show Joseph he wanted things to be different. He took a large skillet from under the counter and set it on the stove. Pulling a half a dozen eggs from the refrigerator, he cracked them into the skillet. He added some green pepper, tomato, cheese, and spices, and cooked up two omelets.

While he was making some fresh coffee, Joseph walked into the kitchen rubbing the sleep from his eyes. He yawned and then stretched. The hard life hadn't been entirely detrimental to his son, Karl thought. Even at forty-two, Joseph had the hard, lean body of a man half his age.

"That smells good," Joseph said glancing at the stove.

"I'm glad you think so. It's your breakfast."

Joseph smiled. "Really? What's the occasion?"

He came into the kitchen and sat down at the table.

Karl shrugged. "No, occasion. I just felt like making breakfast this morning. For both of us."

Karl set a plate in front of Joseph. He filled the two cups on the table with coffee and then sat down next to his son and took a bite of his own omelet. Joseph watched his father eat. He glanced down at his plate and then back at Karl.

"Well, don't just look at it. Eat it," Karl told him.

Joseph tasted the omelet and nodded. "It tastes great."

Karl smiled. "I've been thinking about how nice it is here."

"It's beautiful. I like scenic views."

"How would you like to stay here after I've finished my business?" Karl asked although he already knew the answer. Joseph had already expressed his opinion yesterday when he asked their landlord if she would be willing to sell the house instead of just rent it.

Joseph stopped chewing. He swallowed what he had in his mouth.

"In this house?" he asked.

Karl shook his head. "Not in this town or house, but in this region."

Joseph looked suspicious. "Why?"

"Because you like it here. Shouldn't that be enough?"

"It never has before."

Karl didn't blame his son for doubting him. Karl hadn't proved too reliable in the past. It would take a long time to rebuild Joseph's trust. Maybe a longer time than he had.

"It means a lot to you if we stay here."

"What if someone discovers who you are?" Maybe Joseph still cared for his father in some small way.

Karl shrugged nonchalance. "What will they do to me? I'm old. I'm dying. Happiness is more important to me now than staying free."

Joseph thought for a moment. "Yes, I'd like to stay here. I like America and the mountains."

Karl slapped his hand on the table. "Then it's settled. I'll have my business settled in a few days, and then we'll find our new home and start all over again."

CHAPTER 22

JULY 8, 1993

Kendall's Country Store opened at eight in the morning, six days a week. Some customers had asked for it to open earlier. In a farming town like Fleetwood most of the day's business was done before noon, but Brad Kendall didn't want to have customers walking around the store while he was unloading a delivery. Tina Rourke came to work at seven to help with the daily deliveries. Brad liked to have everything unloaded and shelved before the store opened. Most of the time, she and Brad could have it done by eight. If not, finishing had to wait until business slowed enough so that she could get away from the cash register for a few minutes and finish shelving the order.

On Thursday, the shipment was a large order of canned fruits and vegetables and another order of pasta. Because shelf space in the front of the store was limited, these two orders could be stored more easily than items with short shelf lives, like bread and meats. The reason the order was so large was that Brad ordered these items in bulk and sold them at a greater profit than perishables. He might not manage the store well, but he definitely knew how to make a profit from it.

Brad and Tina took only ten minutes to fill the gaps on the shelves out front. They would store the rest of the twenty-case order in the back. Because the canned goods were heavier items, Brad stored them on the lower shelves so that it required little heavy lifting to stock them. Leave it to Brad to find an easier way to work.

Brad broke open a case of peas and began handing cans to Tina in pairs. She took them and bent over to place them on a bottom shelf. Each time she bent over, Brad stared at her butt or tried to find a gap in her blouse top through which he might ogle her breasts.

"How are things going for you, Tina?" he asked, looking away in time so that she wouldn't see him staring.

"Fine, Brad. Just fine," she said as she took two more cans of peas from him.

She bent over to stack the cans. Brad eyed Tina's shapely calves that showed beneath her skirt.

"You know, I have you working mornings on both Friday and Saturday," Brad remarked. Working weekend mornings was considered a privilege because it meant you didn't have to work weekend nights, and to have off both Friday and Saturday nights was almost unheard of.

Tina stood up. "You didn't have to do that. I don't mind taking my turn working weekends." She took two more cans.

"I know, but I thought you could study Friday night and then Saturday night you and I could go out."

Tina looked up at Brad from her bent over position. "I have summer finals next week, Brad. I'm going to be studying both nights."

Brad rolled his eyes. "But you can't study straight through. You need to take a break sometime. Why don't you go out with me?"

"I told you Brad. I don't feel comfortable going out with the boss's son. This is a small town. People talk."

"That's not it at all. I know why you won't go out with me. You'd rather have some ego-maniac bodybuilder stand you up than go out with a man who could really make you feel like a woman."

Tina straightened up. Where had she heard that before? Brad moved closer to her, and she stepped back. He stepped closer again, but she was up against the shelves and couldn't step back any further.

"Brad," Tina said trying to ignore his aggressiveness. "It's not that I like bodybuilders. I just don't think we would get along well outside of work." Which was a diplomatic way of saying she didn't like Brad, but of course, Brad was no diplomat.

Brad put his hand on Tina's bare arm. It raised the goosebumps on her arms. He let his hand slide down her arm to her wrist.

She thought she heard someone knocking on the door and realized the time was nearly eight o'clock. The store should be open. Talk about saved by the bell. She wished that the store was already open, and she wasn't alone with Brad. The absence of windows kept anyone from seeing what was going on in the stock room.

"You ought to give me a chance before you say no," Brad said.

Suddenly, Tina realized where she had heard the line before. The obscene phone caller had said the same thing to her last night.

"It was you, wasn't it?" Tina said.

His grip tightened slightly on her wrist.

"It was me, what?" he asked. His voice sounded innocent, but his face looked anything but that.

"You made that obscene call."

Brad smiled. "Not obscene, Tina. I was just expressing my affection for you."

He reached out to grab her through her blouse. Feeling Brad's fingers on her chest, Tina acted instinctively and kneed him in the crotch. Brad howled with pain and bent over holding his hands between his thighs. Tina stepped over him and moved toward the door to the storeroom. As she did, Brad reached out and grabbed her ankle. Then with his other hand, he grabbed her skirt and yanked it hard. It slid down over Tina's hips, but she freed her ankle from his grip. She yanked the skirt out of his hands and then she ran out of the storeroom.

CHAPTER 23

JULY 8, 1993

Daniel Levitt woke at six-thirty Thursday morning in his room. He lay in his bed staring at the ceiling. He wasn't studying the ornate ceiling work in Maryland house; it just happened to be where his eyes looking.

Why was he in Fleetwood chasing another old man, especially after what had happened to Greg Heinz?

Mueller had been seventy-six when Daniel had last seen him in 1981. Somehow, an eighty-eight-year-old man who bounced his grandchildren on his knees just did not seem like a Nazi war criminal to him. He knew the difference might only be a matter of appearances, but he doubted it.

Men caught up in the throes of passion sometimes do things they wouldn't ordinarily do. Hitler's influence was something like passion to German men in the early part of this century. The passion had exploited their weaknesses and doubts and caused them to act like Jung's "shadow self," the dark side that is normally kept under control.

When World War II ended, people were forced to face up to a lot of skeletons in the closets whose doors the Allies had opened. Not everyone had, but Daniel believed many of them had. Time and perspective had done the trick. People had mourned and gotten on with their lives, and the wounds had begun to heal.

But not for him. He didn't even have any war wounds to heal. His wounds had been inflicted on him by his father and Adam. They had fueled his hatred and molded him into their vision of a patriotic Jew. Now that his father was dead, Daniel had begun his own recovery, a recovery that his father had never completed or even started. This hunt would either free him or condemn him to a life of hunting old men.

That brought him back full circle to his original question: Why was he here chasing an old man? Why was he willing to reopen his old wounds by reopening someone else's? It wasn't right, but it was something he had to do. It was that last strand of hate that was the strongest, and to break it, would also put him in the greatest jeopardy. He would either be free or trapped forever as a hunter.

Karl Mueller was the man who had nearly ended his father's life.

Mueller had certainly destroyed Ira Levitt's life without killing the man. Now Ira Levitt's son would destroy Mueller the Mauler. It was Daniel's duty as his father's son.

Daniel sat up in bed and swung his legs over to the floor. He propped his elbows on his thighs and then rested his head on his hands. What would he do when all this was over? His parents were dead so very little was left for him in Israel. He doubted if Israel would even feel like home now. He had spent very little of the last twenty-two years there. Usually only a few months between assignments, but even that was minimal because Adam Goldstein usually had him jetting all over the world to dig into archives and interview old witnesses, all to expose Nazis. His entire life had become a vendetta. The longest time he had spent in the homeland had been when his father had gotten sick and eventually died two years ago.

He had spent three months tending his father, then arranging his funeral, and finally closing his father's affairs.

His traveling had taught him one thing, though. While Adam was concerned with the six million Jews who had died fifty years ago, people were dying today who Daniel might have saved had he turned his attention to them. Now he was too old to try and finish medical school, but the people he had seen in Africa and South America didn't need a specialist. They needed someone who would help; someone who knew simple first aid, nutrition, and hygiene. He could do that. A chance for him to heal and not destroy would be a positive change. That was where he belonged, not here.

The phone rang. Daniel knew who it was without answering it because only one man knew his phone number. He let it ring four more times. It gave him a small sense of satisfaction making Adam wait.

He picked the receiver up. "Hello."

"Good, you're there. I thought you might have already left," came the older voice on the other end.

"I just woke up."

"Do you think you'll be able to identify him today?" Adam wanted to know.

"I have to find him first. I was thinking about asking around the grocery store in town. I think that would be the hub of activity; and if he is in town, he will probably show up there at some time. Either him or Joseph. Even a Nazi has to eat."

As he said that, a quick image flicked in his memory. A tall, blond-haired man with blue eyes. The image of a perfect Aryan and he had seen this man in Kay's Kitchen last night when he had come out of the diner. Joseph Mueller?

"Good," Adam said. "I've contacted some other people in Maryland about that guy who attacked you yesterday. From what I've been told, there's an active Klu Klux Klan chapter in the county. This man may be a member so be careful. His name is not on a list of known members, and I couldn't find any psychiatric reports on him that might explain his violence, either."

"I intend to be careful," Daniel assured him.

"Then I'll wait to hear from you tonight." With that, Adam hung up. Daniel shrugged and dropped the receiver into the cradle. After he had showered and shaved, he dressed in jeans and a T-shirt and drove into town on Hanover Road. He saw an unexpected amount of activity in Fleetwood. He was surprised since it was still only seven-thirty in the morning. The feed store was open and doing business. So was the hardware store. Most of Fleetwood's early birds appeared to be farmers, and businesses that catered to them.

Daniel parked in Kendall's Country Store parking lot and crossed the street. He stopped in front of Kay's Kitchen when the smell of eggs and coffee reached his nose. As soon as he saw the sign for food, his stomach rumbled. He walked in and ordered coffee and a bagel with cream cheese. Kay, who worked as the diner's only waitress, told him he would have to settle for an English muffin. They didn't stock bagels.

After his quick breakfast, he was out on the street again walking toward the main intersection. He wondered if the grocery store opened as early as some of the other businesses.

He tapped on the glass of the front door even though the sign on the door said he was ten minutes early. But even as he looked in the window, he saw a young woman run from the back room. She paused for a moment and disappeared behind the shelves in one aisle and then she reappeared, running toward the door.

At the time, he didn't wonder why she was running; he thought she was just hurrying to open the door. He tapped on the glass. The woman looked over at him. He saw fear in her eyes. He had seen the same panicked look in a dozen pairs of old German eyes when he asked about their past. She altered her course and ran toward the door nearest him. He stepped over to it and waited.

The girl reached the door and stopped. Daniel thought he heard a male's voice yell something, but he couldn't understand what the person said. The girl looked over her shoulder. Daniel saw a man come up the aisle toward the girl. Daniel couldn't decide if the expression on the man's face was one of pain or anger.

The girl unlocked the door. Daniel opened it and said, "Good morning. I know you're not open yet, but..."

Saying nothing, the girl hurried past him, bumping into him as she passed. "Excuse me," Daniel said as she brushed him. She glanced up at him, and the sea-green color of her eyes struck him.

The man rushed up to the door and seemed about to reach out and grab the girl. At the last moment, he decided against it. He stopped at the door and stared after her as she ran around the corner of the store.

"What do you want?" the skinny man snapped when he noticed Daniel standing off to the side.

Daniel was sure he had missed part of the scene. Something had obviously happened before he arrived that had upset the girl. He assumed the man, and the woman were having a lover's spat.

"I am looking for someone, and I was hoping you might help me," Daniel explained.

The man's brow wrinkled as he stared at Daniel. He waved his arm inside the store. "Do I look like the police chief? There's only one person in here now, and I'm busy. So if you don't mind, I have to get back to work."

"But I am looking for..." The man shut the door in his face and locked it. Daniel stared after him and watched the man walk back toward the stock room. He walked slightly bent over holding his crotch as if it hurt him. Daniel had an impulse to smash his fist through the glass and unlock the door. Then he would throttle the ill-mannered shop owner. He managed to hold his anger in check, though.

He leaned his opened hands against the glass door and yelled, "Small town hospitality leaves much to be desired."

CHAPTER 24

JULY 8, 1993

Fleetwood Police Chief Steve Montgomery stood at the head of the trail looking at the two bodies sprawled out in front of him. He thought he could smell death in the air, even though he knew it was probably just the musty smell of rotting wood. These bodies hadn't been dead for more than a few hours. No signs of putrescence. The trail was still hot. A lucky break for him.

He frowned. If he was so lucky, why was he so scared?

He glanced at the bodies. Maybe a lucky break for him but certainly not for Shannon Gardner and Billy Stillwell.

Steve had been police chief of Fleetwood for just six months and had thought this would be an undemanding job. Catch a few speeders. Arrest a few drunks on Saturday night. Write up reports about car accidents. Being police chief had been easy money. Until today.

Now, one thought kept going through his mind: Something God-awful strong did this. His eyes strayed to Shannon Gardner's body and to her flattened head, the skull crushed as if it had been an eggshell or a flattened basketball. Steve glanced quickly away when his stomach jumped and threatened to empty itself on the ground.

Shannon had gone to school with his daughter. Steve remembered Lisa telling him how nice Shannon had been to her. Not everyone in town had been so friendly to the Montgomerys since their arrival in Fleetwood. He hadn't wanted to get back into law enforcement when he first moved out here, but he thought it would be a way to show any bigots in town that a black man could work just as hard as they could without asking for special treatment. To run and win his election had cost him most of his savings, but it was worth it. Steve thought he had done a good job so far. However, he sensed that this case would prove just how good he was.

Lee Hoskins, Steve's only patrolman, walked back toward the chief on the dirt trail. He kept his eyes noticeably averted from the bodies off to the side of the trail. At least Steve wasn't the only one with a weak stomach.

"I found Billy's shirt on a blanket off to the side there. It looks like they were probably studying the birds and bees ... or at least getting ready to," Lee said. Normally, he would have smiled at catching a pair of kids trying to be adults, but no one thought of this situation as humorous.

"Is this federal land?" the chief asked.

Lee shook his head. "Not county, either. This is still within the town's border for another hundred yards."

Bad luck for Steve.

"Any sign of what killed them?" Steve asked.

Lee shook his head. "Not much. Apparently, he came in from the opposite side of the trail, but I can't tell you how tall he is or how heavy. Only that he has to be the strongest man I've never met."

"What about rape?" Steve asked.

"The M.E. says 'no.' He could find no signs of forced entry or semen on Shannon. He'll do a more in-depth analysis at the morgue."

"What about him?"

Lee looked surprised. "Him?"

"Yeah, him, Billy Stillwell." Steve answered Lee's unspoken question by saying, "Number one, we don't know whether there was a killer or killers. Number two, we don't know whether a man or woman did this. Number three, there's no law that says a murderer has to be straight. We can't close any possibilities," Steve explained to the patrolman.

Lee snorted. "I know you've got perverts in the city, Chief, but this is the country. Those types of things don't happen up here. We've never even had a murder."

Lee's continual second guessing angered Steve. His patrolman was trying to teach the police chief how to be a law man. Lee might have experience as a patrolman but the town hadn't chosen him as their police chief. When the votes had been counted, Steve had won by eighty-seven votes. He had asked Lee to be his patrolman because he wanted to have access to Lee's knowledge and experience. Although Steve had been a cop for more than a dozen years in a place marked by dangerous crime and lots of it, Lee Hoskins knew the area and the people. Not to mention the fact that Lee was white and certain people would say more to him than they would ever say to Steve.

"Nothing like this, huh? Ever see *The Silence of the Lambs?* That was set in West Virginia, which is just on the other side of the river. Just because you're a redneck doesn't mean you don't like to probe in the out hole. And who cares if there were no murders before? That's history, man. This year there are two murders," Steve snapped.

Lee nodded reluctantly. "I'm not sure if the M.E. checked Billy out. I'll have to find out."

"You do that," Steve said, his anger already fading.

Lee turned and started back down the trail. Steve wondered what his patrolman thought about these murders. Seeing the bodies upset Steve and he had seen more crime in a month in Baltimore than a law man on this side of the state would see in a career. Children being shot. Drug deals. Gang violence. Racial tensions. Robbery. Rape. Child molestation. He thought he had seen it all, but this was something new. Steve didn't like to see fresh ways to destroy life. People were already too creative in that regard.

"Lee?" Steve called.

His patrolman stopped and faced Steve.

"Better bag 'em up. I've made a positive ID, so have you. Don't let the parents see them unless they insist. It'll be better if they remember their kids the way they looked yesterday."

Lee sighed. "I only wish I could."

Steve nodded his agreement. He walked back on the trail a hundred yards. Richard Merrill was sitting on a log. The man looked up when Steve approached. Richard looked like another man who wished he could remember Shannon and Billy the way they had looked yesterday. Now when he thought of them, all he would see would be the crushed skulls, blood, and ugliness of the crime scene.

"Was it an animal, Chief?" he asked.

Steve sat down on the log beside him. "Yes, we just don't know if it has two legs or four."

Bill's eyes widened. "You think a person could have done that?"

Steve nodded slowly. "'Fraid so. Nothing chewed on them, so they weren't killed for food. I don't know of an animal that kills prey the way Shannon was killed. Do you?" When Richard didn't answer, Steve continued. "Of course, I don't know a person who could do it either. Still, it was done. Now I have to find out how."

Richard ran his hands through his thin, brown hair. His hands shook nervously.

"Do their folks know?"

"Not yet. Her dad's worried about her. He thinks they may have run off to get married. How am I going to tell him this?" How could he tell a mother something had slammed her son's head against a tree so hard that it dented the tree, let alone how you describe the son?

As if reading Steve's mind, Richard put his hand on the chief's shoulder. "You have to look them in the eyes and tell them you'll find the killer. Then find him. You're the experienced law man. The people here voted for you because they thought you knew what you were doing. They believed a big-city cop could keep the peace in a small town. You have to prove that now."

Steve turned toward Richard. "What happened? Tell me again. Everything from the time you came into the woods until the time you called me. Don't leave anything out."

"I was headed down to the river to go fishing. I know this sweet little hole where the perch jump into my basket. I parked up by the bridge and hiked down the trail. There's lots of other fishing spots along the way, but mine is out of the way. It's almost a mile away from the bridge, but it's worth the walk." He glanced down the trail where Lee and the coroner were lifting one of the green body bags to walk it out to the coroner's car. "At least it used to be. The Drucker's boy told me about the spot. The trail splits off a ways back. Most everyone uses the upper path if they are hiking. The only ones who come down on the lower path are kids who want to fool around and me."

"When I came around the bend in the path, I saw their legs sticking out onto the trail. Well, I stopped because I didn't know what to do. I've never caught any of the kids in the act before. I mean I've found condoms and stray clothes here and there, so I knew they came here, but I've never actually seen them here. They use the trail at night, and I use it during the day. So I stood there for a bit until I noticed they weren't moving. I figured they were asleep, and I might be able to sneak by without embarrassing them and do my fishing. As I walked by, I noticed the blood stains. Then I saw their heads. I threw up my breakfast on the spot."

"I thought that maybe there was a mountain lion on the loose or maybe a bear. Either way, I didn't want to be nearby if it was hungry. I dropped my pole and ran back up the path to the fork and then took the path to my car and then I came and got you."

Lee and the medical examiner walked by. Richard and Steve fell silent as they watched the body pass them. Steve found it hard not to feel nauseous knowing what was inside the bag even if he couldn't see the body.

"You didn't touch anything?" the police chief asked when Lee and the coroner had passed by.

"Of course not!" He wiped his hands off on his pants as if just the thought of touching the bodies made him feel dirty.

"Don't get upset. I have to cover all the bases. If I don't ask the questions, someone else will."

Richard's head bounced up and down in a nervous nod. "Okay. I just don't like having a finger wagging in my face. I'm trying to help you out here."

"I know and I appreciate it. So cool your jets. These bodies might never have been found or found long after their murders if you hadn't found them. I don't believe you did it. I've seen you arm wrestle. No way you could have done what's in there." Richard ignored the slight jibe. It didn't even raise a smile from the usually good-humored man. "Did you see anything? Unusual tracks? Smoke?" Richard shook his head. "Hear anything?"

"No. Even when I stopped to figure out what I should do, everything was real quiet."

Steve was silent for a moment, then patted Richard on the back and said, "Why don't you go on home? I'll call you if I have any more questions. I don't want you telling anyone about this, though, until I've told their folks. If I catch wind of it, I'll know who to come to."

Richard nodded. "I don't think I would tell anyone, anyway. That sight's gonna give me nightmares for a month. I wouldn't want to pass that feeling on to anyone else." Richard started to walk away, then he stopped and turned back to the chief. "Do you think you'll find who did it?"

"Eventually," Steve answered, but what he didn't say was he hoped he could do it before this person struck again. Stopping a random killer would be hard, and from everything he had heard, Shannon and Billy didn't care about anything but each other. They didn't have any enemies. Just a killer.

CHAPTER 25

JULY 8, 1993

Daniel Levitt turned away from the closed glass door when the skinny, sandy-haired man disappeared into the back room. Clenching his hand into a fist, Daniel rapped on the door again to attract the man's attention. The man looked over his shoulder at Daniel, waved him away, and went into the back room.

Daniel walked around the corner and saw the red-haired girl who had just come from inside the Kendall's Country Store walking toward the end of the street. She might know if Mueller was in town. Someone in Fleetwood must have seen the old man and his son. Fleetwood wasn't that large. Daniel hurried down the street after the woman, crossing Hanover Road to come up beside her.

"Excuse me, miss," he said as he fell into step on her right side. The girl looked over her shoulder but kept walking. For a moment, Daniel saw fear in her face, but then her expression relaxed.

"Do you work in the grocery store?" he asked.

She looked at him, then turned her attention back to the sidewalk.

"Not anymore. I quit this morning."

"That must have been your boss, then. He seemed a little upset at your leaving," Daniel noted. Actually, the man had seemed a little more than just upset, but Daniel didn't want to put the girl on the defensive. He needed her help.

"Serves him right," she said.

Daniel wondered if she would give him the answers to his questions, but he asked, anyway. "Would you mind helping me? I am looking for someone. He is new in town, and I thought that the best place to find out where he lives is to ask at the grocery store."

He liked the way the girl's red curls bounced around her head as she walked.

"Good guess, but I haven't seen anyone new in town except you," the girl told him. "And you sound like you've come from *way* out of town."

Daniel couldn't help his mash-up of accents from all the places he had lived over the years. "This man would be about eighty, and he would have a son in his mid-forties, a little older than me. He would be hard to miss."

"Does this man have a name?"

"He does... but he probably is not using the name I know him by."

The girl stopped walking. Daniel had gone a few steps further before he realized she had stopped walking. He backed up to where she stood.

She turned to Daniel and said, "I don't like the sound of that. I've got enough troubles of my own. I don't want to be dragged into anyone else's."

Daniel shook his head. "You do not have to worry. I am not doing anything illegal," he assured her.

Cocking her head to the side, Daniel noticed how her hair framed her face. There were a few freckles on her cheeks and nose, but they seemed only to add to her beauty, not detract from it. The freckles also made her look a few years younger than her actual age. He guessed she was probably in her early twenties, though she looked like she could have been a teenager.

"It sounds like your friend is, though," the girl said.

"I never said the man was my friend," Daniel snapped.

The girl straightened her head and stepped back, preparing to run or scream. Daniel wasn't sure which.

She looked directly into Daniel's eyes and asked, "What are you? A cop or something?"

Daniel saw Kay's Kitchen over the girl's shoulder. "May I buy you a cup of coffee? I will try to explain things to you. You might know more than you think you do, and finding this man is important to me."

The girl hesitated, then shrugged. "Well, I guess I owe you something for keeping Brad from following me. Besides, I don't think you'd try anything in Kay's, or she would hit you upside your head with a frying pan."

Since the girl seemed like she might help him, Daniel decided he would not tell her he had done nothing to help her.

They walked into Kay's and sat down at the counter that ran the length of the diner. A middle-aged woman whose name tag on her uniform read "Kay" called the red-haired woman "Tina" when she greeted them. Kay took their orders for two coffees.

"So you never answered me," Tina said once Kay had left. "Are you a cop?"

Daniel shook his head. "My name is Daniel Levitt. I work for an organization that tracks down war criminals."

"Vietnam?"

That one word made Daniel realize how far away from everyone's memories World War II was. He was no longer an avenging angel in the hands of God. He was now a bounty hunter looking for an old man.

"No, World War II," Daniel answered.

The girl was surprised. "You mean there are still war criminals from that war? It ended in 1945."

"They are still alive."

"Probably not for much longer." Tina paused. "Wait a minute. Are you saying this old guy you're looking for is a war criminal?" Daniel hesitated momentarily, then nodded. "What did he do?"

"He experimented on and killed a lot of Jewish prisoners in a concentration camp called Auschwitz."

Tina frowned. "Ugly stuff, but what makes you think he is here in Fleetwood?"

"The organization I work for knew he was in Brazil, but we never seemed to get close to him there. A week ago he left Brazil for America. We have tried to keep tabs on him since then, but we have to make a positive verification before I can go to the police."

Tina sipped her coffee and said, "Well, I think your information is wrong. No one new has come to town other than hikers and bikers taking a break from the canal towpath, and when someone does come, everyone knows about it."

"I talked to someone yesterday who seemed to recognize the man. His name was Jacob," Daniel told Tina.

The girl smiled. "Tall man with long arms? Really built?" When Daniel nodded, she said, "That's Jacob Lachman. I don't think I'd put too much faith in what he tells you. He thinks like a ten-year-old. He and his mom live on a farm off Hanover Road north of town."

"Being as familiar with this town as you are must be nice."

Tina shrugged. "It has its disadvantages, too. I know I'm not going to hang around once I get my degree. Too many people know too many other people's business."

Daniel remembered his two years in college when he was studying medicine. Then Adam Goldstein had entered his life. College was now just another one of his dreams that had to be sacrificed for him to become a member of the Committee for the Prosecution of War Criminals.

"What are you studying?"

"I'm a marketing major."

"Good luck. I am sure you will do well. I, on the other hand, am not having much luck." Daniel stood up. "Thank you for trying to help me. I have enjoyed speaking with you."

He drained his coffee and then walked over to the cash register and paid the bill. He waved to Tina as he walked out the door. He would have liked to stay and talk with her some more, but what was the use? He would be leaving in a short time. Daniel wished he had a place that he could put down roots in like Tina did with Fleetwood.

CHAPTER 26

JULY 8, 1993

Daniel wasn't sure why he drove back to the forest after he left Tina sitting in the diner. He would have much rather preferred sitting and talking to her. But she was too distracting. The sound of her voice hypnotized him. Her red hair enchanted him. Her green eyes swallowed him up. Her trim, fit body aroused him.

He quickly shifted his thoughts back to Mueller. Better he didn't think of the girl. She was too young for him. As if he had time to get involved with anyone. He had tried that route once. Long-distance relationships are certainly not long term.

He had been head over heels for a political science professor at Stanford University. Her name was Robyn Friedman, and they had met while he was tracking down an old Gestapo officer named Rolf Bretzl. Then Adam had sent Daniel to Spain chasing after another septuagenarian Nazi. Robyn and Daniel had tried to carry on a relationship. One would fly to meet the other, and they would spend a few awkward days together. Awkward because they had barely known each other to start with and they only grew further apart, the longer they were separated. In the end, they had been making up lame excuses not to visit each other.

Daniel parked his car on the side of the road again. He tried to tell himself Jacob was his only clue to Mueller, and he had last seen Jacob in the forest. Therefore, to pick up Mueller's trail, he had to follow his last clue, which meant going into the forest.

Bull!

In the back of his mind, he knew the excuse didn't wash. Tina had told him where Jacob lived, and it wasn't out in the woods. It was on a farm off Hanover Road. If Daniel wanted to pick up Mueller's trail, he could pick it up at that farm house.

He didn't want to find Jacob's trail, though.

Daniel wanted to find the beast that had scared Jacob off. He wanted to find the thing that had left those odd footprints in the dirt. Right now he was more curious about the beast than about Mueller.

When Daniel reached the clearing where Jacob Lachman had attacked him, he stood silently in the center and listened. He could hear the birds chirping warnings to each other of his presence. In the distance, he also heard a river running over rocks. A place like this would be a nice place to live. A place like this minus a tree-pushing beast, of course.

He continued past the clearing and looked at the footprints behind the brush line again. They were still there. He wasn't sure if they would be. He thought he might have imagined seeing them, but there they were in bold relief in the soft dirt. What had made them? He wanted to answer that question, and that was why he had come back.

He moved back onto the trail and followed it deeper into the woods.

This was the direction Jacob had run away from the beast. It didn't seem to go anywhere except deeper into the woods. It probably turned and ran back to the road at some point.

Daniel pulled his gun and held it in front of him as a precaution. He didn't think Jacob would still be in the woods, but he hadn't thought Jacob would attack him either. This time he would be prepared.

The trail stayed level for about one-hundred yards, then dropped off steeply as it moved toward the river. He stood at the brink of the descent and looked down the trail. He saw nothing. Certainly no beast the size of a grizzly bear.

A branch snapped somewhere in the woods off to his right. It sounded loud enough to be a gunshot in the quiet forest. He wondered if he would learn anything more by going down to the river.

Shrugging, he started down the trail to the river and stopped. He felt the ground shake underneath his feet. It wasn't an earthquake tremor, but something heavy dropped onto the ground. He crouched down and put his hand on the ground. He couldn't feel the tremor now. He looked around. Whatever it was, it had to have been close by for him to have felt it. He scanned the branches of the trees, hoping to see movement that would mark from where something had fallen. They were all still. He was alone.

He turned around to look in the direction he had come, figuring that was the most likely spot for anyone to be.

"I know you're there so you might as well come out, Jacob. Besides, I've got a gun. If you try anything, I'll shoot you."

The bluff was so apparent that Jacob probably could see through it.

Still, he waited, hoping the retarded man would show himself. He wasn't sure what he would do if Jacob showed himself, but he would rather know where the man was than where he was not.

He wondered if Jacob might have been closer to the river. He started to turn and a huge, dark-skinned hand hit his gun hand from beneath, knocking it up into the air. Daniel's reflexes allowed him to fire a single shot, and then the pistol went flying from his hands. Daniel himself was falling backwards, away from his attacker. He hit the ground, tumbling down the hillside. He managed to roll to his side and into a crouch. He was prepared for an attack. Jacob wouldn't catch him totally unprepared this time, but no attack came.

Instead, standing in front of him was a huge gorilla. No, he thought, it was not quite a gorilla. The hair was shorter, and the skin was not as black. The face had a human quality to it, but it was still definitely an animal.

As he watched, the beast reached out for him.

CHAPTER 27

JULY 8, 1993

Karl Mueller watched his son Joseph drive down Deer Run Road toward the town, off to God knows where. Karl tried not to be bitter at the secrets remaining between them. Joseph might have secrets, but so did he. Still, he'd made progress this morning. A small amount, but more than had been there last night. They still had a chance to make things better if God would grant him the time.

Although he knew he had little choice in the matter, Karl would have preferred they stay isolated, not venturing too far beyond the house. The fewer people who saw them, the better. But they had to eat. Better to let Joseph go. Karl would harness his son's natural tendency to wander by having him also run the essential errands. No one would recognize Joseph. No Nazi hunter sought Joseph Speer, a Brazilian immigrant visiting America on vacation. In this case, the sins of the father would not be visited upon the son.

When Joseph had turned the corner of Deer Run Road and driven out of sight, Karl walked into his bedroom. The cedar chest beckoned to him as it always did. While his memory faded with time and disease, his past continued to happen within the pages of his journals. All his thoughts, feelings, and motives were captured forever. In the end, this would be all that was left to tell his story. It would verify his studies, brand him as a murderer, and redeem him in the eyes of God and Joseph.

Karl unlocked the padlock and kneeled down in front of the chest. He pulled the metal box out and opened it. The luger was on top of the piles of notebooks, letters, and pictures. He picked up the pistol. Although the metal was cold, it seemed to burn into his hand. Many years had passed since he had felt the need to carry a pistol. Now his arm was too feeble to hold it steady. He hoped for an easier way that he might carry out his mission, but he could not be sure. Darwin had almost killed Eva Lachman during the last experiment, and Karl had to shoot the poor beast. He had to be prepared for Darwin's sons. If things went wrong, he might be left defenseless. He was not sure what he would face when he found Darwin's sons, but he was sure they would be aberrations even in the sight of God.

He gently set the pistol on the floor beside him as though he was afraid that it would go off if he held it too tightly or set it down too hard.

He was about to close the metal box when he saw Aria's picture. Her angelic face stared at him, poking out from under a notebook.

He uncovered the picture and lifted it out of the box. It was his and Aria's wedding picture from 1936. Aria never looked better than she did in that picture. The photographer had seemed to capture Karl Mueller's new wife's true essence on the film. She had tied her blond hair up in a bun on the back of her head, which showed the curve of her neck. Her mother had helped her apply her makeup that day. She had been too nervous to do it herself. Aria's mother had done an excellent job. Not too much as to look cheap, but just enough to highlight Aria's features. Even in a black-and-white photo, he could see the intensity of life in his wife's eyes. How quickly that had been extinguished by the Jew pig!

He held the photograph up to his cheek, hoping to feel some ancient wisp of her presence through the paper and chemicals. Aria had been dead almost fifteen years and the only place she still lived was in the hearts of her husband and son.

So why couldn't Joseph understand what Karl needed to do? Aria would have understood. She might not have liked it, but she would have understood. He was sure of that. To repent of your sins, you must correct them wherever possible. He had committed his greatest sin over fifty years ago under the guise of medical research. Now was his last chance to correct it, his only chance to correct it. Through quiet and inconspicuous research, he had uncovered Eva Lachman's address and phone number. He had the pictures of her taken during the experiments to recognize her by. Now he must act on his information.

CHAPTER 28

JULY 8, 1993

The beast held his hand out toward Daniel, who scrambled backwards on his hands and feet. He wanted to stand up and make a mad dash for his car, but he couldn't take his eyes off the thing in front of him. It was tall, muscular, and hairy. It reminded him of the blurry pictures the American tabloids always showed of Bigfoot. He had always thought it was a legend, but here it stood in front of him.

The beast easily kept pace with his scrambling. His stride had to be at least seven-feet long. The thing seemed amused by his inability to escape. Daniel could see it smirking. It might have infuriated him if he hadn't been so scared.

"If you stood up, it might be easier to run," the beast said.

Daniel almost screamed. Instead, he was so startled he collapsed onto the ground. The beast squatted on its haunches next to Daniel, letting its hands rest on the ground. The action was definitely ape-like, but the beast brought a human quality to it.

"Don't worry. I won't touch you if you don't want me to," it said.

Daniel lay still. Confusion had stolen his voice.

"I'm sorry about pushing you down back there," the beast said. "I just meant to knock the gun out of your hand. I was afraid you might actually shoot something... like me. I'm so used to fighting with my brother, I don't realize just how strong I really am."

The beast smiled, and it struck Daniel how human his face looked at that moment. His eyes gave him his humanity. They revealed a range of emotion unmatched by an animal. The beast looked familiar, too, but Daniel knew he had seen nothing like him before.

The beast continued talking, not caring if Daniel responded.

"You'll have to forgive my appearance. I was born this way. As for my clothes, they're too restrictive for me when I'm running and jumping." Cocking his head, he paused and stared at Daniel. "Actually, I'm surprised to see you back here again. After what happened to you yesterday, you must have a very strong reason to come back here. Either that, or you're very foolish."

Daniel's gaze shifted for an instant to the beast's feet. The foot was broad and the big toe stuck out to the side, almost like another finger. It was him! The beast who knocked down the tree. "You saved my life yesterday. It was you in the trees. You scared off Jacob."

The beast shook his head. "I didn't scare him off. He chased after me. He didn't catch me, though. Boy, was he mad!"

The beast chuckled at the memory, but it sounded like rumbling thunder. Daniel cringed, and the beast covered his mouth.

"Then he knows what you are?" Daniel said cautiously.

"Who? Jacob?" The beast nodded. "He should know who I am. He's my brother."

This was another shock for Daniel. Even as he tried to assimilate it, he realized why the beast looked so familiar. The beast looked like Jacob. Jacob's brow was not as pronounced, nor his jaw. His skin was not as dark and he certainly didn't have the same amount of body hair, but the similarities were there. The same look in the eyes. The same size. The same elongated face.

They could be two sides of the same coin. Civilized and uncivilized. But which one would play each role? Daniel thought.

"What are you?" he asked.

The beast shrugged and lowered his eyes. "To my mother, I am a secret she can never reveal. To you, I am a monster. To most people, I do not even exist. Except in their nightmares, I suppose."

"That is not what I mean."

"I know." The beast was silent and Daniel sat up. "I am the product of an experiment in genetics. I don't know whether I am a successful experiment or a failure. I am not even sure whether I am a man or an animal or something in between."

Daniel could sense the despair in the beast's voice. He would have liked to have been able to solve the creature's dilemma, but he wasn't sure how he could answer.

"How can you be a genetic experiment? You look older than me. That would mean that you were born during a time when the knowledge to produce you did not exist," Daniel said, making some quick calculations in his head.

"But the knowledge did exist. It was simply not realized by anyone. It has been known for centuries. It just has always gone by a different name, if it was even given a name. Did the female horse ask the male donkey that mounted her if the mule they made should actually exist? I am a mule. I am the product of crossbreeding between a gorilla and a human."

Daniel's eyes widened with amazement. "And your brother?"

The beast nodded slightly. "Him, too. We're twins."

"Why does no one know about you, but everyone knows about Jacob?" Daniel asked.

"If you were my mother, which one of us would you allow the public to see and which would you hide?"

Daniel pushed himself into a sitting position. "Your mother keeps you in hiding?"

"No, not all the time, but I am kept in what amounts to a cage, so that no one else will see me. Jacob, on the other hand, is far more dangerous than me, but Mama allows to move around freely because he looks human or close enough to it to pass as a human. Looks can be deceiving, as you well know."

"But she must let you out sometime. You're here." The beast said nothing, and Daniel realized the truth. "Did you break out?"

Ashamed, the beast turned away and nodded. "I realized two days ago that I am nearly fifty years old, and I have never known a full day of freedom. The closest I came to it was a half day of freedom when I was fifteen years old. Yet, time is not waiting for me to experience what it's like to be free. I am becoming a silverback." He pointed to the streak of silver hair bisecting his back and running from his neck to his waist. "In the wild, that would mean I am an old gorilla, but in the wild, most gorillas would be dead by now. I realized I might not have much more time to live, and I wanted to know freedom before I died."

Daniel stood up and approached the beast. When he was only a foot away, he reached out. Before he touched the beast, he asked, "May I?"

The beast nodded. Daniel touched the beast's shoulder. The hair was thick, but it did not feel coarse like most animal hair. He touched his cheek. It felt soft. More like human skin than animal.

"Why would someone crossbreed a gorilla and a human?" Daniel asked. "What purpose would it serve?"

The beast shrugged. "I don't know. Many of the experiments that took place in the concentration camps made little sense. Why should Dr. Mueller be any different?"

Daniel stepped back. "Mueller? Dr. Karl Mueller?" The beast nodded.

Now Daniel knew the reason Mueller had come to Maryland.

CHAPTER 29

JULY 8, 1993

Tina Rourke wasn't sure why she decided to go swimming, especially after someone had stolen her underwear the last time she had gone. She only knew that she needed to relax and unwind from her confrontation with Brad Kendall this morning, and swimming helped her do that. It was too hot to run and running was exhausting, not relaxing. Also, she didn't feel like driving out to the college to work out in the weight room which was her other way of relieving stress.

She tried to tell herself that an animal had walked off with her underwear, but she knew it was a lame excuse. Her panties had been under her clothes, so if an animal was going to take something, it would have taken what was on top.

Nothing bad had ever happened in the immense forest bordered by Fleetwood and Hanover Road, though. The forest covered most of Polish Mountain, and a lot of hiking trails wound their way up to the many scenic overlooks the mountain offered. The trail was a favorite place used by over-amorous kids who wanted to be alone. Younger kids came to the Hanover Road bridge to swim. No one had ever been hurt out here before except for the kids who belly-flopped off the bridge into the water. Of course, no one had ever reported their underwear stolen either.

This time, her swim was planned. Tina had gone home and changed into her bathing suit and was wearing it underneath her clothes. She unbuttoned her blouse and slid out of her jeans, revealing her green bathing suit. It wasn't as revealing as a thong bikini, but it was sexy and it showed off her trim body most flatteringly. Not that she had worn it to impress anyone. She had only two bathing suits, and she wore the other one when she wanted to impress a guy. This bathing suit she wore to swim in.

She walked into the water until she was waist deep. Her teeth chattered at first, but she quickly got used to the cold water. It felt good compared to the stifling humidity. The cold water cleared her mind so she could think. That was why she came to the river to swim. She dove into the water and surfaced with a loud sigh. Then she rolled over onto her back and floated.

Foremost on her mind was what she would do about Brad.

Filing a complaint with Police Chief Montgomery would put his word against hers. No one had seen Brad try anything, not even Daniel Levitt. If she complained to Chief Montgomery, Brad would probably say she was just fantasizing because of his reputation with girls. And the Chief would believe Brad's word against hers. Brad's dad would make sure of that. Earl had a lot of power in this area, especially in town. She definitely wouldn't go back to work, but she'd warn Brad to stay away from her. She'd also ask the phone company to start tracing all her calls so she would have another source to back her up if Brad made any more obscene calls. That would be her only way to have proof against him if he continued harassing her.

That solved the problem to her satisfaction. Tina rolled over and dove beneath the surface again swimming downstream. When she came up for air, she considered her next problem. Actually, it wasn't so much a problem as it was a curiosity.

Who was Daniel Levitt and was he for real? Her first thought when he had approached her had been that he was trying to pick her up, but he was a stranger in town. She wasn't vain enough to think that he would come to town just to hit on her. Then when she had heard his story, she thought he was crazy. A Nazi war criminal in Fleetwood? War criminals, if any were still around, hung out in cities in Germany, Austria, and South America. Right or wrong, though, he had seemed honest, but his heart hadn't quite been into the search. Either that, or he was a rank amateur.

He revealed his cover to her even though he didn't know her. She had seen enough movies to know that could be a problem. She could easily tell anyone about him. If the Klan ever found out a Jew was in town hunting a German, they'd make Daniel's life miserable. Tina decided she wouldn't say anything for now. She'd keep it her secret. Daniel wouldn't find his man, and he would leave in a few days. He'd be just like the politicians that came into town for the weekends.

Tina dog-paddled back toward the shore until she could stand on the gravel bottom. She waded back ashore, and as she bent over to pick up her towel, someone pushed her from behind. She only had enough time to grunt as she hit the ground on her chest.

As she screamed, a hand clamped over her mouth. She looked over her shoulder and saw Brad straddling her. He rolled her onto her back keeping his hand over her mouth. She shook her head trying to shake his hand loose, but it didn't work. Tina wondered if the same trick would work twice, figured it was worth the try and hit him in the crotch with her knee. He grunted, but instead of rolling off her, he fell on top of her.

"Kick me in the balls, will you? You need some training on how to be a woman, and I'm just the man to give it to you," he told her.

Tina bit into his fingers and he jerked his hand away. She screamed again, and Brad slapped her hard across the face jarring her teeth together. She didn't want to cry in front of him because that would only encourage him, but she couldn't help it.

Brad smiled. He kept one hand on her throat. "If you try anything, I'll choke you. I swear I will." His free hand moved down to her breasts and squeezed. She tried not to shiver but was again unsuccessful. This was not how she had ever imagined herself handling herself in this type of situation. She was scared and couldn't control her feelings. She couldn't even fight off a wimp like Brad.

Brad leaned close to her and licked her ear. Then he said, "If you don't try to fight me, you'll enjoy this. You know you've wanted it for a long time. No one's watching. Let loose and have some fun. I know I will."

He chuckled as his hand moved down between her legs.

CHAPTER 30

JULY 8, 1993

Karl Mueller sat in a rocking chair in the corner of the room and read through his experiment journals. He cried softly and tried to keep his tears from falling into the journals where they might smear the ink. Entries he had written fifty years ago brought fresh pain to him. How could he have been so stupid as to tamper with nature? What had given him the authority to interfere with what God had created? Hitler? Hitler had been partially right, but he shouldn't have feared interracial breeding. Interspecies breeding was what would contaminate the human race.

When Karl had come to Auschwitz in 1943, he had dreamed of creating the perfect soldier. A drone that would kill on command, march fearlessly into battle, strike fear into the hearts of the enemy, and be completely expendable. With his list of needs, he began trying to find the way to achieve them.

Humans were excellent soldiers because of their intelligence, but that same intelligence also kept them from blindly obeying orders. Animals could be trained to do specific tasks, and they were expendable but their lack of intelligence did not make them optimum soldiers. There seemed to be nothing in between the two.

Then one day while walking around the perimeter of Auschwitz, thinking on the problems involved with finding a perfect soldier, Karl watched a guard struggling to keep a huge shepherd under control. He noticed the shepherd was much larger than the other dogs. Its brown-and-black hair had streaks of gray throughout, and it seemed much more aggressive whenever someone approached the fence. The soldier had to walk with his heels dug into the ground to keep the dog from pulling him over.

"That dog," Lieutenant Mueller had said pointing to the large shepherd, "Why is it so different from the others?"

"It's a wolfhound. Its sire was a huge, gray wolf, and it passed its size and temperament onto its son. It makes for an excellent watchdog, though it takes every ounce of my strength to control the beast. I'd hate to be attacked by it," the guard told him.

Karl nodded and watched as the guard continued on his rounds.

The wolfhound strained at its leash, and the guard had to lean back against the dog's strength.

This sight started a cascade of thoughts in Karl's mind. The normal shepherd had been improved by cross-breeding with another species to create the ultimate guard dog. Perhaps, something could be cross-bred with a man to create an expendable soldier. Then the question became: What?

This was in the days before biology and biotechnology became popular fields of study in the scientific arena. There was no such thing as DNA. Genetics was an infant. Darwin had developed his theory of evolution, and Mendel had introduced the idea of dominant and recessive genes through peas. Carver had cross-bred different plants to come up with heartier breeds, and dogs had been cross-bred to bring out different traits.

But this wolfhound represented interspecies cross-breeding. Karl knew it could be done. The wolfhound was proof of that. The question was just how could it be done with a human? Dr. Mueller took the first logical step and tried to follow a known pattern. The best chance of finding an animal compatible to crossbreed with a human should start with finding an animal that looked as similar to the human as the wolf looked to the dog.

This too, proved to be a problem. Primates were the obvious choice and of these, the great apes, particularly, the gorilla because its size and strength was the best choice, but since they were not native to Germany, subjects were in short supply. Most of the gorillas were in zoos. To import one might raise eyebrows, but Karl thought the gamble would be worth the risk.

He made as much initial preparation as he could. When his shifts for selection duty came, he kept his eyes out for a suitable mother. He wanted a young, healthy girl, a girl he could isolate from the normal goings on of the camp. He did not want the rumors of his experiments spreading throughout the camp. The rumors might reach the wrong ears.

Many of the women coming off the trains were older or in ill health.

When he had finally found the girl he wanted, he made a special selection of her. He kept her in isolation from the rest of the work camp. To everyone but Mueller and his immediate staff, she did not exist. He befriended her and examined her to make sure she could conceive. That the woman was named Eva Lachman, he took as a good omen, for she would be the mother to a new species just as Eve had been the mother to humanity.

All the while, he made inquiries for test animals. He avoided military channels because that would draw more attention to his experiments than he wanted to deal with. Some officials asked him why he looked for experimental animals when he had all he wanted surrounding him. Mueller told them his tests were to compare nonhuman responses to human.

It took nearly six months of searching, but he finally took delivery of an adolescent gorilla that he promptly named Darwin since this ape would show the world a new branch of evolution.

He knew the experiment would have a high risk of failure, but it seemed most other animals could interbreed with a similar cousin. The horse and the donkey. The wolf and the dog.

The closest cousin to a human appeared to be the gorilla. If it worked, he could save the Third Reich's young men. If not, no one would ever know. He could burn everything in the incinerators.

The next obstacle he had to overcome was how to inseminate Eva.

Humans did not sexually attract Darwin, and at the time, Mueller didn't think the knowledge existed to perform an operation to remove sperm. He spent another six months trying to find out what aroused the ape. He began his search with images, but was unsuccessful. He then tried the other senses. Touch was unsuccessful and in fact, quite dangerous. The gorilla did not like being poked and probed especially in his genitals. Sound proved just as unsuccessful. Only when he began to investigate smells did he begin to see the signs of success. With fine tuning, he developed what he considered a noxious formula that never failed to arouse the ape.

Now his experiments began in earnest. He spread the substance on Eva and allowed the ape to have her. The first time, Darwin just sniffed around her body and walked away. Karl fine-tuned the formula some more and the ape fondled the girl. Once more, he fine-tuned the formula and retried it. This time the ape entered the girl, but he became too excited from the scent and became violent with the girl. Eva screamed in pain and Karl saw his experiment being killed in front of him.

He shot Darwin before it killed Eva, but he did it regretfully. Finding a woman to be the mother would be easy. He had hundreds to choose from every day. But to find another ape... that would be difficult. Still, when faced with choice, Karl's own humanity forced him to choose Eva.

Allowing her to live proved to be the right choice, though, because the girl became pregnant. Nine months later, not one, but two babies were born. The twins looked almost like their father except their hair was shorter and their features were not as harsh. The twins amazed Mueller, and he was eager to experiment on them to discover their intelligence levels and their personalities. These would be the first of his perfect soldiers.

Before the studies of the twins could happen though, the Russians liberated Auschwitz. Mueller had barely escaped with his life. However, Eva had also escaped with her sons.

Over time, Karl Mueller had thought often about the twins and what had become of them. He had also realized his mistake in creating the twins. He was not God, and his exile from the Fatherland was God's retribution against taking such a lofty role to himself. Nature was not his to change and mutate, and yet two mistakes of his ignorance continued to live. Before the Lord would forgive him in Heaven, the twins had to die here.

CHAPTER 31

JULY 8, 1993

Esau Lachman squatted in front of Daniel Levitt. His hands hung on the ground as he absent-mindedly swirled small circles in the dirt.

"I know what..." Esau stopped in mid-sentence.

Daniel heard the scream, too. He turned his head in the direction of the scream. The sound cut off abruptly. It sounded as if a woman was in trouble. Daniel turned back to tell Esau he wanted to investigate, but the beast was gone.

He wondered for a moment if he had imagined it all. Maybe Jacob throwing him yesterday had hurt his head more than he thought. Daniel stood up and ran along the path toward where he had heard the scream. That had been real. It took him a few minutes to reach the general area where he thought he heard the scream. He paused, hoping to hear another scream so he could pinpoint the person's location. Instead he heard thrashing and a male's voice mumbling something. Daniel followed the trail until it dropped closer to the river then it only took a moment until he saw the problem.

He saw the back of a man as he sat on top of a thrashing woman. It took little imagination to know what was happening.

Daniel jumped forward and grabbed the man by the back of his shirt.

He yanked hard nearly choking the man, as he pulled the attacker off the woman. Daniel glimpsed the woman's face and was surprised to see Tina Rourke lying on the ground. The man turned toward Daniel with his fist raised, and Daniel punched Tina's former boss in the face.

Tina opened her eyes and saw Daniel holding Brad Kendall up by the shoulder as he punched him a second time in the stomach. Brad tried to fall to the ground, but Daniel wouldn't let him. Daniel punched him three more times and then finally let go of the thin man.

Brad fell over on his face. His ragged breaths sounded loud, and he tried to protect his head between his arms.

Daniel stepped over toward Tina. "Are you all right, Miss Rourke?" he asked.

Gasping, Tina covered her exposed breasts and nodded. Daniel had noticed them but tried not to stare.

"Did I get here... He didn't..."

Tina shook her head and glared at Brad.

"I was up on the trail when I heard you yell. I got here as fast as I could," Daniel explained.

"I was swimming. He came at me as I was coming out of the river." Daniel stared at Brad hoping the gagging man would give Daniel an excuse to strike him again. "I thought he was your boss at the grocery store?" Tina nodded and started crying. "Get dressed and I will walk you into town."

Daniel rolled Brad over onto his back and slammed the rapist back against the ground. Brad cried out in pain and held his hands up to protect his face. Restraining his anger, Daniel started unbuttoning Brad's oxford shirt and pulled it off of him with little complaint. Then Daniel started to pull off Brad's pants. Brad resisted, but Daniel made a fist and Brad let go of his pants.

"Underwear, too," Daniel said.

Brad pulled off his underwear and waited.

"You stay right where you are. If you try to run, my fist will finish what it started a few moments ago."

Daniel tossed Brad's clothes into the river. When he walked back to Tina, she was buttoning her blouse. Daniel turned away to give her some privacy.

When she had finished, Daniel said, "Can you walk? I do not know where the police chief's office is. You will have to lead me."

Tina stood up, glanced in Brad's direction, and started walking.

Daniel snatched up her torn bathing suit and stuffed it into his pocket. He motioned toward Brad.

"Get up. You have some walking to do."

"But I don't have my clothes on," Brad complained.

"Be glad I left you your shoes. I would not want you to cut your feet."

Daniel nudged Brad with his foot. "Get moving."

Brad stood up slowly. He tried to cover himself with his hands, but he found it hard to walk that way and gave up before they had even gotten out of the forest. Daniel walked beside Brad in case he tried to run. Tina walked about two yards in front of them. She didn't look back at Brad even once. The three of them exited the woods at the rear of Kendall's Country Store.

Tina looked over her shoulder and smiled. "Let's see what your customers think about your produce, Brad."

Brad flushed red and covered his face as he walked. Daniel doubted Brad could hide his identity, but that didn't stop the grocer from trying. As they walked past the side window and onto Main Street, people stopped along the road and stared. One car slowed down and beeped its horn, but Brad wouldn't look up. An old woman screamed and covered her face with the newspaper she was carrying.

Someone yelled, "Hey, peanut man!"

Another said, "Is that a man or woman? I can't tell from the body," Tina crossed the street and turned left. Daniel followed trying not to smile at Brad's discomfort. He wondered if Tina were leading them through town the long way just to embarrass Brad. He didn't blame her if she was. Tina walked past the hardware store, the five and dime, and the bank.

When Daniel walked into the small storefront that served as the police chief's office, the dispatcher looked up from her work and nearly lost her dentures. She stared fixedly at Brad's shrunken genitals with her mouth hanging open.

"We are here to see the police chief," Daniel said.

"He's..." The dispatcher glanced at Brad's face. Then her eyes wandered down again and quickly shot back up. "He's on the telephone."

"We will wait." Daniel pulled Brad back and made him sit on the wooden bench. Brad jumped up when his backside touched the splintery wood, but Daniel put a hand on his shoulder and pulled him back down. Tina sat on the other side of Daniel so that he was between her and Brad.

The dispatcher picked up her phone, punched a button, and said, "Chief, you better get out here..." She turned her back toward Daniel and whispered into the phone. She hadn't even hung up before the door to the back offices flew open and a tall, black man rushed into the waiting area.

He took one look at Brad and stopped dead in his tracks. "What's going on here?" he demanded.

Daniel nudged Tina. She stood up and said, "I was swimming in the river, Chief, and Brad attacked me."

"I did not!" Brad shouted. "She and this kike were..."

Daniel elbowed Brad hard in the ribs. The skinny grocer winced and shut up.

Chief Steve Montgomery waved his hand at Daniel. "Hey! No more of that!" Steve said.

"He can say what he wants, but the lady is telling the truth," Daniel replied.

Tina smiled slightly at him. Daniel realized he would do almost anything to see that smile. One smile like that seemed to erase most of the misery he had seen throughout the world.

"Brad tried to rape me, Chief. He ripped my bathing suit off." Daniel stood up and pulled the torn bathing suit from his pocket and handed it to the police chief. "He slapped me when I tried to yell, too. He would have raped me if Daniel hadn't stopped him."

The police chief looked from Tina to Daniel. "You're Daniel, I take it?" Daniel nodded. "I don't know you."

"I got in town only yesterday. I am staying at the Maryland House." Chief Montgomery nodded. "How did you happen to be down in the woods in time to save Tina? It's not a frequented tourist attraction around here, especially for someone staying at the Maryland House."

"I was investigating something. One of your friendly townsmen took me into the forest yesterday and jumped me. He might have killed me, except..." Daniel stopped. He didn't dare mention Esau or the Chief might think he was crazy instead of Jacob. "I think he heard someone coming through the forest and got scared off."

"So why didn't you come to me after that? I could have taken your statement and arrested the man," Steve asked.

Chief Montgomery almost seemed more interested in Daniel's attack than Tina's.

Daniel shrugged. "I've always been one to settle my own disputes. Besides, it would have been a stranger's word against a townsman's word. I do not think anyone would have believed me."

"The law doesn't care whether you're a stranger or a hometown boy," the chief said defensively.

"I'll keep that in mind when I see how this case is handled."

"Where were you attacked?"

"In a clearing about a half a mile from the road where the trail through the forest meets Hanover Road."

"In the woods?" Daniel nodded. "Then I have to ask you what you were doing in the woods."

"Chief, I am not here to lodge a complaint. Miss Rourke is." Daniel nodded in Tina's direction.

Chief Montgomery turned his attention to Brad. "Before you say anything, you've got the right to have a lawyer present when you speak, otherwise you don't have to speak at all." The chief pulled a small laminated card from his wallet and read Brad his Miranda rights.

When he had finished, Brad said, "I'll wait for my lawyer." Chief Montgomery nodded. "I figured you'd want to. Okay then, I'll call your dad and let him know where you are. You two can handle things from there."

Steve Montgomery grabbed Brad by the arm and led him down the hallway into what Daniel guessed would be one of the jail cells at the back of the office.

"Margaret," Chief Montgomery said to the dispatcher when he came back, "Track down Earl Kendall and tell him his son's in jail, and he has been charged with rape."

Margaret nodded and picked up the telephone. Punching in the numbers, she mumbled to herself, "He's not going to like this."

"What was that, Margaret?" Chief Montgomery asked.

"I said Big Earl is not going to like this. We'd better hide anything he can throw or break because he's going to be in a mean mood when he gets here."

"Not my fault his boy's in jail. Maybe Earl should have raised him better and taught him to respect women."

Margaret looked frightened. "Oh, please, don't say that to him, Chief. It will just set him off."

Steve patted Margaret's shoulder as if to reassure her. "Don't worry. I don't want to set him off. I just want to let him know what's going to happen with these charges against Brad. It's Brad he's going to be mad at."

Margaret sighed with relief and finished dialing the telephone number. The police chief looked at Tina and Daniel who were still sitting in the reception area. He waved them toward the back. "You two want to come into my office? I need to get statements from you."

The chief's office was not much more than an eight-by-eight cubicle. It was filled with file cabinets and pictures of his family. There was barely enough room for the chief's desk and chair. Chief Montgomery opened his desk drawer and took out a tape recorder.

"Do you mind? I'll have Margaret transcribe it later. You can read it over then and sign it," Steve explained.

Tina and Daniel nodded. The police chief pressed the record button and said, "The following statement was taken from Tina Rourke against Brad Kendall. I am Chief Montgomery, and it is 1:33 p.m. onJuly 8, 1993." He then allowed Tina to tell her story.

She told it simply and without a lot of elaboration. Her voice quavered only when she described the actual attack. Steve asked her questions on points that needed clarifying. Following that, he did the same thing with Daniel. However, Daniel left his conversation with Esau out of his version. He wasn't sure what he would do about that yet.

As Tina and Daniel started to walk out of the chief's office forty-five minutes later, another man slammed open the front door. He was tall and muscular, and he looked like an older Brad Kendall in the face, though Brad had definitely inherited his mother's small, skinny body.

Earl Kendall saw Tina and said, "You led him on, didn't you? Did you think you could lead him on and blackmail him? Well, I won't stand for it you bitch!"

"Wait a minute, sir. Your son is the one in the wrong here, not Tina,"

Daniel said in Tina's defense.

"And just who are you?" The man scrutinized Daniel's face. "My name's Daniel Levitt."

"Oh, you're the Jew who helped the bitch plot against my son. Well, you won't get away with it. We know how to handle your kind in these parts," Earl said as he poked his finger in Daniel's chest.

Angry at the man's reaction to what his son did, Daniel shoved Earl against the wall and grabbed him by the throat.

"Do not make the same mistake you son did and act stupidly," Daniel warned Earl. "I would hate for this kike to make sure you never have another son."

"Let him go," Chief Montgomery ordered, his hand resting on his holster.

Daniel released his grip and Big Earl rubbed his throat. Daniel led Tina out into the street.

"I will walk you back to your car. Where is it?" Daniel offered.

"I parked near the bridge."

"Good, that is where I parked, too."

They walked a few minutes in silence. Tina kept her head down not staring at anyone as they walked.

Finally, she looked up at Daniel and said, "Thank you."

"You are welcome."

"I mean, if you hadn't come by..."

"I know."

"I always thought I could handle myself in that type of situation, but when he attacked me, I fell apart."

"He terrified you. He is a lot stronger than he looks." Daniel lied about Brad's strength, but he hoped it made Tina feel better.

Tina smiled half-heartedly, but the smile quickly changed to a frown.

She stared at the road again. Daniel hated to see that frown almost as much as he loved to see her smile.

"He'll get off you know," Tina said.

"I do not think so."

"His father has enough money to make bail, so he'll be out by tonight. They'll also be able to afford an expensive lawyer to talk his way out of this mess."

"But you know you are the victim." Tina nodded. "The evidence will certainly support you. If you get your lawyer digging into Brad's past, he will find out you are not the first person Brad tried to rape. From what you told the chief, Brad does not like being told no, and I am sure you are not the first one who has said that to him."

"I guess it's a good thing you came to town. For me at least. I'm just sorry the man you're looking for isn't here."

"I am not so sure about that. Or if he is not here, I am sure he will soon be," Daniel said.

Tina stared at him as she climbed into the car, but he was looking off into the forest wondering where Esau was.

CHAPTER 32

JULY 8, 1993

Daniel watched Tina make a U-turn on Hanover Road and drive off toward Fleetwood. He waited until her car disappeared and then walked further down the road to where he had parked his own car. He unlocked the door and climbed into the hot interior.

What had he seen today? It was like something out of a horror movie. Esau Lachman reminded him of the gorillas from Planet of the Apes. Those gorillas could speak, too, but that had all been make-believe. Things like that didn't happen in actual life.

Then he remembered an article he had read in the *Chicago Sun-Times* a few years ago. It said that advances in genetic research had determined that a man and gorilla were genetically close enough to interbreed. Like the wolf and the dog. Like the horse and the mule.

He could hardly believe that something as monumental as the offspring of a human and gorilla could live for so long without being discovered and reported in the press. Yet, he had seen the evidence. Someone had actually done interspecies breeding with a gorilla. No, not anyone... Mueller.

He climbed out of his car and started into the forest again. In a few minutes, he was standing in the spot where he had been lying when he first saw Esau. He listened hoping to hear some sound that would tell him the ape-man was near; but he heard nothing. He saw his pistol laying on the ground and picked it up.

"Esau!" he called out.

He heard a rustling behind him. Esau stepped out of the brush. "You had better not yell my name. Jacob might hear you."

"Sorry. I meant to thank you for helping me yesterday."

Esau sat on a log with his knuckles resting on the ground. He scratched his left arm picking off some sort of insect.

"My brother can be mean, but he has a short attention span. He can be easily distracted. I could tell he was going to hurt you as soon as you walked into the woods. His thoughts are confusing and I thought he might think he actually had Dr. Mueller with him," Esau said.

"What do you mean 'his thoughts'? Can you read his mind somehow?"

A day ago, no one could have convinced Daniel that a man and gorilla could interbreed. Now that he had seen the proof of how wrong he had been, he began to doubt some of his other beliefs, like psychic powers.

Esau shrugged. "I don't know if it's that or if I simply know my brother so well, I can tell what is happening to him. I can only sense things from him, though, and only sometimes."

"What is it like?"

Esau peeled some of the bark off the log he was sitting on while he thought. "Feelings, mostly. I can tell when he's really mad at me even though he smiles and pretends to like me because Mama hates to see us fight. Sometimes it's words and thoughts like yesterday with you. He kept thinking you were Dr. Mueller's friend. I suppose he can read my feelings, too. He hasn't ever said anything about it, but he might not realize what's happening. Esau's not too smart, you know."

Daniel nodded. "So I have been told. However, he is very strong. What is your brother thinking now?"

"I've never actually tried to find out what he is thinking."

"Can you try? I am curious."

"I'll try." Esau closed his eyes. When he opened them, he looked confused, "I'm not sure, but I felt like he was having fun. Maybe playing in the woods. He's not anywhere near here, though. The feeling is very faint, like he's far away."

Daniel scratched his neck. "It is nice to know he won't come charging in here after me."

Esau laughed so hard he fell off the log backwards. "What is so funny?" Daniel asked.

"You're afraid of him," Esau said through his laughter.

"I should be. He almost killed me yesterday."

Esau looked at Daniel across the clearing and smiled. "Well, from what I saw today, you're not totally defenseless. You did more than hold your own back there when you helped that girl. I would have helped her, but you did better than I could have. I didn't know how I could help her without someone else seeing me, and Mama's going to be mad enough when she finds out I talked to you."

"Why? I will not tell anyone about you. I know what would happen. I would like to talk to your mother. I have some questions about Dr. Mueller she may be able to answer."

"Mama hates to talk about the war or Dr. Mueller. If I didn't know better, I would think she wants to forget about it all. But how can she, with me and Jacob around to remind her all the time?"

Daniel sat on the ground across from Esau so that he could watch him. At moments, he would have sworn Esau was just a hairy human, and at others Esau looked like the beast part of him was. Was he a deformed human or a smart gorilla? Which one was the real Esau?

"You said Dr. Mueller is responsible for you. That would be Dr. Karl Mueller?" Daniel asked.

Esau nodded. "You know of him then. My mother has warned my brother and me about him since we were old enough to understand. He terrifies her. She always has been. My mother, as you can probably guess, was the guinea pig for one of his experiments."

"Your mother was not the only one?"

Esau shrugged as he stood up and stretched. "No, I suppose not, but she may be the only one still alive."

"Did you know Mueller is coming to Fleetwood if he is not here already?" Daniel asked.

Esau jumped to his feet. His chest broadened as it filled with air.

"No, he can't be. He's dead, and even if he were alive, he wouldn't know where we live." Esau's voice was slightly higher now and edged with panic. He seemed just as obsessed with Mueller as his brother and mother.

"My sources tell me that if he is not in town already, he soon will be. That is why I am here."

"Why would you know about an old Nazi?" Esau asked.

"Because I am what many people would call a Nazi hunter."

Esau sat down hard on the log. "Then you're serious about this. You're not just curious about Mueller, you're hunting him." Daniel nodded. "This will kill mother if she finds out. I was hoping she was finally forgetting about Mueller finding her."

"It may kill more than your mother. There is only one reason I can guess that Karl Mueller would risk being arrested and come to America, especially when he is coming to Fleetwood. He has to be coming after you and Jacob."

Esau thought for a moment and nodded. "You're right, but what does he want with me and my brother?"

Daniel shrugged. "I can not say. Maybe he wants to finish what he started during the war. Maybe you are only part of an experiment that is partially complete. I do not know for sure. Maybe he just wants to see how you two turned out," Daniel conjectured.

Esau thought on that for a moment. He rested his elbow on his knee and his head on his hand. "Do you think he knows more about what he did now than he did back then?"

"Science knows a lot more. He probably does, too, if he has kept up at all with all the advances. If nothing more, the methods have been refined. I can only imagine what he did to impregnate your mother with gorilla sperm, and all the ways I can think of scare me."

Esau nodded his agreement, but then he said, "Maybe he would know how to make me human, so I could walk into town without being afraid."

Daniel shook his head. "Even if he knew what was needed to change you to a human, he is too old to have the dexterity to do it. I certainly wouldn't trust him, especially considering how he used his medical degree during the war. He's a doctor in name only. No doctor should have done to people like your mother what he did."

Esau scratched behind his ear. "You're going to arrest him then?"

"If I can find him, I will have him arrested."

"Why?"

The comment took Daniel aback. "You of all people have to ask why?"

Esau shook his head. "I'm not asking why for me. I know why I should hate him. I'm asking why are you hunting him? You're too young even to have been born during the war. You're younger than me and I was born right at the end of the war."

Daniel was silent.

Finally, he said, "He may have been the one who killed my brothers and sisters. He changed my father. My father died a bitter man who spent all the time I knew him hating Germany and the Germans. People who knew him before the war said he was not always like that. Mueller, or someone like him, changed my father into someone who lived only to hate."

"So you want vengeance, not justice?"

Esau's question sounded too close to the things Greg Heinz had said to Daniel in the Baltimore Zoo. Daniel stood up and began pacing back and forth along the trail.

"He is a monster. Look what he did to you. He killed sadistically, and the law says murderers must face their punishment. He has avoided his for too long," Daniel said a bit too defensively.

"You seem too gentle to hate so much. Are you letting Mueller change you into someone like your father? It would be a pity because I like you the way you are."

"Did Mueller also crossbreed you with a psychiatrist?" Esau lowered his head. "I am sorry. That was a low blow. I am on edge. I have to absorb too many things. You and Jacob. This mission Mueller seems to be on, and whether I really want to be here in Fleetwood."

"But you're right. I am asking questions that are too personal. It's just that I have never spoken with anyone other than my mother and brother. I'm not sure how to act in this type of social situation."

"I am still sorry I snapped at you." Daniel stood up. "I have to go into town now, but I would like to speak with you again. Can we meet here again tomorrow at this same time?"

Esau glanced at his watch. "That would be good. If I can."

"Oh." Daniel was disappointed.

"It's just that I have to go home sometime, and when I do, my mother may punish me for leaving the way I did," Esau explained. "I'll try my best to come, though. It's nice to have someone different to talk to."

Daniel smiled. "Good, then I will see you tomorrow."

"See you tomorrow."

When Daniel had walked a short distance, Esau said, "You're sure Mueller's in town?"

Daniel turned around. "He is here. I know it."

CHAPTER 33

JULY 8, 1993

Tina Rourke spent most of the afternoon in her apartment exercising so she wouldn't have to think about how close she came to being raped. She exercised. She cried. She studied. She cried. She cleaned. She cried. By early evening, she didn't have a tear left. Only anger was left. She was angry at herself for not fighting Brad harder, but she was even angrier at Brad for attacking her. He was the criminal and yet she felt as if she were the prisoner, not Brad.

As soon as she had gotten home this afternoon, she had taken three showers and scrubbed herself raw trying to get rid of the feeling he had left on her body. Even now, she could still feel his touch on her body.

By six o'clock, Tina needed to get out of the apartment. She didn't care where she had to go; she just had to get away. Tina parked her car in the lot behind the Dollar General, rather than in her usual space behind Kendall's Country Store. She didn't want to chance running into Earl Kendall again. He would certainly have something to say to her, and she was sure it wouldn't be pleasant. Walking out onto the street toward the hardware store, she thought she might walk over to Kay's for a milkshake. When she was depressed, something fattening always helped cheer her up. Ice cream, by itself or in any of its varied forms, was her favorite depression cure.

As she crossed Main Street, she stopped in the middle of the road. From inside Kendall's Country Store, Brad stared at her though the large plate-glass window at the front of the store. He was out on bail. Of course she had known he would be. His father had enough pull to get bail set quickly. He was standing at the window with his hands on his thighs staring at her. When he saw Tina had seen him, Brad quickly grabbed his crotch and smiled. Then he moved his hands back to his thighs. No one had seen him do it but Tina.

A horn blared at Tina's side and she jumped. She realized she was standing in the middle of the lane. Tina hurried across the street and past Kendall's, trying not to look panicked. She walked into Kay's Kitchen hoping to lose herself among plenty of people, but besides Kay, only one other man was in the restaurant. Where was everyone?

The man was tall and lean, not thin like Brad. He was about Daniel's age. She found herself thinking about Daniel more often, but after what he had done for her this afternoon, it was understandable. Daniel might not be as muscular as some guys she dated, but he certainly was heroic.

Tina sat down at the counter on a stool. On the other side of the counter, Kay walked up next to her. Kay Mitchell was a divorced mother of three. Two of her children were grown and moved away. The third was in Tina's calculus class at college. Tina had grown up with Sarah Mitchell and had known Kay even before she opened the diner.

"I heard what happened to you this afternoon, honey. Can't say I would have figured Brad for a rapist, but I believe you," Kay told her.

"Does everyone in town know?"

Kay arched her eyebrows and leaned on the counter across from Tina. "What do you expect? You and the new guy paraded Brad through town, and those who didn't see Brad in all his glory certainly heard big Earl shouting about how you were trying to trap his son."

Tina groaned and laid her head on her folded arms.

Kay patted her head. "I take it you want a chocolate milkshake?"

Kay knew her too well.

"Kay, do you think I was wrong to have him arrested?" Tina asked.

Kay stopped dipping out the chocolate ice cream and walked over to Tina. She waved the ice cream scoop in Tina's face. "Now you listen here, young lady. Rape is rape, no matter how you look at it. I knew a girl when I was in high school. She went out with a tackle on the football team. Anyway, from what she told me, he forced her to have sex with him. I mean this guy was 200 pounds of muscle, and she weighed only 110. She just couldn't keep him off of her. It was like an ant trying to keep someone from stepping on it. She told her parents about it, and they called her a whore. They said he wouldn't have done it if she hadn't wanted him to, that she could have fought him off. Bull. Don't get tricked into that good-old-boy thinking, Tina."

"But if that's what everyone else thinks..."

"It's not what everyone else thinks. It's just that those who are talking loudest right now are the idiots and Earl's friends, which is the same thing. Those who agree with you aren't saying anything because they don't have to. You had Brad arrested. You did the right thing, so they've got no complaint," Kay lectured her.

The small bells on the front door jingled as it opened. Tina turned around and gasped. Brad was standing in the doorway still wearing the full-length blue apron all the employees at Kendall's had to wear.

"Brad Kendall, you get out of my restaurant right this instant," Kay ordered.

Brad laughed. "You can't make me leave. It's a free country, and I'm a free man. Besides, I'm not causing any trouble."

He walked up next to Tina and sat down on the stool next to hers.

Tina moved over to the next stool, but Brad only followed her. Tina refused to look at him.

"I'm gonna call the police," Kay warned.

"Go ahead. What can they do? I'm a law-abiding citizen. I'm innocent until proven guilty you know." He turned his attention to Tina. "How did you like it? You know we're going to have to finish what we started before."

Tina couldn't help blushing, but she said, "Go away, Brad, before I kick you in your balls again. That is, if I'm able to find them."

"I wouldn't be so sassy if I was you, you little red-headed tramp. I also wouldn't testify against me in court. My daddy's friends may have something to say to you if you do."

Brad didn't have to explain who his "daddy's friends" were. The Klu Klux Klan had gone out of fashion in many towns, but Fleetwood still had a strong chapter. Everyone knew Earl Kendall was a big man in the Klan, but no one could prove it. Much to the anger of Chief Montgomery.

"Come on, Tina, you don't want to see me go on trial. You know you like me."

"Go away, Brad," Tina said again more forcefully.

She stood up and turned to go, but Brad grabbed her arm.

"That's it! I'm calling the police," Kay said.

Brad started to say something, but a hand clamped over his and squeezed. Brad winced and let go of Tina. The other stranger Tina had seen in the diner was squeezing Brad's hand.

"I don't believe the lady wants to talk with you," the man said. His voice had a Spanish accent, Tina thought, but he looked European or American.

Brad shook his hand free and stared at the man. Tina thought they might fight for a moment, but Brad probably already had taken too much of a beating today.

"I hope you're not staying in town long, mister. We don't like people who put their noses into other people's business."

Brad turned and walked out slamming the door behind him.

Tina turned to the stranger. "I could have handled that myself, you know." She was tired of someone else having to step in between her and Brad."

The stranger nodded. "I am sorry. I didn't like how he was treating you."

The man turned away. Kay gestured at Tina, indicating she should say something.

"Wait." The man turned. "I'm sorry. Brad has me frustrated and angry, and I took it out on you. Thank you for what you did."

"You're welcome."

"Can I buy you a milkshake to thank you?" Tina asked. It was a small token of her gratitude, but it was something.

The blonde-haired man smiled. He sat down on the stool that Brad had just vacated.

"It's been many years since I've had a milkshake," he said.

Tina held out her hand. "My name's Tina Rourke."

The stranger shook her hand. He had a firm grip, and Tina realized how he had squeezed Brad's hand to the point of pain.

"I'm Joseph Speer."

"Speer? Then you're German. I thought your accent was Spanish," Tina said.

Joseph blushed. "My name is German, but I've never lived in Germany. I lived in Brazil and Africa, though."

"Wow!" Tina said.

Kay brought over the two chocolate shakes.

"So what brings you to Fleetwood? I mean I'm going to school to find a way to get out of this town, but you've been out in the world and you wind up here," Tina said.

"I wouldn't be so critical about your town. It's nice to have a place where you can have roots. I've never really had strong roots anywhere."

"Is that why you came to Fleetwood?"

Joseph hesitated. "No, I came because of my father. He wanted to come here. He's an old man and I try to humor him."

Tina stopped in mid-slurp with her shake. Old man. German name.

Stranger in town. No roots. Was this nice man the son of the war criminal Daniel was looking for? Daniel had seemed so certain that Karl

Mueller would be in Fleetwood, and this was the only other stranger in town. What would happen to this man when his father was arrested? He had to know that his father was a war criminal.

"Are you staying at the Maryland House?" Tina asked innocently.

Joseph slurped at the shake and shook his head. "We rented a house out on Deer Run Road. It's a beautiful place. I wish we could purchase it, but my father only wants to rent. He may break down, though. We may wind up staying in the area, just not in that house."

"Is that the house with the wraparound porch?" Joseph nodded. "It's used to be Davis McKinley's place. He was killed in a car accident a year ago, and his widow moved back to Lehigh to be near her relatives. She's the one who rents out the house," Tina told him.

"I met her when we signed the lease. I told her how much I liked the place, and she said she would sell, but my father said no."

Tina finished her shake and stood up. "Well, I've got to go. Maybe I'll stop by and see you at your house sometime. I'd like to meet your father and tell him what a gentlemanly son he has."

Joseph smiled. "I look forward to it."

Tina walked down to the cash register to pay Kay for the shakes.

"On the house," Kay told her, "After what happened in here, I couldn't take your money for the shakes. You earned them."

"I didn't earn them. Joseph did. Give him whatever he wants to eat, and I'll pay you for it tomorrow."

Kay nodded. Tina thanked her and turned to leave. She waved at Joseph. He returned her wave and went back to sipping his chocolate shake. Outside, she looked down the road toward Maryland House. Daniel was staying there. It was the only place nearby to stay.

She wanted to tell him what she had found out. It would be her way of thanking him for helping her today. Besides, she had to admit she wouldn't mind seeing him again.

CHAPTER 34

JULY 8, 1993

Eva Lachman's stomach growled loudly. She had eaten nothing in over a day. How could she think about eating when Mueller had her babies somewhere, doing his experiments on them?

She paced through her sons' bedrooms, ignoring her empty stomach. She didn't know what she hoped to find among the toys in Jacob's room and computer magazines in Esau's room, but she couldn't just sit still and wait until Mueller killed her sons. Pictures of male models filled Jacob's bedroom. He had torn them out of *Gentleman's Quarterly* and saved them over the years by taping them on his walls. Various bottles filled with lotions and creams covered the top of his bureau. Jacob took a lot of pride in his appearance and did everything he could to appear completely normal. Jacob's bedspread showed the Teenage Mutant Ninja Turtles fighting other mutated animals.

Eva stared at the bedspread for a moment. She had never understood why Jacob liked the cartoon about the four half-turtle, half-man superheroes. Eva closed her eyes and rubbed them gently. Of course, that was the answer. It had always been there in front of her, but she had never noticed it before. Jacob identified with the turtle-men. She had known always that the pictures of models and Jacob's extensive grooming habits came from his need not to look like his father or brother, but the half-man half-turtle creatures seemed to show her he knew he was an oddity and it was never far from his mind.

Eva moaned as she reached down and yanked the bedspread off the mattress and tossed it to the side of the room. She fell onto the bed hugging the mattress and buried her face in the sheets. Had Jacob left his scent with the bed? Was there something still left that would tell her that Jacob had been here? That he had been a part of her life?

She heard the bedroom door open behind her.

Eva's aging reflexes acted with uncanny speed. She rolled onto her back, pointing the pistol at the sound of the voice behind her. And, even as she saw she was pointing the pistol at Esau, she fired.

Luckily, he dropped to the floor, and her aim was poor. With a loud "thwack," the bullet embedded itself in the doorframe to the left of his head as he fell.

"Esau!" Eva shouted as she dropped the pistol on the floor.

"Mama?" Esau peered around the side of the doorjamb like a chastised dog that was now being called lovingly by its master. Eva stood up and rushed over next to her son. She kneeled down beside him and hugged his furry neck.

"I thought you were dead, but you got away. You got away." She drew herself away momentarily and looked around. "Did you bring your brother with you?"

"No, mother..."

Her grip around his neck tightened as she tensed. "He's not dead, is he? Mueller didn't kill him?"

"I don't think so. Why do you think Mueller killed him?"

Eva stood up and held onto Esau's hand. "I saw him. I saw Mueller in a car while I was buying food, and I just knew he was coming for you and your brother." She hugged Esau. "But you got away. You're so clever Esau. I never thought I'd see you again."

"Mother, Dr. Mueller hasn't been here," Esau told her.

Eva stared at her son blankly. "But he had to have been here. Why else would you and Jacob have left?"

Esau hesitated with his answer. "I left on my own. Jacob must have followed me to bring me back."

Eva laughed and Esau stared at her. She saw his stare and fell quiet. "You're serious, aren't you?" Esau nodded. "But you haven't run away in over thirty years! You know what might happen. Those idiots almost shot you because they thought you were a monster the last time."

Esau's dark skin turned a shade darker with shame. He remembered his half day of freedom with crystal clarity because it had been the only freedom he had known until two days ago. They had lived on a farm in Poland after the war until he had run away from the house to go into the nearby town. He had worn a disguise: a hat, coat, and gloves. He had thought that would be enough to allow him to walk among people other than his mother and brother, but he hadn't been able to hide his face. A woman in the bakery had looked beneath the shadows of his hat and seen a monster looking back. The woman had screamed, and Esau had run. Another shop owner had fired a rifle at him. The bullet had passed through the edge of his overcoat as it flapped around his legs while he ran. After that, his mother had no choice but to leave the country. Hunters scoured the forests looking for the monster. All of them wanted to shoot Esau and mount his body as a trophy in the homes. So Eva had moved her family to Israel for a few years and then here.

"I had to leave. Jacob had been teasing me playing around outside the inner fence so I could see him," Esau tried to explain.

"He's done that before, but it's never made you do something so stupid as leaving the house."

"He didn't make me run away, but he did start me thinking. I'm almost fifty years old, and I'm half-gorilla. Most gorillas live to be about forty, so for a gorilla, I'm ancient."

"But you're human, too, and humans live a lot longer than gorillas," Eva countered.

Esau nodded. "I know, but even though I'm going to live longer than a gorilla, I probably won't live as long as a human. I'm an old man... thing. I don't want to die never having lived. If I die regretting I ever lived, then everything you've gone through to keep me alive will have been wasted. I need to be free. Not all the time, but sometimes. Jacob has his freedom. I deserve as much or don't you love me as much?"

Eva slapped her son across his face. "How dare you say something like that! What I do... what I've always done is for your protection. What if someone had seen you while you were playing outside the farm? You might have caused a panic in town. A hunter might have shot you. There's lots of them in this area, you know?"

Esau rubbed his cheek. "But I did meet someone, Mother."

"What?"

Eva grabbed onto the door frame and pulled herself to her feet. She paced back and forth in the bedroom waving her hands in the air.

Esau stood up and said, "His name is Daniel Levitt. Jacob was trying to kill him, but I scared Jacob off. I wasn't going to let the man see me at first, but my curiosity at how he would react to seeing who had helped him was too great. I had to see if people would accept me. Then maybe by chance, I might be able to live free like Jacob."

"And you scared him off, I suppose? How could you be so foolish, Esau? He'll tell Chief Montgomery now for sure."

Shaking his head, Esau said, "I don't think so because he was scared only until he realized I wasn't going to hurt him. Then he wanted to know what I was." Eva looked doubtful. "Talk to him, Mother. He's looking for

Dr. Mueller. I think that's why Jacob tried to kill him. He must have thought Daniel was a friend of Mueller's, but Daniel is a Nazi hunter."

Eva was silent as she walked over to the bed and sat down. She began gnawing on her nails.

"Did you tell him where you lived?" she asked.

Esau walked over and sat down beside his mother. "No, but he can figure it out if he wants. I think he is a very smart man. He knows Jacob's my brother, and everyone in town knows where Jacob lives."

"What if he tells someone about you? What if he happens to mention he met Jacob Lachman's brother?"

"I don't think he will. He's looking for Dr. Mueller, nothing more."

"Then I did see him in town, didn't I? Dr. Mueller, I mean?"

Esau nodded. "Probably."

Eva wrung her hands together. "Oh, I wish Jacob were here. I don't like him being away from the house with Mueller out there, too. What if Mueller has him? Mueller would recognize Jacob if he saw him. Anyone who knows what to look for can see the beast in either of you."

"Mueller is an old man. I don't think he can be that dangerous," Esau said.

Eva looked up at her oldest son. "Don't ever think that power always goes to the strongest, Esau. Dr. Mueller is older so he is probably smarter, too. The fact that he is in Fleetwood means he must be looking for us. Why else would he come here? A smart man will find us no matter what we do. He's traced us this far, hasn't he?"

Esau put his long arm around his mother and hugged her gently being careful not to crush her.

"Everything will be all right. Jacob will come home safely." However, knowing what he knew now, knowing that feeling of hate he had felt from his brother's mind, he wasn't so sure he wanted to see his brother again.

CHAPTER 35

JULY 8, 1993

Charlie Hardesty sat in his rocking chair on the porch of the Maryland House when Tina drove up and parked in the small parking lot on the side of his nineteenth-century mansion. The sun was setting, and he was reading with the help of the porch light. Charlie glanced around the side of *The Washington Post*, saw who she was, and went back to reading.

The house originally had been built by Benjamin Weaver, who had owned a half-interest in many of the area coal mines west of Fleetwood and the flour trade east of town. He had died at the turn of the century, and Charlie's grandfather had bought the house.

Charlie had turned the house into a bed-and-breakfast inn in the late 1970s when he realized farming was becoming a tougher business to keep going. So he had become the epitome of a Southern gentleman, letting his beard grow long, wearing summer suits, and catering his new business to people who lived inside the Capital Beltway and wanted to get away from big-city pressures to a time when life was simpler.

When Tina stepped onto the porch, he lowered his paper and said, "I hear you're looking for another job, Tina."

Despite having lived in a small town all her life, Tina was still amazed how fast news could travel. People must spend their free time on the phone keeping everyone else up to date.

"I suppose so."

Charlie nodded. He pulled his cigar out of his mouth and blew a circle of smoke into the air. He was dressed in a dark-blue suit that looked like it belonged on a politician. But Charlie's customers expected to be greeted by a respectable-looking proprietor, not someone who looked like a farmer. He obliged them.

"I could use some help here. My housekeeping staff is short-handed. It's hard to find the kind of help I need."

Tina smiled. Maybe something would go right for her today. Everyone knew Charlie paid his employees more than their jobs were worth. "I'd like to work here, but I'd have to work around my school schedule. I'm taking classes at Allegany Community College."

Charlie held up his chubby hand. Sixteen years of living a gentleman's life had added thirty extra pounds to his body. When he had farmed the land, he had been a lean man.

"I haven't offered you a job. I'm not sure you're the kind of help I could use."

Tina put her hands on her hips. Why'd he bring it up if he didn't want to hire her?

"Well, what you did with young Kendall in town was impressive. Everyone got a good laugh from seeing what that boy is made of, so to speak. And, he probably deserved what you did to him, too," Charlie continued.

"But..." Tina said as she shot him a hard look.

Charlie met it unflinchingly and said, "But it was high profile, too. You aired your problems in front of the whole town. Not that the whole town wouldn't have found out by now, anyway. I need help cooking, cleaning, and the like, and my pay is high, higher than you were probably making in town. A lot of people think I'm crazy to pay twice as much for something when I don't have to, but I'm not just paying for a housekeeper. I'm paying for discretion and silence. Now, I know you're a good worker, Tina, but can you be discreet? Can you stay in control without letting my customers think you have lost it? I mean if someone pinches you on the butt, you won't parade them down Hanover Road into town, will you?"

"There's a difference between a pinch and what Brad tried," Tina told him.

Charlie nodded. "True, and I know there is. But you know what I'm getting at, don't you?" Tina nodded. "Do you know where to draw the line without offending anyone?" Tina nodded again. "Okay. We'll give it a try if you're interested. Why don't you stop by tomorrow morning, and we'll work out the details?"

Charlie shoved his cigar into his mouth and went back to reading his newspaper.

"I appreciate the job, Mr. Hardesty, but I came here to see one of your guests."

"The Jew?"

"His name is Daniel Levitt."

"You and him got a thing going?" Charlie asked.

"That doesn't sound too discreet to me."

Charlie frowned and thumbed her through the door. "He's in room four."

Tina thanked him and walked into the foyer area of the Maryland House. Again, she was amazed at how elaborate the place was. A wide staircase ran up to the second floor where half a dozen rooms had been turned into suites so that, if the inhabitants chose, they did not have to be seen in the halls. Each suite had a bedroom, a bath, and a sitting room. Each suite also had a dumbwaiter, adding to the privacy. The first floor had the kitchen and offices. One wing, Charlie Hardesty reserved for his own living quarters. The other wing served as a lounge area. It featured an enormous fireplace, three sofas and four chairs. A bartender tended a fully stocked bar during the evening hours.

Tina climbed the stairs and turned to the right. Room four was on the left- hand side of the hallway. She knocked on the door and waited. The light showing through the peep hole disappeared as someone looked through from the other side. The light reappeared, and she heard the chain rattle against the door as Daniel undid the lock. The door opened, and he looked up and down the hall before looking at her.

"You seem awfully suspicious," she said.

He stepped back and opened the door wider. "Part of the job, I guess. Please come in. Or, if you would rather go down to the lounge so we can be out in the open, I understand."

Tina stepped into the room. "Don't be foolish. You did nothing to me this afternoon. In fact, you kept something from happening to me. That's part of the reason I'm here."

Daniel closed the door and locked it behind him. "What are you talking about?"

"Well, I feel like I owe you a big favor after what you did for me this afternoon," Tina told him.

"I did it because you needed help."

Tina sat down in a chair next to the window.

"I sure did. Like the Chief said, you just happened to be on the trail when I needed help. I still feel like I owe you. Besides, I found out something I think you'll want to know about why you're here."

Daniel grabbed her by the hands and sat beside her. "You saw Mueller? Where?"

Tina pulled her hands away. "Wait a minute. I didn't say I saw Mueller. I had a conversation with a man about your age about an hour ago. He's a very nice man. He spoke with a Spanish accent, but his name was German." Daniel's eyes widened. "He's also a stranger in town. He said he wasn't sure why he and his father came to town, just that his father wanted to."

Daniel nodded slowly. "Was his name Mueller?"

"Speer."

"Did he have sandy-blond hair and blue eyes?" Tina nodded. "Average build, but very wide shoulders?"

"You know him?" she asked.

Daniel stood and walked to the window beside her and looked out onto the expansive backyard. "His real name is Joseph Mueller. His father is the man I'm after."

"He seems like such a nice guy. I wouldn't think he could be a Nazi," Tina said.

"You know as well as I do people are not always as they seem."

She rubbed the cheek Brad had hit. "Yeah, I guess I do."

Daniel blushed and turned away. "As far as I know, Joseph Mueller is not a Nazi. From everything I know about him, he hates the Nazis almost as much as he hates the Jews."

"That's odd, seeing how his father is a Nazi."

"His father is the reason he hates them. Joseph blames his father for causing him to live his life on the run. He also blames his father for putting his mother into the situation that got her killed."

"How was she killed?"

"I shot her," Daniel nearly whispered.

Tina gasped.

He turned away from the window and walked over to the bureau and looked at himself in the mirror above it.

"I did not mean to, but she stepped in the wrong place at the wrong time and a ricochet hit her." His hands squeezed the edges of the bureau. "But Mueller left her there. I could see Joseph trying to go back and help her, but Mueller pulled him away trying to get away from me. So I ran to help her, but she was already dead. I had nothing against her. I was only trying to capture Mueller." He clenched his eyes shut and lowered his head.

Tina walked over beside him. She put her arm around his shoulders hugging him. "If you say you didn't mean to kill her, then I believe you."

Daniel turned to face her. His body pressed up against her and looked into her eyes. "How can you believe me? You do not know me."

"I know what kind of person you are. I'm a fairly good judge of character. Maybe that's why I never wanted to date Brad."

"So what kind of person am I?"

Tina thought for a minute. She stroked his cheek once and then brushed a wisp of hair off his forehead. "You're not a killer. That's for sure. And you don't like what you do, that's obvious. What I don't know is why you keep on doing it."

"How can you just look at me and know the kind of person I am when I do not even know myself? I can say I did not mean to kill Aria Mueller all I want. I can get you to believe it. I can get the police in Africa to believe me, but it doesn't matter. Whether or not I meant to, she is dead, and I killed her. Joseph is not the only person who cannot forgive me for that fact."

He slammed his hand against the bureau and Tina jumped. Daniel put his hand on her shoulder. "I am sorry. I did not mean to scare you."

She sagged against him with relief. "You didn't. Not really. I'm just a little jittery after everything that has happened today." She paused. "They live at a house on Deer Run Road. I can show it to you if you want."

Daniel glanced back at the mirror. "Not today. Tomorrow. And then I can finish this mess."

Tina glanced at Daniel's reflection in the mirror. "What do you see when you look in the mirror?"

Daniel's head snapped back to face her. "Nothing," he said quickly. "Just my reflection."

"But how do you see yourself? You don't look happy when you look into the mirror, and from where I stand, you have nothing on your face that should cause you to look so sad."

"Maybe I don't like what I see." He glanced over his shoulder toward the mirror.

Tina turned his face away from the mirror and kissed him. Daniel hesitated a moment and then slid his arms around her.

Tina pulled away and smiled at him. "I don't know what you see, Daniel Levitt, but I like what I see. You may be a little confused about things right now, but I know you'll find out that you are a likable guy."

She walked to the door and unlocked it. Daniel stood by the bureau watching her leave.

As she opened the door, she paused in the doorway. "Maybe you should get a new mirror," she said. Then she closed the door and was gone.

CHAPTER 36

JULY 8, 1993

Joseph Mueller walked to the cash register, taking out his wallet as he did.

From behind the counter, Kay saw him coming and held up her hand.

"Put your wallet back in your pocket. Tina already paid for your meal," she said, smiling.

Joseph looked surprised. "But how? I hadn't eaten it when she was here."

Kay continued wiping down the counter top. The night looked like it would be a wash. Joseph was the last customer. She'd be lucky if she broke even tonight.

"She told me to put it on her tab," Kay said.

"Tab? I don't understand what you mean, but I can't let her pay for my meal. I can afford to pay for it."

Kay shook her head. "I don't doubt that, but Tina wants to thank you for helping her this evening. Just be grateful and put your money away."

Joseph slid his wallet back into his hip pocket. He still looked a little puzzled. He scratched his cheek.

"She's very kind. Most people around here seem to be like her, but a few are like the man, too, no?"

Kay nodded in agreement. "Tonight, you saw one of the best and one of the worst Fleetwood has to offer. Tina Rourke and Brad Kendall."

"I would like to do something more for her if I could. I didn't expect her to pay for my meal when I helped her. I just didn't like how that man was treating her."

"Neither did I. If you want to help her, help her find a job. She'll be needing one. Until this morning, Brad Kendall-the man you scared away from her-used to be her boss. What do you do for work, Mr. Speer?"

Joseph shrugged. "I don't have a profession, so I doubt I could help her in that way. I've spent my life traveling."

Kay stopped cleaning and leaned across the counter. "Oh? Born with a silver spoon in your mouth, huh?" Kay was not known for her tact. She simply spoke her mind. Most of the people in town had learned to expect it, but her approach sometimes set strangers back.

"I wouldn't say that. I've had my own struggles. Finding peace and happiness. Those things go beyond money. I know, I have money but I have neither of those things."

Kay had noticed how detached Joseph had seemed while eating his cheeseburger and French fries, but she couldn't figure out the reason for it. She had simply assumed it was because he was a stranger. Now she realized he was not only a stranger to Fleetwood but a stranger to himself. Though he looked like an adult, he sounded like a teenager trying to find out what sort of person he was. She wondered how a man could become his age without learning that, though.

"Now me, I'm just the opposite," Kay said. "I work like a dog in here some days from six in the morning until eight at night. It doesn't bring home much, especially when you look at the work on an hourly wage, but I'm happy. It keeps me going, and I'm my own boss. I've three lovely daughters who are my happiness. And I'm at peace because I got rid of my lousy wretch of a husband who used to drink away his paycheck."

"What about Tina? Is she happy and at peace?"

"Tina?" Kay thought a moment. "At peace, maybe. She's fairly level headed and makes pretty good decisions, so not much comes back to haunt her. As far as happy goes, though, I don't think she is. At least not yet. She thinks she knows what's going to make her happy, and she's got a plan to achieve it, but I think she'll hit a few detours along the way. I sure know I did." Joseph nodded and smiled. "That is what I need... a plan, but I have no idea how to get what I want."

Joseph sat down on a stool so that he was sitting across from Kay. She was used to being a country counselor, except that the townsfolk, like Tina, were usually the ones talking to her, not strangers. Joseph must desperately need to talk to someone.

Kay laughed. "That's easy. Start by asking yourself, what would make you happy?"

Joseph didn't even hesitate. "A home, a permanent home. A wife, children. A job."

Kay drew back a little. "Those aren't too grand plans. It must not take much to make you happy."

"No, it takes a lot. Those things are as much out of my reach right now as you becoming president of this country."

Kay laughed at the image of her sitting in the oval office. "Well, the two easiest things for you to concentrate on right now would be a job and wife. The other two flow out of those. You can't buy a home around here unless you can show you've been working for a job for a few years or pay for it with cash up front."

"I can pay for it."

Kay's eyes widened. "Wow, maybe I should have let you pay for the meal."

"I still will."

He reached for his wallet. Kay put her hand on his arm. "Just kidding, Joseph. Loosen up. We're not so formal or serious in this town. So you can buy your house. Well then, you just have to find the perfect one for you. That should be easy enough. There are plenty of houses for sale right now. As for the wife, you'd better not go around asking women if they want to marry you. Date for a while. That's what I tell my girls. Eventually, you'll find the right woman for you. When you find the right person both of you will know it. God works in mysterious ways you know."

Joseph nodded. "I know. My father feels God brought us both here."

"See what I mean? Just work on finding the house you want, then you can find a job close by it. As for the wife, keep your eyes open, but don't rush it. Love moves at its own pace."

"Thank you." Joseph stood up and turned to go. He stopped and turned back to Kay. "You're a nice person to talk to. I appreciate you listening to me talk."

Kay smiled. "That's what I'm here for. My job is part cook and part bartender. I'm Fleetwood's answer to 'Dear Abby.'"

"I think you do your job well."

"You might not after I start poking my nose around in your business," Kay warned him.

"It's customary to tip waitresses and waiters in this country, isn't it?"

"In most countries, as far as I know."

Joseph took a fifty-dollar bill out of his wallet and handed it to her.

Then he was out of the door before Kay could say anything. Not that she could say anything, for once in her life, Kay was speechless.

CHAPTER 37

JULY 8, 1993

Daniel stood staring at the door to his room even after Tina had left.

His lips tingled from her kiss. His mind raced. He touched his fingers to his lips and then ran his fingers through his hair. He thought he heard a car engine roar to life outside, and he assumed it was her car. He finally turned away from the door.

What had just happened?

Had he dreamed he kissed her? No, she had done it with no urging from him. She had done it.

He went to his bed and collapsed onto it. The phone on the nightstand rang. He ignored it. Let it ring. It could only be Adam, and Daniel had no desire to spoil his good feeling by talking to Adam Goldstein. The phone rang ten times before Adam finally gave up.

Daniel smiled. One small victory for him.

How long had it been since he had kissed someone? His mind drifted back to Marla in college. He had met her his sophomore year, and they had dated until Adam recruited him during his summer vacation between his sophomore and junior years. After Marla, about five years had passed until he had met Robyn in California. His relationship with her hadn't lasted because the very thing she thought was noble at their meeting, she later felt was obsessive and vindictive at their parting. That was ten years ago. Now, he mused, God seemed to have given him yet another chance to break away from the wandering-and-hunting life he had led for so long and become a normal person again.

He piled the two pillows on his bed on top of each other and lay back against them on the feather mattress. The setting sun shining through the window shined onto his bed. He closed his eyes and tried to imagine what his new life would be like.

Could he even start another life? He knew the time had come to quit Adam's committee. He had been ready to quit for a while but he didn't know how to do it. What would he do once he quit? He thought often about returning to get his medical degree, but every year that passed pushed that option further away. All he knew how to do was hunt men down. He laughed at the idea of being a detective or a police officer. That wouldn't be any better than being a Nazi hunter. He'd be doing the same thing, but with a different boss.

He realized he was kidding himself to even think of being an independent man. He was Adam's trained dog. He might be starving, but he wouldn't take the table scraps unless he was told he could. As long as Adam wanted him on the Committee for the Prosecution of War Criminals, he would stay and honor his father's wishes. Besides, things would never work out between him and Tina. She was at least fifteen years his junior. Much too big a gap to overcome.

He stood up and walked over to the bureau and looked at his reflection in the mirror. Tina had been right. He didn't like what he saw in the mirror looking back at him. He saw his face in the mirror, but his reflected face was changing. His reflection's dark hair grew uncombed and scraggly. His eyes narrowed into slits, suspicious of whomever they fell upon. And across his face spread horrible tattoos like spider webs. Blood-red tattoos radiated outward to nearly every inch of his face spelling out the names of every Nazi he had captured. Only one name was missing. Spengler. Hardy Spengler. Of the seven men he had revealed, only Spengler had been an unrepentant Nazi. Before Daniel had exposed him, Spengler had been an old terrorist trying to blow up the Wailing Wall in Jerusalem. For that man, there had been no guilt, no remorse and so his name did not appear in the web. But the other six carved their memorials once again on Daniel's face, this time including the newest one under his right eye, which read: Gregor Heinsdorf.

Daniel turned away from the mirror. The image attracted and repulsed him at the same time. Attracted, because he knew the reflection was created in his mind by his guilty conscience. On days he felt better about himself, he would look into the mirror and see the same image, but the names would not be such a bright red, the bloodshot eyes not so narrow, and the hair somewhat combed. On the other hand, the image, no matter how toned down it might be, repulsed Daniel because it made him look like a monster.

Was he?

In his mind's eye, he saw the face of an actual monster, Esau with his very human soul trapped in a very animal body. He wondered if Esau knew any more about the experiments Mueller had performed on Eva Lachman.

If Esau did and he told Daniel about them, maybe Daniel could keep Mueller's name from appearing on his face. The less guilt he felt about

Mueller when he exposed him, the less chance he had of having the name scrawled itself on his face. Maybe Mueller was another Spengler.

Would Esau still be wandering in the woods hiding from society, but enjoying his freedom? That would be the first place to look. If he wasn't there, then Daniel would try to find the farm Esau had spoken of. It shouldn't be too hard. Tina could give him directions if he needed them.

He smiled to himself. His reflection didn't duplicate the smile. It never smiled. Esau could help him. If Daniel could depersonalize Mueller in his mind, he could finish his assignment and resign. This would be his last assignment. Then he would give himself a chance to find out what it was like to live, much like Esau had been doing in the woods enjoying his short taste of freedom.

He glanced at the mirror quickly. The reflection grew wilder. The venous web of names grew bloodier.

CHAPTER 38

JULY 8, 1993

Chief Steve Montgomery finished nailing one the few remaining posters onto the tree near the Hanover Road bridge. He had taken it upon himself to post warnings around the edge of the forest. Until he could find out who had killed Shannon Gardner and Billy Stillwell, he would rather everyone stay away from isolated areas like the forest.

He didn't want to have to tell more parents their children were dead. Telling the Gardners someone had murdered Brenda by crushing her skull had been bad enough. Mrs. Gardner had fallen onto the couch crying in her wailing voice. Mr. Gardner had tried to comfort her, but she didn't want to be comforted. Steve imagined he would feel much the same way if someone told him that Lisa had been murdered.

The Stillwells had been another story. Mrs. Stillwell had been rushing off to work. Through tight lips, all she could say was, "I told that boy he'd get himself in trouble fooling around in the woods. He didn't believe me, though." Mr. Stillwell had gotten angry. "Lot of good a big-city cop did us. It looks like you brought some crime with you from the city, boy."

He had reined in his anger for two reasons. The first was that hitting a citizen was no way for a police chief to act. The second was that he had been wondering himself about all the violence. Fleetwood was beginning to be as bad as downtown Baltimore. First, the two murders, then the attempted rape. He didn't think the two were connected, which meant that he didn't have just one criminal to worry about. He had two or more. If he had thought the incidents were connected, he wouldn't have given into Earl Kendall's verbal abuse and veiled threats and allowed him to post bail for his son. He probably shouldn't have anyway just for spite, but Kendall's lawyer had been threatening lawsuits against Steve and the town that Steve didn't want to deal with. Truth be told, Steve was more worried about the lawyer than Earl, although that's not what Earl would tell people.

Steve considered the jump in crime in Fleetwood to be more damaging to his reputation than Earl's boasts, anyway, because it was an increase in violent crime, which was even worse. Fleetwood was a town where there might be one murder every five years, if that. Most of the arrests were for drunkenness and petty theft. His primary duty as police chief was to act as a traffic cop rather than a law enforcer. Now he had serious crimes to investigate and solve, crimes that would put his years of working in the city to use. So what was he doing? He was putting up posters telling people to stay out of the forest because major crimes had been committed within. Leave it to the system to restrict honest citizens because of the actions of the dishonest ones.

He had considered nailing up a poster that warned everyone about rabid bears or some such nonsense. However, he realized by now the entire town probably knew about the murders and would recognize the lie when they saw it. Better to tell them the truth and hope they had enough sense to stay away from Mother Nature for a while.

The one thing he wished he had brought with him from Baltimore right now was nonchalance. The "Look Out For Number One" attitude that was prevalent in the city. He had investigated more than one murder scene where the murder had occurred in broad daylight with two-dozen potential witnesses around, but when he asked anyone if they had seen anything, the answer was no. He wished the people of Fleetwood were like that sometimes. Mind their own business and don't go poking around where you're asked not to.

As he turned away from the edge of the forest, he saw an old Corolla roll to a stop behind his patrol car (Actually, it was his own car with a flashing light he could set on the dashboard). He put his hands on his hips and waited for the driver to get out.

The engine ran on for a few seconds after the driver turned the engine off. Then Steve saw the man who had helped Tina bring Brad Kendall in earlier in the day. What had he said his name was? Something Jewish. Levitt. Daniel Levitt. Not much to him in the way of size and strength. Good thing Brad was even smaller or Daniel would have had trouble subduing him.

"Hello." Daniel waved as he climbed out of the car.

"Wouldn't expect to see you out here, Mr. Levitt. Especially after you said you were attacked in the woods."

"You sound like you doubt what I told you, Chief," Daniel said.

"I said nothing of the sort. It's just that the first thing you did when Tina got attacked was report the incident to me. With your own attack, you only happened to mention it to me a day after it happened. That's inconsistent behavior, Mr. Levitt. I'm a cop. I don't like inconsistent behavior."

"I take care of my own business. Tina's attack was not my business."

"But you helped her."

"Wouldn't you have?"

Steve nodded. "But I would have reported an attack on myself, too."

Daniel shrugged. "Congratulations, Chief. I hope you are regular, too." Steve turned red with anger at Daniel's flippant comment. "But since when has being inconsistent become a crime?"

"It's not, but I've got two murders and an attempted rape to deal with, and I'll follow any lead that I have to solve them."

"Are you saying I am a murder suspect? I did not know the two people who were murdered."

"What are you doing out here, Mr. Levitt? Do you need to talk to me?" Steve's patience was wearing thin. It had been a long day.

"I have some unfinished business down the trail that was interrupted this morning."

Steve nodded. "You know, I've been meaning to talk to you about that. Just what kind of business gets conducted in a forest?"

"It is personal business, Chief."

"In the woods?"

"Maybe. Maybe not. That's what I've come to find out."

Steve rubbed his chin as if he was thinking. "I see." Steve pointed to the sign he had just finished nailing to the tree. "Better take your business elsewhere, I think."

Daniel read the sign and turned back to the Chief. "They were killed at the same time?"

"Boyfriend and girlfriend caught screwing in the woods," Steve said with no humor in his voice. "I figured you might have heard the details about it already. News travels through Fleetwood pretty fast."

"It is not that guy I helped Tina bring in, is it?"

Steve shook his head. "No. Brad Kendall may be a creep, but he's no murderer. In fact, I wouldn't consider anyone in town a murderer, and yet, someone is. Besides, Brad's problem is he thinks he's a stud. There was nothing sexual about these murders, other than what the victims were doing. So you can see why I'm so curious about your business in there."

Daniel hesitated a little longer than Steve thought was appropriate. "I am hoping to find some clues to lead me to a man I am looking for." He paused. "A man who is a murderer," he added.

"Someone who lives here in town?"

Daniel nodded. "For now at least."

"What's his name?"

"Mueller, Karl Mueller."

Steve shook his head. "I don't recognize it."

"He may not be in town yet. Or he may be using the name of Speer," Daniel said.

"Why are you looking for him?"

Daniel shoved his hands in his pockets. "As I said, he is a murderer, and he also is a Nazi war criminal."

Steve's eyes widened. "You're a Nazi hunter?" Was Fleetwood a big enough town to hold the Klan, a black police chief, and a Nazi hunter?

Daniel shook his head. "Just a detective."

"Uh huh. And the Pope is just a Catholic."

"I guess I will have to look somewhere else if I want to find Mueller," Daniel said.

Steve nodded. "That would be my advice."

Daniel glanced at the forest and sighed. Then he turned back to Steve, nodded, and climbed back in his car and drove off. Steve watched him go to make sure that he actually left.

He didn't like Daniel Levitt. Or rather, he didn't trust him. That the increase in violence started when a stranger came into town was just too coincidental. Steve didn't like coincidences. They belied randomness. So the fact that Daniel Levitt came to town just before the trouble started meant something. Steve just had to figure out what it meant.

He finished nailing up his last poster and climbed into his own car.

He drove home to his small brick ranch home on two acres of property. Not much compared to some farms in the area, but it was a world of difference from the row home he had when he worked in Baltimore.

He unlocked the front door, walked in, and waited. The house was too big and lonely for one person. Steve still expected to hear his daughter running across the hardwood floors to greet him. He still hoped to smell the night's meal cooking in the kitchen waiting for him to devour it. He still wanted to see his wife Vickie walking toward him with outstretched arms. Those are what filled a house and turned it into a home.

Had they been gone only a week? It felt like a year. Steve wanted to grab the telephone and tell them he was coming to join them in Philadelphia. He knew he wouldn't, especially not now. He had a murderer to find, a rapist to try, and a Nazi hunter to keep out of trouble. He couldn't enjoy a vacation with those things on his mind. Besides, to leave now would look like he was running away. That was just what the Klan wanted him to do, what they expected him to do; but he had different ideas.

Going into the kitchen, he opened the refrigerator. He pulled out a beer and carried it with him into the living room. He sat down in his armchair and turned on the television with the remote. The evening news was on, but he wasn't in the mood so he switched channels to one that was showing reruns of sitcoms. He settled himself into the chair and sipped at the beer.

By the first commercial break, the tension of the day had eased out of his body, and before the show had come back on, he was asleep.

He did not rest, though. He dreamed he was looking right into Shannon Gardner's face. It was a pretty country girl's face. Then she suddenly screamed. The sides of her face began to press in. Her eyes bulged. Steve heard something crack and knew it was her skull. The blood vessels in Shannon's blue eyes burst and the blue drowned in red. Small rivers of blood ran from her nose. Her screaming stopped, but Steve still heard a noise and he realized it was his own scream.

He woke up with a jerk spilling the remnants of the beer on the area rug. He took a deep breath to calm himself down, and that was when he felt the pain roar into his head from the migraine headache.

"A monster did it," he muttered to himself. No one else could have.

Someone who had given up all his humanity to evil had looked into Shannon's eyes as he squeezed her skull into a pancake. It was the only answer.

No sane person could have looked into her eyes as he killed her.

CHAPTER 39

JULY 8, 1993

With some of her tension released because of Esau's return, Eva fell into a fitful sleep shortly after nine o'clock. Her exhaustion from two nearly sleepless nights had finally overtaken her. However, she would not go to sleep without Esau in the room.

Esau didn't like being in his mother's room. He didn't like the sachet smell. It was too strong. He stayed there only because he wanted his mother to go to sleep. He could tell she needed it. There were dark circles under her eyes and her voice slurred when she spoke.

Sitting in the wooden armchair near the window, Esau stared out across the front yard. He could see only a few yards in front of the house before the thick stand of trees blocked his view. His mother had not cleared most of the land because she used the trees to keep away prying eyes. He watched the fireflies flicker their mating calls to each other. They looked like stars twinkling against a black sky.

He remembered how it felt to be out there in the woods among the trees instead of outside them. He could feel the cool night breeze brushing across his hair and sending chills across his skin. Then he could hear the sounds of the night creatures talking to each other. Owls. Field mice. Rabbits. Deer. Hoots. Chirps. Yelps. Chatter. If he closed his eyes and concentrated, he could almost make out the words they were saying to each other.

Esau looked over at his mother as she rolled over. Her eyes were closed and her breathing slow and steady. Then she stirred fitfully. She was still asleep but just barely. She looked older to Esau, and he knew he was the cause for her appearance... at least partially. The other half of the problem was still outside wandering free somewhere. But his mother. Her skin seemed to have wrinkled in the two days he had been gone. Her eyes, instead of being lively, were now wild. He had seen the same look in the eyes of the animals he had caught in the forest. It was the look of a trapped animal. It was a dangerous look.

The phone rang. The sharp ringing startled Esau, and he jumped in the chair. Eva bolted upright in her bed and screamed, drowning out the last bit of sound from the phone. Esau rushed to her side quickly and held her slowly rocking back and forth.

"It's all right, Mama. It's all right. It's just the phone. Go back to sleep."

"Esau. Esau. Where's Jacob?" she said speaking quickly.

"He still hasn't come home yet. Do you want me to answer the phone?" Esau asked.

Eva turned an ear toward the phone and seemed to hear it for the first time. "No, someone might wonder who you were. You know that. Did you forget all your common sense out in the woods?"

"No, Mama," Esau said sheepishly.

Eva leaned across the bed and picked up the phone on its fifth ring.

"Hello."

Esau saw his mother's grip tighten against the phone. Her mouth went slack, and she clenched her eyes shut.

"Mama, who is it?"

Eva didn't reply. She didn't even move. Esau leaned in closer to her, hoping to hear the person on the other end of the line. As he did, the hair on his arm brushed his mother's bare arm. She opened her eyes wide and screamed. She threw the phone to the floor and scrambled into the corner of her room. She held her arms across her breasts and screamed wildly.

Esau rushed over to her and grabbed her by the shoulders and shook her gently. It only made her shriek louder, a scream of fear. Luckily, no neighbors lived nearby who might panic at hearing her screams.

"What's wrong? Who was on the phone?"

She continued screaming, her voice beginning to get hoarse. Esau turned on the lights. His mother's cries calmed to a faint whimper. She curled herself into a small ball in the corner of the room. He approached her again, but didn't touch her.

"Mama. Mama?" She wasn't responding, so he tried another approach. "Eva. Eva Lachman."

She looked up hesitatingly at Esau. When she saw his face, she whimpered loudly. Her lower lip quivered and for a moment, Esau thought she would scream again. Instead his mother quieted down. Then her body stiffened beneath his grasp.

"Do you know who I am?" Esau asked. Eva shook her head.

"Do you know where you are?" She shook her head again.

He reached out to touch her, and she drew away. Esau stepped back so that she would relax. How was he going to bring his mother to her senses?

She was withdrawing from everything. Esau saw the picture of his grandparents on the nightstand. He picked it up and held it out to his mother. She reached out slowly and took it. She stared at the picture and mouthed some words Esau couldn't hear.

"Do you recognize those people, Eva?" She nodded. "Who are they?"

She clutched the picture to her chest. Her lower lip trembled and Esau wasn't sure whether she would talk or cry.

"Mama and Papa." Her voice sounded higher than usual almost as if she were a child.

"Are Mama and Papa still alive?" he asked.

She nodded, but she clutched the picture even tighter.

His mother had regressed. His touch and the phone call had jolted his mother beyond her ability to handle the shock. Esau picked up the LED clock from the nightstand and held it out toward his mother. She looked at it and then at the picture.

"Eva, do you know what this is?" She nodded. "What is it?"

"Clock."

Esau nodded and patted her arm. She pulled away from his touch as if he had hurt her, but he knew he had been gentle.

"That's good, Mama. Did they have these type of clocks when your parents were alive?"

Recognition happened like a wave passing over her face. Esau could see the return to reality come into her eyes.

"Mama?"

She held out her hands to him, and he took them and pulled her to her feet. When she was standing, she hugged him. He was glad she wasn't afraid to touch him any longer.

"Who was on the phone?" Esau asked.

She hugged him even tighter. "It was him, Esau. It was Dr. Mueller. He knows we're here."

"Did he say his name?"

"Yes. He said he has come to terminate his experiment. He wants to kill you and Jacob. He wants me to help him kill you and Jacob."

She started crying again and Esau stroked her gently on the back.

CHAPTER 40

JULY 9, 1993

Rick Martin woke up with a start. He shook his head and rubbed his bloodshot eyes. At first, he thought the noise from the laughing studio audience had awakened him; but a commercial saying he could already be the winner of ten million dollars was on. His eyes finally focused on the large-screen television in front of him. He had fallen asleep in front of the television set again.

Looking at the clock on the wall above the television, he realized it was almost one in the morning. Why hadn't Gloria awakened him and told him to go to bed? Then he remembered Gloria was in West Virginia. He had been so tired from clearing stumps off an acre of land he cultivated that he had fallen asleep almost as soon as he sat down to watch the evening news. That had been over six hours ago. He'd be up for the rest of the night now.

Then he heard the dogs howling outside. What had stirred them up?

Probably just a raccoon or a deer. He pushed the footrest on his recliner down and stood up and stretched. All three of the mutts were howling, but probably Moe was leading them. Not that it took much to set that hound off. He would bark at an owl or a field mouse as well as a rabbit or a cat.

He turned the television off as he walked by, heading for the kitchen.

Something sticky had spilled on the floor in front of the refrigerator that now tried to hold on to his bare feet. He cursed at himself as pulled his foot free from the floor. After all, it was his fault. He had spilled the soda yesterday and hadn't bothered to wipe it up. If Gloria were here, she would have done it. Of course, Gloria was down in West Virginia visiting her folks and not caring one bit if her husband's feet hurt because the floor tried to grab his skin.

He opened the door to the backyard. The howling got louder with the door open, but he couldn't see anything in the darkness. Even the dogs seemed to be in the dark shadows at the far end of the yard.

He reached to the side of the door for the light switch when he heard one of the hounds yelp. Then, silence. He waited for almost a minute, wondering what had happened.

"Dogs?" he called out hesitatingly.

He reached for the light again when Curly bolted past him into the kitchen. The brown-and-white springer spaniel lost its footing on the linoleum and fell on his side, but he quickly regained his balance and ran into the living room, where he promptly hid behind the television.

"Curly, get out of here!"

The dogs weren't allowed in the house, except sometimes in the winter when it snowed or was extremely cold, but even then they had to stay in the basement. If Gloria came home and saw dog hair all over the upstairs, she would lay into Rick good. She kept a clean house and didn't like Rick, let alone the dogs, messing it up.

He turned to go after his dog when something caught his attention out of the corner of his eye. At first, he thought one of his dogs had jumped the fence and gotten into Gloria's garden (she was going to think he destroyed the place when she got back on Friday). Then he saw it was too large to be one of the dogs. It was a man, an enormous man.

"Who's out there?"

Rick remembered the light and reached for it again. Then he heard a loud, guttural growl. It had come from whoever was out in Gloria's vegetable garden, and suddenly he realized it wasn't a man out there, and he sure didn't want to see what it was. The thing beyond the fence turned and ran toward him. He froze in place for a moment as he watched the creature approach the chain-link fence and push it down as if it was made of Popsicle sticks.

That was enough for Rick. He slammed the door shut and locked it, and ran back into the living room. If there had been room behind the television, he would have joined Curly. He pulled one of his shotguns off the rifle rack. He would not take any chances that his fear might cause his aim to be off.

He heard glass shatter and fall to the floor from inside the kitchen.

He looked through the kitchen doorway and saw a thick arm poking through the window. It was a man's arm, but stubbly black hair covered it. The hand was fumbling around, trying to unlock the door from the inside.

He shoved a shell into the shotgun and ran to the kitchen doorway.

The hand found the doorknob and started fumbling with the lock. He brought the shotgun to his shoulder and fired at the glass panes in the door. With a thunderous boom, the remaining glass in the door and much of the wooden door frame splintered into millions of shards. Whatever was trying to get into the house howled in pain. The voice he heard wasn't an animal's, either. It was a human.

As he listened, the scream faded away. Whoever he had shot ran off into the fields behind the house. He was tempted to run to the door to see who had nearly gotten into his home, but his legs felt like rubber. They would not move.

Rick leaned against the doorway for a few minutes, until his heart slowed back down to normal. Then he managed to walk over to the phone hanging on the wall and called the police.

As the night dispatcher took his report, he looked around and wondered what Gloria would say when she saw what he had done to the house.

CHAPTER 41

JULY 9, 1993

Esau Lachman finally relaxed when he realized his mother had finally fallen asleep. It had taken her awhile to calm down after Dr. Mueller called her. Then something slammed against the front door. Instantly awake, Eva Lachman sat up in her bed.

"What was that?" she shouted.

Esau tried to push her gently back down on her bed. "Nothing. I think the wind probably blew one of the trash cans against the door or maybe a branch broke off a tree," Esau said, not knowing if he was telling the truth, but he wanted to keep his mother calm.

The white-haired woman looked over his shoulder and out the window. "There's no wind blowing. The trees aren't moving. It's him. I know it's him. He's come for you now. He wants to take you like he did Jacob."

Esau held his mother in his thick arms, reminding himself not to squeeze too hard. He could feel her shaking.

She reached toward her nightstand. Her hand groped around the top of the walnut table. Not finding what she sought, Eva pulled away from her son and opened the top drawer. She still wasn't satisfied.

"Where's my gun, Esau?"

"I moved it while you were sleeping. I didn't want you being startled and start shooting again," he told her.

"But I need it now. Mueller's here. Where is it? Where is it?"

"You don't need your pistol. I'll go down and put the trash can in the garage. That certainly doesn't require any shooting."

Eva grabbed his arm, her spindly fingers like talons in his flesh. "You can't go down there by yourself. He'll kill you."

"No one's down there, Mother."

She swung her legs over the side of the bed and put her bedroom slippers on. "If you're going to go down there, I'm going with you."

Esau shrugged. He supposed she needed to see no mysterious Nazi lurked in their front yard. Although Esau wasn't sure what they would find, he knew it wouldn't be Karl Mueller. The first floor was filled with shadows as Esau started down the stairs. Eva flipped the light switch so that the first floor hallway light came on.

Something banged against the door again. It didn't sound like a trash can. Even Esau was not so sure what he would find on the other side of the locked door.

"It's him, Esau. It's him. Let's get the gun before we open the door," Eva said through her tears.

Esau kept walking. He looked out the peephole in the door and saw nothing. He unlocked the front door's double locks and pulled the door open. All the while, his mother whispered in his ear she wanted her gun to protect them from Mueller.

Jacob fell into the hallway, a small pool of blood forming around his large body on the hardwood floor. Eva screamed when she saw the blood. Jacob opened his eyes and blinked.

"Mama. I'm sorry," he whispered.

Eva knelt down beside Jacob and held his face between her hands.

"You're alive. Thank God he didn't get you."

Jacob tried to sit up, and he winced from pain. Esau saw that the right side of his brother's body was bloody, especially his arm and shoulder.

"Get some bandages, Esau. Your brother's hurt."

Esau walked to the first floor bathroom to get the first aid kit from under the sink. When he returned to the front door, Eva had Jacob sitting up and leaning against the wall.

"What happened to you, Jacob?" Esau asked as he handed his mother the first aid kit.

"I was hungry. I tried to eat, but a man shot me," Jacob told him.

"Why did he shoot you?"

"Don't ask questions now, Esau. Get some water and a dish rag from the kitchen. I need to wipe off his arm and see where the blood is coming from," Eva ordered him.

Esau took his time going to the kitchen to bring back the items his mother had asked for. Let Jacob hurt a little. He probably deserved it.

"So why did the man shoot you, Jacob?" Esau asked as he gave his mother the dish rag.

Eva answered for Jacob. "Can't you see it was Mueller? I told you Mueller wants you two dead. He shot your brother."

Jacob looked confused for a moment and then started nodding.

"That's right. It was Mueller."

Eva wiped Jacob's arm clean of the blood. It immediately turned red again from the small holes in the torn flesh. Esau also noted his brother hadn't shaved during his two days of freedom. Stubbly black hair covered his skin. He even had what looked like a short beard and mustache. When Jacob didn't watch his appearance, he looked almost as animal-like as Esau.

"What does Mueller look like, Jacob?" Esau asked.

Jacob sneered at his brother, his lips curling up like an ape's would. "He looks like a Nazi. He's an animal. He's even uglier than you."

"He's an old man now."

"He might be that too. I couldn't see him too well in the house," Jacob said.

"What were you doing in his house?"

Eva cut in. "Esau, stop badgering your brother. He's been hurt."

Esau met his brother's gaze unblinkingly. Jacob was lying. Esau didn't believe Mueller had attacked Jacob. Esau would probably hear on his police scanner that a large man had attacked someone in their house and had finally been scared off by a shotgun blast.

"How did Mueller get into the house to get you?" Eva asked. "How was he able to get through the fences?"

Esau could have told her the answer to that, but he didn't want to give away his own method for escaping the house.

"He didn't get in the house," Jacob said. "I went out after Esau because Esau ran away from the house. I saw a friend of Mueller's in town. I tried to stop him from finding Mueller, but Esau scared me away."

"You didn't try to stop him. You tried to kill him, and he wasn't even a friend of Mueller's. He was a Nazi hunter, but you're too stupid to know the difference."

"Esau, be quiet and let him finish," Eva scolded.

"Can't you see he's lying to you? I bet he got shot when he tried to attack someone else. Isn't that right, Jacob?" Esau argued.

Jacob looked at his mother with a sad expression on his face. Esau wanted to tell his mother how he had felt Jacob killing the girl in the woods, but she would never believe him. She didn't want to believe him.

Jacob said, "I don't want to talk while he's around, Mama."

Eva pulled on Jacob's left arm to help him to his feet. "We'll go up to your room. You must be tired."

Jacob nodded. Then, when Eva looked away, Jacob stuck his tongue out at his brother.

Eva hurried ahead to draw a bath for Jacob, but not before she ordered Esau to help his brother up the stairs. She would do it, but Jacob was too heavy for her to be of any help if he fell.

Let him fall, Esau thought. He wouldn't be any help, either.

As the twins started up the stairs, Esau said, "Are you going to tell her about the person you killed, Jacob? I felt you kill her in my mind, you know. You can't hide what you did from me. I know."

Jacob looked over his shoulder at his brother. At first, Esau saw confusion and fear. Then he saw the pure hatred enter. He didn't need to feel anything in his mind to know that his brother wanted to kill him.

CHAPTER 42

JULY 9, 1993

The first sign of trouble Police Chief Steve Montgomery saw when he entered the Martin's home was the spent shotgun shell lying on the floor. He smelled gunpowder in the air. Rick must have been out of control if he felt he needed to fire a shotgun inside the house. Steve knew Gloria Daniels, and he also knew that she must not be around or she wouldn't have let Rick get away with firing his shotgun in the house.

When Steve bent over to pick up the spent shell, he saw the mess in the kitchen. Most of the top half of the kitchen door was missing. A few tatters of the checkered curtain still hung from the curtain rod, but all the glass panes were shattered. Splinters of wood and glass lay all over the floor by the door, along with five empty beer cans.

Rick Martin sat at the kitchen table with his shotgun laid across his thighs so that it was pointed at the kitchen door. He kept his right hand on the trigger and his left on another can of beer.

"Rick," Steve said gently, so as not to startle the man. He didn't know if the gun was loaded or not, and he didn't want to find out.

Rick rolled his head in the chief's direction as if it were too heavy to hold upright.

"Did you see it?" Rick asked, slurring his words. "See what?"

"Bigfoot." He slammed the can down on the table. Some of the beer spilled out of the can and onto his hand. "Bigfoot tried to kill me. He tried to break into my house and tried to kill me, but I showed him." Rick raised his shotgun slightly and shook it. "I showed him. I did. He killed one of my dogs, though. Maybe two. I still haven't found Larry, but I heard Moe scream. That's what it sounded like, you know. It started out like a yelp, but it turned into a scream at the end. Poor Moe. Poor Moe."

A brown-and-white dog walked into the kitchen. The dog poked his nose into Rick's hand until the man petted him. Then the dog crawled under the kitchen chair and lay down. Steve figured out this dog must be Curly. He was the only one Rick hadn't mentioned.

Steve assumed the dead dog was named Moe. He wondered how much useful information he would get out of Rick Martin while he was drunk.

Bigfoot tried to break into the house. Steve shook his head slowly. He wondered if he could believe anything Rick said.

The police chief walked across the kitchen to the shattered door. The broken glass crunched under his heavy shoes. Not much was left of the door, certainly nothing that could be salvaged.

"You don't have to look, Chief. I got him. I heard him yell," Rick said from behind Steve.

Steve saw red streaks on the bottom of the white door and red drops on the floor. He assumed both were blood. He'd check it out later to be sure. If it was blood, Steve's theory that Rick had imagined the attacker in his drunken state was shot, so to speak, because now evidently something had tried to get into the house.

"Sure looks like you got him," Steve said as he stood up.

Rick nodded. "I did. I did."

"What did... Bigfoot look like?" Steve asked as he turned away from the shattered door.

Rick pursed his lips and took another gulp of beer. "I only saw his arm and shoulder. But they were as big as my legs. It stuck its arm in through the window trying to get in the door."

"What color hair did it have?"

"Black... or brown. I'm not sure. I'm not the best when it comes to seeing colors."

Or when you're drunk, Steve thought.

Steve pulled out his handkerchief and dabbed up the blood on the floor. When he had a three-inch red spot on his handkerchief, he pulled out a ZipLoc storage bag and stuffed the handkerchief into it. He'd send it down to Frederick for testing in the morning.

It is morning, he reminded himself. Ann Card, the night dispatcher, had called Steve an hour ago to relay Rick's call, at two-thirty in the morning.

Then he would send it down later in the morning. "When did you start drinking, Rick?" Steve asked.

"After that thing tried to kill me, I was all nerves, and I needed to calm down."

Steve looked at all the empty cans and thought Rick must be feeling very calm.

"You didn't have anything to drink before Bigfoot came?"

Rick started to shake his head, but it turned into a nod. "I had one beer before I fell asleep in front of the television."

Steve nodded and looked out the shattered door. The back porch light was on. Rick must have turned it on after he phoned into the police office. Outside, the house looked even worse than inside. A section of the three-foot-high chain-link fence had been knocked over. Now how do you knock over a chain-link fence? Just outside the fence, Steve could see a black heap in the shadows. He assumed it was the dead dog Rick had been mumbling about. Moe? Closer to the back door, he saw more wood and glass splinters, as well as some blood spots mixed in with the dirt on the ground.

However, it was the footprint that drew and held his attention. It looked nearly like a human foot. Not quite, though. For one thing, it was far too large. For another, the big toe seemed to jut from the side of the foot rather than from the front of it. He would have to send someone out here to make a plaster cast and try to lift some fingerprints from the door.

He glanced back at Rick sitting at the kitchen table and wondered for the first time if Rick might be right. Maybe he had shot Bigfoot.

CHAPTER 43

JULY 9, 1993

Esau rapped gently on the door to his mother's room. He was careful about how hard he knocked on the wood. Years ago, he had tried to wake Jacob up for breakfast one morning by banging on the door to his brother's room. Instead of scaring Jacob awake with a loud knock, he had awakened Jacob by putting his fist through the door. Since then, Esau kept in mind how strong he was. Things were built according to human strength, not his strength. Rolling a car onto its roof caused him no more strain than a single grunt. He had estimated that he was about two- or three- times stronger than a man his size.

Now that Jacob was settled down in his bed with a full belly of pears and oranges, Esau hoped his mother would be calm. After all, both her sons were home safe so she could relax. Mueller hadn't gotten them. Esau thought talking to her about some of the things he had been thinking about since he talked with Daniel would be all right.

He liked Daniel. Not only was the man easy to talk to, but Daniel didn't run away at the sight of Esau's gorilla-like face. This was the type of person Esau had waited all his life to meet, but he never thought he would. His mother always had told him that people would hate him if they saw him. After his disastrous day of freedom in Poland, he had believed her. Now he wasn't so sure.

When no reply came from inside the bedroom, Esau assumed his mother was asleep. Who could blame her? She was exhausted; and with all the tension released, she must have fallen into a deep sleep almost as soon as she lay down.

He turned to go when he heard her say, "Who is it?"

"It's Esau, Mama. I wanted to talk with you."

Another silence that his mother broke as she unlocked the door to her room. He wondered why she always kept her door locked. Did she want to keep something inside the room or out? She certainly couldn't be so afraid of Mueller to think that if he ever got into the house, he would let a simple door lock keep him from her.

Eva opened the door. She had let her hair down so that it hung loosely around her shoulders. This usually made his mother look ten years younger, but not this time. If anything, she looked ten years older and exhausted. She needed to sleep, and he was taking away from the time she could be sleeping.

"What do you want to talk about?" she asked.

"Dr. Mueller."

She sighed and opened the door wider. Esau followed her inside. Each time he stepped inside the doorway, he felt as if he were stepping back into a different era. His mother's furniture was made of walnut. A large canopy bed dominated the room. It was so tall she used a stepping stool to climb into bed easily. The armoire, dresser with a mirror, and roll-top writing desk filled up the room. Pictures in brass frames showing people his mother never identified hung on the wall. Some of the faces bore a strong resemblance to his mother with their slightly pointed chins and high cheekbones. Esau suspected they were members of his family whose memory Eva did not want to tarnish by associating them with him. The room smelled strongly of rose sachet. In the two windows, the shades were pulled down to the base of the window frame.

Two chairs stood near the window, one with arms and one without. Esau sat down on the chair with no arms so his wide frame could fit into it. His mother sat on the king-size canopy bed with her feet dangling off the side.

Eva stared at her son, waiting for him to speak. Esau tipped the chair back on its rear legs. Eva shook her head, and Esau set all four legs back on the floor.

"Dr. Mueller made me like I am, didn't he?" he finally began.

"Yes, and Jacob, too. You know that," Eva answered.

Esau nodded, as if the confirmation of this helped him solve a puzzle. Actually, it just created more questions.

"Does he know how to finish making me, then?"

Eva blinked. "Finish making you?" she repeated.

"Yes, so I look more like a man." He touched his protruding jaws and heavy brow. "These are not a man's features. I would settle even for looking more like Jacob. He thinks he's handsome even though he's not. Still, he looks better than I do, and when he takes care of his appearance, he can even pass as human."

Eva was silent. Esau wondered if she had fainted. He couldn't see her face clearly in the dim gloom of the room. "Mama?"

"I'm here. I just don't know how to answer you." She paused. "You can't ever look like a man, Esau, because you're not a man."

Esau jumped to his feet. "I am, too. I have opposable thumbs. I walk upright. I talk. I think. Those are the things that make up a man. I read it in a book."

"But can a man flip my pickup truck over on its top? Can a man run faster on his hands and feet than just his feet? Does a man beat on his chest to scare away other animals or his brother? Do other animals accept a man as one of their own?" Eva countered quickly.

"No," Esau admitted, and he sat down on the chair again. He toyed with a tassel on the curtains, batting it back and forth.

Eva stood up and walked over to the chair. She bent over Esau and hugged him. "You're not a beast, Esau, but you're not a man, either. Do you know what your name means?" Esau shook his head. "I named you and Jacob after Abraham's twins in the Old Testament. Esau is Hebrew for 'hairy one.' And just as Esau was the older of Abraham's sons, so you are the older of my two sons."

"If I remember my scriptures right, Mama, Jacob got the better deal at the end of the story just like Jacob gets the better deal now. Jacob's not a man, either, but he gets to go into town. Why does Jacob look human while I look like a beast? We are twins, and yet we're not alike," Esau wanted to know.

Eva shrugged. "It is God's way, Esau. Dr. Mueller tried to play God, and God chose to foul up his experiments as a way of putting Dr. Mueller in his place. Mueller can't make you human with an injection or surgery if that's what you're hoping. He toyed with the natural order of life. You and your brother are the result of that. Yes, God gave Jacob more of a man's outward appearance of a man, but inside he is a child. He endures his trials outside the house just like you have to endure yours inside. But God gave you a man's intelligence, Esau. While your brother will live out his life in his simplistic world, you will think and learn."

"That may not be such a blessing, Mama. I'm forced to live with the knowledge that I am very different from everyone else and that I will never fit in. On the other hand, Jacob looks close enough to a man that his dull wits can allow him to believe that he is one. Who is happier, Mama? It's not me. I would trade all my intelligence just to get off our property when I want."

Eva stroked the hair on the back of Esau's leathery hand. "And what would you do if I let you off the farm to go into town? Would you walk into Fleetwood and apply for a job at F & G Hardware as a handyman? In this town, you would probably be stuffed and mounted in some hunter's trophy room. You're a monster to these people, Esau. They don't know what you are, so they would hate you."

Esau flinched at the thought, but then he remembered not everyone hated him. Daniel hadn't.

"There are other towns. I have made friends through the computer network. They would allow me to live with them. I could live in Washington and only come out at nights." Why couldn't his mother see how much he wanted to roam the countryside? How much he wanted to be free?

Eva shook her head. "You watch too much television. Your friends know the real you, the one that exists in here." Eva tapped her son's chest. "But if they saw the you Dr. Mueller created, the one that exists here." She tapped his cheek. "They would run screaming."

Esau stood up and walked over to the window. He looked between the heavy drapes across the front yard. Through the dense trees, he could see glimpses of the front fence, the boundary of his world. Beyond that was the real world, the world he would never be a part of. Except for the two days he would carry with him until he died.

Eva stepped up behind him and hugged him. "Esau, I'm sorry I upset you, but hurting your feelings now is better than letting you die outside the farm because I couldn't protect you."

"Why do you have to protect me, Mama? Even animal mothers let their young go out into the world to fend for themselves at some point. Why can't you let me?"

"Because I know what it's like out there, Esau. I know what the world can do to you whether or not you want it to happen. Bad things have happened to me, and I don't want something like that to happen to you. Don't you understand? They'll kill you, Esau. They'll shoot you down like the deer they hunt."

An uncomfortable silence rose between them, and Esau felt as if it was a wall separating him from his mother.

"You should have named me 'Tweety,' Mama," he said finally.
"Why?"

"Isn't that a good name for a canary in a gilded cage? And just like that canary, someday I will fly."

Leaving his mother standing by the window, he walked into his own room and slammed the door behind him. It rattled the door frame, and for a moment, he thought the door might fall out.

Esau sat down at his computer and made his clumsy fingers log him into the computer network. He accessed a library database and ran a search on the name: Mueller, Karl. Within the hour, he had printed out all the information he could find. He logged off his computer and took the small pile of papers over to his bed.

He learned little about Dr. Mueller from his reading. The doctor had been a medical researcher before the war. He had been wounded outside Leningrad and had asked for a transfer to Auschwitz as a camp doctor. Apparently, he had continued his medical research experiments while assigned there, though Esau was proof Mueller had branched off into genetics. While Mengele's experiments on twins were widely known, Mueller's work was not. What had happened to the men and women used in his experiments was still unknown.

The assumption was that most of them wound up in the crematoriums when Mueller had finished with them. Very few witnesses had offered any stories about Mueller's experiments, and the stories that had surfaced were horrifying. Only the most general notes about Mueller's experiments were ever found, leading some military investigators to assume that he had burned the evidence incriminating to himself. When the Russians liberated Auschwitz in 1945, the investigators learned that the doctor had killed a soldier for his uniform and posed as a Russian until he could escape from the country.

Mueller had then gone into hiding with his wife. In 1981, a young Nazi hunter tracked Mueller down to a bungalow outside of Moyale, Kenya. It surprised Esau to see that the name of the Nazi hunter was Daniel Levitt. Mueller had stayed one step ahead of Daniel and escaped; however, his wife was killed in an exchange of gunfire. Daniel said later he thought he had seen another man with the old doctor, but he couldn't be sure.

With a grunt, Esau threw the papers aside. They didn't tell him anything about where Mueller might have run after escaping Africa. He doubted it was to America, though. One article said Mueller had fled to Brazil. Another suggested he had gone back to his hometown in Germany. Escaping to America would have been foolish because the Americans would extradite him for his war crimes if they caught him. However, he wouldn't have been the first Nazi to try it.

But Esau's mother was not given to hallucinations, either. She had good reason to fear that Mueller was searching for her again after all these years. He had finally come to Fleetwood. She had seen him driving through town. Daniel had confirmed that Mueller was in the area. And what other reason would Mueller have to come to Fleetwood except to find Eva?

Esau rolled over and grabbed an apple from the bowl beside his bed and began munching on it. He liked to keep a full basket of fruit in his room because both he and Jacob always seemed to be hungry.

His mother had reason to fear Mueller, but Esau didn't. He doubted that a man who was over eighty could do much to harm him. On the other hand, that same man could do a lot to save him if Esau could get the doctor's original research notes. Mueller had to have them with him. Had he kept his laboratory notes for future reference instead of burning them?

Esau fell asleep thinking of how nice it would be to walk through town having no one scream at the sight of him.

CHAPTER 44

JULY 9, 1993

Daniel Levitt woke up on Friday morning feeling disoriented. After a moment, he remembered he was in a room at an inn in Fleetwood, Maryland. He was here to expose Karl Mueller and have him arrested. Daniel rolled onto his stomach and moaned into his pillow. He didn't want to get up. He didn't want to hunt other human beings anymore.

He would rather go into town and find Tina ROutke. He'd jump out of bed if he knew he had a date with her to go sightseeing or eat breakfast together. He pictured Tina's face in his mind. Her curly red hair. Her sea-green eyes. Her full lips. Hers was a face he could wake up to every morning rather than his own face in the mirror when he shaved. The one problem was she was too young for him. She would certainly have younger guys vying for her attentions.

He looked at the clock beside his bed. Nine o'clock. He remembered how he used to wonder what the time would be in California when he woke every morning. During that peaceful time in his life, he had always thought his future would be in California with Robyn.

It would be almost six o'clock in California now. Robyn usually got up at five-thirty in the morning. He needed to talk to her. Not to rekindle a dead spark, but just to talk to someone who knew him as well as anyone could. Although they hadn't seen each other for almost ten years, he still felt close to her. They had been friends before they had become lovers.

He dialed the number he hadn't used in years, wondering if it would still be in service. He should have kept in touch with her. Why hadn't he? Across the country, a phone rang. Once. Twice.

"Hello." A man's voice.

Daniel hesitated to say anything. Had Robyn moved? "Is this Robyn Friedman's home?"

"Yes, but she's not Robyn Friedman anymore. Her last name is Spencer now. You must not have talked to her for a while."

"Oh," was all Daniel could say.

"Wait a minute, I'll get her."

Dead air on the line. Daniel hung up. So Robyn had gotten over him and found a man who could share her life.

Good for her. He was happy for her. He really was.

Did he think she would wait for him or stay single until he got married?

Of course not.

He sat up in bed. He ran his hands through his hair. It felt greasy. He needed to wash it. He needed more than just to wash his hair. He needed a shower. He staggered into the bathroom and turned the shower on, making the water hot and steamy.

He sighed when he stepped into the shower. The hot water soaked into his tense body. It loosened the tight muscles around the spots where Jacob had hit him. Sleep might have restored his energy, but it had done little to relieve the stress he felt. His entire body felt tighter than his old jeans with the thirty-two inch waist.

Life goes on, whether or not he wants to participate in it. Robyn proved that. Her life had been moving forward since they broke up, but his life was still caught in the same loop of hunt and capture. At times, he felt he would never be free from it.

He climbed out of the shower, grabbing a towel off the towel bar. A cloud of steam filled the bathroom. He opened the door to let some of it out. The cool air rushed into the room. He shivered as he dried himself with a towel.

After a few moments, he wiped the mirror off so that he could shave.

He looked at his reflection, wondering how bad it would be this morning. The tattoos were all still there turning his face into a red billboard of shame. He lathered up his face, covering three of the names. As he shaved, the names reappeared on his clean face. He finished as quickly as he could and went back out into the bedroom.

The phone rang.

Although Daniel was in no mood to talk to Adam this morning, he picked up the phone.

"Daniel?"

"Yes, I am here."

"What progress have you made?" Adam asked.

Not even a "Hello" or a "How do you feel this morning?" Strictly business, and it was a business Daniel hated more and more.

"Mueller is in town. I know that for sure. He is going under the last name of Speer. I also know why he is here."

"Why?"

"A concentration camp survivor he experimented on while he was in Auschwitz is here."

"Do you know where he is? Can you lead the police to him?" If sharks had voices, Adam would be a shark who smelled blood.

"No, not yet."

"How much longer do you need?"

"A couple of days at most."

"Good, good. Buerger and Patchen are in Berlin doing some groundwork on another case. We may have a lead on Heinrich Kruger I'll want you to pursue, so tie this up as soon as possible."

No! Daniel wanted to scream. *I am finished. I am free. After Mueller, I have fulfilled my obligation to my father.*

Instead, he said, "Fine. I will let you know when I am finished." He didn't want to listen to Adam try to talk him out of his decision.

"Are you all right, Daniel? You sound odd."

"It must be a poor connection. I have to go, Adam. I have a meeting set up," Daniel lied.

His hand shook as he hung up the telephone.

Another assignment? He didn't want another assignment. He wanted this to be his last assignment. Didn't Adam even care what Daniel felt?

He fell onto his bed. He lay there on his back, pounding on the mattress.

He had a right to live his life. He deserved to see his life go forward.

He had to find a way to break free from this.

CHAPTER 45

JULY 9, 1993

Despite having slept very little during the night, Esau woke up with the sunrise from force of habit. He walked out into the backyard and watched the sun rise above the eastern horizon. He loved the colors of morning as the black, violet, and dark blue of night gave way to the orange, red, and yellow of morning.

He sat in the grass near one corner of the fence. Sitting in front of the fence, he stroked a gray rabbit had hopped up to him. Most of the animals around the farm were not afraid of him. They sensed he was part of them. From somewhere behind him, Jacob suddenly rushed forward, allowing himself to run on both his hands and feet in order to catch the rabbit before it bolted out of Esau's hands. Esau saw his brother coming and tried to cradle the rabbit in the safety of his arm, but Jacob moved too quickly. He snatched the rabbit by the scruff and jumped back away from Esau.

"Let him go, Jacob!" Esau yelled as he jumped to his feet. Jacob danced around out of Esau's reach. The two of them ran around the backyard, Esau pursuing and Jacob taunting.

"Come take him from me," Jacob taunted his brother.

Jacob ran back and forth just outside of his brother's reach and laughed at Esau's inability to catch him.

Jacob held the rabbit up to his face and said, "This pretty bunny doesn't want to look at your ugly face, anyway. He would rather look at my lovely face as I eat him."

Jacob opened his mouth.

Esau stopped running and took a step away from his brother. "Go ahead," he said. "I don't care."

As if to show his indifference, Esau walked back to the fence and sat down in the grass.

"Don't you want to save the poor bunny from me, Esau? I'm going to eat his legs first so that he can suffer before he dies just like I did the squirrel," Jacob said.

"I hope he tastes better than the squirrel, then. Remember how sick you got after you ate it," Esau said without looking up. He picked a dandelion and twirled it around in his fingers.

Jacob stared at the rabbit. Esau watched out of the corner of his eyes. Jacob had stolen a friendly squirrel from Esau months ago. Esau had argued with him and pleaded with him not to eat the squirrel. When his brother had taken the first bite, Esau had cried. Esau hoped he would take the fun out of eating the rabbit if he didn't beg for mercy from his brother.

Jacob tossed the rabbit off the side. The small beast hit the ground on his back, rolled over, and ran off into the trees that surrounded the fence.

Jacob stepped around Esau and up to the fence. He leaned back against it and crossed his arms over his chest.

He said, "I didn't eat the rabbit. I want to let it to live. It's soft and furry and cute. All the things you aren't. Let it remind you how ugly..."

Esau leapt up from his squatting position toward Jacob. Jacob backed away from his brother, but the fence blocked his retreat. This time his brother was faster. Esau grabbed Jacob by the lapels of his shirt and threw him up against the fence. It clattered and shook as Jacob hit it with his face pressed up against the side.

"You're hurting me," he whined.

"Good," Esau whispered in his ear. "Maybe I'll eat you, so the last thing you can see is my ugly face." Esau opened his mouth wide revealing his sharp teeth.

"Don't hurt me," Jacob mewled, his earlier confidence now gone from his voice.

Esau growled in Jacob's ear and then let him go. Jacob slid down the fence until he was sitting on the ground. When he realized he was free, he quickly stood up.

"Stay away from me, Jacob. You may not be so lucky next time," Esau warned his brother.

Jacob growled. He puffed up his chest and beat on it. Esau watched unimpressed until Jacob turned and ran back to the house, this time on only two feet.

At nine o'clock, Esau went back into the house and into the kitchen.

He sliced some of the fruit his mother had bought a few days earlier and mixed it in a three-quart bowl. He pulled five slices of whole-wheat bread out of a plastic bag and toasted them in the toaster. Finally, he poured himself a quart of orange juice.

Nothing caught his attention on the morning news, so he waited until he had seen the national headlines; then he turned it off.

Jacob staggered down the stairs at nine-thirty. He poured himself a half a box of Capt. Crunch cereal, grabbed two bananas and three oranges, and went into the living room to watch Teenage Mutant Ninja Turtles cartoon reruns on television. He completely ignored Esau, pretending that he wasn't even sitting in the same room.

Esau never watched cartoons, but this morning he decided to since the morning news was not offering him anything better. Sitting in the corner of the room, he wound up not only watching the cartoon but his brother. Jacob sat on the couch in front of the television laughing and swinging his arms wildly when the turtles showed their martial arts ability. When Esau had watched about half of the show, he thought he knew why his brother liked the cartoon so much. It was for the same reason he liked to watch reruns of the TV series Beauty and the Beast after the evening news.

"Did you like the cartoons?" Jacob asked him when the show ended.

Esau shrugged. "It was all right, I suppose."

"You didn't laugh."

"I didn't find it funny, just interesting. Why do you like it?" Esau wanted to know.

"I like the turtles."

"Are they turtles or are they men?" Esau asked.

Jacob thought for a minute. "They're turtles. That's why the show is called Teenage Mutant Ninja Turtles."

"But they don't act like turtles. Turtles don't talk. They don't walk on two legs, or eat pizza, or fight crime, or grow to be six-feet tall."

Jacob shrugged. "It's a cartoon. It's not real life. You take it too seriously, Esau."

Jacob stood up and carried his breakfast dishes back into the kitchen. Esau realized his brother really didn't understand why he liked to watch the turtles. Or, maybe, he had answered honestly. Lots of kids liked to watch the Ninja Turtles. They didn't watch it because they identified with the turtles. They watched it because they liked to watch the turtles beat up the other mutants. Jacob probably liked to watch the show for the same reason any other normal kid did. It was fun, and that was all that mattered.

Eva came down the steps from the second floor.

"Good morning, Mama," Esau said as Eva walked into the living room. He noticed the dark circles under her eyes as if she had slept little last night. But both her sons were home and safe; why shouldn't she be able to sleep?

She walked over and kissed Esau on the forehead. "Good morning."

Her voice was missing her normal, bubbly, morning energy. She glanced at the television and saw the cartoon ghost Beetlejuice changing into a variety of different black-and-white-striped shapes.

"How did Jacob convince you to watch a cartoon?" Eva asked.

Esau stood up and stretched. "There was nothing else on this morning. Do you know he watches Teenage Mutant Ninja Turtles?"

His mother nodded. "I try to get him to watch programs that might help him in his studies, but he doesn't like to. His brain has just stopped at thirteen even though his body is fifty."

"But..." Esau stopped. His mother didn't see the significance, either.

Maybe Esau was the only one who was drawn to shows like that. "Never mind." He kissed his mother on the cheek and hugged her. "How are you feeling this morning?"

Eva sighed. "Tired, but better. A night's rest helped me put everything into perspective."

"And what did you decide?"

She tugged gently at a lock of fur on Esau's cheek. "I've decided that your mother is getting old. Her eyes are fading and her mind wanders. You'll have to forgive her if she overreacts sometimes."

Eva smiled and Esau hugged her.

Jacob came back into the room with a second bowl of cereal. "Good morning, Mama. I'm watching Beetlejuice. Do you want to watch it with me? Esau is." Esau shrugged and sat back down.

Eva smiled and shook her head. "No, I'm going to eat my breakfast, then get ready to go into town. I want you to get ready, too, Jacob. I want you to drive me."

"Awww, Mama. I want to watch my cartoons," Jacob whined.

Eva looked at the TV screen then back at her son. "That's fine, but after this one goes off, I want you upstairs changing. Make sure to wear long sleeves. I don't want people paying more attention to you than they usually do. They don't need to know you were shot."

Jacob smiled. "Yes, Mama."

He sat down and was immediately engrossed in the cartoon.

Esau followed his mother as she walked into the kitchen. She took a frying pan from the cabinet next to the stove and set it on one of the stove's burners.

"You were just in town Monday. Why do you have to go back today?"

Esau asked.

Eva took two eggs from the refrigerator and cracked them into the frying pan. Then she turned the gas range on.

"I know, but my investment check came in the mail yesterday, and I want to put it in the bank."

"Is that all?"

Eva looked up from her cooking. "What do you mean?"

Esau reached up and touched the roof of the kitchen with his flat palms. "I mean you wouldn't also be thinking of doing a little snooping around to see if any strangers have been in town lately, would you?"

"Esau, I told you I made a mistake. I didn't see Dr. Mueller. I was just upset about seeing that article in the tabloid."

Esau nodded, but he wasn't convinced, especially since Daniel also said Mueller was in town. She had overreacted, and now was she was under-reacting. Esau stood at the entrance to the kitchen watching his mother fry her eggs. She looked up and saw he was still standing in the doorway. The smell of the greasy eggs made his stomach feel slightly queasy. He liked his eggs raw or mixed with milk.

"Is there something else?" Eva asked.

Esau sucked his lips in and looked at the floor.

"Don't stand there acting like your brother. Tell me what's on your mind."

"I want out of the house again," Esau said in a barely audible voice.

He wondered if his mother had even heard him.

She slowly chewed the piece of egg she was eating. "There's the door to the backyard," she said pointing behind Esau, "But I don't suppose that is what you meant."

Esau shook his head. "I've been thinking about this all night. I want to go into town. If you're not worried about Mueller anymore, you shouldn't be worried about me."

Eva stopped chewing. "I told you I didn't think I saw Dr. Mueller Monday while I was in Kendall's. I didn't say I didn't think he was in town. You even told me he was here in town. Besides, how many times have I told you what would happen if people saw you?"

"I know, but Fleetwood isn't the only town. I could go to New York or Los Angeles."

"No, Esau. Even if they didn't shoot you, they would capture you and put you on display."

"I'd at least have a chance at freedom."

"You're free now."

Esau crossed his arms over his chest. "Really, Mama? Were you free when they put you in Auschwitz?"

Eva had been raising a fork to her mouth. She stopped and laid it down. Pushing her chair back, she stood up and walked over to Esau. She stared at him a moment and then slapped him across the face.

"Don't you ever compare me with a Nazi, do you hear me? And don't you ever think you have the corner on self-pity in the world." She pointed up the staircase. "Now go up to your room and stay there until I tell you to come out," Eva ordered.

Esau's shoulders sagged. "Yes, ma'am."

Esau walked to his room, shutting the door behind him. He fell onto the bed and looked at the large poster of New York City on one wall, then the picture of Zurich, and London, and Paris. He wanted to visit them all. The closest he would ever get were the posters he ordered through the travel guides. If he had been born looking like his twin brother, with a mild brow and muzzle, then he could travel, but then would he want to go? Jacob didn't seem to care if he ever left Fleetwood, but then, Jacob was stupid; he wasn't.

About fifteen minutes later, he heard the garage door open as Jacob and his mother left. He stood up and walked to the door of his room. Ordinarily, he wouldn't have thought of disobeying his mother and leaving the house, but he would not stay locked in his room when outside, the day was beautiful. He had told Daniel he would try to meet him.

Starting down the main stairs, he heard the telephone ring. He was not allowed to answer the phone because whoever was calling might wonder who he was. Instead, his mother had bought an answering machine. He waited for the third ring when the machine would answer. He heard the click as the machine engaged, then Jacob's voice said, "Hello, you've reached 555-6890. We can't come to the phone right now, but if you leave your..."

The caller hung up.

Esau shrugged and finished walking down the stairs. He turned on the television and watched a morning talk show. Obese women in bathing suits talking about how they were discriminated against.

At least people know you exist, he thought. No one but Jacob, his mother, and now, Daniel knew Esau was alive. A few other people who might have seen him when he was a baby, but those people had probably considered him a freak and had forgotten about him.

He stood up and walked over to the back door. He wanted to be free. He wanted to wander beyond the gates without having to worry about coming back. He wanted to walk down a street and say hello to people.

He didn't care whether they replied or ran off screaming. At least they would acknowledge him. At least they would know he existed.

He went back to the couch and finished watching the show. During the last commercial break, the phone rang again, and he heard the answering machine pick up. Before the caller hung up, Esau heard someone say, "Is she home?"

"Nein." Click.

Nein? That was a German word. No one in Fleetwood would have answered a question by saying "Nein." They would have said "no" or maybe "nope", but not "nein."

Daniel was right. Dr. Mueller was in Fleetwood.

What did that mean for his mother? Had Dr. Mueller returned to kill her? No benefit in that. Why would he endanger his life by doing something so foolish?

No, Dr. Mueller wanted to see how his creations had grown up. Maybe he would even have a way to make Esau human. He smiled at the thought.

He leaned over and erased the messages from the answering machine. He didn't want to upset his mother.

CHAPTER 46

JULY 9, 1993

Daniel sat on a bench in front of the Dollar General Store on Main Street in Fleetwood. It gave him a view through the front window of the Farmers and Merchants Bank across the street. Inside, Eva Lachman stood at the teller window.

Eva signed a check and passed it to the teller. She stood with Jacob, who was playing with the chain that held the ball-point pen to the counter. Would Jacob interfere when Daniel tried to talk to Eva? Daniel hoped not. His throat still hurt from his last meeting with Jacob, but Jacob wouldn't create a scene in public. Hadn't he waited until he'd gotten Daniel into the forest before he attacked him? The man wasn't completely dumb.

Daniel took the small tube of mace from his pocket. If he had to use it, he hoped it would be enough to deter someone as large as Jacob.

Taking Jacob by the hand, Eva turned from the teller to leave the bank, and Daniel got a good look at the both of them. Daniel still thought Jacob looked as if he might have severe Down syndrome, but when he studied Jacob's face, he could see the animal features that were so prominent on Esau's face. The small muzzle. The dark skin when Eva's skin was pale. The heavy five o'clock shadow. The slightly longer arms and shorter legs.

Eva, on the other hand, despite her tiredness looked lovely. Even at sixty-four, Eva still had a shapely figure. Her breasts did not sag and her waist did not bulge. Her makeup highlighted her high cheekbones and her eyes. Her gray hair did not seem lifeless, but lustrous. Only her eyes betrayed the strain and anguish she was under.

As she and Jacob stepped out of the bank, Daniel stood up from the bench and walked across the street toward her. Jacob was the first one to see him. He glared at Daniel, who took off his baseball cap as he stopped in front of Eva.

"Miss Lachman? Miss Eva Lachman?" he asked.

Seeing him, Jacob seemed on the verge of jumping at Daniel. Daniel kept his hand in his pocket so that he could use the mace at a moment's notice for what good it would do.

Eva stared at him for a moment and then said, "Yes. I don't believe I know you."

Daniel held out his hand. "My name is Daniel Levitt, and you do not know me. I am an... investigator of sorts."

"My son told me what, or rather who you investigate, Mr. Levitt."

Daniel noticed she used the generic word "son" rather than mentioning Esau's name where other people might hear it and wonder who Esau was.

Daniel glanced at Jacob standing behind her. "Yes, I am sure both your sons had something to say about me. Since you know who I am investigating, do you know where I might find Dr. Mueller?"

Eva's breath caught. Daniel thought he heard Jacob growl but he couldn't be sure.

"Jacob," Eva said and grasped her son's hand.

"Jacob seems to have a strong dislike for Dr. Mueller." *And me*, Daniel thought.

"He has good reason to hate the doctor." She seemed to spit the word doctor out.

"Why is that?" He wondered if she would tell him the truth or fabricate a lie.

Eva hesitated for a moment too long before answering, Daniel decided. "Why, because of what he did to me and to Jacob's grandparents, my parents," Eva said.

Daniel nodded and tried to appear sympathetic. "Was your son born in Auschwitz, then? He looks old enough."

"No."

"But Mama..." Jacob started to say.

Eva squeezed her son's arm. "No, Jacob was born about a year after the liberation."

She was lying to him. Esau had already said that he and Jacob were a product of Mueller's experiments. Could Daniel rely on any information he got from her?

"Miss Lachman, I just wanted to warn you that the doctor may be in this area. I don't think he would try to harm you or anything. He probably would not even recognize you if he passed you on the street, but I thought you should know," Daniel told her.

Eva's eyes widened. She glanced at her son and then back at Daniel. "And just how do you know where he is?"

"I have been tracking him on and off for a dozen years."

"You are really a Nazi hunter then."

Daniel shrugged. "I suppose by strict definition I am. I do not consider myself that, though."

"But you're so young." The comment reminded him of Gregor Heinsdorf saying Daniel was part of a second generation of vigilantes.

"I have personal reasons for doing what I am doing," Daniel said.

"We all have personal reasons where the Nazis are concerned, Mr. Levitt. Who in your family did he kill?"

"My half brothers and sister and almost my father." Eva nodded.

"They were sent to Auschwitz, and only my father walked out. My brothers and sister might have even been killed during one of Mueller's experiments. I will never know. Just as I will never know them."

"And so you grew up wanting revenge?" Again that same tone, that same unspoken accusation, as if he were back at the Baltimore Zoo.

"No, Miss Lachman. I was a medical student at Louisiana State University when I was recruited to help track down Nazis. The last time I saw Mueller was when he was escaping Africa in 1981. He must have been warned I was coming. He was leaving with his family when I arrived, and I saw him. I saw his family. That really made me mad. I thought why should he have a family when he destroyed mine? I tried to capture him but he got away. That even made me madder. Now I am close to him again, and I do not want to lose him this time."

Daniel rarely told his life story to strangers, but it usually helped concentration camp victims to know that despite his age, he had also lost family in the camps and that he deeply hated Mueller. Only now he wasn't so sure it was hate. The hate had died in 1981 when he killed Aria Mueller. He found fanning the fires of hate difficult, having been a victim of it himself for so many years. And even harder was fanning the fires of hate for someone he had seen for only a few seconds. Heinz's comment about him being part of a second generation of vigilantes still rang in his head and struck too close to the truth.

"I see," Eva said.

"Has Dr. Mueller contacted you?"

She tensed up. "No. I haven't seen him since 1945, and I hope I never see him again."

Eva stepped to the side and tried to move around Daniel, but he followed her. "Can you think of any reason he might want to come to town to see you?" he asked.

"I don't want to talk about Dr. Mueller. Please leave me alone."

"But Miss..."

Jacob stepped in front of him. "My mother said she doesn't want to talk about the doctor. Leave her alone."

"I am just trying to…"

"Leave her alone!" Jacob yelled.

Jacob shoved Daniel hard. He felt himself being lifted off his feet and flying back onto Main Street. It was *déjà vu*. For just a moment, he was back in the forest where Jacob had attacked him when Daniel first arrived in Fleetwood. Except he knew that his landing here would make landing on dirt feel like landing on a mattress. He hit the road on his back first, then his head hit the blacktop. The world around him started spinning. He thought he might pass out.

A car coming down Main Street slammed on the brakes. Daniel heard the tires squeal against the road and smelled burning rubber.

From the sidewalk, Eva yelled, "Jacob!"

She ran into the road in front of the stopped car and knelt down beside Daniel. She gently lifted his head and set it on her lap. "Are you all right? Jacob didn't mean to be so rough. Sometimes he just forgets how strong he is."

Strong, Daniel thought, *that was an understatement. The man was an ox. An animal. Then, that's what he was, wasn't he? A hairless ape.*

Daniel tried to sit up. He still felt dizzy and the spot on his chest where Jacob had shoved him hurt. It would probably be bruised tomorrow. Every time he and Jacob met, Daniel seemed to come away from the meeting battered and bruised.

He reached into his pocket and took out his card. On the back of it, he had written his phone number at the Maryland House. He put it in Eva's hand and closed her hand over it. "If you want to talk about the doctor or if he contacts you, call me. I understand what you have gone through and I want to help. I want to stop him."

"Are you all right, Mister? You just flew out in front of me. I almost didn't have time to stop," the young woman who had been driving the car asked.

"I'm fine, thank you." A lie, but why trouble her with his problems? At least she hadn't hit him.

He stood up, took a moment to steady himself and then walked off toward the opposite side of the street from Jacob.

Jacob stared at him from across the street, but he didn't approach Daniel. Eva yelled at her son for pushing Daniel into the street. Jacob didn't look like an ape now. He just looked like a large, middle-aged man.

Back in his room at the Maryland House, Daniel stripped to the waist and looked at his chest in the mirror. Just to the left of a bullet scar on his chest, a large purple bruise was appearing. It hurt him to take deep breaths. He wondered if he should see a doctor. He might have a green-stick fracture on one of his ribs. No, he doubted there were any broken bones. He was just getting too old to play the action hero as if he knew of an age to endanger his life.

He lay down on his bed and thought about Eva. She had been scared. Not of the doctor, but of him. Why? Was the problem just that she didn't want to talk about the camp or was it something else?

And Jacob. Imagining Mueller performing such a genetic experiment was almost impossible. Almost. Esau and Jacob were proof that something highly secret had gone on within the confines of the concentration camp.

CHAPTER 47

JULY 9, 1993

Esau scuttled nervously back and forth sideways in front of the fence that marked the edge of his world. He didn't even pay attention to the two raccoons playing in the field beyond the fence. His mind was occupied with other matters. Pacing was a habit he guessed he had inherited from his father even though he had never met the gorilla Dr. Mueller had named Darwin. Had Darwin even realized what he had given life to?

Esau's pacing helped him keep track of his thoughts. When he was confused, he paced left and right, moving sideways and using his hands to help him move more easily. His direction changed each time he followed a new thought. When an idea clarified itself, and he followed it to its conclusion, his path slowed. He paced the entire length of the yard tracking a thought.

As he paced now, his mind kept chewing on two points. His mother had seen Dr. Mueller in Fleetwood. Daniel said Mueller was in town, and a man who spoke German had called the house. It was not a coincidence. This he knew as a certainty. His mother had never claimed to have seen Dr. Mueller since as far back as he could remember, and she did not associate herself with people who spoke German just as she never associated herself with members of concentration-camp-survivor groups. Daniel seemed fairly certain that Fleetwood was where the doctor was.

So was Esau. Mueller was in town. Esau changed directions.

Why had Mueller come to town? To kill Eva? Esau shook his head. No, that was impossible. Well, maybe not impossible but it made no sense. Nothing could be gained from it. His mother hadn't been trying to have Dr. Mueller arrested. She was afraid of him.

How had Mueller found them? That was a simple question to answer, especially for Esau. Not much stayed hidden in today's world. Even common citizens were losing their right to privacy. Computers could access anyone's most-confidential information. Private detectives could find those who were missing.

Computers, while they made life easier, also made privacy harder to achieve. Someone around the world could break into almost any computer file and extract whatever information he wanted. His mother's monthly investment checks were printed out by a computer, so her name and address was on file with her financial advisor. Her accounts at the bank had her name and address on them. Her naturalization documents were on computers. So were her real estate documents. Plenty of trails led to his mother if a person knew where to look, and obviously Dr. Mueller had known where to look.

If this were true, then why did the doctor wait until now to seek Eva out? Esau spun around and walked back in the other direction.

The doctor would be in his eighties now. Did he still act like a Nazi? Did he want to kill Eva because she knew about his experiments? Esau shook his head. None of that would matter now. Dr. Mueller was old and close to death. Even if he was arrested, he would never live to see his trial. His mother had probably been closer to the truth when she said once that Mueller was as much their father as Darwin had been. As a foster father, Dr. Mueller would want to see how Jacob and Esau turned out. What had they grown up to be like? Had his experiment succeeded?

What was the aim of the experiment?

Dr. Mueller wanted to see his creations. Of course. It made sense.

Esau changed directions.

He was an old man who was dying. He should be allowed to see what he had brought into the world. Maybe, with all of today's advances in biotechnology, he knew of a way to help Esau and Jacob... to finish the job and make his experiment a success.

Esau stopped walking.

Yes, Dr. Mueller could help him be human. Yes! Yes! Yes!

Esau had to call Dr. Mueller and tell him to come right away. Esau turned to run toward the house until he remembered the man on the phone had not left his telephone number.

He sat down on the ground and pounded his fist on the dirt. It wasn't fair. He was close to being human. He could talk to Dr. Mueller. He couldn't let his mother know Dr. Mueller had called because she would panic and take her sons and run as far away as she could. She would never let Dr. Mueller come near him. He would have to find Dr. Mueller on his own.

How hard could that be? He didn't think many houses in the area were for sale. Certainly not a lot that would have just been sold recently. What if the doctor had rented an apartment around town? Some people had divided up the old, large Victorian homes into smaller apartments. Whether Dr. Mueller was in a house or apartment, Esau still had a problem.

His computer! He could access the Allegany County Board of Realtors' multiple listing service through his computer. He could find out for himself if Dr. Mueller had rented or bought a house lately by finding out the houses and apartments that had recently had a contract submitted or had gone off the market.

Esau ran into the house and bolted up to his room, nearly shaking the staircase apart under his heavy pounding. He turned on his computer. He scanned the listing of programs he had on his computer and clicked on the one for the modem. Then he looked up the different database numbers to which he had access. The real estate database was among them.

The program asked for the zip code he wanted searched. He typed in Fleetwood's zip code. The screen showed six houses for sale and none of them even had contracts put in yet. He exited the screen and asked for rental homes and apartments in the same zip code. Three homes and eighteen apartments appeared. One home had been rented and six of the apartments. Two of the apartments and the home had gone inactive two days ago. He looked over the names of the renters.

Nothing rang a bell. Then a thought occurred to him. What if it had been a privately arranged rental? How could he track that? It wouldn't show up on the MLS.

He ran downstairs to the living room and pulled out all the newspapers from the past week. He turned to the classified ads in each of the papers and compared the real estate ads. Most of them ran through the entire week but two stopped running early in the week. One on Monday and the other on Tuesday.

He called the Pennsylvania number for the house closest to the farm that had stopped being advertised. He had to call now before his mother and brother got back from town.

A sleepy voice answered the phone.

"Hello, I'm calling about the house you have for rent on Deer Run Road. I'm moving into the area, and I need to rent a home."

"I'm sorry, but I rented the house early this week."

"Oh." He tried to sound disappointed but he was really excited. He might be onto something.

"When will you be coming to town? I only expect these renters to be in the house for a few months at most," the woman in Pennsylvania said.

"Really? You rent from month to month then?"

"Oh, yes. It's easier to find tenants that way. I rented the house to a father and son who are going to be in town for only a short while. I shouldn't say this, but the old man sounded sick. I hope he doesn't die in my house."

"Well, I won't be moving into the area for another couple months, so if I see the ad in the paper again, I'll call you," Esau lied before he hung up the phone.

An old man in poor health. It could be Dr. Mueller, and the address was only a short distance from the farm. He memorized the address, then folded the newspapers and laid them next to fireplace again.

He smiled. Now he knew where the doctor lived. Now he could be made whole.

Should he ask his mother to leave? She would probably only yell at him for leaving the house and remind him what a monster he was. She probably had to find someone to put up a higher fence, Esau thought.

Did he have a choice? Could he live outside of the house? Without his mother?

A choice always existed. So what were his choices?

The phone rang and interrupted his thoughts. On the fourth ring, the answering machine clicked on and Jacob's voice stiffly told the caller no one was home to take the call so could he please leave his name, number, and a brief message after the beep. The machine beeped and Esau waited to hear who was calling.

"Eva? Eva, this is Dr. Karl Mueller. Do you remember me? I need to speak with you. You can't avoid me forever. You'll have to talk to me sometime. I won't go away," the voice said through the answering machine.

Esau stopped daydreaming and listened. He sat down next to the phone.

"Eva, if you're there, please answer me. I don't mean you any harm, but I need to talk to you about the twins. Something needs to be done. You know it as well as I do."

Esau's hand reached out for the receiver and hovered a few inches in front of it. One of his mother's cardinal rules was that he could never talk on the phone. If she ever found out he not only had talked on the phone but also he had talked to Dr. Mueller, she would be furious.

"My number is 555-1876. I'm staying here in town, and I'll be here until I finish..."

Esau picked up the phone and held it to his ear. "Hello?"

"Oh, I'm sorry. I must have dialed the wrong number. I meant to talk to Eva Lachman."

"This is her house. I'm her son."

"Her... I didn't think you would be able to talk," Mueller said. "I'm half-human, Doctor, so there was a fifty-fifty chance."

"No, I doubt the odds were that favorable. May I speak with your mother?" Dr. Mueller asked.

"She's not at home."

"Then can you have her call me?"

"I will tell her you called, but I have something I would like to ask you," Esau said.

On the other end, Dr. Mueller hesitated. "What do you want to know?"

"Is what you did to me reversible? I was thinking that with all the recombinant DNA technology available today, you might be able to insert human genes into a virus and inoculate me with it. That would work, wouldn't it? Wouldn't my body gradually turn into a human one? I try to read the scientific journals, but they are over my head."

Karl Mueller hesitated again.

"You obviously have your mother's brain." He paused. "Perhaps, there is a way. Would you and your brother like to discuss the options? As I said, I'm staying here in town. If you two would like to come by my house to talk, I believe we can find the answer to your problem. We could surprise your mother," Mueller offered Esau.

"I can't say whether Jacob would want to talk to you or kill you, but I would like to meet with you. I believe that if anyone can help me, you can."

After an awkward silence, then Mueller said, "Yes, I suppose since I am the one who started it all, I should finish it. Let me give you the address to my house."

Esau wrote the address down on a piece of junk mail. It matched the house that the woman in Pennsylvania had rented.

"When can you be here?" Mueller asked.

"I'm not sure. I can't let my mother see me leave. I'll be there sometime this evening."

"I'll be waiting."

CHAPTER 48

JULY 9, 1993

Margaret Dobson frowned when she saw Chief Steve Montgomery walk into the office at eleven o'clock. He opened the door and stood in the doorway for a moment trying to decide whether or not he should go in. Margaret watched him with an odd look on her face. He'd better decide before she jabbed him with one of her wisecracks. His choice made, Steve nodded his head in her direction and shuffled across the floor.

"You look like a hairball the cat threw up," Margaret said as she typed away at the old Smith-Corona typewriter. Fleetwood was too poor a town to afford a word processor.

Steve stopped. "What did you say?"

"I said you look like a hairball the cat threw up."

Steve shook his head slowly. "I thought I just misunderstood you. That's a new one."

Margaret grinned. "I'm nothing if not original. I heard you had a call last night, but it looks like you didn't go back to bed. Checking out a prowler doesn't take all night."

Steve settled himself into one of the reception area chairs. It was wooden and uncomfortable, but he needed to sit down. He closed his eyes and sighed as he settled into the chair.

"Do I look that bad?" he asked when he opened his eyes.

Margaret rubbed her chin in thought. "Well, you look like you're ready to fall asleep standing up. You're probably undernourished since Vickie is out of town. Your eyes are bloodshot. If you were a white man, I could probably see the circles under your eyes. And your shirt is unevenly buttoned."

If someone else had made the comment, Steve might have been offended, but he was used to Margaret's blunt assessments. For her to be surprised at his condition must mean he really looked bad. Steve knew he was a workaholic. He shouldn't have been surprised he couldn't go on vacation with Vickie and Lisa, although he needed the time off more than either of them.

He looked down at his shirt. Margaret was right. He had mismatched the buttons and the button holes in his semi-conscious state, and he was the man this town expected to track down a murderer. How much faith would they have in their police chief if they could see him now? How much faith would they have in him if they knew how little progress he had made on the case?

"I spent half of last night at Rick Martin's place. He shot something trying to get into his house, and he claims it was Bigfoot. Whatever it was, it made a big mess of his kitchen."

"Rick's a sot. You know that."

Who better than the police dispatcher to know the dirt on everyone in town? No, not quite on everyone. Seeing Brad marched in here in the buff had surprised even her.

"I know that," Steve said. "But he hit whatever he shot at. I saw the blood, and I saw the weirdest footprint it left behind. No one checked into Memorial or Sacred Heart hospitals with a gunshot wound either. I'm not sure what to think anymore."

"So maybe Bigfoot has moved from the Pacific Northwest to Western Maryland, or maybe you have to find another explanation for what Rick shot because you wouldn't want to write in your report that the prowler was Bigfoot." Margaret frowned at that thought. "Want me to set up a meeting with the state police and the county sheriff?"

Steve shook his head. "Not yet. I want to work on this awhile by myself. That's what I get paid for."

He felt his eyelids getting heavy. Falling asleep in the chair would have been so easy. He could forget about everything. Let everyone who walked by the window wonder what was wrong with him. He didn't care.

But he did care. Steve forced his eyelids open.

"Did Dr. Noble call in the autopsy reports on Shannon and Billy yet?" Margaret shook her head. "Did you call him?"

"Yes."

"What did he say?" Steve asked.

"Verbatim or the censored version?"

Judging by the look on her face, Steve decided he would rather hear the censored version. He was too tired to work up a good anger at the county medical examiner.

"Censored please. I'll fill in the details," he told Margaret.

"He said, 'Tell the blank boy he'll have to wait his blank turn like everyone else.'" Margaret rolled her eyes. "He makes it sound like he has bodies dropping left and right all over Allegany County."

Steve rubbed his eyes. He was going to have to go into Oakland and look over the medical examiner's shoulder while he did the autopsies. And even then, he might need to give the good, white doctor a swift kick in the backside to get him working.

"Why don't you go home?" Margaret asked.

"I will. I came in only because I expected those autopsy reports to be ready. If by some miracle they do come in, call me."

"I have a feeling you'll be sleeping at the house if I call," Margaret said.

Steve stood up and shuffled back to the door, already dreaming of what his bed would feel like. He might count one lone sheep before he fell asleep.

He stopped and turned back to Margaret. "I also sent some stuff from last night to the state lab for processing. If anything comes in on that, call and let me know. I've got to get a lead on something."

"Okay, Chief."

"I bet you never thought it would be so busy in here," Steve said.

"It could be busier," she told him.

"That's what I'm afraid of," he said as he closed the front door.

CHAPTER 49

JULY 9, 1993

I'll be waiting. The words replayed in Esau's head like a tape loop. *I'll be waiting*.

Dr. Mueller wanted to see him. Esau's dream of being human was only a few miles, maybe only a few hours, away. He should be talking to Dr. Mueller right now. Instead, he was in his room, grounded.

He lay on his bed reading through the information he had collected from his computer databases about Dr. Mueller.

Mueller had caused him to look the way he did, and he said he knew how to reverse the process. How long had Esau waited to hear someone say that to him? Now when he had finally heard the words, he couldn't take advantage of them because he was being punished.

He had realized his mother had been upset as soon as she had walked into the house earlier that afternoon. She had been unnaturally quiet and her hands shook as she closed the garage door behind her. When she had looked at Esau, he could see her eyes were red as if she had been crying.

"What's wrong, Mama?" he had asked.

"You told him everything, Esau. I can't believe you told him everything. He knows. He knows, and I'm so ashamed," Eva had said right before she started crying.

She sat in one of the kitchen chairs and sobbed into her hands.

Esau went to comfort her, but Jacob blocked his way into the kitchen. Esau tried to push past his brother, but Jacob wouldn't let him pass.

"Let her alone, Esau. Haven't you upset her enough for today?" Jacob told him.

"I have done nothing."

"You told Mueller's friend about us, and he came to talk to Mama while we were in town."

Esau stopped pushing. "Daniel? You saw Daniel? You should talk to him, Mama. He can help us," Esau said over his brother's shoulder.

Eva wiped her eyes. "Go to your room, Esau. Go to your room and stay there until I tell you to come out. I don't know what's gotten into you. First, you left the house, and now you've told someone about us."

Not about us, he wanted to say, about me. He figured that would only anger his mother more, though. Esau went up to his room without saying anything. He had been in his room since three o'clock and now it was nine o'clock. His mother had let him come down to eat dinner, but she had sent him back to his room immediately afterwards. He could hear Jacob downstairs watching television, probably another of the stupid sitcoms he liked so much. His mother had gone to bed about a half an hour ago without even saying goodnight to him.

He took a peach out of the bowl next to his bed and bit into it. The juice dribbled down his chin, and he wiped it off on the back of his arm. Of course, after he'd done it, he realized he was only making the hair on his arm as sticky as the hair on his chin.

Eva suddenly screamed from her bedroom. Esau dropped the peach and sat up in bed. His mother screamed again and despite his grounding, he ran out into the hallway.

Jacob bounded up the stairs. "Mama screamed," he said.

"I heard her."

Esau hurried to his mother's door and tried to open it. It was locked of course; she always kept it locked. He knocked on the door.

"Mama, it's me. Are you all right? I heard you scream," Esau said through the door.

His mother answered him with another scream. "Keep him away from me! Don't let him touch me!"

"She's in trouble, Esau. Mueller must be in there with her. He wants to kill her," Jacob said excitedly. He was running back and forth sideways with his shoulders hunched forward.

Esau pounded on the door. "Mama. It's me. Open the door."

From inside the room, she screamed again. Esau took a step back from the door. He jammed his arms straight out at the door. Because of the power of his thrust, his hands passed through the wooden door and into his mother's room. He reached around and unlocked the door from the inside. Jacob rushed past him into the room, turning on the lights as he did.

Esau turned and saw his mother sitting up in her bed, holding her blanket up to her chin. Jacob, Eva, and Esau were the only ones in the room.

"Where's Mueller, Mama?" Jacob asked. He looked under the bed to make sure the German wasn't there.

"What are you talking about?" she asked. Her voice trembled as if she was on the verge of crying again.

"You were screaming. We thought you might be in trouble," Esau answered.

He didn't like the way his mother was looking at him. Almost as if she didn't recognize him.

"I'm fine. I'm fine. There's no one here."

She didn't sound fine to Esau. Her voice was shaky and her eyes darted around the room, but they always seemed to end up staring at Esau. Why was she looking at him like that? Was she mad at him for being out of his room?

When Esau finally realized why she was staring at him, he was ashamed. Since his mother was alone in the room, she had obviously been having a bad dream. She had probably dreamed about Jacob and Esau's father. Why else would she look at him so oddly? Of the twins, Esau most reminded his mother of Darwin, the gorilla. He looked away from her, ashamed of his appearance and ashamed that he caused his mother such terrible memories. He would always be the beast to her. No matter how much she denied it in words, her wide, brown eyes told the truth. She would always fear him because he looked less human than Jacob.

"Are you all right, Mama?" Jacob asked.

Eva patted his arm. "Yes, I was just having a bad dream. I'll be fine. Now please leave me alone."

Jacob nodded and left. Esau quickly followed, turning out the light as he left.

In the hallway, Jacob turned to Esau and said, "She's angry at us, Esau, and it's your fault."

"What did I do?"

"You broke her door. You've been a bad boy, and now she thinks I'm a bad boy, too."

Esau shrugged and left his brother standing alone in the hallway. He was in no mood to argue with his brother tonight. He had things to do. Besides, Jacob didn't understand most of his brother's arguments.

Esau went into his room and opened up his closet. Unlike Jacob's closet, his closet wasn't stuffed with expensive clothes. He didn't need them. He never dressed up to go out anywhere or meet anyone. Besides, casual clothes were easier to find in his size than trousers and shirts. He pulled out a pair of black sweatpants and a blue-and-white rugby shirt. He felt most comfortable in loose-fitting clothes.

He thought about leaving his mother a note to tell her where he was going, but that would only panic her more. If he didn't leave a note, she might think he just got fed up with living inside the fence and broken out again. However, if he confirmed her fears about Dr. Mueller, she might have a breakdown. She looked close to it now.

He wanted to surprise her. He wanted to return to her whole and human. Then she would look at him the way she looked at Jacob. When she hugged him, her eyes wouldn't show any repugnance, only love.

Esau sneaked downstairs as quietly as he could. Unfortunately, the hardwood floors creaked under his heavy weight. Jacob had gone to bed, so the downstairs was empty. Esau went out the back door and ran to the farthest corner of the yard.

He looked at the barbed wire running across the top of the fence. He could easily reach up eight feet, but he doubted if he could pull himself over the top safely. His gaze moved down to where, until Monday, the metal wires had held the chain-link fence to the posts. They were gone because he had pulled them off when he left the last time. Since they were still missing, obviously neither his mother nor Jacob had figured out how he had gotten free.

He kneeled down and lifted the fence up as high as he could.

Because he had pulled the fasteners free, he could pull it up to his chest. That was as high as he needed. He ducked under the fence and onto the other side.

He let go of the fence and stood up. He was outside, and he couldn't even tell that he the fence was broken.

He was outside!

He jumped up as high as he could. He was free again! He cheered out loud. It was a rumbling, throaty growl.

He stood still for a moment and waited. He half-expected to see his mother and Jacob come running after him, but no one came.

He was really free once again.

Esau looked toward the forest. He would still have to go under the outer fence, but that would not be any trouble. If the breach of the inner fence hadn't been discovered, then the outer fence probably hadn't been noticed either.

Once on the road, he could go anywhere he wanted, and he wanted to go to Dr. Mueller's.

CHAPTER 50

JULY 9, 1993

Esau stood in the shadows of the towering oak trees, which during the day provided cool shade for the residents of the Maryland House. He was a dark shadow that made the trunk of the tree look thicker.

He found himself much more comfortable moving around in the shadows and woods now than he had been a few days earlier. All the sensations that had overloaded his senses before–the crickets' chirping, the reflection of the moon on the water, the trembling of the ground as a small herd of deer ran nearby–he now took as commonplace. In turn, nature had accepted him as one of her own.

What occupied his senses now were the windows of the Maryland House. He saw twenty-four, three rows of eight, on this side of the building, and half as many on the other three sides. Some were lit with the light from within the rooms spilling through them and some were dark. Most of the lit rooms had the curtains drawn so the light Esau saw was muted. The people were shadows on the fabric. He suspected some of the dark windows might have people in the rooms beyond them, but he couldn't be sure. His night vision was no better than a human's.

He sat and watched the windows for most of an hour trying to figure out which one of them was Daniel's room. After he had managed to eliminate only four of the windows (the people in them had moved to the window so Esau could see them), he moved around to the side of the house hoping he might have better luck.

He did not know what else to do. He needed to talk to Dr. Mueller, but at the same time he was scared to visit the old man. Daniel knew Mueller was in Fleetwood, so he also probably knew where Deer Run Road was. He hoped Daniel would go with him to Dr. Mueller's house. The trouble was that even though Esau knew where Daniel was staying, he didn't know how to get in touch with him. He couldn't very well walk into the Maryland House and ask for Daniel. The sight of him would send the place into a panic. Esau needed to find Daniel without being seen.

The telephone! That might have occurred to him earlier, but before today, he never used the telephone except for his computer modem. His mother didn't want people wondering why they heard two different male voices at the Lachman farm when everyone knew Eva had only one son. So again Esau had become the invisible son.

The problem he had now was trying to find a phone that wasn't in a public place. However, most phones were in public places. That's how the phone company made money off of them.

His problem was solved when Daniel walked out of the front of the Maryland House toward the parking lot. He paused under the porch light to scan the parking lot, and Esau clearly saw his slightly long face with his straight nose. His first impulse was to rush out into the open to greet Daniel, but the man was still in front of the Maryland House where the yard was well lit. Someone might see a beast approaching Daniel and scream. Instead, Esau reached down and picked up a stone and threw it at Daniel. The rock missed Daniel, but it hit a nearby Jaguar with a resounding "thwong."

Daniel dropped to a squat and dodged behind a car. When he dared to look over the top of the car, Esau jumped up and down silently waving his arms. Daniel stared at him for a moment, then stood up and walked over to the side of the building.

"You should not be here. Someone might see you," was the first thing Daniel said.

"I need to talk to you. Can we go someplace?"

Daniel hesitated. "Meet me at the main road. I will take you with me in my car."

Esau nodded and disappeared into the darkness. He ran back into the trees, then circled around the edge of the property and jogged down to Hanover Road. A car stopped at the edge of the Maryland House driveway. Esau waited until he was closer to the car so he could make sure the driver was Daniel. When he saw it was Daniel, Esau opened the door and slipped into the passenger seat beside the Nazi hunter.

Daniel pulled onto Hanover Road and headed toward Fleetwood. "I saw your mother and brother today."

"So I heard," Esau said. "You're lucky Jacob didn't kill you."

"I know. He pushed me out into traffic. I only wanted to talk to your mother, but she treated me like I was a Nazi."

"She's scared of anything from the war or anything that reminds her of the war."

"She is going to have to face up to things sometime. What happens to you and Jacob when she dies?" Esau shrugged and let a long silence come between him and Daniel. Finally, Daniel said, "What was so important you had to come and see me about?"

"I want you to go see Dr. Mueller with me."

"Funny you should mention that. I am heading out to look at a house I think he might be renting."

"To see Dr. Mueller?"

"In a way."

Esau smiled. "Good."

"Why do you want to see him?"

"I have to talk to him."

"What!"

"He has seen me before. He's responsible for me being the way I am."

Daniel pushed on Esau's shoulder indicating that Esau should slump down in the seat so that anyone who might be on the streets of Fleetwood couldn't see him. Esau took hold of the lever on the side of his seat, pushed the seat back, and laid back on it.

"Have you thought about why Mueller has come to Fleetwood after all this time? It sure is not because of all the nightlife. My guess is that he wants to finish what he started in Auschwitz, which means he wants to kill you and your brother and maybe your mother, too."

"That's what I thought at first, but I've talked to him on the phone. He called the farmhouse today, and I talked to him. I think he can finish me, make me human. He made me like this. He can make me like you. He said he could help me."

Daniel ran his hand over his brow. "You were an experiment, Esau. Just because he made you one way doesn't mean he can reverse the process. Besides, he is an old man. Even if you could trust him, you couldn't trust his memory or his skill."

"Then again, he might do just what I hope he can," Esau said quickly.

"Esau, I can only guess at what your life must be like, but I cannot see that any risk would be worth what you are figuring. Mueller could just as easily kill you."

"Then I've got nothing to lose." Daniel didn't reply to that statement.

"All my life I have lived a nonexistence. My mail is addressed to Jacob. I don't get phone calls. I don't get to go into town because I don't exist. You can't kill something that doesn't exist."

Daniel slowed the car. He squinted as he looked out the window, trying to read the numbers on the doors. When he saw the one he wanted, he stopped the car.

"Is that Mueller's house?" Esau asked as he raised himself up on his elbows.

"Maybe. That's what I am here to find out." Daniel reached behind Esau's seat and pulled out a pair of binoculars. He held them up to his eyes and adjusted the focus.

"What's the number on the house?" Esau asked.

"It is 8189 Deer Run Road."

"This is his house. He told me his address when I talked to him. Do you see him? Is he home? He said he would wait for me."

"I do not know. No one has even walked in front of the window." Esau stared at the lighted windows of the house. Daniel drove two houses down from Mueller's house and parked on the opposite side of the road.

"If it's him, what will you do?" Esau asked.

"I will call the police and give him all my evidence against Mueller. Then I will go home."

"That's all?"

Daniel nodded. "I do not have any authority to arrest him."

"Don't you want to talk to him? Aren't you even curious about why he made me? I know I am."

"I have talked to too many Nazis." Daniel raised his binoculars quickly. "I saw an old man walk past the window. It could be him. I will have to get much closer to study him. Maybe I can catch him in town or walking down the street and make a positive identification," Daniel mumbled to himself.

"You're not going to do anything now?"

Daniel shook his head. "What would you have me do, Esau? At night, anything I did now would look suspicious. I had better wait for the daylight when more people are around and one man will not be as suspicious looking."

"Maybe I'll go talk to him then." Esau reached for the door handle to open the car door.

Daniel put his hand on Esau's arm. "I think you had better talk to your mother about this. I am sure she would have more than a few things to say about you visiting Mueller."

Esau shook his head. "The decision is not hers to make."

"True, but your decision will affect her life, especially if he shoots you." Daniel imitated a gun with thumb and forefinger. "You know what

Mueller did to your mother. He is called Mueller the Mauler for a reason, you know.

Esau stared at the house, then back at Daniel. "But I want to be human. I want to live."

"Esau, you are living. Your life is what you make it, but you are not making it anything. If you are not happy with it, change it. You are letting your mother live your life."

"But you just said..."

"I said you should talk to her. She will have a viewpoint about this man neither you nor I have. It may open your eyes. You see an old man, but you have to remember what this man did." Daniel heard himself talking and couldn't believe it. After what had happened to Greg Heinz, how could he ever believe a man couldn't change?

Esau sighed and lay back in the seat.

"You have waited this long. Just think about it," Daniel said.

Esau nodded. "Okay. Let's go home."

CHAPTER 51

JULY 9, 1993

Daniel stopped his car on the side of the road. The light spilling from his headlights illuminated the fence gate.

"We are here. What now?" Daniel asked Esau, who was still lying on the seat beside him.

Esau shrugged. "I guess now I go home and face the music again. Maybe I'll get lucky, and no one will have noticed me missing this time. I've only been gone only about two hours."

"You could always go away somewhere."

Esau raised his seat to an upright position. "Where? I'm not fit to live either as an animal or a human. I've got no choice. People would either shoot me or study me. My mother points that out to me time and again."

"You always have a choice."

Esau opened the door and stepped outside. "Not for me. I don't have a choice." He closed the door and leaned in the open window. "Daniel, when you arrest Mueller, can you see if he has any notebooks or diaries describing what he did to my mother? If he can't help me, maybe someone else can. They'll need his notes as a starting point, though."

Daniel smiled. "I will check."

Esau straightened up. Daniel put his car in reverse and backed onto Hanover Road. Esau watched him drive off until the red taillights disappeared. Then he turned and walked along the outside of the fence. When he found the loose section of fence, he slid under and walked toward the inner fence. He was in no hurry to get back to his prison. He hoped his mother and brother were asleep. If they were, maybe he could sneak back in without them ever knowing he had left.

That idea blew away with the wind as soon as he saw the house. It was lit up like a Christmas tree. Every light in the house had to be on. Obviously, his mother had discovered he was gone.

Luckily, the place where he had broken through the fence was at the far end of the yard in the shadows of the trees. He still didn't want anyone to know how he left the house. He slipped under the fence and started walking across the yard.

He heard a loud growl in the direction of the house. Jacob burst through the back door running in the bent-over, animal-like stance he sometimes slipped into when he wasn't careful. Esau resisted his natural urge to charge his brother in return. He simply kept walking. Jacob stopped suddenly in front of Esau and began beating on his chest. Esau felt his lip twitch as he wanted to bare his teeth, but he maintained his control. He stepped around his brother and walked toward the house.

"You made her cry again, Esau," Jacob called from behind him.

"Does that make you happy? You made her cry."

Esau said nothing. He could see his mother through the back door pacing back and forth in the living room. He paused for a moment at the back door and took a deep breath. Then he opened the door.

His mother stopped walking when she saw him enter. The relief showed on her face for a few moments and then was replaced by anger.

"Where have you been?" she snapped.

"I needed to go talk to someone."

"You talked to someone? Who?"

"Daniel. You remember, you were very rude to him today," Esau said with a hint of sarcasm.

"The Nazi hunter? Why would you need to talk to him?"

"I wanted to talk to him about Dr. Mueller. He also wanted to check a house he thought Dr. Mueller was renting."

Eva stepped forward. "Does he know where Mueller is?" Esau nodded. "What's he going to do?"

"He has to make a positive identification, but that may take time. Then he's going to report Mueller to the police and hope he gets extradited back to Israel."

"We can't wait that long. Mueller is here to kill us. We can't give him the time to come for us."

Why was everyone so sure that Dr. Mueller meant harm? Couldn't people change? Dr. Mueller truly seemed to want to help him.

"We have to give him time seeing how he has to find someone who will identify Dr. Mueller," Esau said.

"I can identify him."

"But you won't testify to it. You would never face Mueller," Esau pointed out.

He crossed the living room and started up the stairs to his room. He wanted to go bed and think through everything.

"Esau, don't leave while I'm talking to you," Eva shouted.

Esau turned to face his mother. She looked even angrier than she had this afternoon. He could see veins bulging through her skin and she was chewing on her lower lip.

"I want you to promise you will never ever run away again," she demanded of him.

"I can't. I enjoy being free. I may want to go out again." Then he turned and walked up to his room.

Maybe Daniel was right. Maybe Esau should do what was right for him.

CHAPTER 52

JULY 9, 1993

When Joseph Mueller walked into Kay's Kitchen for a dinner and a break from his father, the first person he saw was Tina. She was sitting at the counter talking with Kay and sipping on a chocolate milkshake. He liked the way her red curls bounced around her head whenever she nodded. She differed from Regina, at least on the surface. Under the skin, Joseph felt Tina and Regina were probably more alike than not.

He liked the diner as a place to get away from his father. The old man was too afraid to come to a place where people met. He still thought someone might recognize him after all these years. The diner smelled delicious with all the different aromas from the kitchen mixing.

Kay saw Joseph and nudged Tina's arm. Tina looked over her shoulder, saw Joseph and waved him over to the counter. Her smile looked almost exactly like Regina's.

"Thank you for paying for my meal last night," Joseph said as he sat down beside Tina.

"Don't thank me. I owed you one. You saved me from getting hassled," Tina said.

"Nonetheless, your gesture was kind."

Tina shrugged. "So what brings you in here tonight? Are you such a bad cook that you can't stand your own cooking? I know that's why I come here so often."

Kay snorted. "And I thought you were just too lazy to pop a TV dinner in the microwave," Kay said as she walked off to wait on another customer.

Joseph laughed. "Actually, I'm quite an excellent cook. Sometimes I just need to get out of the house. It's such a big house, and yet sometimes, I think that even if I lived in a mansion, it would be too small for me and my father to live in together."

"You're a little old to be having parent problems, aren't you?"

She slurped the last of her milkshake and waved for Kay to bring her another one. Joseph asked for a malted.

"I suppose as long as I have a parent, I can have parent problems," Joseph answered her.

"What about your mom?"

Joseph's head drooped. "She's dead."

"Oh, I'm sorry."

He could tell the revelation embarrassed her, and he said something that would put her at ease.

"I got along fine with my mom. When she was alive, she used to keep my father and me from getting on each other's nerves. She was the peace-maker in the family."

"I never had too many problems with my parents. I can't say the same about them having problems with me, though. They're good people. They live in Fort Ashby over in West Virginia. When I think back on the grief I put them through while I was in high school, I feel like the most-ungrateful kid alive."

Joseph smiled. "So you were a free spirit?"

"You may call it that. My father called it 'Hell on wheels.' I stayed out all night sometimes. I got drunk. I dated jerks. I skipped school so much I barely graduated. That's why I'm going to a community college and not a four-year school now."

"You don't seem like that person now."

Tina shook her head. "I'm not. At least not totally. When I graduated high school, I moved away almost immediately. I thought I was an adult, and I wanted to be on my own." She sipped the milkshake Kay brought her. "Being on your own gives you a sense of responsibility. I had to get a job and keep it. I had to get my grades up so I can transfer to a four-year college next year."

"Do you still want to leave here?"

"Not as much as I did a few years ago, but I still want to do and see things that can't be done or seen from Fleetwood or Fort Ashby. I'm just not rushing to do them."

"I'm hoping that in a few months my father and I might actually buy the house we are renting."

Tina looked surprised. "Really? Aren't you going to miss living in different places around the world, though? I know I would."

"To me, this is a different place."

Tina changed the subject. "Speer's a German name, isn't it?"

"Yes," Joseph said with a nod.

"Are you and your father German, then?"

"Yes, by birth, but I've never considered myself German. I have never lived there. My father is a true German, though."

"What's your father like? He can't be all that bad."

Joseph nodded. "Oh, yes he can. He's a fanatic."

"What's he fanatical about?"

"He's..." Joseph stopped and stared at Tina. How had she gotten around to asking so many questions about his father? She seemed to hang on his pause, anxiously waiting for his answer. Why was she so anxious if they only had a conversation?

She knew!

His breath caught. She knew or at least suspected. But how? He had said nothing before that would have exposed himself. His father hadn't been in town. What had made Tina suspicious of his background?

Joseph stood up and left two dollar bills next to his malted. "Please, excuse me. I just remembered something I have to do at home."

He turned and nearly ran out of the diner. Had Tina told the police about her suspicions? Were the police even now heading toward his house ready to arrest his father? They had to get out of Fleetwood now whether or not his father wanted to.

CHAPTER 53

JULY 9, 1993

Daniel stifled a yawn and straightened up in the seat of his car.

Parked off the road in front of the gate that led into the Lachman Farm, he had been watching the farm since he had dropped off Esau earlier. Daniel had planned on staying until morning. He figured that once Eva was awake, Esau wouldn't try to run away again, at least not while she was awake.

But Esau would run away again. Of that Daniel was certain.

Now he had just been proven right. He wasn't sure why he expected Esau to break out through the front gate. He guessed that location because that was where he had dropped Esau off. Seeing Esau running down the road already outside of the fence was a mild surprise.

Daniel let the man-ape run past the gate and into the forest. He wasn't too worried about tracking him. Not that he thought he could easily follow Esau through the forest. The big man-ape was quick and silent, just like most animals. However, Daniel knew exactly where Esau was heading. His destination was a brown house on Deer Run Road.

When Esau disappeared from his view again, Daniel started his car.

He pulled out onto Hanover Road and headed into Fleetwood. He hoped he could get to Mueller's house before Esau.

Esau hesitated at the edge of the woods. He could see Dr. Mueller's house about 100 yards away. The problem was that between the forest and the house was very little cover. If neighbors happened to be looking out of their back window when Esau started across the yard, they might see him.

He looked at the houses that flanked Dr. Mueller's. They were each at least 200 yards away from Mueller's house. Esau wondered how clearly anyone would see him from that distance in the darkness. He would have to take that chance.

He took a deep breath and started running. He expected to hear someone yell at him at any moment. Floodlights would wash him in bright light, exposing him to the world. To his surprise, he reached the sliding glass door at the rear of Mueller's house with no one seeing him.

He rapped on the glass, careful not to knock too hard and shatter the door. He didn't want to make a poor impression on Dr. Mueller the first time they met. Then he waited nervously to see what Dr. Mueller would look like.

He wasn't at all what Esau had expected. Esau knew he would be old, but this man looked ancient. His hair was white and limp. He was very skinny and his clothes hung loosely on him. Imagining this man as the animal he had once been was hard even if his mother and Daniel were to be believed. Esau didn't see him that way. This was the man who could make him human.

The doctor looked startled when he first saw Esau standing outside his window. Then his fear turned into a smile. He shuffled over toward the door and unlocked it.

"You must be Esau. Come in, I've been waiting for you." He waved Esau into the house. "I thought you would be here earlier."

"I'm sorry. I had to make sure my mother didn't see me leave," Esau told the German.

Esau stepped into the house, and Dr. Mueller closed and locked the door behind him. Then he drew the curtains shut so no one could see in.

Jacob Lachman was dreaming when he suddenly sensed danger. He wasn't in danger, but Esau was. No longer was he in his dream. He saw a neighborhood he recognized as one on the north side of town. Somehow, he knew Esau was there. In that house, not in the farm house. Esau had left the farm house again. Esau was being a bad boy.

Jacob reluctantly woke up and climbed out of bed. He walked down the hall to Esau's room. When he peeked in through the door, the room was empty. The lights were off downstairs so Esau wouldn't be there either.

Bad Esau.

Jacob knocked lightly on his mother's door. He heard no response from in the room. He knocked again. From inside the room, his mother stirred. She turned on her nightstand lamp. The light came through the holes that Esau had punched in her door.

"What is it, Jacob?" she asked groggily.

"Esau left the house again."

"How do you know that?"

"He's not in his room and the lights are off downstairs."

"Do you know where he's gone?" Eva asked.

Jacob nodded again. "I think so."

Eva climbed out of bed. "Get dressed Jacob. We have to go after your brother."

"Is Esau a bad boy?"

Eva nodded. "Yes, Jacob, Esau's a very bad boy," Eva said.

Jacob smiled. He only took a few minutes to get dressed. By then his mother was ready, too. As they were getting ready to climb in the truck, Jacob grabbed his head.

Pain shot through his head. Then the words "Mueller" and "Danger."

It almost sounded like a warning. Esau was sending a message like Jacob had sent Esau a message when he killed the girl. Esau was trying to warn him about Dr. Mueller.

"Jacob, what's wrong?" Eva asked.

"Esau's in trouble. Dr. Mueller has him."

Eva's face paled, and she sagged against the truck. Jacob ran around to her side of the truck to keep her from falling.

"You'll have to drive," Eva said. "I don't think I can right now. Can you get us to where Mueller has Esau?"

Jacob helped his mother into the cab of the truck. "I can get us there," he promised.

Jacob climbed into the truck. He started it up and pulled onto Hanover Road, and drove toward Fleetwood.

"Mama, maybe we should go somewhere far away from here and hide," he suggested after a few moments of silence.

"We will, Jacob. We can't stay here any longer."

"But I mean maybe we should leave now."

"What about your brother?"

Jacob shrugged. "Maybe we should let Dr. Mueller have him. He's the reason we can't live normally. He's not like us."

Eva slapped her son. Jacob was so startled he swerved into the opposite lane. He pulled back onto the right side of the road.

"Esau is your brother. You may not like him, but he is just the same as you. Don't you forget that I love him just as much as I do you."

"Yes, Mama," Jacob said as he rubbed his cheek.

He couldn't believe his mother had hit him. She hadn't hit him in years. Why had she hit him? He hadn't let Esau get out again. His mother should hit Esau, or better yet, let Dr. Mueller hurt him. That would teach him not to run away.

He pulled onto the street he had seen in his mind image. “This is the road, Mama.”

Eva reached into the glove compartment and took out the small pistol she had bought when she had gone to the bank to deposit her investment check.

Karl Mueller gave Esau a tour of the lab he had set up in the basement. A large examining table in the middle of the room was surrounded by cabinets filled with bottles and instruments. Esau walked slowly around the room, looking in each cabinet. He didn’t like the feel of the room. He felt closed in and imprisoned, but then he had never been in a place like this before so he was not sure how he should feel. The room smelled damp and sterile, nothing like the basement in the farm house.

“Do you still do research?” Esau asked.

“Very little, I’m afraid. However, I still can’t resist a few projects.”

“Like me and my brother?” Esau glanced over his shoulder and the doctor shifted uncomfortably.

“Yes. As I told you over the phone, I believe I can help you.”

Esau turned and faced the doctor. “How?”

“I have a few theories based on new information that has been discovered about gene manipulation. In theory they will work, but they have never been put to the test because I’ve never had the proper subject.”

“And I am that subject?” Esau asked.

Mueller nodded slowly as if it hurt him to do so. “I think so, but I still must make sure some conditions exist even with you. May I examine you?”

“If the examination will help me become human.”

Dr. Mueller pointed to the examining table and Esau lay on it. Mueller began his examination by looking into Esau’s eyes.

“How much do you weigh, Esau?”

“Three-hundred-and-twenty-five pounds.”

The doctor moved onto examining his mouth and teeth. “Impressive. You are the size of a small ape or a huge human. Do you have any allergic reactions to drugs?”

“None that I know of.”

“Good. Good.”

Behind his head and out of his line of sight, Esau heard the doctor open a cabinet. A moment later, he saw the doctor standing over him again. Esau felt a sharp pain in his arm. He looked down and saw the doctor had jabbed a needle into his arm.

"What did you give me?" Esau asked.

"Something to make you sleep."

"Sleep?"

"Yes," Mueller said as he uncovered a set of surgical instruments. "I wouldn't want you to wake up while I was operating."

"Operating..." was all Esau managed to say before he passed out.

"What is that?"

Karl spun around at the sound of the unexpected voice and found himself facing his son. He smiled and stepped to the side so that Joseph could see Esau Lachman.

"This is why I came to Fleetwood, or at least part of the reason," Mueller announced.

"Is it a gorilla?"

Joseph moved closer to the table.

"It is half gorilla and half human," Mueller told his son.

"Human?"

"A result of a failed experiment during the war. The experiment should have been terminated but wasn't. The Russians interfered with my plans."

"Is it one of yours?" Karl nodded. "What were you thinking of? What sort of twisted mind could create this?" Joseph asked.

"I wanted a soldier who would be willing to die in place of Germans," Mueller explained.

Joseph couldn't take his eyes off Esau. "You didn't create a soldier, Father. You created a monster." He paused. "This thing has been living here all this time?"

"His mother has protected him as she does his brother."

"There's another one?"

Karl nodded. "They are twins."

"If anyone ever knew this existed, this would shatter a lot of scientific theories, I think. All those scientists looking for the missing link, and you've created one."

"This is not a creature God meant to exist, Joseph, but I have created it. Now I will destroy them both, and then my notes. I have created either a sub-class of humans or a superior class of beast. Neither is natural. I must destroy both of them."

As the pickup truck screeched to a stop in front of Mueller's house, Eva saw the Nazi hunter running across the street toward her. He stopped beside her window.

"What are you doing here, Miss Lachman?"

Eva turned to stare at him with wide eyes. "You! Did you bring him here to kill him?"

She should have let Jacob kill him in town. Why hadn't that car hit him harder? Just a bit harder might have put him in the hospital. Instead he was alive and helping Mueller kill Esau. Maybe Jacob was right. Maybe Daniel was Mueller's friend.

Daniel backed away from the truck. He was probably going to warn Mueller that Jacob and she were outside.

"I followed Esau from your house. I was just getting ready to see what is going on inside," Daniel told her.

Lies! Lies! Were lies all he could speak?

"Mueller's trying to kill him! That's what's happening, and you let him go into the house," Eva shouted.

She climbed out of the truck and started running toward the house.

Daniel grabbed her by the arm to stop her. Jacob growled and back-handed Daniel across the mouth. Before Daniel had realized what had happened, he flew back onto the road. His head hit the blacktop leaving him dazed while Eva and Jacob ran toward the house.

Facing the locked front door, Eva said, "Open it, Jacob."

Jacob smashed both his fists against the door. The wood offered little resistance, and his arms went through the panels. Then he reached down and unlocked the front door. The door swung open, and he ran inside in front of his mother.

A middle-aged man came up the stairs and Jacob grabbed him by the neck, lifted him off his feet, and held him up against the wall. The man grabbed for Jacob's hand, but he couldn't break Jacob's grip.

"Where is Esau?" Jacob asked.

The man pointed down the staircase. His face turned red as Jacob choked him. Jacob let go of the man and hurried down the stairs with Eva. In the center of the basement, Esau lay unconscious on a metal table. Mueller was nowhere to be seen. The middle-aged man hadn't been Mueller so where was he? He had to be down here somewhere.

Eva rushed to the table and unbuckled the straps that held Esau to the operating table. Was she too late? He didn't look alive. Then she noticed his broad chest was still moving up and down. Good, she wasn't too late. He was just unconscious.

"Jacob, you're going to have to carry your brother out to the truck," Eva said.

Jacob paused from the job he had set himself to do of smashing everything in the lab. He knocked over cabinets, crushed instruments, and threw bottles against the walls. He looked at his brother in disgust. He toppled one last cabinet of drugs and then went to the operating table. Jacob slung Esau's limp body over his shoulder and turned to go back up the stairs.

As he did, the man he had attacked upstairs came running down the stairs holding a pistol in his hand. Eva lifted her own pistol, pointed it at the man, and fired. The man's chest blossomed red, and he fell back against the stairs. He started to rise off the stairs, and she fired again.

Outside, Daniel heard the shots just as he staggered to his feet. That was three times Jacob had gotten the better of him, and Daniel had come out of each time only battered and bruised. If it happened again, his luck might run out.

He thought about going inside the house to see what was happening, but he knew it would be too dangerous. If Mueller didn't try to kill him, Jacob would. Daniel staggered back to his car and climbed in. He needed to think about what he should do now. Things were out of hand.

He turned the car around and started back past the house. As he did, he saw Jacob run from the house with Esau slung across his shoulders. He was followed closely by Eva. Jacob put Esau into the truck bed and then he and his mother climbed into the truck and drove off.

Good. At least Esau was alive. Maybe he wouldn't be so foolish again.

Karl Mueller waited for a few minutes in his hiding place even after he had heard Jacob and Eva leave. He had wedged himself in between the hot-water heater and the wall in the darkest corner of the basement. He had been afraid Jacob would find him during his destruction of the lab, but luckily, Eva had stopped him in time. Jacob would not be as easily fooled as his brother. Esau was driven by reason, but Jacob was driven by hatred. When Mueller was sure the others had gone, he worked himself out from his hiding place.

His lab was destroyed. Very little remained unbroken. Now not only was Jacob alive, but Esau was gone and still alive. And...

Mueller saw Joseph lying on the stairs. He rushed over to his son and saw the two bullet holes in Joseph's chest. He grabbed a handful of gauze bandages off the floor next to overturned examining tray. Wadding the bandages up, he tried to stop the flow of blood out of his son.

"Joseph! Joseph. What have they done to you?"

Joseph's eyelids fluttered momentarily at the sound of his father's voice, but they did not open. Karl felt for his son's pulse. He found it just barely. It was irregular and faint. He needed to get Joseph to a hospital right away.

Karl covered his face with his hand and took a deep breath. He had to think. He couldn't let Joseph die. He had to stop the bleeding and call for an ambulance. Surely, a nearby hospital would help his son.

"Why, Lord? Why?" he cried out. "I am only trying to set things right before I die."

First Aria, and now Joseph. He couldn't let this happen. Not twice. He couldn't let another member of his family die.

"Father?" Joseph whispered.

Karl looked at his son. "I'll get help, Joseph. I won't let you die. I'm not leaving you. Don't you see, I'm not leaving you. I'm right here. I'm not going anywhere this time."

"Thank you for staying with me." Blood trickled from the corner of Joseph's mouth.

Somewhere in the distance, he heard a siren. Someone must have called the police. Good. Maybe they could help Joseph. They could use all their new technology and keep him alive.

Karl bent over and started coughing. A mouthful of green phlegm fell to the floor, but he was unconcerned with that right now. He had to help his son. He caught his breath and sat up. When he turned back to Joseph, he saw his son was dead.

CHAPTER 54

JULY 9, 1993

Steve dreamed he was sleeping in the hammock in his backyard.

The day was sunny and a light breeze blew across his face. He took a deep breath, inhaling the fresh air. No air like that in Baltimore. Just a faint hint of his wife cooking steaks on the grill.

If only he could get rid of the bee buzzing around his head. Then things would be perfect. The bee dive-bombed him buzzing louder as it closed in for the kill, then fading as it flew off. Steve swatted at it as it came in close again. This time the buzzing turned into a ringing.

He woke up in his bed, disoriented from his dream. He grabbed the telephone off the nightstand. Glancing at the clock, he saw he had been in bed only two hours, not near enough time to make up for all the time he wanted to sleep.

"This had better be good," he said into the phone.

It was Ann Card, the night dispatcher. "Chief, I'm sorry to wake you up, but there's been shots fired at 189 Deer Run Road. I've been getting calls from everyone in the neighborhood."

"Is Lee nearby?" Steve asked.

"He's at the movies. You gave him tonight off."

"I did?"

"That's what the duty roster says."

Steve rubbed the sleep from his eyes. "I must have been delirious." He yawned. "Okay, I'll be in as fast as I can. For now, get an ambulance out there."

"Yes, sir."

Steve splashed cold water in his face, ran his fingers through his hair and got dressed. He wondered if Big Earl had a plot to have him drop dead from exhaustion because he couldn't get enough sleep. Sometimes he thought it might be true. He was in his car ten minutes after he hung up the phone and on Deer Run Road another five minutes later.

The house at 189 Deer Run Road was easy to identify. The house had a crowd of spectators gathered around it. If someone committed a crime in the middle of the desert, Steve was sure the crowd would be at the crime site before the police arrived. However, he was the first official at the house. The ambulance hadn't arrived yet.

The crowd parted for him as he hurried up to the open front door. He pulled away a man who looked like he was about to go inside. By the looks of the door, it had been beaten open. With what was anyone's guess. He didn't want any foolish civilian walking into what was a potentially dangerous situation.

Steve drew his revolver and stepped inside the hallway. The hallway and what little he could see of the living room were empty. He swung his gun arm into the kitchen and scanned it quickly. It was empty, too. Then he heard a sob.

He moved into the kitchen. He couldn't see anyone, but he still heard the sobbing. He moved toward the open basement door. An old man sat at the bottom of the stairs crying over a younger man.

Steve hesitated only a moment before rushing down the stairs. "Are you all right, sir?" he asked.

The old man stopped crying and looked up. "She killed my son." Steve reached the bottom of the stairs. The basement looked like a laboratory. Whatever had happened in the house this was where it had transpired. Steve looked at the younger man and saw the blood-stained shirt.

"Who killed your son, sir? Is she still in the house?" he asked. The old man shook his head.

Steve holstered his pistol. He reached over and took the old man by his elbow. "Let's go upstairs, sir. The ambulance will be here in a few minutes to pick your son up. I need to talk with you about what happened here tonight."

Karl Mueller shook his arm free. "No, I want to stay with him. I had to leave his mother, but I won't leave him. I won't. Not this time." He hugged his son's lifeless body.

Steve decided not to press the issue. "Okay, then. I need to call in upstairs, but I will need to speak with you later."

Steve hurried up the stairs and called for the medical examiner from the kitchen phone. He got a small delight when he found out Dr. Noble was on duty. Steve only hoped the good doctor hated being roused out of a sound sleep as much as Steve did.

He walked out to the front porch and looked at the door again. His initial observation was that the woman who had broken in used some sort of battering ram to get through the door.

Watching the crowd out in the front yard, he realized he could not keep this incident quiet. People would talk, and they would start making connections. Three murders in three days, and two attempted murders. The situation was getting out of control. Something was very wrong in Fleetwood, and he needed to find out what it was before anyone else died.

He finished his call and walked back to the basement stairs. He saw the old man holding the dead man's hand and patting it.

"Do you see, son? I didn't run this time. I stayed with you," the old man said.

He stopped crying when he heard the siren marking the approach of the ambulance. Then Steve heard something that worried him because it meant more trouble.

The old man said, "I will kill them, Joseph. As much for you now as for me. I will kill them. Then I will join you and your mother. We will be a family again."

CHAPTER 55

JULY 9, 1993

When the Lachmans arrived back at the farmhouse, Jacob Lachman pulled his brother's still-unconscious body from the truck bed and slung it over his shoulder. He carried his brother up the stairs to his bedroom, knocking Esau's head against the wall occasionally.

"Not upstairs, Jacob. In the basement, and be careful with him. He's your brother, not a bag of potatoes," Eva Lachman directed her son when he was halfway up the stairs.

Jacob turned around, letting Esau's head hit the wall as he did. Eva sighed and threw up her hands. Maybe Jacob would get lucky and knock some sense into his brother's head.

Jacob walked back through the kitchen to the stairway that led to the basement. The basement was unfinished. It had no windows in it, so it was very dark and seemed smaller than it actually was. Eva only used it when she needed to wash clothes or she wanted to store food away for the winter. The walls were made of stone, which helped keep the temperature in the basement cool, no matter how hot the temperature was outside. While the basement might be nice in the summer, it made Eva's elderly joints stiff.

The wooden stairs complained loudly under the combined weight of both Jacob and Esau, but they held as Jacob walked down.

Eva hurried upstairs and brought a blanket, a thick comforter, and a pillow into the basement. She arranged a makeshift bed in the middle of the floor and pointed to it.

"Put Esau on this," she told Jacob.

Jacob did as she asked. This time, he was careful not to abuse his brother since she was watching. Eva laid her head on her Esau's chest to listen for his heartbeat.

She stood up and said, "Jacob, I want you to tear these stairs down."

"What?"

"You heard me. Tear these stairs down. Get a saw or an axe out of the garage if you need to, but all I want left when you're done is a pile of firewood," Eva explained.

"But if I do that, we won't be able to get down into the basement," Jacob complained.

"We can use a ladder, but right now, I want you to tear those stairs down. We'll use the wood in the stoves."

"Yes, Mama."

After Jacob climbed to the top of the stairs and went into the garage, Eva went upstairs to the kitchen and filled a glass with water. Her hand shook as she raised the glass to her mouth, but she steadied it with her other hand. Even so, some of the water spilled onto her dress.

She had to do this, she told herself. Esau was making her do this.

He was being a bad boy, and he had to be punished.

She had both her sons back. She had escaped from Mueller, and now she would make sure he never had a chance to get them again.

Jacob came back from the garage with an axe and started down the stairs. "You'll let me out once I knock the stairs down, won't you, Mama? I don't like it in the basement. It's too cold."

Eva nodded. "I'll put the ladder over the side so you can get back up," she assured him.

Jacob went down the stairs and Eva moved to the edge of the doorway to watch him. His first swing of the axe took out one of the banister supports. He grabbed hold of the loose wood and pulled it free from the wall. The destructiveness seemed to excite him and he swung the axe faster and harder at the lowest step, smashing through it. He laughed and continued his assault on the stairs. When he finished, all that was left of the staircase was small blocks of wood, just as she asked. He always did what she asked, unlike Esau.

Jacob lowered the axe reluctantly and looked up at his mother. He looked as if he doubted she would lower the ladder for him…

"Now stack the pieces in the corner, Jacob, and I'll let the ladder down for you."

Jacob did as he was told and began stacking the pieces on top of each other against the far wall. Eva disappeared from his view and returned a few minutes later. She pushed the metal ladder through the doorway and let it dip slowly toward the ground.

"That's good enough. Come on up here."

Jacob climbed the ladder to the kitchen. When he was standing on the floor, he pulled the ladder up.

Eva hugged him and said, "You're a good boy, Jacob."

Jacob grinned. Eva picked up a five-dollar bill from the counter and handed it to him. He took it and looked at it.

"Why don't you go into town and get yourself some ice cream? Kendall's should be open by the time you walk into town. But don't talk to anyone you don't know and don't go anywhere but to Kendall's and back. No playing around today. Do you understand me?"

Jacob nodded, still smiling. He hugged his mother lightly and then hurried out to the garage. Eva watched him leave and hoped she wasn't letting him get himself into more trouble.

Jacob got his reward for being good and Esau got his punishment for being bad.

Once Jacob had left, Eva returned to the kitchen. She pulled one of the kitchen chairs up to the edge of the doorway and sat down. She waited for the drugs Mueller had injected into Esau to wear off. When he stirred, Eva stood up and pushed the chair away from the doorway.

Esau came awake with a start. He sat up straight, swinging his fists at an imagined enemy. When he realized he was alone, he stopped swinging. He looked around the basement in a slight daze, then he looked up and saw his mother watching him from the doorway.

"Mama?" he said.

"Yes, Esau."

"Am I in our basement?"

She nodded. "Yes, Esau."

"How did I get here? The last thing I remember was Dr. Mueller sticking a needle in my arm. Then everything went fuzzy and dark."

"He was going to kill you, just like I told you he would do if he had the chance. Why didn't you listen to me? I warned you so many times about him, but you didn't listen to me. You were a very bad boy, Esau," Eva said as she shook her finger at him.

Esau looked at the cement floor in shame.

"I want to be human. All human, not just part. I want to outside of the yard. I can't do that when I look like a monster. I thought he could help me. He said he could." Esau lowered his eyes to the floor.

"Help you? I thought your brother was the stupid one in the family, but even he wouldn't have gone to Karl Mueller for help. Mueller made you what you are!"

"Then he would also be the most likely person to make me human," Esau said.

Eva shook her head in frustration.

"Where are the stairs?" Esau asked.

"They're gone. I had Jacob break them down." Esau moved up under the doorway. "Because now the only way in or out of the basement is on the ladder," Eva said.

"But why?"

"Because I want you to stay in the basement."

"What!"

"You've been a bad boy, Esau. I can't trust you to stay in the house when I'm not home or even when I'm not watching. So at least now I'll know where you are, and Mueller won't be able to get you. You'll be safe. Don't you see? I'm protecting you so Mueller can't get you again."

"But you're imprisoning me even more than before. It's unfair."

Esau's lower lip stuck out in a childish pout.

"To let Mueller kill you would be unfair. If you behave yourself, maybe I'll let you come upstairs occasionally. Of course, either your brother or I will have to keep an eye on you."

Esau suddenly jumped up and grabbed hold of the bottom of the doorway and tried to pull himself up. The linoleum tiles were too slick to hold and so his fingers slipped from the ledge.

Eva panicked when she saw him trying to get out. She hadn't expected him to react like that. Didn't he see that she was only protecting him?

He jumped up and grabbed the ledge again. She had to keep him in the basement, so she stepped on his fingers. She had on leather loafers with thick rubber soles. Even though she only weighed 120 pounds and Esau could have lifted her easily, the sudden pressure on his fingers felt more like 300 pounds. She wouldn't break his fingers, just hurt them. Esau yelled as he pulled his hand away.

Then Eva stomped on his right hand. He refused to let go of the ledge this time. Eva stepped on his fingers again and he started to slip.

"This is not the way to be a good boy, Esau. Now I told you to stay in the basement until I say otherwise."

"I don't want to stay in the basement. I want to be free!"

Esau's right hand slipped off the ledge. He grabbed wildly at the ledge, but his fingers slid off the linoleum. Then they found something solid and grasped it.

Esau heard his mother yell and saw her fall through the doorway over his head. He was even more surprised when he saw his hand holding her ankle. He hit the hard floor on his butt and saw his mother fall on the concrete a few feet away from him.

He cried out and crawled over to her side. She was conscious, but her breaths were ragged. One of her arms was bent in an odd position, and Esau realized it was broken. Eva's nose was also bleeding, and she was crying.

Esau started crying, too. He dabbed at his mother's blood with his shirt.

"I'm sorry, Mama. I didn't mean to hurt you. I was just trying to grab onto anything I could. I'm sorry. I'm sorry."

Eva reached out with her good arm and touched Esau on the cheek.

"I only wanted to protect you. I want you to be a good boy. I don't want Mueller to hurt you," Esau said.

"He won't, Mama. He won't. I promise. I'll stay down here as long as you want me to. I won't even say anything or do anything, so he can't hear me. I'll be good."

Eva smiled and then her hand fell from Esau's face. After a moment, he figured out what had happened; and he screamed in his deep voice. He had killed his mother.

CHAPTER 56

JULY 10, 1993

Fleetwood Police Chief Steve Montgomery wasn't sure what disturbed him the most about Dr. Barry Noble, the county medical examiner: his totally detached, unemotional manner as he examined the crushed head of Shannon Gardner or his very emotional manner toward blacks.

Noble's delays at performing the autopsies on Shannon and Billy Stillwell had forced Steve to come to Memorial Hospital in Cumberland and look over the coroner's shoulder while he performed Brenda's autopsy. Steve would have much rather preferred reading the autopsy. As it was, he felt like a necrophile looking at the nude girl on the stainless steel table.

Noble only glanced at Brenda's head, tilted it from side to side, and made his diagnosis. "Someone busted this girl's head open, boy," Noble told Steve in a condescending tone.

Steve bit down on his tongue. He reminded himself he was here to get information, not get into a fist fight with a redneck coroner. He had followed Dr. Noble back to the hospital from Albert Speer's to grease the wheels, not kick them.

"I can see the obvious, doctor. What I'm curious about is how she got that way," Steve said slowly.

Noble touched her head as if he were doing a faith healing. Pulling his hands away, he took a deep breath and said, "The breaks in the girl's skull would seem to indicate that someone crushed her head between their hands."

Steve made some notes on his pad. Hands? How could someone's hands crush a girl's skull? "What do you mean 'seem to indicate'?"

He hated the antiseptic smell of the morgue at Memorial Hospital, but even more than that, he hated the smell of death that permeated the place. He tried to take as few breaths as possible without passing out. Besides, he didn't want to let Noble know he had the home-court advantage while they were in the morgue.

Noble frowned. "While the breaks roughly indicate a hand shape on either side of the skull, she could not have been murdered in that way."

"Why?"

"A person can only generate so much pressure between his hands. No one could generate that much pressure, not even someone the size of Arnold Schwarzenegger," Noble said in an exasperated tone.

"Then how can you say it looks like someone squeezed her head?"

Noble put his hands on his hips. "I'm not stupid. I'm just telling you what it looks like, not what it is," the coroner snapped. Steve could tell by the doctor's tone that the man was just as confused as he was.

"Have you examined the hairs and blood samples I sent you from the Daniels' farmhouse? Are the two incidents connected?" Steve knew he was grasping at straws, but he had trouble believing so many people in Fleetwood had gone crazy at once.

"I examine bodies, boy. I'm a doctor, not a technician. I assigned one of my assistants that job."

Steve leaned forward across the examining table. He made sure not to touch the body. "Your initial report stated you found animal hairs on the girl. I want to know if those hairs match the ones found at another crime scene. A doctor would call it doing a follow-up. I'll expect to hear your results by six tonight, doctor. In addition, I want the hair samples from the Speer home compared to the other samples by this evening, or I'll have a talk with Dr. Sampson."

Steve relaxed, but he stared unblinkingly at the coroner. Barry Noble's face turned red, then purple. Steve knew he wanted to say something, but he knew better. Dr. Sampson didn't tolerate racism with his staff, and Noble had already been put on notice because of an earlier encounter with Steve.

Noble stood up. "Fine, I'll fax you my findings this evening."

He spun on his heels and stormed out of the morgue, leaving the door open behind him.

CHAPTER 57

JULY 9, 1993

A ring of chocolate ice cream covered Jacob's mouth when he walked into the kitchen. It had dried into a tasty stain that was the same shade as his skin. He had walked into town and bought a pint of Ben and Jerry's Super Fudge Chunk ice cream at Kendall's and eaten it sitting in the shade on the side of the grocery store. He swirled his tongue around his lips to see if he could still lick the ice cream off his face. When he couldn't, he went to the sink and rinsed the sticky ice cream off his mouth.

"Mama, I'm home," he called as he turned off the faucet.

He expected to see his mother walk into the kitchen, but no one came. He wondered if she might be in the backyard or upstairs taking a nap. Jacob looked through the window and didn't see anyone outside. Hurrying upstairs, he found the door to her room open, but she wasn't inside the room. She couldn't have gone anywhere. The truck was still in the garage.

Maybe she had told Esau where she was going. He would be awake by now and probably mad that he couldn't get out of the basement. Esau had been a bad boy, though, and bad boys were punished.

Jacob walked to the doorway of the basement and looked down. He thought Esau would be awake and wandering around in a daze. Maybe he would be yelling about being punished. Instead, Jacob saw his mother sleeping on the blankets she had brought down for Esau.

"Mama?" he called. "What are you doing down there?"

She didn't answer him, and that was when Jacob worried. His mother was usually a light sleeper. She should have opened her eyes when he called out to her.

"Esau? Esau, are you down there? Answer me!" Jacob shouted. He stomped his foot on the floor and walked away from the stairwell.

He saw the ladder leaning against the wall. He would have to go down into the darkness again and wake his mother up. He didn't want to go down there, though. It was dark and damp and... creepy. She must have fallen asleep, and Esau had escaped from the basement.

He slid the ladder through the doorway until it touched the floor of the basement. He climbed down and walked over to his mother. He wanted to tell her that Esau had run away again. Esau was bad, but Jacob was a good boy. His mother would be proud of him, but mad at Esau like she was when he ran off to Dr. Mueller's. Jacob was always a good boy.

He shook his mother's shoulder, and she did not stir. He touched her cheek and felt her cold skin. A cold, damp basement was no place for his mother. She might get sick.

Something was odd about his mother. She looked like she was asleep, but he felt she wasn't. Then he noticed his mother's chest wasn't rising, and he screamed.

As the scream died on his lips, he heard something rattle behind him. He spun around and saw Esau pulling the ladder up into the kitchen.

Jacob raced across the basement to catch the end of the ladder and pull it back down, but he was too slow.

"I didn't mean to do it, Jacob," Esau said.

Jacob noticed his brother's face was wet and his eyes were red. Had Esau been crying?

"Mama's dead, Esau," Jacob said.

Esau started crying again. "I didn't mean to, Jacob, but she was stepping on my fingers. Jacob's brow creased, and he squinted. Esau was telling him something, but not saying it. Jacob had to think carefully about what Esau was saying.

"You killed her? You killed her!"

He ran to the open door and jumped at his brother. He grabbed onto the edge of the doorway but he swung in the open air with nothing for his feet to grab onto.

"I'm going to kill you, Esau. I'm going to kill you! You can't hide from me, you know."

Esau closed the door on his brother and then turned and left the house. This time, he would go out through the front gate.

CHAPTER 58

JULY 10, 1993

At the sound of a knock at his door, Daniel Levitt sprang from his bed. He never slept soundly anymore. After nearly being killed when he first started working for the Committee for the Prosecution of War Criminals, Daniel had learned that deep sleep was a luxury he couldn't afford. At least not if he wanted to stay alive.

He hesitated, then called out, "Who is it?"

As soon as he spoke, he ducked behind the bed. If Mueller started spraying bullets through the door, he didn't want to be a target.

"It's Tina."

Daniel hurried to the door, opened it, and pulled Tina Rourke inside. Then he locked the door again.

"Did you see anyone on your way up?"

"Just Charlie."

Daniel nodded.

The redhead crossed her arms over her chest. "What's going on, Daniel?"

"What do you mean?"

"I mean, I told you where your Nazi lived, and a few hours later his son is dead. I thought you were after the father, not the son. Did I misjudge you? This wouldn't be the first time I've misjudged a man."

Tina spoke so quickly Daniel had trouble absorbing what she said.

"Joseph was killed?" he asked.

"You mean you didn't know? The news is all over town. People are talking about Bigfoot killing him. Of course, they don't know that a Nazi hunter was after him. Why did you have to kill Joseph? He was a nice man. Maybe nicer than you."

The last barb hurt Daniel. His blissful feeling of peace in Fleetwood looked like it had just ended. Even Tina assumed he had killed Joseph. What if she told the police? Chief Montgomery was all too willing to use the reason to run Daniel out of town or arrest him. What if Tina told him? What good would his incredible story be against the more-reasonable story of a local citizen?

Daniel sat down on his bed, shaking his head. "I did not kill Joseph.

Believe me. I was there, but I never made it into the house. I drove away when I heard the shots. But if Mueller is still alive, then they are still in danger."

Tina sat down beside him. "Who's still in danger?"

"Eva Lachman and her two sons."

"I know Eva, but she only has one son. His name's Jacob. He's a little slow. I told you that."

Daniel shook his head. "No, Eva has two sons, but she keeps one at the farm all the time. He is not allowed to go out. He saved me from Jacob the first day I was in town."

"That sounds cruel. Eva isn't cruel. Why would she do something like that to her own son?"

"Eva cannot let anyone see Esau. You see, Mueller performed some experiments on her when she was in a concentration camp during the war. Eva's sons are the result of one of those experiments."

"Is this hidden son deformed or something?"

"Or something. He looks like the Bigfoot the people are talking about."

"Then he killed Shannon and Billy!"

"No." Daniel laid his hand on her arm. "Esau Lachman is not a killer. He is intelligent. Inside, he is as human as you or I. He just looks different than we do. I know he did not kill Mueller's son. I told you I was there. I saw Jacob carrying Esau out of the house unconscious. I am just as sure he did not kill the two teenagers in the forest."

"But everyone is saying..."

"I do not care what everyone is saying. Esau saved my life. I have talked to him. I do not think he could kill."

"Everyone can kill."

Daniel shook his head. "You need to meet him. You will not believe me if I tell you about him, but you might accept what I say easier if I introduced you."

"Why?"

"Because he cannot stay where he is now. He is like a prisoner. I want you to meet him, so if Esau needs your help after I leave left town, he will know someone he can go to. I have to keep Mueller from killing Esau."

CHAPTER 59

JULY 10, 1993

Esau leaned against a large tree and cried. He slid down until he was sitting on the ground and cried loud, wailing sobs that silenced the animals nearby. He didn't care if they were scared. He didn't care if someone heard him crying.

He had killed his mother. He had killed his mother, and he didn't deserve to live.

Maybe Dr. Mueller was right to try to kill him. He was neither man nor ape, but he was a killer. Killers deserved to be put to death. Isn't that what the law said? His mother should have let Dr. Mueller kill him. Then she would be alive, and he would be dead like he deserved to be.

He raised his head to the sky and said, "I won't kill ever again, God. Just let her be alive. Let me be wrong that she was dead. Let it be a bad dream that I'll wake up from. And if it's not, kill me. Punish me for doing this to her. I don't deserve to live when I have killed the one person in the world who loves me."

He sat silently then, half expecting to hear God speak to him or hoping to see his mother searching for him. If she would only come, he would stay in the cellar for the rest of his life. He wouldn't try to leave ever again. He would die in the basement if only his mother would be alive and he could see her and talk to her every day for the rest of his life.

He clenched his eyes shut and concentrated, trying to feel Jacob's mind. His thoughts searched for their matching pattern. When the thought patterns met, he could tell Jacob was still trapped in the basement.

He tried to tell his brother what had happened. *I'm sorry. I'm sorry, Jacob. I didn't mean to kill her. It was an accident. I didn't mean to kill her. I love her.*

He lay back against the maple tree and waited. He wondered if Jacob had heard him. Maybe Jacob didn't want to hear him. Then he felt a tickle on his brain. Jacob was trying to reach him.

You're a bad boy, Esau. I hope you die. I hope I get to kill you.

Jacob paced around the edge of the basement, never straying further than an arm's length away from the wall. He wanted to stay as far away from his mother as possible. Her body lay near the center of the basement on the cold cement floor, still looking as if she were asleep. Jacob didn't want to be close to the dead body. It was not his mother anymore. This was just her dead body, a shell. He didn't want to touch it. It was cold and clammy, not at all like his mother had felt.

He backed himself into a corner and roared as loud as he could. His hands rested against the cold stone foundation of the basement. He swung his fists backwards, pounding the wall. The wall shook slightly under the pounding, but it remained intact. All he succeeded in doing was bruising his hands.

Esau was gone. He had run out of the house through the garage door, using the remote controls on the truck's dashboard to open the gates. He had heard the garage door slam shut when his brother had escaped.

"But I'm good!" Jacob yelled as he wiped the tears from his eyes. He pounded on the wall again, ignoring the pain in his hands.

When his hands started throbbing, Jacob stopped and his cries lessened to a whimper. He licked his sore hands, hoping the pain would go away. Then he wrapped his arms around his legs and rocked back and forth on the cold floor.

He looked up and saw his mother's body on the blanket. He could see the top of her head and the graying hair. He had trouble thinking of the body he was looking at as his mother.

"I was a good boy. I was a good boy," he mumbled.

Hearing himself say the words did little to soothe his fear. His mother needed to tell him he was a good boy. She knew the truth, but she would never tell him he was a good boy again. How would he know when he was doing something good unless she told him so?

He pushed himself to his knees and took a deep breath. "Esau!" he yelled at the top of his voice.

He had felt Esau's words in his mind. Esau trying to pretend he was a good boy. Esau apologizing for what he had done. Too late for that now. His Mama was dead.

In his mind, he felt his anger congeal into a solid rage. How dare Esau act like he was sorry! What good did that do now? He pictured the anger in his mind as a sledge hammering away at the stone walls of the basement. Even though he didn't see it, he felt his anger free itself from the basement and sail into the outside air, searching for Esau.

He felt Esau's sorrow first. Even if Esau had accidentally killed their mother, it changed nothing. Their mother was still dead, and Esau's sorrow wouldn't bring her back.

Esau was a bad boy.

Jacob felt Esau sensing Jacob's presence and trying to shut Jacob out. Then, he could no longer feel his brother's emotions, but he could sense Esau out there somewhere.

He looked at the closed door. He knew he could reach the ledge because he had already done so when Esau pulled up the ladder. He stared at the doorway through narrowed, brown eyes.

He had to get out. He had to get Esau.

Punish Esau.

Kill Esau.

He shook his head and pounded on his chest. He growled deep under his breath.

In the dark corner of the basement, he saw the pile of wood scraps he had stacked there earlier after breaking up the stairway. It looked two- or three-feet high. If it was under the doorway, it would be high enough so that he could manage to pull himself out of the basement.

He smiled and giggled. Esau wasn't the only smart one.

Jacob could think, too. He would get out of the basement.

He ran over to the pile. From behind the pile, he tried to push it along the floor. Instead of sliding, the pile tumbled and spread out along the floor.

He grumbled and grabbed an armful of boards and carried them over to a spot on the floor underneath the doorway. Several more trips back and forth across the basement rebuilt the pile of scrap wood under the doorway.

He stepped back and admired his work. He turned to his mother's body and said, "See, Mama. I can think. I'm smart, too."

He stepped lightly on the pile and climbed to the top. He reached up and grabbed the edge of the doorway, which came to just below his chest.

He smacked his open hand as forcefully as he could against the door. The wood around the doorjamb splintered, and the door swung open. Jacob jumped up and fell forward onto the floor. He squirmed forward on his stomach until he was safely on the floor and out of the basement.

Rolling onto his back, he sat up, then stood up and looked into the basement. His mother's body was still there. She was still dead.

He could still feel Esau's presence. His brother was moving farther away from the house with each moment. Jacob picked the truck keys off the table and slid them into his pocket. He would find Esau and Jacob the good boy would kill his bad brother.

CHAPTER 60

JULY 10, 1993

Daniel thought Tina was sitting unusually close to him as they drove down Hanover Street through Fleetwood. Not that it mattered to him. A man could get ideas when a pretty girl sat that close to him, and he didn't need any help coming up with ideas.

As they passed Kendall's Country Store, Daniel saw Brad Kendall standing on the front patio area, sweeping it clean. The thin man looked up and saw Daniel and Tina turn the corner. His eyes hardened and narrowed to small slits. Daniel had seen that look enough times to recognize it for what it was. Hate. Brad hadn't learned his lesson about anything. He only blamed Daniel and Tina for his being in trouble for attempting to rape Tina. Beside him, Daniel heard Tina's breath catch momentarily as she saw Brad.

That's the problem with the American justice system, thought Daniel. There is no justice. Criminals have all the privileges while the victims have very few. In America, a man could commit a crime and the odds were in his favor that he would get away with it.

Daniel pulled his car into an empty space in front of the police station. He got out, went around to the other side of the car and opened the door for Tina. She climbed out and together they walked into the police station. He watched Brad over Tina's shoulder to make sure the grocer didn't start toward them.

Chief Montgomery stood at the front desk talking to his receptionist when Daniel opened the door. The chief looked up, saw the two of them, then straightened himself up. He looked tired.

"Well, speak of the devil. I was just telling Margaret I was going out to pay a call on you, Mr. Levitt."

"Well then, it looks like I saved you a trip," Daniel replied.

The chief glanced at Tina. "Are you having some trouble with Brad again, Tina?"

Tina's earlier fear gave way to irritation. "Does it matter if I did? You couldn't do anything about it. Not unless Earl gave you permission," Tina told him.

Chief Montgomery stiffened at the implication. "I do my job the way the law says I can do it, Miss Rourke. The law says Brad is 'innocent until proven guilty' and that if bail can be posted, he can be released on bond. While I may not like Earl Kendall, the law and he agree on this point. Not much I can do about that."

Daniel interrupted before Tina could yell something back, which he had no doubt she was planning to do. She needed to vent her anger about Brad on someone, and the chief seemed like the perfect target.

"Chief, I heard there was shooting on Deer Run Road. I came to see if I could get any information about it."

"For a stranger in town, you sure seem to be tapped into the grapevine." Steve glanced at Tina.

Daniel shrugged.

"Okay," Steve said, "Come back into my office. It just so happens that I wanted to talk to you about that shooting."

Had someone seen him at the house, Daniel wondered. The chief wouldn't need to talk to him about the shooting unless the police chief could connect him to it.

Why was he worried? He had done nothing wrong. He had been in a daze out in the middle of Deer Run Road when the shooting happened.

Daniel and Tina followed the Chief Montgomery into his office. It was a small room. The desk was clean except for an open folder filled with some papers and photos. The gray-steel file cabinets were shut. Two frames hung on the wall. One held Steve's university diploma from the University of Maryland and the second was an 8 1/2-x-11 photo of Steve Montgomery, his wife, and his daughter.

The chief pointed to the two wooden chairs in front of the desk.

When Daniel and Tina sat down, the chief walked behind his desk and remained standing. He held his hands behind his back and stared down at Daniel.

"Let me be frank with you, Mr. Levitt. I don't like you. I don't like what you represent, and I don't like the chaos that you have apparently brought to my quiet town. Nazi hunters, in my book, are no better than the Ku Klux Klan. Since I already have to deal with the Klan, I could do without the Nazi hunters."

Daniel remained calm. "What have I done, Chief? I have come into town and asked a few questions. Nothing more at this point."

Steve's voice slipped up a notch in intensity. "You're nothing more than a politically correct bounty hunter. What's more, since your arrival in Fleetwood, I've had to deal with five murders, three of them in town, the assault on yourself, an attempted break in at Rick Martin's, and the attempted rape of Miss Rourke. That's more crime than this town has seen in two years, and it all began when you drove in."

Daniel leaned forward in his chair. "Are you accusing me of something, Chief? I certainly did not tell Brad Kendall to attack Tina, I do not know Rick Martin, and I certainly had no reason to kill two kids screwing around in the forest."

Steve nodded and held his hands behind his back. Daniel would have bet that the police chief was clenching and unclenching his fists.

"I know that. That's why I haven't arrested you. Not yet at least. But I don't believe in coincidences, Mr. Levitt, and it's too coincidental that you showed up when all this trouble started."

Daniel stood up from his chair. He was tired of having the police officer look down on him both figuratively and literally. Daniel's anger was beginning to get the better of him.

"Chief, let me assure you, I want to finish my business here as quickly as possible. I certainly have not received a very warm welcome. The only thing people around here hate more than a black man is a Jewish man."

He meant the comment as an intentional barb, and he was glad when he saw Chief Montgomery take it like that. The black man stiffened slightly and clamped his teeth together.

"What's it going to take for you to finish your business here?" the chief asked.

"I need to find Karl Mueller and have him arrested. Then Israel can request extradition from America."

"I told you there's no one in town by that name."

"I know. I found out he goes by the name of Albert Speer here." Chief Montgomery's eyes widened. "Ah, now you know why I came to talk with you," Daniel said when he saw the look of recognition in the chief's eyes.

"Do you carry a gun?" Steve asked.

"I own one, but I do not carry it on my person."

"What caliber?"

Daniel sighed. The chief thought he had fired the gun at Joseph Mueller. "A 9-mm Beretta. It is registered in Houston where I bought it years ago."

"You won't mind dropping it off here for a ballistics check, will you?"

Did it matter whether or not he minded?

"It is registered, Chief Montgomery."

Steve jabbed his finger at the desk. "I don't care if it's registered. I want to see it right here."

"Did Mueller or Speer say he had been shot at by a Jew with a Beretta?" Daniel asked.

"The older Speer only said something about a woman shooting his son. The younger Speer isn't saying anything. He's dead."

Tina's grip tightened on Daniel's arm.

"So why do you want to see my gun? I am not a woman as I am sure you can see."

"I want to see your gun because I don't trust you."

"Do you have Karl Mueller in custody?" Daniel asked.

"Of course not. I don't know he is who you say he is, and Albert Speer is not wanted for a crime."

Daniel stood up. "It looks like I will be staying around a little longer. You might have gotten rid of me had you bothered to hold the old man, Chief. Now I guess I will have to find him myself."

"Levitt, I won't stand for vigilantes in my town. If you try it, I'll toss your ass in jail."

"This is America, Chief. No one ever goes to jail." Daniel turned and left.

Tina glanced at the police chief. "He's upset right now," she told him.

She followed Daniel out to the car and sat down in the passenger seat not looking at Daniel. Daniel glanced at her and sensed the tension. She didn't look at him but stared forward.

"What did you expect me to do?" Daniel asked. "Daniel, he's the police chief. He was just doing his job."

"You're mad at him, too. Don't pretend that you aren't. American priorities are messed up. I thought a law officer was supposed to protect the innocent and arrest the guilty," Daniel said as he started the car and raced the engine.

"That's what he's trying to do."

"No, what he is trying to do is arrest me and let Mueller go free," Daniel told her. "He thinks I am the easy target, the man he can pin all his problems on. Well, I do not intend to let him do it."

An awkward silence fell between them. After a few moments, Daniel said, "I have to try to find Esau. You can come with me if you want or I can drop you off at your house."

Tina looked at him. He could see her frustration in her expression and he was sure his expression showed the same thing. He didn't want to be a Nazi hunter. He wouldn't be if he could just complete this last assignment.

Tina opened the door and got out of the car. "I'll walk home. I can see that getting your revenge is the most important thing in your life right now."

Daniel started to reply, but she slammed the door. He thought about going after her, but that wouldn't do any good. She needed to cool down and so did he. He would talk to her later, but right now he needed to find Esau. Maybe Esau could tell him why Eva had killed Joseph Mueller.

Daniel turned the car around on Main Street and made a right turn onto Hanover Road. His original intention had been to go back into the forest to see if Esau was hiding out there again. The more he thought about it, though, the more he doubted he would find Esau there. The man-ape had been in no shape for exploring the forest when he had last seen him. In fact, he was probably lying in bed recuperating from whatever had happened to him in Mueller's house. That meant he was going to have to see Eva Lachman to get into the house. He didn't think that would be too easy especially if Jacob was anywhere nearby.

He drove further along Hanover Road until he came to the beginnings of the fence that marked Eva Lachman's land. He stopped at the front gate and blew his horn to announce himself. He hadn't expected her to open the gate, but he had to try.

Daniel stepped out of his car and walked up to the gate. The gate had an electric latch, but it was locked into the closed position. Barbed wire was set on the top of the fence in a V configuration. That would cause some difficulty, but it wouldn't stop him if he wanted to go over the fence.

The problem would be if the fence was electrified. At first glance, it didn't seem to be. He saw no exposed wires running through it, no warning signs, and no hum of electricity through the wires. He reached out slowly and quickly touched the fence. No charge of electricity, either. He laid his hand on it and still felt nothing. The fence was not electrified.

He went back to the old Corolla and opened the trunk. He rummaged through his tool box until he came out with a pair of wire cutters. Shutting the trunk, he walked to the driver's side door and took his pistol from under the dash. Jacob might try to attack him again if he was inside the house. He was determined that this time he wouldn't be on the losing end of the meeting.

He went back to the fence and started to climb it. When he reached the top, he used his wire cutters to cut the ten strands of barbed wire that spanned the top of the fence. He pushed the cut strands aside and went over the top of the fence and down the other side. Nothing to it.

Following the driveway, he walked until he reached another fence.

Eva must be really paranoid about Mueller finding her. Not that the fences had helped her much. Mueller had found her anyway, and he had even come close to killing Esau.

Beyond this fence, Daniel could see the house. The garage door was closed. He climbed the fence, but he didn't have to cut the barbed wire because no wire covered the top of this fence.

When he opened the garage door, he saw that Eva's pickup truck was still parked inside. In the open garage, he knocked on the door to the kitchen and waited for a response. The fact that he had scaled two fences already put him on the wrong side of the law, but he wanted to minimize his illegal actions as much as possible. When he heard no answer, he tried the doorknob. It was unlocked.

He pushed the door open and waited. "Esau!" he called.

Someone had to be home. The truck was in the garage, and Esau was always kept on the property. Were Eva and Jacob waiting to attack him?

Daniel stepped into the kitchen, listening warily for any sound. He moved forward and saw the aluminum ladder propped in the corner of the kitchen. Then he saw the basement door. He moved over to the open doorway and looked through it.

The stairs were missing, and the basement was nearly empty except that in the center of the bare cement floor lay Eva Lachman. She looked asleep, but somehow Daniel doubted that was the case. The hairs on the back of his neck bristled.

"Miss Lachman," he said.

Eva didn't stir. He knew he was going to have to go down there to investigate, whether or not he wanted to.

Pushing the ladder through the doorway, he climbed down into the cool basement. He moved up next to Eva and shook her on the shoulder. She still didn't stir. He felt for a pulse at her neck. He couldn't feel a pulse and her skin was cold and clammy.

Had Mueller finally gotten to her and killed her?

He pulled the blanket back. He didn't see any bullet or knife wounds.

Her back might show a wound, but he decided not to turn her over. She was dead. That was all he needed to know.

The more he thought about it, the more he doubted she had been killed by Mueller. The doctor seemed interested only in the twins.

If so, then who had killed Eva and left her in the basement?

Daniel climbed back up the ladder. He should call in Eva's death anonymously, to the police station. No need letting Chief Montgomery know a Nazi hunter was reporting a suspicious death. The police chief would probably try to blame him for Eva's death, too. As Daniel climbed out of the basement, he saw a large pair of bare feet in front of him. He looked up and saw Jacob towering above him.

Jacob growled like an angry animal. Daniel reached for his pistol, but Jacob grabbed him by the shoulders and pulled him out of the basement. He tried to grab his pistol, but Jacob pinned his arms against his side.

The huge man-ape threw Daniel across the kitchen as if he weighed only a few pounds. Daniel slammed into the counter near the sink. Pain shot through his back and he slid to the floor, his arms numb.

Jacob approached him with bared teeth. "I should have killed you in the woods. You are Mueller's friend."

Daniel wanted to grab his pistol, but his arms were still too numb to move. Jacob came close to his face and roared. Daniel refused to close his eyes. He had always told himself that if he had a choice, he would face death and not cower from it. He was going to have a chance to prove himself now.

CHAPTER 61

JULY 10, 1993

After Tina Rourke watched Daniel turn his car around and head out of town after Esau Lachman, she walked along the road toward Kay's Kitchen. For some reason, she felt as if Daniel had just jilted her. Not that she had any ties on him. She had just begun to wonder: What if? He was handsome, even if he was older than her. Maybe being older wasn't such a bad thing. Maybe being older just meant he had sowed his oats and would be more stable than the guys she dated. His profession and nationality also made him exotic in a way. More than that, when he let down his guard, like when they had talked in his bedroom, he seemed vulnerable. She found that strangely appealing. She wanted to feel needed by someone.

She certainly hadn't ever felt needed before. Even by her parents.

They had given up on her about the time she hit her teens. The way she had turned out wasn't entirely their fault, of course. She had worn them out so much that they were just too tired to need her.

Tina stopped at the curb by F & G Hardware. She looked to her left to make sure no traffic was coming. Then she looked to her right. She saw no traffic, but she did see Brad.

He was watching her through the window of Kendall's Country Store.

When he saw she was watching, he blew her a kiss and thrust his pelvis toward her.

A twinge of fear shot down her spine. How could he still act so cocky? Was he so egotistical to think that she wanted him? After everything that had happened? Or did he simply want to torment her as his way of getting revenge?

As he watched her, she held up her hand so that Brad could see that her thumb and forefinger were only an inch apart. She wondered if he would get the message. When she saw his face go red with anger, she knew he understood.

She quickly jaywalked across the street and headed into Kay's Kitchen. Her friend immediately welcomed her with a smile. Kay looked pretty busy with the lunch crowd, but she still managed to talk to Tina.

"What are you having, Tina?" Kay asked.

Tina sighed and said, "Chocolate milkshake."

"Uh oh," Kay said.

"What uh oh?" Tina asked as she sat down at the counter.

"You order a chocolate milkshake, when you've got man problems," Kay informed her. Kay hurried off to give Jack Michaelson his lunch; then she came back to Tina.

"What are you talking about?" Tina asked her.

"When you broke up with Bo Ridgely a few weeks back, you came in here and ordered a chocolate milkshake. When you wanted Mike Dawson to ask you out, but couldn't figure out a way to encourage him, you came in here and ordered a chocolate milkshake. Shall I continue?"

Tina held up her hands. "No. I admit it. My emotions rule my stomach, but I still want a milkshake."

Kay turned away from the counter and made up the milkshake.

When she handed it to Tina, she said, "So who's the problem now, sweetheart? Is Brad still bothering you?"

Tina shook her head and slurped at the milkshake. The rich-chocolate taste relaxed her like a sedative.

"It's Daniel Levitt."

Kay thought for a moment, trying to match the name with the face.

"Levitt. He's that older guy in town with the dark hair? The one who helped you parade Brad through town."

Tina nodded and smiled, remembering how good showing Brad for what he was felt.

Kay shook her head slowly. "Better forget him. He's too old for you," Kay said.

"That's not the problem. I don't mind that he's older than me. I think I would play second to his work, and his work is killing him. There might be nothing left of him for me when his work is done."

Kay leaned across the counter on her forearms. She closed one eye, and the other seemed to stare out at nothing.

"Has he been married before?" she asked finally.

"I don't think so."

Kay laid her hand on Tina's arm. "Then you may still have a chance to fix him. If he had been married and was still a workaholic, then I would say you have a problem. In this case, though, I think he just might not be used to having someone else make demands on his time. He'll have to learn to set his priorities, and if you want a lot of his time, you have to show him you should be a top priority. You'll have your work cut out for you, though. Someone like that is a 180 degrees from the type of guys you're used to." Kay paused. "So you really like this guy, huh?"

Tina nodded and grinned.

"He's not your usual type," Kay said.

Tina shrugged. "He's still cute."

"But he's not built like Arnold Schwarzenegger."

Tina nodded. "No, but strangely that doesn't really seem to matter. Do you think that means I'm growing up?"

Kay laughed. "Don't you think it's about time, honey?"

CHAPTER 62

JULY 10, 1993

The wooden floor trembled beneath Daniel Levitt as Jacob stomped toward him. Daniel resisted the urge to look away from his killer. He thought he was finally going to get out from under Adam's thumb, only not the way he had hoped.

Jacob grabbed Daniel by his shirt and yanked him to his feet. Daniel slumped against the sink. He wanted to raise his arms to at least present some sort of defense, but they were still numb and flapped uselessly at his side.

Jacob bared his teeth and leaned in close to Daniel's face. Daniel felt the man-ape's hot breath in his face. Suddenly, Jacob's head jerked to the side, and he howled.

Jacob let go of Daniel's shirt and turned away. Daniel saw Esau standing in the doorway.

"Leave him alone, Jacob," Esau said.

Jacob howled. "You killed Mama! You killed her!"

"I told you I didn't mean to."

Jacob howled again and charged Esau. Esau reached up and grabbed the top of the door frame. As Jacob drew closer, Esau jumped up and kicked his brother in the chest. Jacob grunted and flew backwards into the wall, cracking the plasterboard underneath the wallpaper. Jacob slumped to the floor, groggy but still conscious.

"Let's get out of here," Esau said.

Daniel staggered past him and out the door into the garage.

"Are you all right?" Esau asked as he followed Daniel into the garage. "My arms are a little numb, but they will be all right in another minute," Daniel assured him. "At least I hope they will."

Esau ran past Daniel out the garage door and around the front of the house. Daniel had to run to keep up with Esau's long gait. Esau ran up to the chain-link fence at one corner of the backyard. Instead of scaling the fence, he lifted it and held it up for Daniel. Daniel rolled under the fence and waited for Esau. The large man-ape quickly followed and then they both ran for the outer fence.

After repeating the process at the outer fence, Esau said, "Where's your car?"

"At the gate."

"Let's get to it and get out of here. Jacob has the remote control to work the gates. He also has the keys to the pickup. He can be after us in a few minutes once he gets his wind back," Esau warned.

Inside the car, Esau leaned the seat back as he had done the night before so that no one could see him from outside the car.

"Where do you want to go?" Daniel asked.

Esau shrugged and stared at the ceiling. "It doesn't matter anymore. I have no home."

"I cannot get you into the Maryland House. Too many people might see you." He paused as he tried to decide on where he could hide Esau. "I will take you to Tina's. She rents a house, and I think it has an attached garage. No one will have to see you. We will drive right into the garage, close the door, and go into the house."

Esau nodded. "Fine. You were foolish to come here. Jacob would have killed you without thinking twice about it. He's already killed at least two people."

"What happened, Esau?" Daniel asked. "Why is Joseph Mueller dead? Why is your mother dead? Did Mueller get her?"

Esau turned his head away.

"I saw your mother in the basement. I heard your brother yell that you killed her."

"I did," Esau whispered. He couldn't meet Daniel's stare.

"Was it an accident?"

Esau nodded.

"I should call in the accident. Your mother should be buried. I am not sure if your brother will think to do that."

"He won't, but you're right, of course. She deserves to be buried. Can you make sure it's a Jewish burial? Obviously, I can't do anything for her."

Daniel shook his head. "I will report her death, but anonymously. The chief and I are not really on speaking terms. If he knows I am reporting her death, he will be even more anxious to get me out of town. Jacob will be expected to make the arrangements. Hopefully, the funeral director will help him make the right decisions."

Esau looked at Daniel. "I don't think he's capable. To make the right decisions, I mean."

"He will have to be. You cannot do it. You do not exist in the eyes of this town, remember?"

Esau rolled his head to the other side, so he faced the car door.

Daniel saw him wipe his eyes as he began to cry. He reached over and patted Esau's shoulder sympathetically.

"What will you do now?"

Esau shrugged. "Maybe Mueller should have killed me. Either he will or Jacob will, I think. When I'm dead, no one will even miss me. No one will even know I'm gone."

Daniel looked down at the man-ape. He had spent his life chasing after Nazis who no longer had victims. Now he had found a victim. The Nazis were still causing hurt; but in this case, he might be able to help the victim rather than simply punishing the Nazi. He hoped so.

CHAPTER 63

JULY 10, 1993

Tina dumped two bananas, a cup of strawberries, a little honey, and water into the blender and switched it on until the contents turned into a fruit shake. She poured the mixture into a cup and began slurping it. It was one of her healthy indulgences, unlike the chocolate milkshakes she got at Kay's. No one could make a milkshake as delicious as Kay's.

"Looks tasty," came a voice from behind her.

Tina spun around and saw Brad Kendall leaning in the doorway to the kitchen. His smile was broad, but it looked evil to Tina. If the devil ever took a human form, he would look like Brad.

"Get out of here," Tina said as forcefully as she could.

"Make me," he said and laughed loudly.

A few days ago, Tina wouldn't have thought that would be much of a problem. But now, she wasn't so sure she could fight him off.

"If you try something, even your father won't be able to get you out on bail," Tina warned him.

Brad stepped forward and Tina backed up, pressing herself against the counter.

"They have to catch me first. Not that you'll tell them anything."

"Don't kid yourself. I'll be on the phone the first chance I get."

Brad clenched and unclenched his fist. "No you won't."

She threw her shake in Brad's face. He yelled and wiped at his eyes. She grabbed a saucepan sitting in the dish drainer and smacked the side of Brad's head. She heard a dull clang and Brad dropped to the floor like a rock.

She ran around him toward the phone on the kitchen wall. She grabbed the receiver and punched 9-1-1. Before she could press the last digit, Brad ripped the receiver out of her hand and yanked it from the telephone. The side of his face was bleeding, and he looked angry–angrier than usual.

He smashed the receiver across Tina's face. She yelled and fell against the kitchen table. It upended, dumping her on the floor. Brad straddled her and grabbed Tina's throat with one hand and raised the receiver over his head preparing for another blow.

"You won't be able to tell the police anything. If you do, my father will make sure you get a midnight visit from some people who are very unhappy to see you hanging around with that Jew."

Tina couldn't say anything. Her eyes widened as she saw the tall, hairy beast walk up behind Brad. The creature grabbed Brad's raised arm and lifted him off the ground. He kicked as his feet left the ground. Then he looked over his shoulder, saw what was holding him, and started screaming.

"Should I kill him, ma'am?" the beast asked. Esau bared his teeth, growling threateningly.

Too startled to speak, Tina just stared at the beast. It looked like a gorilla, but it was talking... to her! Tina saw Daniel sitting on a high stool at the opposite end of the kitchen. He nodded to her and looked like he was trying to keep from laughing. What did he find so funny?

"Don't let it kill me!" Brad screamed. "Don't let it kill me!"

Brad was crying. Tina could have almost taken pity on him if her face hadn't been throbbing from where he had hit it with the phone receiver. Let him be as scared as she had been.

"No, not this time," she said. "But if he ever comes near me again, he's all yours."

Esau nodded and let go of Brad. The shopkeeper hit the floor running. He was out of Tina's house before she could say anything to him. A few moments later, she heard the engine of his car roar to life as he sped away from the front of her house.

She turned and looked at the beast. It was over six-feet tall. At first glance, it looked menacing, but when she looked at its eyes, she knew differently. It had soft-brown, puppy-dog eyes. Hadn't someone once said, "The eyes are the mirrors to the soul"?

Then she heard Daniel laughing. He was still sitting on the stool holding his sides as he laughed.

"Did you see the wet patch on the front of his pants when he ran out of here? I do not think he will bother you again."

Tina glanced at the beast. "Would it have killed Brad if I had said so?" she asked meekly.

Daniel pointed to Esau. "The 'it' is a 'he.' Why not ask Esau?"

She looked at the beast. "Well?"

"Daniel said I would be better off scaring him. If Daniel had shot him, a wounded man would have only caused more problems for us. Your neighbors would have heard the shot, and the police would want an explanation for the shooting."

That made sense to Tina, especially after hearing what Daniel thought about the justice system. Chief Montgomery was looking for a reason to run Daniel out of town.

Daniel walked over to her and touched the side of her face. She winced and pulled away.

"We should get you to the hospital," Daniel said.

"No. They'll only put ice on it and give me a pain killer. I can put ice on it myself, and I don't like drugs."

Tina walked into the living room and sat down on the sofa. She stared at Esau until he turned away uncomfortably. Daniel stayed in the kitchen and made an ice compress.

"You're Jacob's twin brother?" Tina asked.

Esau nodded.

"Other than size, you don't look at all like him."

"I don't act like him either," Esau said.

"For someone who has lived his life hidden from the world, you've been getting around a lot lately."

Esau shrugged but said nothing.

Daniel walked into the living room and handed Tina the ice pack for her face. "Mueller is after him and Jacob. The doctor created them and now he wants to kill them." Daniel sunk into a big armchair.

"Can't you go to..." Tina stopped. She had started to say "the police," but she realized the answer to that before she even finished the sentence. How could someone who looked like Esau and was not supposed to exist ask the police for protection?

Pandy walked into the living room after having taken a nap on Tina's bed. He brushed by Tina and only gave Daniel a passing glance. He strutted over to Esau. He sniffed at Esau's bare feet then rubbed himself against Esau's black sweatpants. Jumping into Esau's lap, the cat curled himself into an orange fur ball.

"Fickle cat," Tina muttered. "Doesn't even matter to him that I'm hurt."

"He's just more comfortable around an animal," Esau said.

Tina stared at Esau, studying his face. Was Esau an animal or a man?

"What are you going to do, Daniel?" Tina asked.

Esau looked at Daniel as if he, too, was curious about what was going to happen.

Daniel sighed and slid deeper into the armchair. “I am not sure. I came to town to expose Mueller and start extradition on him. Now I am not so sure that is my top priority.”

“What is?” Esau asked.

“Finding someplace for you where you can live peacefully, for one. The other is to make sure Brad doesn’t bother Tina again.”

That surprised Tina. Maybe all was not lost with Daniel after all.

CHAPTER 64

JULY 10, 1993

Steve Montgomery squatted down on his haunches and stared into Eva Lachman's basement. The naked bulb in the basement cast only a small circle of light, but what it revealed was enough. At least the smell of decay hadn't set in yet. Whatever had happened here had happened recently. He shook his head and sighed. What was going on in Fleetwood?

His anonymous caller had been right. The body was there. If Eva had died from a fall, she obviously hadn't landed on her back with her arms on her chest. Someone had cared about her enough to lay her out.

Of course, how the caller had known the body was in the basement was a question that would nag at Steve's mind until he knew the answer. However, finding the answer to that question was at the bottom of his list of priorities right at this moment.

Another murder. That brought the total to four in town and two on the C&O Canal towpath nearby. And he wasn't any closer to finding the killer than he had been after the first two murders. Some lawman he turned out to be.

Steve stood up and stretched. He looked out the kitchen window and shook his head again. Eva Lachman had turned her home into a prison, as most people called it. Everyone in town knew about Eva's outer fence, but he'd never heard anyone mention an interior fence. Had no one known about it? What had she been so afraid of that would drive her to such extremes? Whatever or whoever the killer was, Eva evidently had been right to be afraid. Not that her precautions had helped protect her. She was still lying dead in her basement.

And where the hell were the steps to the basement?

Steve turned from the window and looked around the kitchen again.

Some sort of scuffle obviously had taken place. The table was overturned. One of the wooden chairs was broken. A large dent was in the wall. Still, he couldn't seem to find any signs of forced entry into the house, which seemed odd considering the precautions that Eva had taken to keep people off her land. Certainly she would have locked all her doors and windows? Steve had already noticed the cut barbed wire on the outer fence, so obviously someone Eva hadn't wanted to let in had gotten in. Until he found out differently, he would assume that Eva's killer was the same person who had cut the wire.

His deputy came down from the upstairs rooms and shrugged his shoulders when Steve looked at him.

"Everything looks normal upstairs, but no one's up there. I saw holes in Eva's door, but they're covered up with a sheet so I guess they happened awhile ago. Whatever happened that got Ms. Lachman killed, I'd say it all happened in the kitchen and basement. If this was a theft, the thief left some antiques, a computer, and a couple of television sets," Lee reported.

"I don't care what it started out to be. It's a murder now." Steve glanced at the body. "Better get the ME up here to have a look at the body."

Lee nodded and went to the phone to make a call to the county medical examiner. The hospital operator should have been on a first-name basis with Lee by now. They had been giving the hospital a lot of business lately. Steve walked over to the sink and looked out into the backyard once more. It reminded him of a prison exercise yard. No matter how beautiful the scenery was, the fence told anyone who looked at it that it was there to keep people out.

Lee hung up the phone. "He's on his way."

An abnormal shape on the overturned table caught Steve's eye. He bent down next to the table and touched the dark spot. It was a lock of short, black hair. He pulled a small plastic bag from his pocket and put the lock of hair into it. The hair reminded him of the hairs he had seen at Rick Martin's and at the two murder sites. He wasn't sure whether to be relieved or scared that a connection might be made between all the murders.

Though one killer should be easier to find than three, the idea that the murderer might be the same in all four cases disturbed him. The creature Rick Martin had seen try to get into his house, he called Bigfoot. Though Steve didn't believe it was Bigfoot, the footprint indicated this was not a run-of-the-mill intruder. Had the same creature broken into the Lachmans' house? More damage had been done to Rick's house than this one. Of course, Eva hadn't shot at this creature with a shotgun.

"Chief, I saw something a little odd upstairs."

"You already told me about Eva's door," Steve said.

Lee shook his head. "It's not that. There's three bedrooms that look like they have been lived in. One is obviously Eva's, but the other two rooms both belong to men. One is Jacob's, but the other one belongs to someone else."

"How do you know?"

"Jacob's not exactly the brightest person around, and I saw a computer with a modem in the third bedroom."

"Are you going to wait for the ME?" Steve asked. Lee nodded. "Tell him I'll be in his office tomorrow expecting some answers." Steve paused. "If Noble shows up, tell him I'll be expecting the answers tonight."

Steve climbed back into his car and headed for town. He hoped those hairs didn't match up with the others. If they did, he had connected murders, which might mean a fifth murder. Something was going on in Fleetwood that he didn't understand. He was on the outside looking in and he wasn't seeing much.

CHAPTER 65

JULY 12, 1993

Karl Mueller stood at the edge of his son's grave as the funeral director tossed a shovelful of dirt onto the coffin. His old suit no longer fit him properly and was a decade out of date. It was the only appropriate thing he had to wear to a funeral.

The Catholic priest who had conducted the service had left a few minutes ago after expressing his sorrow to Karl.

"Why are you sad?" Karl asked the priest.

"I am always saddened when someone dies. Death leaves a void in the life of the living," the priest told him.

"Then you must live in perpetual sadness, Father. The world is full of death. As a priest, you should be elated another soul has returned to the Lord."

The priest nodded slowly. "But those who die always leave behind someone who cares and grieves, and those are the people with whom I empathize."

Empathize? The priest hadn't seemed too empathic when he had eulogized Joseph.

"My son is at peace, Father. He knew very little of that when he was alive," Karl said.

"The Lord will bless him, Mr. Speer."

Karl wiped away the tears that seemed to run continuously now. "I know. It is my soul I fear for."

The priest looked like he wanted to ask the obvious question, but he said nothing. He simply nodded his head, patted Karl's hand and walked off toward his waiting station wagon. His life would be unaffected by the ceremony he had just performed. Karl's life, what little remained of it, would be forever scarred by Joseph's absence.

He looked up from the grave. Besides himself, the priest, and the funeral director, the only other attendee at the grave had been Police Chief Montgomery. The large black man looked uncomfortable standing across the grave from him. Imagine what the Fuhrer would have thought if he had seen a black law officer? Times had changed.

Karl turned on his heels and headed for the black BMW. Chief Montgomery caught up with him and put his hand on Karl's arm. Karl jerked his arm away.

"Don't touch me," Karl snapped.

"I'm sorry, Mr. Speer. I know this isn't the best time to talk to you, but if I'm to find out who murdered your son, I need to know what you saw."

"It doesn't matter what I saw. Nothing will bring my son back."

"At your house, you said a woman shot your son. Did you know her?"

"I know who she is."

Chief Montgomery's mouth opened slightly in amazement. "Who?" he asked.

"Her name is Eva Lachman. She lives on a farm near this town,"

Chief Montgomery cocked his head to the side. "Are you sure?"

"Yes, boy," Karl snapped. "I'm old, not blind. I knew this woman long ago. There was bad blood between us. When she saw me in town, she got angry and took the law into her own hands."

"She certainly did. However, someone else took the law into their own hands and murdered her."

Karl stopped walking. "Dead?"

Chief Montgomery nodded. "An anonymous caller told me she was dead. I found her body in the basement of her house Friday. Her neck was broken. Do you know anything about that?"

"What about her sons?"

"Did she have sons, Mr. Speer?" Steve asked.

"Of course she did, she..." Karl stopped speaking abruptly and started for his car again. No one knew about Esau. That's why the police officer was so surprised by the plural reference to sons.

The chief caught up with Karl again. "What were you saying about her sons, Mr. Speer? Do you know where they are? We haven't found either of them yet." He paused. "I take it you hadn't heard that Miss Lachman was dead."

Karl shook his head. "No."

He turned and hurried to the car. Locking himself in the car, he rested his head on the steering wheel.

What was happening?

First, Eva killed Joseph, sweet Joseph. Karl should have bought a house somewhere so that Joseph would have known some happiness in his final days. Karl had killed him just as he had killed Aria. He had brought

Joseph into the danger America meant to him and he had taken Aria on a flight from the law, which had led to her death. How could he ever atone for those sins?

And now Eva was dead, and Jacob and Esau were missing. How could he redeem himself of that sin if he could not find the twins?

He had to locate Jacob and Esau before he died. They could not be left alive, more so now that their mother was dead.

Didn't the Bible say "An eye for an eye. A tooth for a tooth?" Now he had one more reason to kill the twins. Eva had taken his son. He would kill hers.

CHAPTER 66

JULY 12, 1993

Steve slammed the door of his car. He had left Baltimore to escape the crime, and he had escaped it. Except now, he had walked into a town where he was one of a handful of blacks. He was a minority in Fleetwood, unlike in Baltimore.

Damn, that old man. Where did he come off with his attitude?

Wasn't it enough he had to deal with subtle hate from people like Earl Kendall?

Steve drove along Hanover Road headed back into town. At the Fifteenmile Creek overpass he saw half a dozen cars and three pickup trucks parked on the shoulder. It didn't take a genius to figure out what was going on. Things were getting out of control.

A lot of good his posted warning had done. The notice had attracted hunters instead of keeping them away. Rick Martin had added fuel to the fire by going around Fleetwood telling anyone who would listen how he had fought off Bigfoot. Now Brad Kendall was telling people that Bigfoot had attacked him at Tina Rourke's.

Steve couldn't care less about Bigfoot. He was more concerned about what Brad had been doing at Tina Rourke's.

Steve stopped his car beside Ed Rafferty's truck as the man climbed out. The man was holding a Winchester in one hand and a beer in the other. The last thing he needed in those woods was a bunch of drunk hunters shooting at anything that moved, including each other.

"Having a little trouble reading, aren't you, Ed?" Steve said as he rolled down the window.

Ed reached into his truck and set the beer out of sight. Then he swung around to face Steve, holding the Winchester. Steve tensed for a moment thinking that the man might want to aim it at him.

"Did you think we wouldn't find out?" Ed asked. "Find out what?"

"The hair."

"What hair?"

"You are as stupid as they say." Steve almost jumped out of his car at that comment. "Lee told us the hair you took from Rick's place matched the hair from Eva Lachman's house, the old German's house, and those kids you found in the woods. And we all know what tried to get into Rick's house."

The hair analysis must have come back. Too bad Lee had such a big mouth. Steve was the last person in town to know, and he should have been the first.

"I don't believe that. Determining if two strands of hair are exactly the same is impossible. And even if you could, my job is tracking down the killer. Not yours or anyone else's."

"Well, you're not doing too good a job. The only way we're going to keep this thing from killing anyone else is if we kill it first, and you're wrong about the hair. With these hairs, you can tell they are the same. Dr. Noble says they're the thickest strands of human hair he's ever seen. It's almost like an animal's," Ed told Steve. "Just the kind of hair Bigfoot would have, don't you think?"

Steve shook his head. "I don't want you going in there, Ed. If you're right, and I'm going to look into it, then you being in the woods is dangerous. Hunting something that can crush a human skull in its hands is not like hunting a deer. You don't want to meet up with whatever did that."

"Not dangerous for me. Dangerous for whatever has been killing the folks around here. Maybe you don't want to do anything since we're only white folks, but we take care of our own." Ed shook his rifle at Steve.

"I won't let you go in there, Ed."

"What can you do? Your posters don't mean diddly squat. This is still a free country, and the woods are public property. Me and the others are gonna find the thing that killed those people, and we're gonna shoot it if it's an animal and hang it if it's a man."

Ed turned and walked into the woods, almost daring Steve to stop him. Steve couldn't do anything but watch him go.

He grabbed the microphone on his police radio and shouted into it, "Margaret, this is the chief. Get Lee on the box. Now."

His tone had left no room for debate and Margaret hesitated in answering him. "He's not here right now."

That only made him angrier. "Where the hell is he?"

"He went across the street to get some lunch."

"You get him on the horn when he gets in. He's caused some big problems for us. If one of these fools out here kills himself while looking for Bigfoot, I'll make sure Lee joins him," Steve said angrily. "Are the autopsy reports and hair analyses on my desk?"

"Yes, Lee signed for them."

"He did more than sign for them. What about fingerprints?"

"They're back, too. It's weird, Chief."

"Well, what's it say? Might as well tell me seeing as how everyone else already knows."

Margaret didn't respond. She must have been looking for the report.

"The prints at the Gardner-Stillwell site and Rick's house are unidentified. There were four sets of prints at Mr. Speer's. One unidentified. Eva Lachman's. Joseph Speer's and his father's. However, the state also kicked out another name to match Albert Speer's prints."

"Whose name?"

"Karl Mueller."

So Levitt had been right about the old man being a war criminal.

Could the old man be the killer? No. Even if Speer had been healthy, he couldn't have crushed Shannon Gardner's skull. He was just hoping for a reason to arrest the man, partly out of spite for the way Mueller had treated him earlier.

"What about at Eva's house?"

"Four sets there, too. Eva's, two unidentified and Daniel Levitt's." Now Steve had the ammunition he needed to go after Levitt.

CHAPTER 67

JULY 12, 1993

Daniel pushed the accelerator to the floor. The Corolla shuddered under the increased demand, but it sped up. He had to get back to Tina's as quickly as possible. He had left Tina's so that he could be alone to clear up some of confusion and think things through. He'd done that now, helped a bit by what he had heard on his police scanner. He had to get both Esau and himself out of here before anything happened.

Forget Mueller. He wasn't important. He would be dead in a few years, anyway. Then God would be his judge. But Esau might be dead in a few days if Daniel couldn't get him out of the area.

Chief Montgomery had yelled over the police scanner about hunters looking for Bigfoot. That could only mean they were hunting Esau. Not to mention the fact that the state police must have identified Daniel's fingerprints, which would make him a suspect in Eva's murder. Chief Montgomery was probably looking for him right now.

Daniel pulled into the driveway behind Tina's royal-blue Volkswagen bug. He burst through the front door, scaring Tina so badly she dropped the newspaper she was reading.

"Where is Esau?" Daniel nearly shouted. "He left about fifteen minutes ago."

"Where did he go?"

"He didn't say."

Daniel stomped his foot on the floor. Tina laid the paper down and looked worried.

"Why did you let him leave?" Daniel snapped.

"Daniel, he's three times bigger than I am. What could I have done?" She moved over close to Daniel and hugged him. "What's wrong?"

"Hunters are in the woods looking for Esau. If they find him, they will shoot him. Plus, Chief Montgomery knows I was at Eva's house around the time she was killed. I want you, me, and Esau to get out of here now."

"I can't leave right this minute. There's packing to be done."

Daniel threw his hands up in the air. "Pack what you need for now. We will get the rest later."

Tina pulled on Daniel and made him sit down on the sofa beside her.

"Think, Daniel. Don't rush into things. Esau's not here. We have to find him before we can decide what to do. It's his life."

In the distance, Daniel thought he heard shots.

CHAPTER 68

JULY 12, 1993

Esau stood far away from the small group of people standing around the open grave. Hidden in the shadow of the trees, he watched his mother's casket slowly disappear into the ground. Esau cried quietly, cursing himself for killing his mother.

Jacob was among those gathered at the grave side. He was dressed in a suit Esau hadn't seen him wear in years. Esau didn't recognize any of the others. He supposed they were people from town his mother had known. His mother had kept to herself, and the small size of the crowd showed it.

He settled onto the ground to watch the proceedings. His mother was dead, and he had killed her. He could not make up for that mistake no matter how hard he tried. His mother's life wasn't like a door he could replace because he forgot his strength and knocked too hard. This time his strength had broken something that he couldn't fix. He had killed his mother. He was the worst kind of murderer. He deserved to die.

A warm breeze blew across his back and ruffled his hair. He drew his knees up to his chest and slowly rocked back and forth. He wished he could hear what the rabbi was saying about his mother, but he was too far away. He couldn't risk getting any closer or he would be in the open and someone might see him.

Would the rabbi say that Eva was a caring mother? Definitely.

Would he say that she had lived through the most-trying period of Jewish history and overcome the obstacles before her? Probably. Would he say she had spent all of her life afraid that Mueller would kill her, but in the end, her son had been the one who had killed her? Probably not.

As Esau watched the funeral, his emotions flowed openly. No one, except one, would notice. Jacob looked up from the grave directly into Esau's eyes. Jacob had sensed him! Esau closed off his thoughts, but he knew it was too late. Jacob knew where he was.

Esau sat as still as he could, but he did not look away from his brother. If trouble came, Esau would run. His mother's grave was no place for the two brothers to fight. He hoped Jacob would realize that. Esau's body tensed as he anticipated jumping to his feet and running.

Hate... die... killer.

The words pounded in his head as Jacob tried to penetrate Esau's mental shielding. Jacob wasn't attacking him physically. He was attacking him with thought, continually reminding Esau of his unforgivable crime.

The realization only seemed to make the connection between him and Jacob even stronger.

I hate you, Esau. You're going to die, killer.

Jacob looked back to the open grave. Esau realized his brother would do nothing here out of respect for his mother. Even in death, Jacob still behaved well for his mother.

Jacob was the good son. He was the bad son.

He leaned his head forward on his knees and cried. When he looked up later, all the people were gone, and the grave was filled in. Even Jacob had left in the funeral home's limousine.

How long had he been crying? A couple of hours at least.

He stood up and stared at the patch of dirt. He walked out from under the trees. The sun was setting. He stopped beside the fresh grave and kneeled down.

"I'm sorry, Mama. I didn't mean to. Honest. I want to be a good boy like you always thought Jacob was."

He lay on the grave, hoping to feel something from his mother. Did she know how sorry he was? He felt nothing. He was alone. His mother was truly gone.

CHAPTER 69

JULY 12, 1993

Esau stood up from his mother's grave and stretched. To the west, the sun was setting over the tree line, and he paused to appreciate the rich colors.

He would have to surrender his freedom once again. He would head back to Tina's house now. She was a nice woman. He had never met any women besides his mother, and Tina hadn't run away screaming like his mother said people would do. She had accepted him and talked to him.

Going back to her house was an admission of defeat. But her house was the only place he could go. Jacob would be in control of the farmhouse, and Esau would not be welcome there. After everything that had happened, for all he had talked of freedom, he was still a prisoner. Only now he had a different prison.

Would Daniel be his new jailer?

He walked deeper into the forest. Despite the slight chance of meeting someone along the trail, he preferred staying deeper in the forest. He could stay hidden among the trees almost the entire way back to Tina's house, where he would come out at the far end of her back yard. He would still have to cross a half dozen roads to get to that point; but with the light fading, that shouldn't cause much of a problem unless he was spotlighted suddenly in someone's headlights.

He found himself walking slower now than he had on his way to the funeral. He had rushed out of Tina's home almost as soon as he had read about his mother's funeral notice in the newspaper. He had been anxious to attend the funeral then. He had to be there if only to say goodbye symbolically to his mother. That was the least he could do.

Esau had sensed Jacob's confusion with all the details that he was being asked to prepare. Jacob had trouble handling two choices; but when he was presented with a half dozen or more, his mind overloaded. Esau guessed that the funeral director, knowing Jacob's limited capacity, was trying to take advantage of him. His mother had been fairly wealthy when she died, and all the money went to her only known heir, Jacob.

Esau had tried to send thoughts to Jacob's mind on which choices to make about his mother's funeral. In some cases, he got through to Jacob and helped his brother make a better choice. At other times, Jacob made some poor choices. The casket was not of the best quality, and it pained Esau to know that his mother's body was made all that much more susceptible to the earth because he had to remain in hiding.

He waded into the river until it was waist deep. That was as deep as it would get on him. Once across Flipping Creek, he would be only fifteen minutes away from Tina's. As he crossed, he heard a boom behind him then a small fountain of water erupted next to him. In the distance, someone yelled something. He heard another boom, and another eruption of water.

He turned and saw an orange-jacketed hunter a hundred yards away shooting at him.

"I found him! He's over here!" the hunter yelled.

He tried to hurry through the water, but he couldn't move quickly.

He heard more voices and people snapping branches as they tramped through the forest. Then he heard more booms from rifles. Something hit his arm, and he fell forward onto the bank of the river.

Some hunters ran hard trying to catch up with him. They looked like fireflies flitting through the dark shadows that the trees setting sun cast through the trees. But these fireflies were deadly. He turned and ran in the opposite direction.

A bullet hit him hard in the back and he roared. He stumbled and went down on one knee, but he forced himself to keep running. He screamed at the pain again, hoping to scare the hunters, but he didn't stop running.

If he did, he would be dead.

CHAPTER 70

JULY 12, 1993

When Tina heard the thump against the back door, she jumped out of her chair and nearly screamed. Daniel was on his feet and moving toward the door before she even recovered from her initial shock. If Brad had returned to bother her again, he was going to find himself looking down the barrel of Daniel's pistol.

Too many things were happening too quickly. Esau's area of safety was growing smaller. Brad was continuing to annoy Tina, and Chief Montgomery would run him out of town before too long. Fleetwood was a slowly tightening noose around all their necks.

In the kitchen, Daniel could see out the windows on the top half of the door and he didn't see anyone standing outside. Still, that didn't mean Brad couldn't be crouched below the door. In fact, he was so thin he could probably standing at the thin blind spot to the side.

Daniel moved closer to the door with his pistol poised and ready. He looked through the window and saw Esau's hairy feet sticking out from his dark sweatpants.

Fearing Esau was dead, he flung open the door and Esau fell into the kitchen. His eyes were closed, but Daniel could see his chest rising and falling as he breathed. He grabbed the huge man-ape under the arms and pulled him all the way into the kitchen and then kicked the door shut.

Tina walked into the kitchen and gasped. "What happened to him?"

"I do not know. He was lying against your door."

Daniel saw the puddle of blood forming beneath Esau's back. With a grunt, he rolled Esau's 350-pound body onto his side. He saw the two bullet holes in Esau's back and one in his shoulder.

"Damn." He was too late. The hunters had already found Esau and killed him for no other reason than he was different.

"What's wrong?" Tina asked.

"He has been shot, and he's lost a lot of blood," Daniel told her.

"Is he dead?"

Daniel started to nod, but then he put his hand on Esau's neck and felt for a pulse. It was there. Rapid and uneven. Esau must be in shock.

He saw no exit holes for the wounds either. That meant the bullets were still somewhere in Esau's body. He would have to get them out of Esau if the beast was to live.

"I need hydrogen peroxide, a sewing needle, thread, needle-nosed pliers, and a flashlight," Daniel said quickly, his medical training showing itself. "Do you have all that stuff around here?"

Tina nodded. "I think so."

She ran off to find the items. Meanwhile, Daniel took his shirt off and tried to use it to staunch the blood flow pouring from the two holes in Esau's back. Those were the critical wounds. The other bullet had pierced Esau's left bicep and was only a flesh wound.

Tina came back a few minutes later and laid all the items at Daniel's side. He did a quick inventory of the items and said, "Good. Boil some water and drop the pliers in the water."

"What are you going to do?" Tina asked.

"I have got to get the bullets out of his body, disinfect the wound, and stop his bleeding."

Tina frowned at the thought. "Do you know how to do that?"

"I know enough to make me dangerous. I used to be in medical school," Daniel told her.

Esau put his hand on Daniel's. Daniel looked down and saw that Esau's eyes were open.

"You are going to be all right, Esau. I can help you," Daniel told him.

Esau's head moved back and forth almost imperceptibly. "Let me die. I deserve to die. I've never lived."

Then Esau passed out.

When Daniel felt the pliers had been sterilized long enough, he told Tina to rinse them in cold water and bring them to him.

"What about what he said?" Tina asked.

"Would you let him die if you could save him?"

Tina shook her head and handed the pliers to Daniel.

"He still may die after I am done with him, but I've got to try," Daniel said.

Using the pliers like a pair of forceps, he inserted them into one of the wounds. Tina shined the flashlight into the wound, hoping to catch sight of the bullet. The hole filled with blood too quickly. However, when the pliers struck the metal bullet, Daniel heard the sound. He pulled the bullet free and then searched in the second wound for that bullet.

When both bullets were laying on the floor, he checked Esau to see if any major arteries had been nicked. None had that he could see, so Daniel sewed Esau's wounds up with the needle and thread.

"We need to make him comfortable. He is too heavy to move, so he will have to stay right here."

"I can make up a bed and we can roll him onto it," Tina told him. Daniel nodded. "Good. I want him on his stomach so I can keep an eye on those back wounds."

"You did a good job on him," Tina said.

Daniel patted her hand. "For his sake I hope so."

"You should have become a doctor instead of a Nazi hunter."

He shrugged and looked at his bloody hands. Why hadn't he finished getting his degree in medicine? Then his hands could have been healing tools instead of killing tools.

"Sometimes I feel like I did not have a choice," he said more to himself than Tina.

"You always have a choice."

He looked at her, shocked to hear his own words used against him.

"Perhaps, but if I had continued in medical school, I would never have met you."

"Brown noser." She glanced at Esau. "Will he be all right now?"

"I hope so. We cannot very well take him to a doctor. A lot of his recovery will depend on if he wants to live or not, and at this point, I think that question is a toss-up with Esau."

Esau lay on his stomach breathing slowly, his huge body moving up and down with each breath.

CHAPTER 71

JULY 12, 1993

The information that came over the fax machine disappointed Steve.

He picked up the pile of paper and sat down to read through them in detail. He had sent out requests for background information on Daniel Levitt, Joseph Speer, Albert Speer, and Eva Lachman.

He had been hoping that Daniel's background check would show some technicality that Steve could use to arrest the man as a suspect in Eva Lachman's murder, some connection that would give Daniel the slightest motive to have killed her. Steve would have been satisfied with even something unrelated, which he could use to run Levitt out of Fleetwood. Maybe his green card had expired or he might be wanted for questioning in some other crime.

Daniel's sheet was clean but not pleasing. Daniel had been responsible for the arrest of six Nazi war criminals. Then Steve noticed that the youngest of these had been fifty-three years old. Daniel was truly a Nazi hunter, and a Nazi hunter with connections. The only thing noted of interest in the report was that Daniel had accidentally killed a woman in Africa named Aria Mueller. She was the wife of a war criminal named Karl Mueller. Daniel had shot at Mueller and a ricochet had hit Aria. Though Daniel was eventually cleared of murder, the Israeli government had quickly pulled him out of Africa before the case even went to trial.

The Speers yielded more-interesting information because they did not exist according to the state police records. The report stated that Joseph and Albert Speer were suspected of being Joseph and Karl Mueller, which explained why one set of prints at the Speer home had been identified as Karl Mueller's. Karl was an Auschwitz doctor sought for immoral medical experiments. Joseph was his son and not wanted for any crime.

Eva Lachman's background showed nothing unusual. She was a survivor of Auschwitz, had inherited family money and immigrated to America in 1952. The fact that her record showed nothing unusual was disconcerting because it gave no clue why Eva had made her home into a fortress. That's when Steve saw the chain.

Eva Lachman had feared Mueller would come after her so she had made her house into a fortress. Mueller, a.k.a. Speer, had come to Fleetwood with his son to find Eva. Their connection was that Mueller was an ex-Auschwitz doctor and Eva was a former Auschwitz prisoner. Daniel Levitt had followed Karl Mueller from wherever he had been hiding to Fleetwood.

Had Karl killed Eva as revenge for his son's death?

Albert Speer or Karl Mueller had told him that Eva had been the woman who killed Joseph Mueller. Had Eva come to Speer's house to kill Karl and wound up killing Joseph? That made little sense. She was afraid of Mueller, her house testified to that. Going to kill him was an offensive act that a scared woman wouldn't have done. Besides, Mueller's fingerprints hadn't been found at Eva's house; Levitt's had.

What about the unidentified prints? Could they have been Mueller's? Steve doubted that. The lab had identified Mueller's prints from his house. They should have been able to identify them from Eva's house.

But if Eva had killed Joseph, then Mueller might have killed her in an act of revenge over his son's death. Steve shook his head.

Judging by Speer's reaction, Steve doubted the old man had killed Eva. He had been too surprised to hear the news. Someone had killed her, though.

Steve flipped through the various fax sheets rereading them while he drank a cup of coffee.

He didn't like the web that was forming over his town. Even if he was right about the connections between Eva, Levitt, and Mueller, he still hadn't figured out how the murder of the two teenagers and the break-in at Rick Daniel's house fit into all the information he had just learned.

He didn't think he would like the answer when he found out either.

CHAPTER 72

JULY 12, 1993

Mueller sat on the dirty sofa polishing his pistol, lost in his own thoughts of hatred and revenge. This was all he lived for now. The house was dark, but he didn't need light to see what he was doing. Besides, he didn't want to alert the twins to his presence in their house until it was too late.

Karl hadn't used the pistol in decades. This luger had saved his life in 1945 when he had used it to kill a Russian captain during his escape from the concentration camp. Now he would use it to save his soul and cleanse the world of his greatest mistake. Karl slid the clip into the handle and set the pistol on the sofa next to him. It seemed to glow in the darkness anxiously waiting to serve him once again.

One or both of the twins would return here. This was their home; probably the only home they would remember. They would return and they would die, and then Karl would die.

Karl looked at the pistol. One shot each and the twins would be dead, but would that be enough? Would justice be served?

Jacob had nearly choked Joseph to death before Eva had shot him.

Even then, Joseph had lingered for ten minutes or so afterward. No, a quick death would not be right. The twins must suffer as Joseph had. An eye for an eye. Joseph hadn't deserved that. He had never done harm to anyone.

The evil must destroy itself. He must maintain the control of his body long enough to cause the twins to kill each other. That would be justice. Nothing would cause them such pain as to destroy part of themselves.

Evil must destroy itself.

If Jacob and Esau destroyed each other, that would be best, and for the one that survived, Mueller would end it then. With one bullet for the surviving twin and then one bullet for himself.

Then it would be over. His family would be reunited. Aria, Joseph, and Karl. He would return to God with a clear conscience.

CHAPTER 73

JULY 12, 1993

Daniel sat on the wooden kitchen chair with his elbows on his knees and a cup of steaming coffee in his hands. The tendrils of steam carried the coffee's aroma to Daniel's nose, but he barely noticed it. He stared silently at Esau. The beast was sprawled on his stomach. His body twitched occasionally. Once, Daniel even thought he heard Esau moan.

Was Esau dreaming?

What would a half-man, half-ape dream of? Freedom? Being human? Killing Mueller? All of the above?

Tina walked into the kitchen. She laid her hands on Daniel's shoulders and gently massaged his neck.

"How is he doing?" she asked.

Daniel shrugged. "It is hard to say. I am judging his vital signs by human standards, but he is not totally human."

"Does it make that much difference?"

"It might. He had a fever of 105.2. He has lost a lot of blood so his blood pressure is low. He probably should have a transfusion, but would human blood kill him? I don't know. I doubt anyone does. The bullets are out at least and the wound is patched up. I do not think there will be an infection, but time will tell," Daniel said, frustrated that he might not have helped Esau at all.

Daniel didn't take his eyes off Esau as he spoke. During his previous meetings with Esau, he had tried not to stare at the beast. He didn't want to make Esau any more self-conscious than he already was, but now that Esau was unconscious Daniel could study him all he wanted.

Tina squatted down next to Daniel. "Why don't you get some sleep? I can watch him." Daniel shook his head. "I'll wake you if anything happens," she promised.

"Northwest," Daniel murmured. "What?"

Daniel looked at Tina. "I need to take Esau to the Pacific Northwest. We can set up a farm way out in the country with plenty of forest for him to enjoy. He will be safe. Even if someone sees him out there, they will just think he is Bigfoot like they do here. Only out there, it would not be such a big deal. I do not think they would try to kill him."

"Isn't that the same thing his mother tried to do?" Tina said. "I mean, keeping him isolated on a farm."

Daniel shook his head furiously. "No! She kept him behind the fence as if she did not trust him to decide for himself. I do trust him, but for him to have any freedom, a lot of people cannot be around, or he might get shot again."

Daniel thought Esau looked more human unconscious. His features were relaxed. He reminded Daniel of an actor in an old Planet of the Apes movie. He looked like an ape, but you could still tell he was a man underneath all the make-up.

"When will you leave?" Tina asked.

"As soon as Esau is able, and if he wants to go. I can not make him go if he has other ideas."

"What about Karl Mueller?"

Daniel shrugged. "I do not care about him. Let Adam come to Fleetwood and get the old man if he wants Mueller that badly. Mueller will be dead within a few years probably before we could even get him to trial."

An awkward silence fell between Tina and Daniel as if they were each standing on opposite sides of a canyon trying to talk to each other. Then Daniel asked, "Will you come with me?"

"Where?"

"The Northwest. When Esau and I leave, I want you to come too." Tina thought about it. "I've never lived with anyone I wasn't related to. My Catholic upbringing, I guess."

Daniel nodded. "That sounds reasonable to me."

Tina looked surprised at Daniel's response. "That sounds like a vague proposal."

He smiled and took her hand in his. "Forgive me. I am not used to asking someone to marry me."

Tina stood up still holding his hand. "But you barely know me," she said.

"I know more about you than most people, I am sure. During the past few days, I have seen how you react under the worst conditions; being attacked by Brad, meeting Esau. If I can still tolerate you during what has probably been the most-trying time of your life, I think the rest of our lives should be easy. Do you agree?"

Tina went to the sink and got a cup of water. She sipped it without saying anything. She only stared at Daniel over the rim of the cup. "You're serious, aren't you?"

"What do you think?"

Esau growled loudly as his body had convulsion-like shakes. His eyes opened, and he sat upright on the floor. He grabbed at his head and held his head between his hands. He looked at Daniel through clouded eyes. Daniel saw only dim recognition in them.

"He is coming," Esau whispered. "He's coming after me. He wants to kill to me."

Daniel kneeled down next to Esau and put his hand on his shoulder trying to ease the huge beast back on the makeshift bed. Esau refused to be pushed down. And even in his weakened condition, Esau was still stronger than Daniel.

"Who Esau? Who is after you?" Daniel asked. Esau shook his head. He was crying. "Jacob."

His eyes rolled back into his head and he fell back to the floor, unconscious. Daniel barely caught him in time so Esau didn't slam his head against the floor.

"How would he know if his brother is after him? You don't think Jacob shot Esau, do you?"

Daniel shook his head. He lightly fingered the fading bruises on his neck. "No, Jacob is a hands-on sort of guy. Maybe he can sense his brother. They say twins sometimes sense things about each other that other brothers and sisters cannot do."

"Does that mean Jacob's coming now? That he's coming here to kill Esau?" Tina guessed.

"It may. You had better stay here with me. I have my pistol, which should stop even Jacob." Daniel didn't sound so convinced, though.

"Let me lock the doors and windows first. That may not stop Jacob, but it will warn us if he is coming. Besides, I'll at least feel safer that way."

Tina set her cup on the counter and started into the living room. "Tina?"

She stopped and looked at Daniel. He was blushing, but he maintained eye contact with her.

"Will you marry me?" he said.

Tina smiled. "Yes."

CHAPTER 74

JULY 12, 1993

Steve looked at the footprint in the soft dirt and shook his head slowly. It matched the one he had seen at Rick Martin. This was freaky. It was like something out of the Twilight Zone, not Western Maryland.

"Did you see what they shot at?" Steve asked his deputy.

Lee shook his head. "I just heard the shots and came running. Whatever it was, was already gone by then. All that was left were these footprints, which disappear on the rocks, and this." He shoved a branch in Steve's direction. Steve saw the brown spots on the leaves and recognized them as blood.

"Any ideas then at what they shot at? A bear maybe?" Steve guessed. Lee shook his head. "They said whatever it was, was running on two legs and had clothes on."

"Clothes? They were shooting at a man?"

"They swore to me it was Bigfoot."

"Have they been drinking? If they have, and they've shot a man..." Steve started to say.

Lee shook his head. "They are all stone cold sober and mad that they didn't bring down Bigfoot."

Steve looked skeptical. "I've never heard of Bigfoot running around in clothes."

He followed the large footprints until they disappeared on a pile of exposed rocks. He had no doubt these were the same footprints he had, seen outside Rick Daniel's house. The hair samples they collected would probably match those at all the various sites where crimes had happened the past few days.

There's a monster in Fleetwood.

He didn't want to believe it, but what else could make those footprints? They weren't human, not with that side toe. They weren't a bear's footprints since there were toes, not pads and claws. They looked more like an ape's footprint, but there were no apes in this area. Especially not apes that wore clothes.

Steve turned and looked back to where Lee was standing. He wanted to voice his ideas about the origin of the footprints. Maybe a dancing bear had escaped from the circus or some such nonsense, but he was afraid he'd sound like a fool to his deputy.

As he started back towards his deputy, he saw a large form rise up behind Lee. At first he thought it was a person. The form was wearing clothes, and he even looked vaguely familiar. His face was hidden in shadows.

Steve started to raise his hand to point behind Lee, but the large man swung his arm and knocked Lee up against a tree.

The man saw Steve and roared, not yelled, but roared. Steve held his ground. That's when he recognized the man.

"Jacob!" he yelled.

Jacob ignored him and kneeled down on the ground so he could stick his nose in the footprint. Steve slowly drew his pistol, trying not to attract any attention to himself.

"Jacob, just be still. You don't want to get yourself in anymore trouble than you're already in."

Lee stirred and Jacob looked at him, then Steve. Steve fired. The shot went high and Jacob rolled away and ran into the woods.

Steve hurried after him. He reached Lee who was holding his back and moaning. He could hear Jacob crashing through the trees, but he couldn't see anything. The brush was too thick.

He squatted down next to Lee.

"Did you see who it was?" Lee asked.

Steve nodded slowly. "Jacob Lachman, but he wasn't acting like he normally acts. He was acting more like an animal."

CHAPTER 75

JULY 13, 1993

Daniel was on edge throughout the night. He expected to see Jacob smash through the kitchen door at any moment, but that moment never happened. Daniel paced the kitchen, never straying far from Esau in case the man-ape needed his attentions. He continually looked out the kitchen windows into the backyard. Jacob could come at any moment or never. Whether or not he would comenot, all depended on how coherent Esau had truly been when he woke up earlier.

Tina fell asleep some time after three in the morning.

That surprised Daniel because she seemed more afraid than him, if that was possible. After all, he was the one Jacob had almost killed. Daniel was sure Jacob wouldn't hesitate to finish the job. Yet, Tina insisted on locking all the doors and windows. She also put a butcher's knife under her pillow in case Jacob came into her bedroom.

"Daniel?"

Daniel spun around on his heels and lifted his pistol. Esau was lying on the floor, but his eyes were open. Daniel rushed to his side and squatted down beside Esau and felt his forehead. The fever had broken. Esau's face was damp with sweat.

"I'm thirsty," Esau whispered.

Daniel filled a glass of water and brought it to Esau. He rolled over, propped himself up on his elbows, and gulped it.

"How long was I out of it?" Esau asked.

"About twelve hours," Daniel said after checking his watch.

"Are you all right?"

"I should ask you that."

"I remember sensing Jacob coming after me."

"You said as much. I have been walking on pins and needles all night long expecting him to attack us. He has not come yet."

Esau closed his eyes. "No, he's further away now. He must not have been able to follow my thoughts because of the fever. It must have interfered or something."

"So we are safe?" Daniel asked.

"For now, but he won't give up. He wants to kill me. And now he has a good reason."

Daniel relaxed in the chair. "He is not the only one who wants to kill you. For such a nice guy, you have many enemies."

"I thought Mueller could... would help me. I really did." Esau clenched his fist. "I was so stupid. Even Jacob knows enough to hate Mueller. Mama was right all along."

"I want to leave town, Esau, and I want to take you and Tina with me. It is not really safe for either of you here."

Esau drew his knees up to his chest and smiled. "I like Tina. She's nice."

"I think I love her."

Esau nodded. "Where do you want to go?"

"Oregon or Washington. We will buy a farm with lots of land. I have enough money stashed away to afford it. You will be free to roam without scaring anyone, and I will be able to get away from the committee."

"It sounds good, but how will you get me out of town? Half of the men in town are out hunting me. That's how I got in this condition. They hunted me like I was an animal and shot me in the back. Jacob's hunting me. Dr. Mueller's hunting me."

Daniel stared at Esau for a while watching the very human expressions on the very animal face. "Jacob can impersonate a normal person. If we shaved you clean, could you pass for normal?"

Esau shook his head as he rubbed his hand over his hairy face. "I've tried it more than once. With no hair on my face I look like some sort of alien."

Daniel thought for a moment. "What if we left enough hair on your face so that it looked as if you had a beard and mustache? Put a wide-brimmed hat on your head?"

Esau rubbed his chin. "Sort of a Santa Claus look, huh?"

"Something like that." Daniel was getting excited. The more he thought about it, the more he thought it would work. With a little work and night travel, Esau would be a plausible person at least long enough for them to get across the country.

"Let's try it," Esau agreed.

Daniel went into Tina's bathroom and found a disposable razor. Then he took a pair of scissors from Tina's sewing room. He went back into the kitchen. Esau had pulled himself up and was sitting on a chair.

Daniel soaped up Esau's face with dishwashing soap and began his work. Using the razor, He shaved Esau's face down to the bottom of his neck, leaving on the hair above his lip and on his chin. This gave Esau a beard and mustache. Then Daniel combed and styled the hair on top of Esau's head and used the scissors to give it as much shape as he could.

When he was finished, he stepped back and looked at Esau. In the bright light of the kitchen, Esau still looked too odd to pass for a person. Daniel turned off the lights and looked again with only the light from the living room shining. Esau looked more convincing.

"Wow."

Daniel looked over his shoulder. Tina was standing in the doorway. "Good morning, Tina," Esau said. "How do I look?"

"You look better than an ugly cousin I have who lives in Richmond, but at least you look human."

Esau smiled.

"Daniel, you can start a second career as a hair stylist in Washington," Tina said as she wrapped her arms around his waist.

Daniel and Esau laughed. Daniel walked back over to the kitchen window.

"I guess it is time to leave."

CHAPTER 76

JULY 13, 1993

Karl sat on the couch staring out the double doors, which looked out over the fenced backyard. This was the home that Joseph had wanted and it had become the home where he died. Now Karl would wait to die. He knew he would die soon. The coughs had grown steadily worse, convulsing his weak body each time they came. He had known he would die for years. As a doctor, he had recognized the signs long before Joseph had. Karl had had time to accept his fate. He was no longer afraid of the end, only of failing to stop what he had begun.

He held the pistol between his legs. If he could only get those aberrations of nature within his sights, he would complete his final experiment. Then he could die in peace.

How could he find the twins? They had abandoned their house.

Everything was still there. Everything except them. They had left everything they had known and given into their wild sides. The only thing Karl had seen out there was the police chief. Luckily, he had got out of the house before the police officer saw him.

The morning shadows stretched out across the lawn as the sun rose over the trees.

Today. He would have to find them today. They were out there somewhere, probably still in hiding. He had created them so he should know them better than anyone else. He had to flush them out.

He stood up and shuffled toward the bedroom. Right now he needed sleep. He was almost to the doorway when the sliding glass door behind him shattered. He turned and a dark form knocked him down as it ran past. He heard it crash down the stairs into the basement. It screamed and Karl shuddered.

Karl recognized this twin as Jacob. He had the same rage as the Jacob he had seen tear apart his basement lab, but this Jacob looked more animal. His hair had grown out, and he looked even wilder than he had before, if that was possible.

One of the twins had found him. Karl grabbed at his pistol, which he had dropped when he was knocked down. Jacob screamed again. Jacob grabbed Karl by the shirt. As Jacob pulled Mueller to his feet, the old German knew he was going to die. He was going to fail and the twins would live to spread their evil.

"Where is he?" Jacob screamed in his face. His breath was hot and foul smelling.

Karl didn't answer, and the creature shook him.

"Where is he? You brought him here before. Where is he?" Esau. Jacob thought his brother was here.

"He's not here," Karl whispered.

"Where is he? He was here before."

"He wouldn't come back here. I want to kill him," Karl said defiantly.

If he was going to die, he would face it as a soldier.

Jacob looked confused. "Why did you want to kill him?"

"He is evil. He is an aberration of nature. He is not human. He was never meant to be and so he should be killed." Karl wasn't brave enough to add that he thought the same thing about Jacob.

Jacob set Karl on the floor, but still held onto Karl's shirt.

"He's a bad boy. Mama knew he was different from me. That's why she never let him out of the yard. Not like me. I could go into town for ice cream all by myself."

Karl thought he detected an opportunity and followed up on it. "Are you searching for Esau?"

Karl heard a growl deep in Jacob's chest at the mention of Esau's name.

"Yes, he killed my mother. I want to kill him. He's been bad. I want to punish him."

So it had been Esau who killed Eva. That surprised Mueller. Esau hadn't seemed violent at all. If it had been anyone, Mueller would have expected it to be Jacob. Perhaps Esau was not as civilized as he pretended to be. He might only be able to hide his bestial nature better than Jacob.

"I want to kill him too," Jacob said. "Esau's bad."

Mueller nodded. "Maybe we could help each other."

Jacob thought for a moment and then tightened his grip. "Why should I help you? You're Dr. Mueller. Mama said you were evil."

Mueller thought quickly. "I'm not Mueller. My name is Albert Speer." Jacob cocked his head to the side. "Then why did my Mama get so mad at you and have me break into the house?"

"She was mad at me because I was trying to kill Esau. Remember? She didn't think your brother was bad, but we know differently, don't we? Esau killed your poor mother. If I had killed him first, your mother would still be alive."

Jacob nodded and Karl knew he was safe for now. He would use Jacob to find Esau and then kill them both in a way befitting their sins.

"Can you find Esau, Jacob?" he asked.

Jacob nodded and tapped his head. "Sometimes I feel him here, and I try to follow the feeling. It's hard and takes a lot of concentration to follow, but I can do it sometimes when I really want to. Esau can do it, too, and I don't enjoy having him in my head."

"Can you find your brother now?"

"I have to stay away from where other people are, though. They have guns and shoot at me when they see me. They think I'm like Esau... bad, just because I'm his brother. But I'm good. I didn't kill Mama. Esau did."

Karl patted Jacob's shoulder as a gesture of sympathy. "Jacob, if you can track down your brother, I can drive you to wherever you need to go. You'll be able to find him. No one will see you in my car."

Jacob smiled. "That's a good idea. I think Esau has friends now who are protecting him. He told Mama and me about a man named Daniel Levitt he had talked to."

Karl hadn't heard the Nazi hunter's name in years. "Daniel Levitt. Are you sure?"

Jacob nodded.

So Aria's murderer was in town. Would Daniel Levitt be his executioner as well? Not until the twins were dead. That was his priority right now. After that, Levitt could do what he wanted.

"We have to work quickly, Jacob. I know Daniel Levitt. He's a dangerous man. He is a friend of Dr. Mueller's," he lied.

Jacob stamped his foot on the floor and the entire house shook. "I knew it," he said. "I knew it, but Esau said he wasn't and Mama believed him."

"If you can track your brother, Jacob, I will take care of Daniel. He won't interfere with you and Esau. You can punish Esau the way you want to."

"That's good."

Karl nodded. "Yes, yes it is."

Then for the first time in a long time, Mueller smiled.

CHAPTER 77

JULY 13, 1993

Daniel and Tina walked into Kay's and sat down at the counter. Kay had just opened up for the breakfast crowd and she already looked tired. Daniel was nervous about coming into town, but Tina said she wouldn't leave without saying goodbye to Kay.

Kay smiled at both of them. "So what brings you in here this morning?" Kay glanced at Daniel. "Not another milkshake?"

Tina shook her head and smiled sheepishly. Kay smiled and leaned forward.

"You've got a secret, don't you?" Tina nodded. "Well, don't keep it from me, girl. I've got work to do."

Daniel looked around and for the first time noticed all the orange-jacketed hunters sitting around laughing and drinking their morning coffees. These were the men who had shot Esau.

"What's the matter, Daniel?" Tina asked.

"Nothing. Just a little nervous, I guess."

Tina smiled and put her hand on his.

Kay glanced over at Daniel who was grinning now. Then she looked back at Tina.

"I don't see a ring on your finger, so I guess you didn't get yourselves married."

"Not yet," Tina said.

Kay clapped her hands together. "Really. That's wonderful, dear. Settling down a little bit will keep you away from some of the jerks you've dated. And you," Kay turned to Daniel. "I don't know you from Adam, but you had better take good care of this girl, or you'll have me to answer to."

Daniel took Tina's hand in his. "Oh, I intend to. She is helping me get a second chance."

"A second chance at what?"

"A second chance at the kind of life I want to live."

Kay laughed. "Well, obviously you've never been married if you think you'll live the kind of life you want to live. Are you going to get married here in town?"

Tina glanced at Daniel. "No, we're leaving for Oregon."

Kay straightened up. "Oregon? That's on the other side of the country. Why do you need to go all the way out there?"

"That is where my ranch is," Daniel lied, partially. He intended on buying a ranch. He just hadn't done it yet.

Frowning, Kay asked, "When are you leaving?"

"Tonight."

Kay put her hands on her hips. "You're not giving me a chance to throw you a bridal shower or anything."

"We cannot stay around here," Daniel said.

"Why? Brad won't bother Tina again. Everybody's too wound up about trying to find Bigfoot to listen to Brad talk you down."

Daniel wondered if Tina would say something about Esau to her friend. Instead, she said, "Daniel's family also lives in Oregon, and they're going to want to meet me. Daniel was just out here on a business trip. He has to get back to his ranch."

Kay hugged Tina, then Daniel. "We'll wish you both the best. Promise me you'll write and keep me up to date. Name the first girl you have after me."

Tina laughed. Daniel turned red from embarrassment.

"Kay, I also need to ask a favor of you," Tina said.

"Name it, darling. It will be my wedding gift to the both of you," Kay said.

"Since we've got to leave tonight, I won't be able to take all my things with me right now. Can you watch my house until I get everything out?"

Kay nodded. "No problem."

Tina handed her the keys and thanked her again. After a few minutes more of small talk, Daniel and Tina were able to pull themselves away.

Outside the diner, Daniel said, "You are a convincing liar."

Tina giggled. "Would you rather I have said we were going to smuggle Bigfoot out of Fleetwood?"

"No, I am glad you did not." He paused. "I have to go back to Maryland House to get my things. I will drop you off at your house and then come back, ready to leave, in about an hour."

Daniel kissed Tina before she got out of the car. "You can still back out of this if you want, you know. Esau and I are the only ones who have to leave. You are young with a lot of years ahead of you. You are tying yourself down to a lifetime job."

Tina shook her head. "You worry about Esau. I'll worry about you. If I didn't want to go, I wouldn't."

She climbed out of the car and headed toward her house. She heard Daniel's car drive off behind her. It sounded like a roller coaster being cranked up the first hill. She wouldn't be able to handle that noise all the way to Oregon. He needed a new muffler.

Esau was sitting on the sofa watching the television when Tina came in. His chest and arm were wrapped in white bandages, which were actually an old white sheet of Tina's.

"How are you feeling?" Tina asked.

"Stiff. A little achy, but my fever is gone," he told her. "I'll be able to leave."

"Daniel's going back to the Maryland House to pack. I'm going to pack up my stuff, too. We're going to get you out of here to some place where you won't be in danger."

"That's an enormous sacrifice on both your parts."

"I don't know about Daniel, but I needed a change, anyway."

"I appreciate this. You two are the first friends I've ever had, and I can't imagine any friends being better," Esau said.

"Do you need to get anything from your house that you want to take with you?"

Esau shook his head. "I couldn't stand going back there again. It hurt me enough when I went back to help Daniel. Let Jacob have my stuff. It will drive him crazy trying to figure out how it works."

Tina walked into her bedroom and pulled her suitcase from under her bed. She would not be able to take much with her. Maybe she could have Kay finish the packing job and send everything on to Oregon instead of coming back to do it herself.

She had never been west of the Mississippi River. She wondered what it would be like. The pictures she always saw of Oregon showed lots of gigantic trees. She was finally getting away from Western Maryland after wanting to all her life, but she was nervous and a little scared.

She grabbed a pile of her clothes and tossed them into the suitcase.

As she sorted through the drawers in her bureau, she heard a crash and a loud growl from the living room. She headed for the door thinking that Esau had fallen. Something struck the shared wall between her living room and bedroom. The entire house shook under the impact.

Tina stepped away from the wall and headed for the door again. As she did, she saw Esau fly into the hallway and land on his back. He groaned and glanced at her. He waved her back into the bedroom.

She started to move backwards when someone who looked a lot like Esau stepped over Esau and stomped on his chest. The only person it could be was Jacob.

Jacob was going to kill his brother.

CHAPTER 78

JULY 13, 1993

Esau heard his brother's approach a split second too late for him to prepare for Jacob's attack. A heavy footstep, a guttural growl, and Jacob came crashing through the bay window, tearing the curtain down as he landed on top of Esau. Esau had been rising out of his chair, but Jacob knocked him sideways sprawling on the floor. Spikes of pain shot through Esau's wounded arm as he landed on it. Jacob sat on top of his brother, shaking off the curtain.

Esau had never seen his brother look so animal-like. With his facial hair grown out, Jacob barely looked any different than Esau usually did. Jacob growled and snarled and beat on his chest. Despite all his pretense at being human, Jacob was just as much a beast as Esau.

Esau thrust his hips into the air and threw his brother off of him. He rolled to the side and began to stand. Jacob dove into him throwing him into the hallway that led to the bedroom and bathroom.

Esau saw Tina, looking scared, standing in the doorway to her bedroom. He waved her away. Jacob couldn't be allowed to see her. Jacob would kill her as he had done to the teenagers in the forest. Anyone Jacob thought was connected with Esau would be in danger.

Jacob leaped into the air and tried to jump on top of Esau's chest, but Esau pressed himself flat against the wall. Jacob landed on the floor and the entire house shook. Rolling back onto the floor, Esau grabbed his brother's leg and pushed him away. Jacob staggered and fell back into the living room, giving Esau time to stand up and catch a breath.

Besides the pains that Jacob had inflicted on him, the bullet wounds in his back hurt him. Esau could feel himself bleeding so he must have broken open his stitches.

He hurried to the far side of the living room to keep Jacob as far away from the bedroom and Tina as he could. Jacob darted forward and tried to punch Esau, but he ducked in time. Instead of striking his face, Jacob's fist smashed through the wall into the kitchen. Esau took advantage of the moment and punched Jacob in the stomach. Jacob grunted, then growled, as he pulled his fist free from the wall. Esau hit him in the face. Jacob staggered, but didn't fall.

Jacob jumped and grabbed his brother's throat between his hands.

Esau tried to punch Jacob again, but the punches seemed to have no effect on his brother. Jacob was too angry to feel pain. What more could Esau do? Was Jacob the stronger of the two of them?

No, throughout his childhood Esau could remember many instances where he had proven he was stronger than Jacob. Esau had more of his father's strength, but Jacob had more of his father's anger. The two might cancel each other out now. Jacob's anger was strengthening him.

Esau growled, but Jacob squeezed even harder, cutting off his air.

Esau straight-armed Jacob in the chest, but Jacob grunted and held on. He squeezed even harder.

Esau saw stars in his vision and he panicked. He didn't want to die. He was finally free, and he didn't want to waste that freedom. It had cost him too dearly. He wanted to enjoy being free although he didn't deserve it. He had killed his own mother. Maybe he should let Jacob kill him. Maybe Jacob was doing the world a favor. But how many people had Jacob killed? At least the two teenagers in the forest that Esau had sensed die. Wouldn't letting Jacob continue to kill unchecked be the same thing as helping him kill?

Esau raked his nails across his brother's face drawing blood. Jacob screamed and let go of Esau's throat. Esau leaned forward and bit his brother's leg like an animal trying to end its opponent's mobility. Sensing Esau's tactic, Jacob pulled his leg away. But he moved too quickly, and it threw him off balance.

Esau fell onto his brother using all his weight to knock the breath out of him. Jacob pushed him away, and both of them got to their feet. Esau pounded on his chest and kept in a low crouch. He had lost all sense of fighting like a human and he was defending himself in the way that felt most natural.

"Go away, Jacob. Leave me alone," Esau ordered as he bared his teeth at his brother.

"I'm going to kill you just like you killed Mama."

As Jacob charged, Esau clasped his hands together and swung them like a club. His fists caught Jacob on the chin snapping his head to the side. Jacob fell to the floor as if he'd hit a wall and lay still.

Esau waited at a safe distance, circling his brother until he noticed Jacob's chest wasn't moving. He rushed to Jacob's side and felt for his pulse at the side of Jacob's neck. There was none. He turned Jacob's head to the side. It was too loose. Feeling behind Jacob's neck and through the skin, he could feel the odd shape of the spine. He had broken Jacob's neck.

He had killed again. First his mother, now his brother. He had let too much of his animal's instinct take over.

He cradled his brother's head and shoulders in his lap. "I'm sorry, Jacob. I'm sorry. I didn't want to kill you, but you wouldn't stop. I had to. I'm sorry."

He touched his forehead to his brother's and cried.

"It's quite all right, Esau. You'll be joining him in a moment," Mueller said.

Esau looked over his shoulder and saw the Nazi doctor pointing the pistol at his head. Esau took a deep breath and looked away.

CHAPTER 79

JULY 13, 1993

"Move away from him, Mueller."

Karl Mueller turned away from Esau and saw Daniel Levitt standing across the room. He lowered his pistol to his side.

"Do not think that because you need to be close to hit a target with a pistol, I need to be," Daniel warned.

Mueller looked at Daniel standing across the room in the garage doorway. Daniel had his own pistol pointed at the old Nazi.

Mueller sighed. "Go ahead and shoot me then. It doesn't matter. If I die without killing both of the abominations I created, then I have failed. If I live, I will try to kill the beast again. One of them is dead. Let me finish my work; then you can do with me what you want," Mueller said. "I'm not afraid of you anymore. I'm only afraid of failing."

Daniel glanced at Esau. He was squatting in a crouch. His elbows were slightly bent and his hands rested on the floor. He looked as if he were about to launch himself into the air.

"Go ahead, Jew. Shoot me. Or do you only shoot unarmed women?" Daniel's finger tightened on the trigger but he restrained himself. Killing Mueller would be so easy.

"Esau, is Tina all right?"

"Yes."

"And Jacob?"

Tears formed and rolled down the sides of his cheeks. "He's dead. killed him. I'm alone now. All alone."

"You're not alone, Esau. You have us." It was Tina speaking from the hallway. Esau turned his head slightly and smiled weakly at her.

"You are friends, not family," Esau said.

"Don't make it sound like a loss. You haven't had friends to know how dear they can be."

Mueller stepped around from behind Esau and tossed his pistol off to the side. Tina hurried over and grabbed it. Mueller turned his back to Daniel and walked into the kitchen.

"Stop!" Daniel ordered.

"Shoot me in the back if you want me to stop, Jew, otherwise I will walk out that door and choose my next fight."

He continued walking slowly giving Daniel an ample enough target.

Tina stared at Daniel, but said nothing. Daniel's focus narrowed to the nape of Mueller's neck. One shot and it would be over. He would be freed from his obligation to Adam and to his father.

But he would never be freed from the guilt. Didn't Aria Mueller still haunt his dreams at night? Did he really want her husband to join her? What about the face in the mirror? What would he see when he looked in the mirror next? Where would Mueller's name be tattooed?

Daniel lowered the pistol to his side. "Daniel?" Tina said.

"Let him go," Daniel whispered.

Esau looked up. "No!"

Esau jumped to his feet spinning around in mid-air. Mueller started to turn to face him, but Esau grabbed him by the back of the neck and slammed him up against the wall. Mueller's nose started to bleed, but he didn't make a sound. He truly wasn't afraid.

"Esau, no!" Daniel yelled.

"Yes! He wanted to kill me. He wanted me to kill Jacob. He's evil. He deserves to be killed. Mama was right. I should have listened to her."

Esau brought his face right up next to the old man's and growled into Mueller's ear.

Daniel moved up next to his friend. "Maybe so, Esau, but take it from someone who knows. You don't want to be his killer. For him, the pain will be over; you'll be doing him a favor, but for you it will be just beginning. Don't you have enough death on your conscience? Do you want to add another life to the guilt you're feeling?"

Mueller's eyes focused on Daniel, then Esau. The old Nazi closed his eyes.

Esau lowered Mueller so that the old man's feet could touch the ground. "We can't just let him walk away," he said to Daniel.

"Why not? I cannot kill him, for the same reasons you cannot kill him. We both already have ghosts haunting us. Why add his to the crowd? I have bigger plans for my life than trying to atone for killing him."

"He'll come after us," Esau persisted.

Daniel pointed at Esau. "Look at him, Esau. He is an old man. He is sick and dying. The pain that his sickness is causing him will be more than anything we could ever do to him."

Esau hesitated.

"Do not let him finally make you into the beast all these years of living in the farm house couldn't do. Part of being human is being merciful rather than vengeful. If you can master that, you'll be more human than most people, especially him."

Esau let go of Mueller. The old man turned and slid to the floor. He buried his head in his hands and wept.

"I am not a beast," Esau said quietly.

Tina took him by the arm and led him toward Daniel. "No, you're not."

Daniel took Esau by the arm and Tina by the hand and walked out of the house without looking back.

CHAPTER 80

AUGUST 24, 1996

Daniel walked out onto the front porch of the two-story cape cod. He shaded his eyes and looked over the front pasture area. He and Tina owned three-hundred acres of pasture and timber. He had finally found his home.

Tina was in the clearing, hoeing her small vegetable garden. After leaving Fleetwood, she had discovered she enjoyed many of the things she thought she had despised in Maryland. Like gardening and being fat from pregnancy. Her swollen belly made movement difficult, and Daniel wished she would stay off her feet until the baby came, but Tina was a hard-headed woman. He knew that when he married her, but he hadn't quite realized just how stubborn she could be.

"Going somewhere?" Esau asked.

Daniel looked around, but he didn't see Esau. Then a movement high in the tree caught his eye, and he saw Esau shimmying down the towering redwood. The man-ape dropped the last ten feet and landed on the ground in a crouch.

"I just got a call from Larry Hijab. His stud is down and looking pretty sick," Daniel told him.

Daniel had gotten his DVM degree last year. He had to do some finagling to get into veterinary school at his age, but Adam had called in some markers for him and wished him well upon his retirement from the Committee three years ago.

"Daddy, don't go. Stay here and play," Cody called from the other end of the porch. The two-year-old came running across the porch and grabbed his leg, hugging it tightly.

Daniel picked up his son, tossed him in the air, and caught him.

Cody laughed and kicked his arms and legs.

"Cody want to fly, Daddy. Want to fly," Cody yelled.

"Esau, heads up," Daniel said.

Daniel tossed his son at Esau. Cody squealed with delight as Esau caught him and set the boy on his shoulders. Cody grabbed two handfuls of Esau's hair and held on.

"Don't worry, Daniel. I'll keep him occupied until you get back,"

Esau promised.

"Thanks," Daniel said.

Esau loved Cody almost as much as Daniel and Tina. A little over three years ago, they had all come to Oregon. Each year Esau thought he would die. He would get depressed for a week or so when he thought about all that had passed, but then the depression would disappear. And each year he continued living with little sign of slowing down. Daniel hoped his friend had inherited his mother's ability to age.

Daniel no longer feared looking in the mirror. All traces of the blood tattoos had disappeared by the time they had moved into the house they had built on the property. Knowing he had showed mercy to someone who hadn't deserved it freed Daniel from his personal demons.

Esau was another case, though. Daniel heard him cry out some nights from the bad dreams he was having. Hopefully, Esau would find his own ways to come to terms with what he had done.

Daniel walked across the yard to Tina who was standing straight now massaging her lower back. "I have to go over to the Hijabs'. I will bring a couple of pizzas back for dinner," Daniel told his wife.

"Sounds good to me." Tina kissed him on the cheek. "Make sure to have them put some oats on one as an extra topping."

"I have heard of pregnant women having weird cravings, but this takes the cake," Daniel said.

Tina laughed. "It's just a little pregnant veterinarian's wife's humor." He pulled a letter out from the pocket of his shirt and handed it to Tina.

"What's this?" she asked. "Read it."

She did. The letter was from Chief Montgomery. Daniel had received it a week ago. Kay had forwarded it to them along with her own letter. The chief's letter had been in a sealed envelope addressed to Daniel. Jacob had been connected to all the murders in Fleetwood. The hair samples and fingerprints placed Jacob at all the crime scenes. The courts had posthumously convicted him of all the murders, clearing Daniel of any wrong doing.

Karl Mueller had died after an extended battle with cancer. He had caused no more problems in town after Daniel and Tina left, and he hadn't tried to follow them. Instead, he had chosen to live out his time in the house on Deer Run Road, and he visited Joseph's grave weekly. Daniel hadn't known whether to feel relieved or saddened at Mueller's death.

"Knowing he's dead doesn't bring me the pleasure I thought it would." Daniel turned around. Esau was standing there reading over his shoulder.

"I guess you were right, Daniel," he added. Daniel nodded saying nothing. "What should I do with this?" Tina asked.

Daniel shrugged. "It doesn't matter to me. I read it, and after a few days I realized that the information in that letter would only interest Daniel Levitt, Nazi hunter. That man stayed in Fleetwood. Daniel Levitt, veterinarian, came to Oregon."

Cody tugged on Esau's arm and held his hands up. "Ride."

Esau lifted the boy up and held him upside down by one ankle. Cody laughed and kicked.

Tina dropped the letter onto the ground and chopped it into small pieces with her hoe. Then she tilled the ground until the white pieces of paper were covered with soil. Daniel smiled.

About the Author

J. R. Rada is the Amazon.com bestselling author of *Kachina, The Man Who Killed Edgar Allan Poe,* and *Welcome to Peaceful Journey.*

He works as a freelance writer in Gettysburg, PA, where he also lives with his wife and sons. James has received many awards from the Maryland-Delaware-DC Press Association, Associated Press, Maryland State Teachers Association and Community Newspapers Holdings, Inc. for his newspaper writing.

To see J. R. Rada's other books, visit his website (jamesrada.com/jrrada).

If you would like to be kept up to date on when J. R. Rada's new books are published or ask him questions, you can e-mail him at *jimrada@yahoo.com.*

PLEASE LEAVE A REVIEW

If you enjoyed this book, please help other readers find it. Reviews help the author get more exposure for his books. Please take a few minutes to review this book at Amazon.com or Goodreads.com.

If you enjoyed *Beast*, keep up to date on new releases, news, and specials from J. R. Rada by joining his mail list. When you sign-up at https://bit.ly/3CILHI6, you'll get *Polderbeest* as a FREE gift.